SILK & SINEW

A COLLECTION OF FOLK HORROR FROM THE ASIAN DIASPORA

EDITED BY

KRISTY PARK KULSKI

Bad Hand Books
www.badhandbooks.com

For our ancestors. For us.
For the ache of loss, we cannot name.
For home—
wherever we've built it.
We belong.

EDITOR'S NOTE

To retain the diversity of our Asian diaspora, all work in this book retains the English of preference of individual authors.

TABLE OF CONTENTS

TREACHERY FOR THE FORLORN

Saba Syed Razvi

On this the night of a thousand echoes,
the moon hangs bright and low in the sky like a coin,
ready to pluck for the ferryman.
Which voice would you invoke into the walls
of your heart, if the wayward would listen?
The lover won and lost, or the one kissed
only in dreaming?
Your mother, with her lullabies
and chastisements, hearth and harvest for your braids,
a faith in your rising star beyond others,
your vanquishing fist raised in rebellious defiance?
Your father, dancing like que sera sera, smiling
with a hand held to lead you to shore
beyond the doldrums of your lost path?
Your own self, broken by the teeth
of time's illusions, tearing mask from apron
and string, from the labyrinth's gaze?
Every touch of leaf and breeze and cormorant lingers
in the clouds, the moon flickering beyond reach

with every thought. Will you look for the glow of pebbles
under breadcrumbs if there is no more home to follow?
Will you take the boat over stormy waves
and through the fog of forgetting?
A shrouded figure waits by the crossroads,
calling out your name.
He stands between. An east. A west. A land of monstrous
shadows and the bloodied bliss of conquest.
He stands, a reminder of the allure of transgression.
His eyes look out through yours
in mirrors and still waters and polished stone.
A demon slips stark over rice fields and mangrove forests,
roots billow in water and against the chaos of men's hands.
A goddess tends the sacred fecundity of everything green
and sleek, an undulating snakelike dance into balance.
His sleeves billow behind him in the shadows.
They were never wings.

FOREWORD

As I sit down to write this foreword, calls of "Your Body, My Choice" ring out across social media from young, predominantly white, men celebrating the success of the most mean-spirited, misogynistic presidential campaign of my lifetime.

Feelings of unease give way to fear, as memories of the 2020 pandemic come rushing back to me. Insults like "China Virus" and "Kung Flu" drawing derisive laughter from mostly Caucasian audiences, followed by a spike in harassment against Asian Americans that seemed surreal in its fury. To make matters worse, these cowards seemed to direct their violence against Asian American women, making us fear for our safety every time we left our homes.

Like many artists, I felt a sense of helplessness. What could I do? In those troubling times, I found comfort in books and stories, and eventually I found myself writing. It was cathartic. I wrote about women who were wronged, who were in pain, and who fought back, finding their power in the metaphorical violence of my stories. And so, when Kristy first approached me to write a foreword for *Silk & Sinew*, telling me that the work was her response to the anger, sorrow, and frustration over what had transpired, I instantly understood the importance of this anthology. Like me, Kristy has refused to let go of the steadily growing anger over the continued violence against Asian women. She has refused to let our experience be overlooked and ignored.

Being a second-generation, Korean American woman, the stories in this anthology resonated with me deeply. The themes relating to identity, the cost of immigration and assimilation, and intergenerational trauma are ones that I—and many other Asian people—know personally, whether through our own experiences or from those of our parents and grandparents.

In *Mother's Mother's Daughter* by Audrey Zhou, I could plainly see my own mother, who immigrated from Seoul in 1985. Like the mother in the story, my umma worked tirelessly, giving up her dreams and breaking down her body to feed, house, and care for my brothers and me. And as an eldest daughter, I could relate to the story's depiction of our parentification—in other words, how Asian cultures force daughters to grow up before our time and to take on caretaking roles in the family, while the boys are often free to enjoy their childhoods.

I've always understood, however, that my mother's sacrifices reached beyond the obvious. When she became an American citizen, she not only left behind her family and friends and homeland, but also a big part of herself. She had to become a person who would forever be caught between worlds, having given up her birthright across the ocean as a Korean and never having the English-language ability or cultural capital to feel confidently American. I could see this aspect of my umma in Rena Mason's *Mindfulness*, where the main character returns to Thailand and is reminded of the identity she lost, realizing that her affinity for ghosts manifests because they exist "somewhere in between, like her." Similarly, in *Fed by Earth, Slaked by Salt*, Jess Cho captures how immigrants are often diminished in their new countries, the protagonist at one point explaining: "Both my parents lived small lives, in the way that only those who understand the weight of uprooting know how."

To a certain extent, my generation can relate to our parents' liminality. Even in Los Angeles, I have been asked if I speak English, if my family eats dog, and so on, all meant to emphasize my—and our—"otherness." But when I visited Seoul for the first time in my twenties, it was not the magical experience I had imagined. My unbelonging was conspicuous, with my clumsy Korean pronunciation and my American clothing. Like Della in Nadia Bulkin's *Things to Know Before You Go* surmising that "she was not a real Indonesian," I had to wonder whether I was Korean or American, or perhaps neither.

Here in the United States, I have long been frustrated by how Asians were portrayed in popular culture. For example, from *Breakfast at Tiffany's* to *Sixteen Candles* to *Full Metal Jacket*, Hollywood has for years enjoyed presenting us as clowns or prostitutes. These frustrations were well entrenched by 2020, when the Covid-19 pandemic brought out the very worst in many people. My friends, family, and I watched in horror as our elders were attacked in broad daylight and Asian women were followed home and stabbed to death. Then, on March 16, 2021, the anti-Asian fervor in our country reached a boiling point when six Asian women were brutally murdered at spas in Atlanta, Georgia by a white man who claimed that he had a sex addiction and was trying to "eliminate" the "temptation." My writing became a vehicle for me to express the rage that consumed me. Female rage is a common theme in *Silk & Sinew* as well, and as expected, I really enjoyed the vengeful tales like Ayida Shonibar's *An Unholy Terroir* and *The Fox Daughter Comes to Glenview* by Seoung Kim.

Finally, no anthology involving Asian families would be complete without at least a couple stories about dark secrets or family demons. This anthology has both. Geneve Flynn's *If I Am to Earn*

My Tether is a fascinating intergenerational story about sins of the past, and *The Squatters* by Shawna Yang Ryan is a ghostly tale that confronts Taiwan's violent and tragic history. *Silk & Sinew* provides a reminder that, as we all deal with dark times of our own, we can face our fears and uncertainties by taking solace in one another and standing together. To quote Angela Yuriko Smith in *Neither Feathers nor Fin*, "As long as we find each other, we will survive."

I hope you enjoy these stories and take comfort in them like I did. Furthermore, I hope that you not just survive but find ways to thrive in these coming years.

Monika Kim
November 2024

SOIL

A POCKET OF SOIL

Geneve Flynn

you bring with you a pocket of soil
your mother's ghost, and nothing more
you plant your heart, hoping it takes
but the alkaline shale
turns it all to calcified stone

your father wept behind his door
when promises came, along with gifts
you married away the dirt-poor girl
one last thing to anchor you home—
you bring with you a pocket of soil

but the voices are strange
all the faces, white stone
you listen hard for a kindness or two
but all you hear—a dying sigh
your mother's ghost, and nothing more

she fades away on loamy breath
replaced by quiet that eats you whole

it creeps up your legs
it crushes your chest
you plant your heart, hoping it takes

you dig your fingers into the dirt
searching for roots, for cassava leaves
too many edges, grinding your bones
and nothing grows here
but the alkaline shale

soon, it swallows you up to your chin
crawls into your ears
films over your eyes
it hardens around you, this arid place
and
turns it all to calcified stone

MOTHER'S MOTHER'S DAUGHTER

Audrey Zhou

Mother inventories her body once the weather gets cold, to see how we'll get by when winter comes.

She keeps a notebook with the precise cost of everything in our home: the home itself— which took two of her ribs scattered in pieces into the earth until day by day, they grew into the walls. The very chairs we're sitting in, in the living room, grown from locks of hair. I'm alright with woodwork now, but before me and before there were customers willing to pay us with gold for our work, Mother had to furnish it somehow.

And then there are the things that gold cannot buy: myself, born of her left foot. My older sister, Yuling, born of three fingers from Mother's right hand. All witches are their mother's daughters, made of magic. And as all magic is, it was a contract: my mother planted the flesh and bone, hewn neatly at the ankle, in the garden. In return for her sacrifice, I sprouted after a year. Yuling was five years old then, old enough so that she can recount, now, how she watered me every two weeks like clockwork until I emerged from the garden.

Yuling's incubation took nearly two years—Mother says because there had been less buried, it took longer for Yuling to grow. She always laments that she should have given Yuling more.

"But I saved it to give to you instead," she told me, when I asked why she hadn't.

Mother stares into the hearth instead of at either of us as she lists what we already have: "The dried stuff in the storage room should last for a month, food-wise. We're doing fine on medicine. Maybe we could get something for the drafts in the house, more repairs."

I consider what we'll need: food can be bought from the market with a handful of coins or grown in the garden with enough fingernails. Clothes are much the same.

I can't help but glance at Mother's ankle, where the firelight shines off the wooden prosthetic I carved for her. Glance at her hands, swathed in bandages; her graying hair, pinned up to hide the patches from where she took too much hair too soon.

Yuling catches my eye. She's braver than I am. "That doesn't seem enough for all three of us," she says, but she's not brave enough to ask what we're both thinking: what is Mother going to give up so it is? I wait with her, tense, wondering if Mother's going to snap.

But Mother doesn't yell, or shout at us about how we're ungrateful, or ask what more we could want from her.

"I'll be dead," she says, as easily as if remarking on the weather. "So, you'll only need enough for two."

I'm not sure how to think about what it means for Mother to be dead, or dying, which is just as well, because she doesn't give me the chance. She approaches death the way she does everything else: cryptically, with conviction, and with no patience for our questions.

"Everyone dies," she tells us the next morning, on her way out the door to do her usual routine of visiting customers. "Everything goes back to the earth eventually, so stop worrying about it. It's my time, not yours. How are you going to survive the winter if you don't start thinking about it now?"

So Yuling and I think about winter.

The stuff we really need is food and warm clothes, nothing that will require anything drastic. Mother raked in some money during the summer, whispering charms—the kind of contracts that only take words—over farmers' blighted fields, but magic is most effective when it costs something physical. The crops never turned out. I buy wool with the gold she earned, but though there's enough left over to fetch a basket of root vegetables during a normal season, the farmers have no crops we can spend it on.

One week before we're due to run out of food, Yuling plucks out long tresses of hair, because Mother won't let us use flesh or bone. I join her in the garden, shoveling little concave half-moons into the dirt.

"I don't get why Mother won't let me help," I tell Yuling. It's cold but not too cold; the sun beats down on our backs, unrelenting.

I know the contracts— three strands of hair and a spill of blood for a length of fur; sliver of knuckle bone for a basket of root vegetables— but Mother doesn't even like me to use my hair, never mind that I'm of age. Never mind that Yuling was doing it all long before, for me.

Yuling hums, placid, but her slender jaw tightens up. "You help plenty, Yulan," she tells me, and she pinches my nose. "You care for everything we plant, and you take care of the house. There's more to life than just surviving."

I favor Mother more than Yuling does: I got my moon-face from Mother, round-cheeked and full, and the same long, thick hair. Yuling was incubated near the willows: I think that's why she came out all slender angles, hair falling in wispy sheets, like the trees laid claim to her more than Mother's blood did.

25

I consider the worth of flesh and bone. How do you measure love once you've pulled it out of your body? Yuling and I— we're both our mother's daughters. But am I more my mother's daughter, for the extra skin she put in? For where it shows?

"Did Mother treat you like me, before I was born?" I ask. "Give you the easy jobs?" Did she handle Yuling with softer hands? Mother tries to be more present for me, now, but she can't manage it all the time. She isn't pleasant to be around all the time either.

Yuling's expression clouds. "No," she says. "No, not really. She's always been Mother."

"Do you wish things had been different?" I ask. If Yuling had been born of a foot too, or if I'd been three fingers. If I looked less like Mother, or Yuling more.

"She's our mother and you're my sister," Yuling tells me, smoothing a hand over my hair. Yuling has always been tactile in a way that Mother is not; I don't know if that's her nature, or if Yuling developed that because she could tell that it was mine. That I needed more than just Mother's half-kind words.

Yuling isn't the type to hold onto her resentment too tightly, but letting go of something doesn't always mean it goes away. We fought a lot when we were little—me, because Yuling's face twisted up when she looked at me, and Yuling because Mother always told her to be nicer. Sometimes Yuling looks at me like she did back then. But she always brushes my hair in the mornings and tears out her own when Mother instructs her to.

Two contrasting truths can still exist in the same place.

As the leaves fall off and the cold crowds into everything—the walls, under the covers at night, inside our clothes—Mother wilts with the season. There's not a contract that exists that can stop time.

Mr. Li down the road needs his crops to grow, wants something for his fields that'll work. So, Mother comes home and goes straight to the bathroom where we keep the stuff that sterilizes... the stuff that cuts; the knives not meant for cooking.

"You can't be serious," Yuling says, when Mother tells us about the contract, clear-eyed and set jaw, the wrinkles around her eyes drawn taut at her temples like strings.

It's a bad bargain no matter how you look at it, no matter how you turn it around. A field can grow better the next season if you give it enough time, but Mother isn't going to get the remaining two fingers of her right hand back, no matter what. I don't think there's any amount of Mr. Li's gold that can make up for that.

"I'm certainly old enough to make my own choices," Mother says. When she goes to the garden, holding the sterilized knife, we follow her.

I resort to begging. "Let me do it," I tell Mother. "Come on, Mama, what's worth this much—please, let me see it."

"Stop," she snaps back at me. Steel flicks out, an arc of motion like lightning. Bone crunches. Mother's sweating—blood loss, exertion—and pale. One finger down.

Yuling gags. I fumble for the blade, blindly, and Mother grips me by the wrist when I get the handle in my hand, faster than I thought she'd be capable of.

"You think I did this to myself so you could do it too?" Mother asks, fury and pain sharpened to a point, the sound of her voice like steel.

"We don't need this," I say. "You didn't—was this necessary? Is this necessary?"

I mean that we don't need Mother to sacrifice like this, that she doesn't have to pull herself apart like that. But Yuling sucks in a breath through her teeth, like a whistle, and Mother's face closes like a wound, raw.

Mother doesn't hit me but when her hand moves, for a wild, suspended moment, I think she will. But she only lifts her skirt so I can see her foot, afternoon sunlight reflecting muted and glassy off the wood; lambent. What she gave up for me before I was even myself; what I have, in some failing capacity, tried to give back to make up for it.

"You're young, Yulan," Mother says, grip tightening until my hand falls open. I only notice how badly I'm shaking because of the steadiness of her hand when she takes the knife from me and makes the next cut. White-knuckled. "How could you understand? You don't know what you need."

The second finger falls to the ground. Yuling hauls Mother to the bathroom to fix her up. It takes me the whole evening to bury the flesh in the ground, even though the task isn't physically taxing at all. My brain catalogs details that weigh me down like lead—the weight of each finger, the smoothness of the flesh, the pink and the red and the white—but I try to remember anyway, for when I'll make a new prosthetic for Mother.

I make my limbs move: I dig a hole into the ground, two meters deep. Put the fingers in. Cover them up again. Use the boiled well water to hydrate.

Inside the house, Yuling must be looking at Mother right now, at her face all twisted up. Must be telling Mother to breathe as Yuling disinfects and bandages as Mother clamps her mouth shut and doesn't make a sound.

So, I guess I got the easy job, again.

Apparently, for the cost of Yuling's birth contract, it took Mother a month to recover. It takes her three weeks this time before life resumes as usual.

In this household, forgiveness is more of pretending to forget. Mother's new wooden, metal-hinged fingers bend like they should once her knuckles heal enough to have attachments. She hands over a pot of salve with her right hand one morning— for the bruises she left ringed around my wrist.

It occurs to me that I've never heard Yuling or Mother talk about how a witch dies. It's the little things that come first: Mother spends less time doing her rounds outside; her skin takes on a cold, constant pallor. She oscillates between being uncharacteristically kind and ruthlessly practical.

"You know I'm proud of you guys," she says, one day. The next: "Better sell my clothes, when I'm gone. If you can't get coin for it, repurpose the cloth."

Then the big things come: Mother spends a full morning telling us what to do for her funeral. She starts spending more of her time in bed than out of it.

"It doesn't have to be a spectacle," she tells us. "Just lay me down."

We follow her instructions: the first witch, my mother's mother's mother all the way to the start of the line, came from the earth; all witches return to it. The hole we dig is person-tall and two meters deep; we consider the nearby forest, but Mother says the garden is fine. Less trouble. Even so, the frost means it takes the better part of a day to break through the soil, which has chilled together into hard chunks.

"It reminds me a little of when you were born," Yuling says, soft. "When we were preparing the ground, to plant you."

We spend a lot of time indoors, now that Mother is bedridden, talking about stuff that doesn't matter: the weather and how it seems the worst of the cold will be over soon. She reminds us of contracts we've long had memorized, of what customer relationships will need to be kept up.

"You can use your fingernails if you really need to," she tells us one afternoon. "But nothing more permanent than that."

"What if that's the only way?" I ask. Yuling glances at me.

"It won't be," Mother says. "Times are different now."

I think, somehow, that Mother must be saving up all her words for when they matter. I wonder what secrets she might have been keeping, what advice she might leave behind. She's been like an opaque screen my whole life—but maybe that just means the fault is mine, for never learning to figure her out.

But Mother doesn't tell us she loves us. She doesn't say anything at all when she goes, because she goes overnight, and the evening before she's too tired to sustain conversation. Like a bad dream, I go to bring Mother breakfast one morning and find her unresponsive. Find that the only breathing in the room is my own.

My own words, which I've been saving up, waiting to see if they'll take new shapes—*I didn't mean what I said, before; I love you; I'm sorry for what you gave up for us*—have nowhere to go.

"Do you think she would have lived longer if she hadn't had me?" I ask Yuling later, when we prepare for the burial.

"Maybe," Yuling says. "But she wanted you. I wanted you."

We put her body to rest in the ground. The days pass like water.

Now that Mother is dead—not dead, I correct myself, just returned to the earth—there's no one to lecture me for making contracts with my hair.

I get away with it for a few weeks: a few strands from the base of my neck each time, planted in the garden after Yuling goes to bed and then the literal fruit of my labors plucked at dawn and smuggled into the pantry.

I don't know what gets me in the end—my own carelessness, overconfidence, or some sort of sixth sense on Yuling's part—but Yuling catches me one night. It's a full moon—I can't hide in the dark or claim that Yuling's seeing things. There's me, crouched over the earth, scissors in hand, looking up. There's Yuling, standing over me.

For a long moment, there's silence. Yuling breaks it first.

"You think we don't have enough?" she asks. Her voice is even, but the look in her eyes—I think about Mother looking at me, when I tried to stop her from cutting her fingers off.

That's not it. I cast about for an answer. "It wasn't fair that you had to do this and I didn't," I say finally, voice a little wobbly.

Yuling looks at me, teeth gleaming in the moonlight. "Maybe," she allows, "but you're still my little sister." Two truths can exist in the same space.

"I don't want you to think like—god, Yuling. you don't have to give all of yourself up," I tell her. "Not like Mother."

"I don't want to be like Mother," Yuling tells me. "But what do you think you're doing? I don't need you to make up for anything."

"I'm not—"

Yuling continues, relentless. "All you did was live," she says. "And that's all anyone wanted for you. That wasn't a crime."

We develop new routines. Yuling doesn't let me use anything of my own, but she doesn't use anything permanent, either.

We start to deal in charms and the wooden trinkets and furniture I make. I water the garden, even the corner where Mother is buried.

Mr. Li comes to visit after it all.

I am prepared to dislike him when I see the familiar farmer's hat coming around the bend to the house, but he's carrying a basket of turnips and cabbages. "There will be beets and lettuce in the spring," he says. "I'll come when they're ready."

We invite him inside, as reciprocity for the gift if nothing else, and he reveals that he's brought sunflower seeds to snack on. We have idle conversation over our tea.

"Sorry," Yuling finally asks, interrupting Mr. Li's anecdote about the best fertilizers, "but why have you come?"

Mr. Li grows quiet in awkward surprise, eyes glancing from Yuling to me, throat working. He looks like a wounded raven I found in our backyard once, its wing clipped. Numinous, like even though it was a hurt thing, it was divine.

"Your mother," he says. "She asked me to take care of you after she passed on, and in exchange, she said she'd see to my field. I would have done it anyway, of course, but—"

"She wouldn't have liked that," Yuling says, for the both of us. My throat is too thick to speak.

How do you give back a thing like what she's given us? I can't fall asleep that night. I watch the shadows on the wall move, and then I think about Mother all alone, under the earth. I think about how before I was myself, I was just Mother's foot in the ground, how I didn't know anything but the soil around me and Yuling pouring water overtop me.

I get up and set a pot of well-water to boil. Yuling stirs, eventually, probably awakened by the sound of the fire crackling. She doesn't say anything, but she helps me fill the watering can up. Helps me water Mother, as if we can still reach her now.

As the weather warms, something moves underneath the earth's surface.

Subtle things. A plant displaced a few centimeters over. A shovel left outside ends up half-buried in the earth. It occurs to me that though I had never seen a witch die before Mother, I have never seen a witch's birth, either.

"How did it go again?" I ask Yuling, the two of us staring slack-jawed at where the fresh dirt of Mother's grave has shifted. "When you were watering me? When I was born?"

"A little like this, actually," Yuling says.

I think of how Yuling and I have kept watering Mother's grave, almost by habit. There must exist a contract that involves an entire body.

How much is a second chance at life? I don't know if there's anything worth that, if anything can be traded for it. But it must be possible to get close—to find some approximation.

On the first day of spring, the ground splits apart. My little sister comes up from the earth, all tufts of hair, already screaming.

She is our mother's daughter through and through, even still red and covered with afterbirth and soil. I'm willing to bet her round face isn't all baby fat, that she'll end up looking like me. Like Mother. Out of the three of us, she'll probably look the most like her.

She grows. We name her Yuli. Yuling and I, we don't know sometimes, if we are looking at the favored sister or our mother, reincarnated. I don't know if it matters.

We do what we would have liked growing up. When Mr. Li comes around with a cart of fruit, Yuling mashes peaches so Yuli can eat them. I make wooden toys.

The seasons pass. I inventory my own body: my hands develop calluses from the wood and the house repairs and I've put on more muscle and fat now that we're eating better. There's a cut on my foot from where I dropped the box of knives from the bathroom—we don't use those anymore.

Yuling and I keep watering the spot we buried Mother, never mind that there's nothing there anymore. When Yuli starts to walk, she toddles after us in clumsy imitation. We'll explain, eventually, what it means and who our Mother was and how Yuli came to be. But there's no need for her to learn the kind of contracts we did. No need for her to carry the same things we do.

Life goes on. Nothing we can't get back goes into the garden.

THE SQUATTERS

Shawna Yang Ryan

The government begins excavating the bones in late February to coincide with the events planned to commemorate the massacre. It is meant to gesture that they truly do intend to follow through on their promise of "truth and reconciliation" and with the upcoming election, a way to score political points for the candidates of the ruling party. The site is one of a number of mass graves that have been located in the past two decades, and now there is an official governmental department in charge of identifying the victims and honoring them with a proper burial and headstone.

I would like to tell you we were always solemn as we cataloged and analyzed these lost lives, but we made jokes because laughter is what made us human, alive. Dissociation was part of the job.

When I told my mom I was heading to Taiwan, she was both delighted and dismayed. Neither she or I had been back to Taiwan in almost a decade, and we both longed for it. She warned me to not mix myself up in the island's contentious politics. "It goes so much deeper than you can understand, Alex," she said. I told her the very reason they were allowing me in was because of my neutrality. And my elementary Taiwanese, *Tâi-gí,* which no one in my American organization spoke.

There were no direct flights to Taiwan from the United States. They'd ended three years before as part of the expansion of "strategic ambiguity," so I took a seven-hour flight from Honolulu to Narita, passed five hours in Narita eating udon and wandering past shops selling meneki-neko and ceramic Totoros. I bought a plastic No Face charm and hung it from my computer bag strap.

After the final flight to Taipei, I was fingerprinted and photographed, and greeted at the customs exit by a man sweating through his white dress shirt and holding a sheet of paper with my name scrawled across it.

I was once again home.

The earth smells rich and damp as we cut away the green and turn the soil. My colleague, Pei-chun, works with a small trowel. A heavy rain has swept away part of the hillside, but she thinks she can determine the parameters of the original grave. The washed bones have been strewn by the drifting mud, but we cannot touch them yet.

It was a dog—a Golden Retriever—that made the discovery. It galloped down the hill with its newfound toy—gleaming like a sanitized pet-store bone—in its mouth. Wrestling the object away, its human discovered a jaw in her hand. A tibia could be mistaken for an animal bone, perhaps. But not a human jaw. She called the police. The news crews were there before the police could rope off the area and Pei-chun now picks up gum wrappers and bottle caps with a snort.

I have been to a number of mass graves. At each excavation I am newly struck by an inarticulable sense of loss. Certain things hit hard: the skeleton of a teenager in a Jon Bon Jovi t-shirt and moldering jeans in Bosnia; a skeleton in Myanmar still wearing a stack of beaded bracelets, an open hand of bones that had slipped from the baby it held; a heap of bodies outside of Mexico City without hands. Sometimes the cadavers are partially fleshed, and I can almost see their lives. A tarnished barrette still holds back a hank of chestnut hair from a decaying forehead. A Pokémon watch sinks into a softening wrist. Maggots stream out of Nike Air Force 1 high tops.

The bones today are clean though Pei-chun finds scraps of cloth. I photograph each piece, record it in my notebook and on my laptop, and put it in a plastic bin. Clean bones are usually old bones, so we have an idea of what we are looking at.

"How many of these have you done?" I ask Pei-chun in my stilted Taiwanese. I have known Pei-chun for three days, since the briefing at the university. Bleary-eyed, we shared an awkward breakfast this morning in the hotel slurping rice porridge and eating fried eggs.

"This is my third." Pei-chun answers in English.

"Are there ever any surviving family members?"

"With DNA testing, we find quite a few, but they are usually distant relatives. Many family lines ended in these graves."

So it often is. Change by degrees is too hard; some prefer to do it in one fell swoop, a sweep of bullets, a community destroyed, rubble to build a new country out of. I have seen it in a dozen places around the world.

I call my mother back in California and tell her where I am staying. I flip the phone camera and slowly spin around the room so my mom can see the soft buttery walls, the recessed lighting, the black tiled bathroom. Out the window a few random lights twinkle up the hillside.

"Gong Gong and Po Po had a country house over there," my mom says. "We went when we were kids, but when Po Po died, we stopped going. I don't know what happened to it. You should go look at it. Send me a picture. I remember we spent whole days catching crickets."

My heritage here in Taiwan is only partly known to me, obscured by language and my mixed-race blood. I want to see a piece of my mother's life. Her childhood home had been bulldozed decades before for a high rise. I'd only seen slivers of it in the background of old photos, and I thought it would reveal something important to me about her, and maybe us.

"There wasn't an address." My mother continues. "But I can tell you how to get there. There's a small town that the highway cuts through. It was called Camphor Grove then. Just past it, the road veers to the left and goes into the forest and up a hill. You'll pass a small temple, like a garden god altar really. Well, who knows if it's still there. It's been, what, forty years? Fifty? But the house had a gigantic banyan in the courtyard. It took five of us to reach our arms around it. If you see the banyan, you will know it's the right place."

I know Camphor Grove. It is where the woman who had found the original jaw lives. It is mere hundreds of meters from the excavation site. I will go after work tomorrow.

Pei-chun is friendlier today, jokes with me and with Yan-ting, who is the other archeologist on the dig and comes from what I assume is a rival university.

After work, Pei-chun asks me to join her for a beer.

"I have to run an, uh" I search for the word "errand" in my Tâi-gí vocabulary, "*job* for my mother."

"What a filial child," Pei-chun says.

"I'll go with you," Yan-ting volunteers.

Pei-chun pretends not to hear him.

After work, we walk back to the main road where Pei-chun has parked her car, and Yan-ting and I have our bikes. I wave goodbye. Then I continue up the road and find a small opening in the tall grass where it looks as though there might be a path. I look over my shoulder and a woman sitting in front of the town's last shop, which sells dusty bottles of sarsaparilla and Pocari Sweat, stares at me. I wave and the woman gives a barely perceptible nod. I turn into the grass.

To the most attentive eye, there is a path. As I push my bike through, I consider going back to the work site for a machete. The birds call, the sky grows darker as if rain clouds have moved in, and I have already lost the sounds of other humans. After a while, I see a large stone partially obscured by the grass. I push aside the blades and see a small paint-chipped god nestled in the alcove beside two melted red candles. This must be the god altar.

It gets dark faster than I anticipate. I am usually back in the hotel after a cheap meal of noodles or an individual hot pot eaten under a blaring news report at the shop two doors down from the hotel. I flick on my bike light and keep going.

The canopy of a giant banyan appears on my left. I can't believe I have found it. The grass ends at a fence with an arched gateway. I push through to a dirt courtyard where the giant banyan stands, a hundred trunks roping down into the earth. A flock of quieting birds murmur in the boughs. A house stands just beyond the reach of the banyan's canopy. The rounded black roof tiles are disrupted, broken, and one corner of the overhang is cracked, exposing its inner workings. An open veranda surrounds the house, in a Japanese style. Shingles have fallen from the exterior. A flat bicycle tire lies half under the veranda.

I could leave. I should leave. It is even darker now and the mosquitoes have bitten me in half a dozen places. I'm hungry. But I have come this far, and I'll have to wait until Saturday before I can visit in the daylight. I unclip the light from my bike and head to the front door. Respectfully—or reflexively—I sit on the veranda and take off my muddy boots before opening the door.

What do I expect to find? A discarded table, thick with dust? A forgotten calendar? Nests of chewed straw and grass holding tiny pink newborn rats?

For a moment, my grandfather's face flashes in my mind. General Hwang Chang Wei, war hero. He had died when I was just ten, but his presence echoed on. He commanded a room. He was taller than average, with thick shoulders, a hard jaw, a shock of white hair. My mother adored him. He was hard on his sons and indulgent with his daughters, especially my mother, the youngest. I'd heard from my cousin stories of him beating my uncles, of his rage, of the creative cruelties he inflicted for obedience. But from my mother, it was all adoration. The charm he effected on women also applied to my grandmother, Po Po, who forgave him the ways he made her cry with his infidelities and when he stonewalled her for complaining, how he withheld money or love or acknowledgement. Po Po could only remember the glow she felt when he looked upon her.

I brace myself as I open the door.

It's just as I imagined. Torn tatami. Overturned furniture. The smell of old cat piss. I cough.

A moment later, my light flashes on a child's face, glowing blue in the dark doorway. Startled, I drop my light.

"Sorry." I sink to my knees and grasp around for the light. "I didn't know someone was here. Sorry."

The child echoes me. "Sorry?"

I scurry through the front door. My hands shake as I clip the light and roll my bike through the gate.

I look over at the banyan—I am an archaeologist, not a botanist. I don't know how many trees of this size can exist in one community. Either I have the wrong house, or my mother is wrong, and the home belongs to others already. *Nostalgia*, at its root, means the pain of returning home. I know the past is dreamy in her mind, some Thomas Kinkade vision of glowing windows, meadow flowers, dewy stone pathways. She doesn't think of how mold creeps across the walls, mildew furs on fabrics, softens beams, lures termites.

She forgets that this is a place where flesh disintegrates in a matter of days.

We stake off the site with plastic yellow ribbon, build scaffolding out of uniformly cut bamboo, and drape a large blue tarp to keep the late winter rain from turning the grave into mud. With string, we mark off a grid over the excavation. Under another canopy, we set up two tables with our cameras, tools, notebooks and computers. Plastic bins sit stacked beneath the table. Even up this vine-tangled slope, our cell reception is strong, and we tether our computers to our phones. A rainbow of colored labeled flags flutter down the hillside, marking the placement of each artifact.

The week passes quickly. A man from the government comes to survey our progress and take down a report. So far, it looks as though we have the bones of at least three separate people.

"A mass grave," he says. He looks at me and explains, though I am familiar with the history: After Japanese colonialism ended, the Chinese Nationalists came in from China. A brief bright window of hope for Taiwanese self-rule was shut by the military rule of the Nationalists, who violently suppressed any suspected "dissidents" in what was known as the 1947 March Massacre. The executions and repression continued on for years, including thirty-eight years of martial law.

"Or maybe it's just an ordinary domestic murder-suicide," I offer.

The man clears his throat. He doesn't understand the caustic humor of people who hold death in their hands on a daily basis.

"We'll tell you soon enough," Pei-chun continues.

"Of course, of course," the man says.

Like any child of the diaspora, I suppose, there was a lot I didn't know about my family. Despite my mother's favored daughter status, she left Taiwan for America, with no plans to return. Marrying my father, a Jack Mormon from Iowa, ensured it. My knowledge of Taiwan was limited to a few childhood visits and a couple trips as an adult; the rest of it came from books. Taiwan was a history reported on by white men, a list of restaurants in the Lonely Planet guide, children's picture book images of water buffalo and rice paddies and crowded cityscapes.

My grandmother was a thin woman, impeccably dressed in qipaos long after they fell out of fashion. She wore pantyhose exactly one shade darker than her legs, block heeled shoes. She had her hair washed and set once a week at the local salon. She claimed to have been part of Madame Chiang's mahjong circle. She was a devout Christian.

My grandfather had what was considered a lucky, masculine face: square jawed, with a broad forehead. His face portended his authority and his ability to endure hardship. He grew into his physiognomic destiny, was promoted and promoted through the army ranks until he made General. He was deeply superstitious and fixated on etiquette, protocol. Once, when I ignorantly left my chopsticks standing in my rice, like an incense offering to the dead, he swiped it so briskly that the chopsticks flew off the table and clattered to the floor. The room went silent. *Never do that again*, he said in his beautifully accented English. I knew better than to cry.

Back at the site, I look at bone fragments, teeth, bits of fabric, jewelry. The dead come alive. Identified so far: Female, 20s, scraps of a blue crepe dress. Male, 30s, wristwatch. Female child, approx. 10-12 years old, jade bracelet. A shattered rib bone indicates gunfire.

Ulna and radius wrapped around the child's skeleton, draped in disintegrating fabric, haunt my dreams.

Child skull resting on the women's ribs, a pile of decomposing hair hanging through like seaweed.

Of course, these details come into focus slowly. Usually, it is just bone by bone, scrap by scrap, so we are shielded from the immediate horror of the story of this trio.

We find bullets. Yan-ting takes them and turns one over in his hand, inspecting with a squinting eye. "Early 20th century. It's actually an American bullet, so the killer wasn't Japanese. Must have been Chinese."

At the night market with Pei-chun, we shuffle past stalls selling cell phone charms, cheap hair ornaments, t-shirts for 100NT. Pei-chun buys a candied haw. I munch on a skewer of squid balls.

"Miss! Foreign Miss!" a middle-aged woman, sitting at a table with a large physiognomy chart hanging behind her, calls out.

Pei-chun nudges me and nods toward the aunty-prophet: "I think she's talking to you, 'Foreign Miss.'"

"Me?" I ask.

The woman beckons me over.

"Sit, sit."

"I don't…" My protest dies. Because of my unusual face, I am always being called over into one hustle or another.

"This one is free of charge. Tell her it's free," she says to Pei-chun. The woman reaches across the table and strokes my face. "You need my help, Miss. It's all over your face." She takes a small, embroidered pouch, the kind from a temple with a paper blessing folded inside, and dangles it on her finger. "A wanderer. You don't belong here."

"Oh shut up, you old—" Pei-chun begins.

The aunty shushes her and folds my hand around the charm. "You'll need this for wherever you're going."

In the lead-up to the island-wide commemoration of the March Massacre, a journalist and photographer come by to interview us and write a laudatory piece about confronting the past. The story elicits hundreds of comments, many of them lamenting the poor child. Instead of reconciliation, it triggers anger anew at the government.

On our next call, my mother asks if I've found the house.

"Someone lives there, Mom."

"What do you mean?"

"Someone is living there."

"It must have been the wrong house. Did you see the banyan?"

"Yes."

"That's our house. If there are squatters, we have to tell Oldest Uncle. I loved that house. We slept with the doors open in the summer." She sighs.

"But if we aren't using it..."

"It belongs to us! If we want to let it fall apart, it's still our house! Go back. I carved my name in the banyan. Then you will know for sure. Let me know."

Ever filial, I reluctantly return to the house. The banyan roots that grow from canopy to ground look like vines of hair. I wriggle my way between these, trying to find the center. Caged within the roots, I finally spot what I think is the primary trunk. It's so dark here in this grotto that I must turn on my phone's flashlight to see. I run the light up and down the bark, looking for a sign of characters, something that might distinguish them from the usual knots and cracks. My light catches an old etching. My mother's name.

I extricate myself. The sun is low in the sky.

I go back to the house. Again, I leave my work boots by the door. Knock. I call out a greeting.

A little girl opens the door.

"Sor-ry?" she says, and laughs.

"Is your mother home?' I ask in Mandarin. She shrugs.

"Is your mother home?" I ask again, this time in Tâi-gí. She nods and beckons me in.

A moment of dizziness and panic. The tatamis are pristine. The furniture gleams. In the alcove, fresh lilies bow their white heads, and the room smells of spring. A folded futon in the corner. Am I lost again?

A woman enters—wire-rimmed glasses, hair pulled into a low bun—startles to see me, and asks my name, what I want.

I try to explain with my elementary language skills. I ask the mother how long they've been in the house, if they are the owners. I explain how I am looking for an old family summer home.

She answers in Japanese. I shake my head. "American," I say.

She tries again in Tâi-gí. From what I understand, the house is theirs. They have lived in it since they built it. *But my mother's name in the bark?*—I apologize for my mistake, for bothering them.

I guess my Americanness is a novelty though, because she asks me to stay for dinner.

She brings out a bucket of freshly steamed rice, sets out boiled chicken, a stack of pomelos, and a teapot. Kiyo, the girl, talks to me in a mix of languages that amuses and confuses me, and her mother tells her to quiet down and eat.

The food feels like air and leaves me hungry.

I thank her for her hospitality.

At the courtyard gate, I turn for another look at the house. The door opens and I glimpse Kiyo's face, ghostly in the shadow. She shouts my name.

I wake up ravenous and drenched in sweat. The AC is dead, and a spear of light falls between the blackout curtains. I find a bag of chips in my backpack and devour it while standing naked in the bathroom.

I'm kneeling on dirt, working, when my phone vibrates. I send it to voicemail.

Another call. It's my mom.

I ignore it, but she calls a third time.

"Mom, is everything okay?"

"Baba" my mother begins. "I had forgotten this. I had a kitten. One day, Baba was painting and she walked across his ink, leaving little footprints. I ran to grab her but before I could, he had broken her neck. I can still hear the snap. He dropped her in my arms and told me to watch my next cat better."

"Mom, that's horrible."

"Maybe I've lived too long. I can't distinguish my memories from my dreams. Did it happen? Did I make it up?"

"The house isn't ours, Mom. Someone lives there. They say they built it."

"They are liars. They'll leave. They have to leave. We'll make them leave."

"Mom."

At lunch, I am finishing my fourth rice burger when I notice Pei-chun watching me, bemused.

"You're really hungry." she says.

My stomach growls. "I think it's the heat."

Later that night, unable to sleep, I go out alone for hot pot. I order plates of chrysanthemum stems, cabbage, clams, and sliced raw beef. My mouth fills with saliva at the blood pooling in the meat dish. I don't bother to cook it.

My phone buzzes on the nightstand.

"Is everything okay? It's two in the morning."

"There was a doll with a porcelain face in the room I slept in. I found it under the tatami during our first summer there. And writing in the corner of shoji. *Qing. Pure.* Why would someone write that?"

"I don't know, Mom."

Deep in the night, I go to the house. Kiyo's mother feeds me: peanuts, rice, steamed chicken, rice wine. I recline onto the tatami, satiated.

"Wake up, lazy ghost," Pei-chun says, using a literal translation. "You look like shit."

Pei-chun plops down next to me. "Check this out." She switches to Mandarin and tells me about her visit to the national archives in Taipei.

She tells me that in March 1947, at Camphor Grove, as in a number of locations in Taiwan, mass killings were carried out by Chinese Nationalist forces. This was the infamous March Massacre. Troops, led by General Hwang Chang Wei, went home to home in the town that was suspected of harboring supporters of Taiwanese home-rule, and systematically killed all residents, including women and children. Because the community was so small, the story did not have the same lingering legacy as the murders in Taipei.

I shuffle through the photocopies that she hands me. My grandfather's face looks back at me from a newspaper article, standing proudly next to his Generalissimo, Chiang Kai Shek. The flag of the Republic of China is caught in mid-flutter behind them.

I shove the papers back into Pei-chun's hands and turn away to vomit.

I wear the night market charm tied to my belt loop. Kiyo sits in the front room. She practices her characters, writing each one inside of a pre-printed square. Her jade bracelet taps across the paper. This is how I learned to write Chinese too: *Blue sky, white sun.*

A woman trudges up the hill toward us.

"Stop! This is a research site. Step around!" Pei-chun waves the woman over toward the left.

"I'm looking for the Foreigner," says the intruder. She is the face reader from the night market.

I meet her at the edge of the site.

"Time haunted." She searches my feverish face. "Some places are haunted by ghosts; others by time. Like layers atop each other. The past is hanging over you."

"We're excavating a grave," Pei-chun shouts. "The past is not just hanging over her—it's under her fingernails and in her hair. Aunty, please leave us."

My aunty-prophet, with her frizzed-out perm and polyester blouse, ignores Pei-chun. "Believe what's before your own eyes. Stop fooling yourself." She surveys our work. "None of you are mere bystanders. You're all implicated!"

"Every time." Pei-chun says after the woman leaves. "At every site, every time, some shaman, some seer, comes with a warning. Such a cliché."

B elieve what is before my eyes.

I find thirteen tiny phalanges. A child's toes. I don't know where the fourteenth bone is. With a gloved hand, I remove them carefully and place them in a bag to send to the lab.

Today is March 13, I realize. Two days from now, but many decades ago, troops came and murdered my little friend, Kiyo. And the troops will be led by my own grandfather, who will take over their home as a country house for his family for the next few generations.

I will take Kiyo and her mother and hide them before my grandfather and his men arrive. I will do what I couldn't do for the teenager in Bosnia, for the mother in Myanmar, the child in Rwanda. I will change the trajectory of the future.

It is spring in the mountains. The air is bright and warm, the humidity weighing down again. The house looks freshened up. New flowers sit in the alcove. Kiyo is delighted to see me. I tell her that she and her family must leave the house.

She protests and I grab her arm. I drag her across the room, and she yells at me to stop, to let her go. She cries for her mother.

I yank her across the threshold. She looks at me with startled eyes—betrayal—and then her face begins to collapse in on itself, breaking into a million fragments of bone. Her hair disperses like a black halo. Her arm scatters through my fingers and onto the porch in a pile of sand. Her dress diffracts into a rainbow.

In just a moment, I stand before a litter of dust on the porch of a dilapidated house.

After the lab confirms the identities of the bones and their living relatives are found (some distant cousins in Taoyuan), the government pays for a quiet burial. Our crew goes, along with a few reporters and some of the long-lost cousins. There is one surviving cousin who remembers them—she is in her 90s, and she speaks carefully about her aunt, her uncle, her cousin. How their disappearance meant an assumption of death in those days, how they came to search for them and found the home occupied by the KMT. She holds a photograph of them, Kiyo and her parents, uncanny in sepia.

The day before my flight home, I visit the house for the final time. I slip between the roots of the banyan and find my mother's name. With a pocketknife, I carve my name below hers.

At the bottom of the hill, I call my mom.

"You were right, Mom." I confirm. "It's ours. The house belongs to us."

AN UNHOLY TERROIR

Ayida Shonibar

I.

This is a fable. Or rather, a warning.

II.

Like all dangers, the disease arrived without notice. Nobody had encountered anything quite like it before—the loss of appetite, the shifting bones, the crumbling of features we recognise as human. It was entirely foreign to us. We forced gruel down the throats of our mothers, confined our children to the safety of their soft-blanketed beds, but none of us knew how to contain the sickness once it chose to take root in our loved ones.

In the end, all we really did was grieve and watch them disintegrate.

Such desperate times called us to prayer, to convene together, under the guidance of our Provost—the man who navigated our community through troubled waters like these. At the end of each week, we congregated in the Atrium to pay him our respects, goodwill, and a healthy portion of our earnings.

The Provost began his ceremonies by taking attendance. We welcomed newcomers who had married in from neighbouring towns, and we reminisced over leavers who pursued work opportunities along the trade route or, even more unfortunately, passed away from the illness.

Then the Provost listened carefully to our reflections. He identified reasons behind the things our simple perspectives were too close to, or too far from, to understand. He shepherded us toward the good lives we sought.

Most importantly, he made sense of things that were otherwise too painful for us to bear.

"Otto was a good child," he explained to Mrs. Ludwig, Otto's mother, "but sometimes he succumbed to laziness. Last month, he postponed his turn to draw water from the well, and the Brinkhof family was unable to complete my laundry on time. And now, Otto is no more. The heavens sent him the sickness as a punishment to us, for not teaching him well. Let this serve as a lesson to us all. We must do better."

Hence, out of the unknowable, the Provost procured an actionable warning. We were never again late to deliver on his requests. His grey shirts were cleaned first, his blonde hair trimmed before anybody else's, his daughter Angelika's pale face moisturised as soon as she entered the salon.

Still, we were not a perfect village, for the illness continued its cull. Week by week, the crowd in the Atrium thinned. All of us villagers—the ones well enough to leave our homes—appeared faithfully. Our prayers to the Provost lengthened, our donations deepened.

The last week before the winter solstice, twilight sank thirstily over our district. When we opened the Atrium doors after the service, lightning cracked ominously across the dark sky. We gasped as one.

An unexpected shadow shuddered outside. Although we knew our friends and neighbours—respectable citizens, all of them—were inside the Atrium with us, something else lurked amongst the copse of trees.

Something new, something alive moved toward us.

The silhouette of what seemed a woman—a young one—split away from the vegetation. Night-black hair plastered against brown, shivering skin came into our focus. A shawl of a peculiarly shining texture hung over her shoulders, appearing to us a woven exoskeleton repelling rainwater and resplendent in contrast to our uniformly monochrome attire.

She was unlike anything we had ever seen. We could not bring ourselves to cease staring.

Titli had travelled from a faraway land. Having learned her family's craft of creating vivid fabric out of a sleek material she called silk, she sold her wares across three continents, seven countries, and countless towns before happening upon ours.

Stories about her spread through our village like the disease. Some were directly sourced from discussions with her in the local tavern. Others mere speculation. Most were spun out of our own expectations and fantasies.

"Her countenance is rather lovely," said Angelika in a hushed tone. Her father was collecting the first spring fruit from the grocer around the corner, and clearly, she did not want him to overhear how she had caught Titli's gaze over the apothecary's display case for several moments longer than was appropriate. "I thought the southern peoples were meant to look beastly, but I find her most becoming."

"You've never seen her without a shawl, though," Mrs. Ludwig remarked. "I've heard they don't have real human skin. That underneath those shapeless fabrics, they're hiding something fibrous, something scaly."

"I think it's far more sinister than that. Have you consumed their piquant cuisines? I'll wager she breathes fire like a dragon," Georg Brinkhof said.

Mr. Hartner hastened to add, "Their food is spiced for good reason. They eat the flesh of other *people*."

"Do you reckon? How shocking!"

"What do you think it tastes like?"

"Chicken. All meat tastes of chicken."

"Would it pair well with lettuce? I'm searching for ideas to encourage sales from my large harvest."

So we carried on, giggling and whispering, until a long shadow fell over our group and silenced us immediately. Angelika withered under the Provost's stare. The rest of us clamped our mouths shut guiltily.

"Cannibalism is no laughing matter," the Provost said. "If you joke about degeneracy today, tomorrow it will tempt you into deviant behaviour and destroy this parish."

"I'm certain nobody here would fall prey to such things," Angelika reassured him. She was a soft-spoken daughter, the fairest maiden of us all. As she approached marrying age, the entire village waited with devout anticipation for the Provost to choose which family would be blessed by her sweet hand.

"You are too foolish to understand what that girl can do to us," he said. "She could corrupt our way of life. She will turn us against each other, if you let her, twist you into my opponents instead of my disciples. Only if you refuse such perversion and stand strong in your convictions can you withstand such an influence."

"Yes, sir," we mumbled.

Yet curiosity proved a challenge to the integrity of our convictions. With our relatives falling to the illness at home, Titli's strange clothes and scandalous customs were a welcome distraction. Conversations about her continued out of the Provost's earshot.

"Which organ in her body generates the fire?" Angelika asked Georg.

"It comes out of her mouth."

"Can she control its direction?"

"Not any more than you control your own tongues," a new voice said from the tavern's entrance.

Titli's thick brows pulled together in a furrow. She glared at each of us in turn, as if memorising our faces, before storming back outside. The door slammed behind her.

Angelika blushed a deep scarlet. The Provost was the only person who had ever reprimanded her before. "We should follow her. Find out what she heard and apologise. This is no way to welcome a newcomer to our village." She stood, brushed her grey skirt into prim folds, and made for the exit.

"Wait!" Georg jumped to his feet heroically. "It's dark outside. Let me accompany you."

The rest of us trailed behind, reluctant to face Titli's temper but too chivalrous to allow the youths into a confrontation on their own.

Titli walked quickly, several paces ahead and oblivious to her entourage. She had almost reached the end of the main road, only a few steps away from the well, when she came to an abrupt halt.

Angelika squinted into the darkness. "What is she doing?"

The indigo shadows of dusk wrapped around Titli, a second cloak of silk. The late hour must have crept up on her, for she opened her mouth in a wide yawn—or so we thought, at first.

There was something wrong in the movements of her face. The cheekbones shifted audibly, her jaw unhinging with a pneumatic snap as if preparing to dilate for a birthing.

Angelika pressed a shaking hand to her lips. "Why—"

"Shh!" Georg's eyes were uncharacteristically wide. "She might hear."

Titli's skin glowed warm in the cold night. She retched, knees buckling. Her tongue lolled out of her mouth, red and bruised like a rotting berry. Saliva dripped down her chin and sizzled where it landed on the ground. A golden sheen spilled past her open lips.

Mrs. Ludwig uttered a word we had never before heard her speak.

Flames spewed from Titli's mouth and skittered onto the open road. They were a strange hue, a spiral of yellow and green and purple, like the colours of her silks. Dry leaves littered across the floor sparked, then incinerated into ash. The varicoloured fire roared to the end of the street and tumbled down the well. We watched water bubble up the cylindrical wall, smoking and overflowing like volcanic lava. The liquid flared hot and bright, and crept toward us. The heat seared our vision and the tips of our loose hair.

Angelika cried out. Georg's hands flew up to shield his face from the glare. The smell of something burning coated our throats.

Titli coughed, her lungs depleting. Her hands and knees splayed on the ground. The blaze sputtered out. Slowly, the frothing water settled back into the depths of the well.

Mrs. Ludwig edged back. A twig cracked loudly beneath her heel.

We ducked behind a building as Titli's head spun in our direction. She had taken note of our faces once already that evening. We didn't dare invite more attention from such a dangerous creature. At any moment, she might inhale deeply and roast us alive.

Mrs. Ludwig made a run for it, throwing herself to the other side of the building. We sprinted after her, careening back to the tavern, glancing around at each other to gauge reactions to what we had observed. Georg's expression was alight with glee. For all our speculation, most of us could not have imagined anything like this. But Georg had insisted from the beginning that Titli was a fire-breather.

And now she had proven herself to be just that.

Later that week, the Provost arrived to collect his cleaned shirts. Instead of encountering the quiet courtyards and subdued households from his previous visit, he came upon us yelling to our neighbours from open windows, bustling with errands, even making love in partially concealed alleyways. The smell of roasting lamb—a rare luxury—wafted from the tavern. Our mouths watered in anticipation.

"Has something happened?" the Provost demanded of Mr. Hartner, who was passing by with his cart of vegetables.

"We are cured!" said Mr. Hartner. "The sickness consumes us no longer."

The Provost's lips thinned. His gaze flitted over to Georg, who poured coins into the florist's hands while speaking animatedly of his sister's revitalised health.

Georg wasn't the only one inclined to festive purchases. We emptied our purses for our favourite sweetmeats, to stock up on mead for toasting. Hope and joy had seized our hungry, thirsty spirits.

The Provost alone remained untouched by the commotion swirling about him. He turned back to Mr. Hartner with a disapproving frown. "What, pray tell, is this supposed cure?"

Georg glanced over. "Sir Provost, it's the southern girl. She breathed fire just like I said she would and boiled all the water in the well. It seems something rotten was growing deep inside, poisoning us, but now no trace of it is left."

One of the Provost's eyes twitched. "She breathed fire? Like the devil himself?"

"Well, I admit she gave us quite the fright when we witnessed it happen last night," Georg said. "I've never seen anything else like it. But—excuse the pun—all's well that ends well, no? Perhaps there's some benefit to her oddities."

The Provost's face went dangerously white. When he spoke, his voice was thin and sharp. "I warned you not to succumb to her dishonour. You would reject a malady the heavens sent to guide us toward a noble path? Mark my words, when this demon's hellfire spreads to your homes and to your precious families, you will no longer deem beneficial her *oddities*."

Unbeknownst to us, Titli had just stepped out of the dressmaker's shop on the next block. Hidden behind the awning, she overheard this last part of our conversation. Had we crossed the street, traversed the line of fir trees, and spotted her at that very moment, we would have seen the smile fade from her lips and the gentle light in her eyes darken into something ugly.

The Provost's worries accompanied him late into the night. He perused our local newspaper for information about the southern colony but found nothing specific. No accounts of fire-spitting savages, no records of natives overthrowing civilising authorities through arson.

But he recognised Titli's attributes as unnatural. The way her indecent mannerisms amused and attracted his parishioners could quickly adulterate the village's delicate lifestyle. He would no longer be able to care for the people he took responsibility for if they were to stop listening to him. To prevent this, the Provost needed to understand Titli in great detail. He intended to operate two steps ahead of her hazardous mechanisms.

Any such exhibitions from her ancestors would surely have been noticed by the governing outposts in the southern territories over the last century. With more extensive sample sizes to study, their observations must have contained deeper knowledge than anything he could hope to glean from Titli's case alone.

Our Provost had just finished penning a letter to send to the southern colonial authorities when he smelled something burning. He lurched to his window.

The crackling sound reached him first, the noise of peckish flames gnawing at his front door.

The Atrium was not the only building affected. Golden fire stalked after our houses like a beast of prey. Its green teeth gnashed through our thatched rooves, its purple talons tore into our wooden walls. The air filled with acrid smoke and our bitter cries.

We rushed to and from the village well to load and empty buckets of water. The Brinkhofs brought their large laundry tubs. Mr. Hartner lent his vegetable cart to facilitate transport. Angelika ran down the street ringing a bell to wake everyone.

And the bravest of us, our Provost, climbed ladders to our upstairs windows and reached inside the smouldering caverns to rescue our children.

Between coughs and sobs, we cursed the monster who brought this upon us.

III.

One hundred years ago they came over the horizon with pitchforks and firearms to scrape the crops from our lands, pry the jewels out of our earth, wrest the fish from our rivers, wring the life out of our bodies. For a hundred years, we were squeezed in their fists, crushed under their boots, broken by their pressure—until our organs found a way to bend.

Our bones shifted to diffuse the blows of their clubs. When they called us beasts and threatened to beat us, our fangs lengthened to daggers, our nails sharpened into swords. We bit and scratched our way out of detention. Blood dripped down our chins, fulfilling their prophecies of our savagery. Our changing skeletons reached for any possibility of freedom.

Titli's family spun cotton into fabric for generations before the northern traders confiscated the premises under the steely gaze of their guns. Chaperoned by the traders and their weapons, our cloth travelled across three continents, seven countries, and countless towns to a faraway land.

Without our textiles, we shivered through the nights and hungered through the days. Our fingers, previously so deft at turning spinning wheels, began to unravel at the tips. The skin disintegrated into thin, flexible columns. These were durable and shimmered in the light. If we closed our eyes and imagined different colours, the threads became infused with vibrant shades.

Titli watched her parents tear the strings off their fingers with their teeth and weave them together into geometric patterns. Together we twisted tunics and scarves, trousers and skirts, until everyone in the village became adorned with custom-made clothing. These were given out of devotion, a sharing of something we were able to provide for our loved ones while the northerners snatched everything else away. Though we turned reticent after the loss of our original livelihood, Titli felt our affection stitched into each row of silk we created.

When the northern traders arrived again with their guns to shut down what they deemed an illicit textile production, we clutched little Titli in our hands. The threads from our fingers wrapped around her body in a shell. They spun over and under her limbs like fitted armour until no bullet could pierce their barrier.

By the time Titli clawed her way out of the cocoon, we were gone and so was her childhood.

The fire from her mouth was new. Nothing like it had erupted out of Titli's body before. It stung as it scorched its way up her throat, leaving behind burned, inflamed flesh that made it difficult to swallow.

Titli didn't know what brought it forth. It began with a sudden cramp in her abdomen that intensified into a rising white-hot pain. She tried to press her lips closed when she felt it swell up the second time, but a mere layer of flesh charred fast and offered little obstacle against her internal conflagration.

Pressing trembling hands to her bleeding mouth, Titli watched in horror as the curtains in her inn room caught fire. She rushed to beat at the flames with her pillow, but something about the golden, greenish, purpling blaze made it spread more swiftly than other flames. It burst through the window and raced to the nearby buildings.

"Fire!" she tried to scream, but her raw vocal cords tore wetly around the word. She hurtled down the stairs and tripped onto the street. Alarm bells pounded a warning. An elderly man struggled with a cart overloaded with water pails. Titli rushed toward him to help stabilise it.

Running back and forth between the burning street and the well blurred into a continuous haze of activity. Hands loaded sloshing containers into her arms, and she passed emptied ones back down the relay line. Folded tightly into a chain of human beings, Titli felt the ends of adjacent bodies blending into the beginnings of hers. She worried about her spontaneous ignition but buried like an ember in the dense throng of people, it remained dormant.

When the flames in the area were finally under control, the pealing alarm clattered to a halt. Titli glanced up to search for the source. Angelika was sprawled on her knees by the Atrium steps, head in her hands, bell discarded at her feet.

Titli sat down beside Angelika and handed her a fresh glass of water. The maiden drank deeply, droplets leaking from the corners of her mouth and neck bobbing. Purple shadows lined the skin over her rippling tendons like the ghost of a hand refusing to relinquish her. Titli pictured her own fingers tracing their path, though in a caress too reverent to leave marks.

After a long moment, Angelika finally lowered the glass and wiped a dainty thumb over her lips to dry them, gazing coyly at Titli through yellow lashes. "That was very thoughtful of you." She gestured to the ashy dust around them. "Especially since your thirst must exceed mine, given your glowing oral talents."

Titli stilled.

"The gem-like colours, the remarkable speed—I'm familiar with your work."

Titli's throat ached, both in its flesh and somewhere deeper. "Do you despise me?"

"You make me nervous at times," Angelika confessed. "But you're here helping us put out the fire, aren't you?"

"But I—I was the one to—"

"This isn't the first fire to run wild in the Atrium." Angelika bit her lip, chewing on her words. "I started one in my father's study when I was a child. It wasn't anything quite like yours. But still, it happened. Because I was playing by the hearth even after he forbade it. You see, it was the only fireplace in our house in the dead of winter, and my fingers were turning blue with cold. I was so afraid to tell him what I had done that I hid in my room until he came across the fire himself. By then, half of the upper floor was irreparably damaged, and to this day he doesn't know why."

Titli moved without thinking. Their hands touched on the warm ground between them, her little finger crossing over Angelika's. "It was an accident. You were young."

"I've never told anybody this before." Angelika craned her head to gaze up at her father's building. "I helped sweep up the debris and everyone told my father what a good girl I was. You probably think I did it out of guilt. But all these years later, I'll be doing the same thing again." Her hand turned and gripped Titli's tightly. "Soon this won't be my home any longer. But as long as I live here, I ought to help fix it, I think."

Titli was exhausted but her mind was too heavy for sleep. The silk forming from her fingertips was thicker and tougher than usual, less thread for fine clothing and more strings of rope. She twined them together into a solid cord. By the time the sun rose in the morning, she had constructed countless such cables.

People were already busy with repairs outside. Titli lugged her pillars of rope into the bustle and offered them up as reinforcement beams.

Georg regarded her coldly. "This is the material you use to make those colourful outfits? Do you mean to dress up our buildings in frippery after setting them on fire?"

Titli considered retreating to the inn to save face. The villagers weren't thrilled by her appearance, and enclosing herself inside a cocoon had protected her life before. But she had missed the opportunity to make a difference in the outcome of her family's survival. Instead, she had emerged into a world without her community in it.

This time, she had the choice to remain present. Her strange new fire had caused a devastation she had never intended. At the very least, she should stay and make repairs.

"My silk is load bearing and moisture-resistant," she said hesitantly. "You can set it up as temporary scaffolding or use it to seal exposures."

Wordlessly, Georg picked up one of Titli's cords. They fed it through a pulley, then secured more along walls and to knit cracks together. By evening, Titli's silk wove through most buildings on the main street like multicoloured surgical stitches drawing wounds closed. And as the neighbourhood healed, so, too, did its residents.

Georg wiped his dusty hands with a handkerchief. "This was a nice idea, Titli." He pronounced her name with the hard *T* sound of his language. "If you have more silk to spare, I hope we can continue tomorrow."

They perched on scattered wooden crates to rest their feet. Angelika came by and arranged plates of bread and sausage, mugs of wheaty beer, to share. Her lavender fragrance lingered with Titli all the way back to and from the inn as Titli grabbed a sachet of curry powder, which they took turns sprinkling over their meal.

The three of them were halfway through their supper when the Provost stepped out of the Atrium.

In ten long strides, he was upon them. "Angelika, what are you doing? I warned you all this day would come. And now you break bread in the smoking wreckage this outsider created."

Titli stopped chewing, unsure how to react. The curl in the Provost's lip unnerved her.

"We're just eating," Angelika said softly.

"*Eating.*" The Provost's hand flexed at his side. "Have you forgotten what they consume down in the southern colonies, Angelika? Any day now, she will begin eating *you.*"

"Excuse me." Titli rose to her feet. The Provost's anger wasn't making only her uncomfortable; beside her, Angelika's shoulders hunched. "I think I'll take my leave."

IV.

A large letter arrived for the Provost the following week. The stamp marked it as originating from the southern colonial authorities.

The natives of these lands are false people, read the personalised note included with the official records. *Fruit that grows here is as unholy as its terroir. Provost, you will see from these documents how we have our hands full maintaining civilisation in this region.*

There were diagrams included. Drawings of faces with inhumanly extended teeth, which curved over the lower lip, past the chin, and were shaded with insinuations of dried blood.

Illegal Manufacturing of Silken Textiles read the heading of one report. It described a material suspiciously similar to the fabrics Titli was spreading wantonly throughout the Provost's village. He should have anticipated her so-called trade dealt in contraband. *All fabric production and distribution must be regulated through the appropriate authorities. Anything operating outside of these regulations is strictly prohibited.*

The Provost flipped through the rest of the pages, pausing at statements about *demonic vipers shedding artificial skin* and *beastly wings protruding out of the shoulder blades.* Worst was the confirmation that *bloodstains around the dental projections verify their consumption of human flesh.*

He tossed the stack of papers onto his desk. With this, there was plenty of justification for him to act. Nobody could read through these detailed accounts from the southern governing station and believe someone like Titli should be allowed to exist in his village.

V.

The knock sounded late one night.

Titli sat up in her bed. She never received visitors at the inn. "Who is it?"

"It's me," answered Angelika.

It was a small room. The only place to perch awkwardly was on the bed. Angelika's perfume thickened the miniscule space between them.

"What brings you here?" Titli asked after a long silence of them staring openly at each other.

Angelika bit her lip. "Do you truly eat people?"

"Well, what do you think?"

"Am I someone you would eat?"

Titli's mouth twitched. "I can, if you'd like me to."

Angelika's gaze lowered. It slid from the stack of incomplete embroidery projects to Titli's lips to the rumpled bedspread. "Would it hurt?"

"No. And I would stop the moment you signaled me to."

"All right." Angelika's eyes lifted again. A faint blush tinged her cheeks. "Eat me, then."

"Which room is the outsider staying in?"

"Sir Provost, good evening!" The innkeeper hopped to his feet. "Second floor and down the hall."

The Provost stormed upstairs and threw open the door.

The sight that greeted him took him several moments to comprehend. His daughter's head thrown back over the pillow, knees pulled upward, a moan on her lips. Between her legs, Titli bent as Angelika's elegant hands tangled in her black curls.

"What is the meaning of this!" he bellowed.

Angelika squeaked and dived under the covers. But the damage was done.

The Provost curled his unforgiving fingers around Titli's upper arm and hauled her off his daughter. Titli shouted, but the Provost heard nothing beyond the furious rushing in his ears.

By the time he got her out to the street, their scuffle had drawn a crowd. Georg planted himself in the Provost's path. "Where are you taking her?"

"Get out of my way, Brinkhof. She's a winged demon we must cast out of our society."

"I've never noticed anything like that, and we've worked together every day."

"Time and again, I've cautioned you not to let her linger around us. I told you she would pit us against each other, turn you into my adversaries. You mustn't let her win."

"Wait!" Angelika chased after them.

The Provost ignored his daughter. He yanked the struggling Titli to the well and pinned her against the rim.

"Stop!" cried Angelika. "Leave her alone!"

Titli twisted, digging in her elbows and reaching out with her knees. A kick connected and the Provost grunted. The pouch fastened to his belt came undone. Its contents spilled onto the ground—a journal, a sack of gold, and a tinted bottle.

"Father." Angelika stooped to retrieve the bottle. "This is one of my cosmetic tinctures from the apothecary. I've been missing it for months."

Georg peered at the container. "Why would your father have that?"

"I don't know. It's poisonous if ingested." Angelika tucked her nail into the stopper and pried it off. "The bottle is empty. He must have used quite a lot of it somewhere. It couldn't be on his own short hair. For—" Her voice caught. "Father. *Father*, was it you? The well water—did you pour this in?"

The Provost screamed. From the timing, it could have been a response to his daughter's question. Then he reeled back with gashes gored into his palms.

"I knew it." His eyes bulged. "Look at her real form."

Titli's hands scrabbled for purchase on the well's wall as her back arched and her shoulders elongated. Scales erupted through the back of her tunic, tracing bones that contorted into multi-pronged, webbed limbs. Soft, downy fur coated her skin. When she threw back her head in agony, canines stretched out of her mouth like stalactites. The ends were stained with the Provost's blood.

Mouth twisting with contempt, he lunged at her. His ragged hands closed around her neck.

An animalistic shriek rose out of Titli's throat, a cawing, wordless expression of pain. Instinctively, her wings stretched open and gave an enormous flap. Her feet lifted off the ground. Still clutching at her furiously, the Provost rose with her, his legs dangling uselessly in the air.

"Help me!" he said. One hand dug into Titli's neck, fingers shifting cords of muscle and nails drawing blood. His other hand reached out, searching wildly for something to grab hold, for someone to anchor him back to the ground. "Angelika!"

Angelika, bottle still clenched in her hands, turned her face upward.

The Provost's grip around Titli's thickening body loosened. He howled as his body fell straight down into the well with a splash.

Water crashed around his thrashing arms.

VI.

That dawn, we tracked Titli's flight across the lightening sky. Her figure loomed large in the beginning, but the shadow of a shape shrunk the farther it moved from us. Our eyes squinted into the horizon until we could no longer make out any part of her.

We whispered "goodbye," though she probably didn't hear.

Morning dew saturated the air with the perfume of spring flowers. Birds woke in the trees and started up their choir.

As we turned toward the main street and our homes, the shouts of a drowning man faded into the background.

IF I AM TO EARN MY TETHER

Geneve Flynn

a gundarim (Malay poetic form):
>*if I am to earn my tether*
>*first I must trace the line*

There are lines in our city-state you will not cross. You are bound within Singapore, forever trawling like an ancient catfish growing increasingly too large for its pond, suffocating even as your wealth expands. Land reclamation is no help. Those artificial grounds are the places you cannot go. When I steer your wheelchair to one such perimeter, sometimes facing the soaring triple towers of the Marina Bay Sands hotel, sometimes looking over the utilitarian silos of the Jurong Island petrochemical plant, your lips peel back, exposing yellowing teeth and receding gums. Your usually somnolent eyes widen.

The panicked noises you make are dreadful.

I try to catch a glimpse down your throat. Even immobilized and draped in a blanket, you still withhold that from me.

You are lucky. You have edges to your world: borders and limits that tell you who you are and who you are not.

I have no such blessing. I can go wherever I please, fly across the continents, traverse great distances—as long as my passport is current and my credit is good.

On the rare occasions when I am relieved of your care, I visit the peripheries of your world. I stop and wait, hoping to feel something that holds me back, hoping for the stretch of an unseen tether tugging on my insides, but there is nothing. I step from the old island to the new and I am the same Felicity on either side.

You died, Ngoi Goong. *Grandfather.* It's happened before, but this time, it took the doctors and nurses four minutes to revive you. I stood by your bedside, hands pressed to my stomach, gaze lowered. It must have looked like I was mourning you.

Instead, I fretted that I had left it too late to tell you your story.

Now that you're settled on clean sheets, the froth of failing systems wiped from your chin, and all the paraphernalia for prolonging life tucked away, I shall begin.

You don't even need to be awake. I think she will hear.

It was not greed that shone from your eyes when a broker approached you with a contract to deliver sixteen hundred tons of sand to the zone that would become Marina Bay.

At least, not at first.

Your mother had fallen ill with emphysema and as the oldest son, it was your lot to care for her. Your wife was also pregnant with your first child and your fledgling business as a sand merchant was foundering. How were you to know that the licenses to mine legitimately were so costly, or that you would have to cross so many palms to build guanxi. *Favor.*

"The original crew absconded," the broker said with a too-casual shrug in reply to your question and signaled for another coffee from the market stall vendor.

You looked up from the sheaf of papers with a frown. "All of them?"

The broker sniffed. "You know how these people are."

It was common for one or two crewmen to desert; they most often came from the kampungs and poorer neighboring countries, forced from their coastal villages by the very industry that now took them in and promised a fair wage and steady work. In reality, their contracts were little more than debt bondage. The men had to pay for their lodging and supplies and work visas, but the interest was exorbitant, so they were forced to sign on for more work, which meant more fees. And so it went, on and on.

"Bodoh." *Stupid.* He continued in Singlish: the mishmash of Indian, Chinese, Malay and English that made up the Singaporean tongue. "The authorities just catch them and imprison them, or deport them. Or bring them back to us. Then they're worse off than when they crawled off their boats."

Still, an entire crew? You hesitated, cool despite the crowding and humidity of the open-air arcade.

The broker took a bite of his toast, slathered with coconut jam, and slurped his coffee. "Can you do the job?"

You thought of your mother, gasping for air as she steadily turned blue; your wife, growing more gravid with each day. You looked down and saw the name on the contract: Chao Yap Seng, the minister for Future Building and Land Development. The most connected man on the island.

You folded the papers and tucked them under your arm and shook the broker's hand.

"I'll make it happen."

"Thank fuck," Shi Lei, your brother and second-in-command, muttered when the *Fanrong* finally chugged out of port.

It had taken three days to ready the barge for departure, weighed as she was with repairs you'd arranged under lien from the broker. Your stomach twisted as you watched the crewmen hurrying across her deck. If you failed to deliver, you would lose her and be no better than them: drowning in debt and owing more than when you started. The southwest monsoon season was only weeks away so the window was narrow, to say the least. With a tight laugh, you clapped Shi Lei on the neck, shaking him like a dog because you had to release your nerves somehow. "We'll make it. Don't I always have a plan?"

Three hours later, the sun was directly above, beating down fierce and hot, when the scarred coastline of Dibaham Island hove into view.

Shi Lei gestured with his chin to the south of the island. "Should we put down at Letong Beach as usual?"

You peered through the binoculars. "Shit." On the edge of the peninsula, a glint of glass reflected sharply. "Coast guard. We can't risk it."

"Should we turn back?" Shi Lei squinted against the glare.

"I'll be ruined." You gripped the rail, heart thudding. You had harvested the sand from this island for months. Why, today of all days, would the Malaysian Coast Guard be patrolling this very stretch? What did it mean? Was it fate? You stared at the open sea beyond Dibaham Island, as if you could see your destination.

Did you dare?

"Laoban?" *Boss.* Shi Lei preferred to call you this rather than your name. Your little brother, always looking to you to lead, to take care of things; just like everyone else. The weight of it bore you down like a sinker.

"How far is it to the Riau Archipelago?"

Shi Lei paled. "Three hours north-east. But the crew will baulk. They say it's pantang." *Taboo. Forbidden.*

You shook your head. "Superstitious nonsense. You know better than that." You straightened, determined to pull yourself upright. "This is our only chance. Set our course."

The light had deepened to indigo by the time the *Fanrong* arrived at one of the unnamed islands in the archipelago, but the evidence of other sand miners stood stark: chewed, half-collapsed cliffs and churned shoreline; the stink of dead fish washed up on the beach.

The seven men in your crew huddled in small knots on deck, whispering amongst themselves. Berhantu. Berhantu. *Haunted.* Most were indigenous to Malaysia and Indonesia, and their belief that all things have spirits—even the land itself, especially in this isolated cluster of islands with nothing but black water for miles all around—was hard to dislodge.

Shi Lei came up alongside you on the bridge. "This is going to be impossible."

You peered out into the darkness. The spine of a rock formation jutted from the west of the island, outlined in the setting sun and shaped like the curve of a woman's body. This was the right place. "Power up the lamps. Things will look better to the men in the light." You took a deep breath. "And start the dredger."

"Now? Can't we wait until tomorrow morning?"

You closed your eyes. It was more effort to get these men to do the work than to do the work yourself. You could pilot the *Fanrong* yourself but there was no way you could mine the necessary volume of sand without them. With a controlled sigh, you gripped your brother by the nape again. "It took us five hours to get here, in a barge with the current against us. How long do you think it will take the coast guard to arrive?"

Shi Lei shrugged out of your hand, then went to do your bidding.

A huge white maw swam up from the murk, snapped and missed, as a mudskipper was caught in the scoop of the dredger. The tiny fish tumbled, pulled up into the belly of the barge which chewed through the underwater shelf of the island, disgorging a steady sludge into its innards. For the past six hours, the roar of the machine filled the air, shaking palm fronds and echoing across the water, non-stop.

Flipped far from the main flow, the little creature lay on its side on the sand, broken and gulping. Its scales coated with a thin, nacreous film of diesel. The crew labored through choking fumes and under the halogens, crawling over the vessel, checking the engine and making sure the extraction ran smoothly.

The fish managed to right itself and dragged its body a few inches. If only someone would have noticed and tossed it back into the sea, it might not have been too late. Then, the sand flexed like a muscular tongue, and with a red pop and a squeak of agony, the mudskipper was gone.

Shi Lei looked up from the winch he was trying to unsnarl under a stuttering lamp. He shivered. The world had just shifted, as if an unseen cloak that kept him concealed had suddenly vanished. He felt the cool regard of something caress his back and spun, forgetting his gritty eyes and aching feet, forgetting the incredible tension straining the damaged cable. He stared out into the night. The light had exhausted the receptors in his vision, so he saw nothing, not even the metal cord as it finally gave and whipped across his chest, shattering his collarbone and tearing a broad strap of skin and flesh free.

You scrubbed the blood from your hands, thankful that the sedatives had finally kicked in and the screaming had stopped. You rested your forehead on the mirror above the sink in the tiny restroom aboard the barge.

If you left the island now, you could be back on the mainland by midday at the latest, and Singapore General was only minutes away from Jurong Port. You could get Shi Lei into hospital, give him the best chance of recovery. He could still regain the use of his arm. Wasn't that what a big brother should do?

Yet there were others in the family counting on you, and the hold was only a third full. What had Shi Lei been thinking, doing repairs under such poor light?

His shoulder was strapped and his wounds had been disinfected and bandaged. A camp had been set up thirty meters from the barge where the forest met the beach for the men to eat and rest. Exhausted and ashen, looking younger than he had in years, Shi Lei now slept on one of the camp beds.

It wouldn't do to move him; better to let him rest.

This contract benefited him too. It would expand the business and make you both wealthy beyond your dreams. You just had to stick the course. He would understand.

You stared at the hold in the chill light of dawn, wondering if the lack of sleep was making you see things; the silence after hours of constant roaring grind seemed to ring with questions. Even though you and the crew had worked through the night, only just now powering the dredger down because a boulder had become jammed in one of the buckets, the *Fanrong* was still only a third full.

Something must have gone wrong. Shit. Shi Lei did most of the maintenance on the machine, you would have to ask him.

You knew something was wrong when your feet took you within earshot of the camp. There was a persistent fluttering and agitated tapping at the canvas enclosing the tent where Shi Lei slept. *What on earth?* You flipped back the entry flap and jewel-green insects exploded from inside, tangling in your hair, scratching at your neck with long, spiked legs, brushing your lips with gossamer wings. You dared not open your mouth to cry out, only folding yourself into a tight ball, arms clamped over your head, eyes squeezed shut. The rich, throat-coating smell of earth and vegetation pressed around you, and it seemed it would smother you completely.

As suddenly as the swarm erupted, it evaporated. In the quiet that followed, you cowered, flinching at the prickle of grass, at the trickle of sweat down your cheek.

"Boss!" One of the crewmen hurried towards you, his steps squeaking in the sand.

You cracked an eye, then the other, and straightened. There was no sign of the grasshoppers. No broken wings, no twitching backwards-bending legs, no gleaming multi-faceted lenses reflecting their agonized deaths. You turned in a slow circle.

Aayiz paused and followed the line of your sight, his expression mirroring yours. "What is it?" he asked nervously.

"Nothing. I was startled by a bird. What's the problem?"

He cast another worried glance around then focused. "The boulder's cleared but we can't start the motor. We checked the fuel and pump. It all looks okay but it refuses to kick over."

"All right, don't worry. Shi Lei can walk us through the repair." *Shi Lei.* He had been trapped with the swarm. Before you could pause to think about what it had been like, you stepped inside the tent.

"What…" Aayiz stumbled into you.

The camp bed was empty except for what looked like ordered rows of golden rice, concentrated around the blood stains from your brother's wounds. Where was Shi Lei? You crouched beside the bed and leaned forward, then jerked back.

Insect eggs.

"Hantu sedang mermerhati." *The ghosts are watching,* Aayiz muttered beside you as the crew crept through the thickening jungle. He peered at the merbau trees and tangled strangler fig roots that laced their trunks in sinewy cages.

"Quiet!" It had taken every bit of persuasion to convince the men to form a search party. Finally, you'd had to promise a share of the profits once the *Fanrong* returned to port. "Let's find Shi Lei, then we can go back to the barge."

"Then we leave?"

"First we find my brother."

The dense forest canopy cut much of the midday sun's light, but seemed to trap all of the island's heat and humidity. Mosquitoes and midges sang around your ears and sipped at the sweat on the back of your neck. You frantically swept them away; you could still feel the scratch and claw of the grasshoppers. You hadn't imagined it. Salt from your perspiration found stinging lines on your skin and told you it had been real.

"Boss! Look!" Kadek called.

You hurried to the crewman's side and followed the line of his pointed finger.

"Kampung," he said.

It was little more than a few stilt houses and a circle of stones to contain the remnants of a fire in a clearing, not enough to call a village but it still tightened the skin over your body.

You ventured into the houses, the crew hovered outside at a distance, but found no sign of Shi Lei. The buildings were dim but freshly swept, with the few communal belongings neatly stowed. There were no animal droppings or cobwebs, nor other evidence of abandonment. You felt ghosts. Not spirits as Aayiz meant, but the echoes of people who had been here only moments—seconds—ago.

"Spread out!" You pushed through the men and turned in a circle. "There may be someone we can question."

The men glanced at each other then reluctantly departed to search.

You stared up at the entrance to one of the houses and with a quick look to check that no one was watching, you climbed the stairs.

The dark interior was cut through with fingers of light from gaps in the roofing. The breath of loamy, green petrichor washed over you and you hastily brushed at something trailing across your cheek. It was only a stray rope hanging from the beam. You returned to what had caught your eye the first time: a row of glass bottles lined along a shelf at the rear of the house, their interiors blackened halfway up their sides from within by some viscous substance. You forced yourself to step closer, your heart tripping in your chest. You leaned in, feeling the press of the darkness, the specters of the people who lived here.

"Boss! Tuan!" *Sir.*

With a sharp inhale, you stumbled backwards and fled, seeking the daylight, the air that didn't reek of chitin and soil.

You stood blinking down at your crewman from the top of the stairs. "What? What is it?"

Aayiz beckoned anxiously. "We found another barge."

The vessel had come to ground on a beach a few hundred meters from the kampung. It had missed the jagged rocks at the mouth of the bay and, somehow, had been interred up to its deck. Apart from the sand that obscured its name and swallowed half of its hull, the barge appeared unharmed. Its dredger was still submerged, as if the ship had been caught in the act of pillaging.

"Was there a storm?" Aayiz asked. "Where's the crew?"

You shook your head. "Let's check inside. Shi Lei might have sought shelter."

The same insectile stink greeted you as you climbed aboard. You and the men were forced to enter from the far side where the sand covering the deck was treacherous: you sank up to your knees in some places and slipped in others, risking a turned ankle. The men refused to go inside, so it was up to you to search the operating room.

It was the *Naga*, the barge and crew who were originally signed on for the contract. You flipped through the logbook with a frown. How could the ship have become so buried in only one week? And where was the crew?

A grinding shudder worked from beneath your soles, into your shins, your thigh bones, your groin, all the way up to your teeth. You threw your arms out to steady yourself. From the deck, your crew cried out, high-pitched and terrified. You dropped the logbook and tried to clamber out. It was only the hull shifting on the unstable ground, what had frightened them so? The sand drained away beneath your feet, sucking you down, even as you clawed at the levers, the cabin edge, racing to get higher. You scrambled onto the roof of the operating room and clung on as the barge continued to sink and keel. Your men had leapt free and you saw that it was not the failing ship that had frightened them.

Uncovered by the movement, and rolling and sliding bonelessly into the collapsing, eddying vortex, were the bodies of the missing crewmen. Their eyes were frozen open, speckled and crusted with grains of sand in place of tears, and their mouths were forced wide with the carapaces of many jewel-green grasshoppers. A final body tumbled toward the center of the draining sand. An arm had come free from the sling you had applied only last night, and his bandages had unraveled, exposing the torn flesh at his chest.

"Shi Lei!"

You saw with a lurch that rows of golden eggs had been laid in the wound with efficient, biotic order.

"Jump!" Aayiz screamed.

Broken from your horrified trance you leapt, landing gracelessly, knocking the breath from your lungs.

Aayiz grasped your arm and dragged you upright. The other men were sprinting for the cover of the trees. Together, you staggered, feeling the ground slipping away from your heels, sensing its hunger as the barge groaned and screeched behind you. You didn't dare stop, even though your chest burned and your head pounded. You and Aayiz crashed into Kadek at the edge of the jungle. He stumbled but caught you; your diaphragm finally unlocked and you sucked in a huge breath. Turning, you watched just as the stern tipped up into the air, then with an enormous grinding sigh, the sand closed over and consumed everything.

"We have to go, boss." Aayiz pulled you away. "We have to get off this island."

Your legs dragged as you blundered back into the clearing: the same one you and the crew had returned to time and again for the past two hours. The same giant merbau tree soared into the sky from its center, fighting to escape the shadows of the forest below.

"Fuck! It can't be!" Kadek sobbed. He charged in the opposite direction from where you had come.

"Kadek!" Aayiz cried, himself close to tears. "Wait! Stay close!"

Too late, the forest swallowed him and you and the others were forced to give chase.

You pulled up, not quite believing your eyes.

The kampung.

Kadek had skidded to a stop and the other men huddled close despite the sticky heat. Dotted around the clearing and stationed on the stairs and peering from the dark doorways of the houses were men, women, and children, all short in stature. They stared at you in blank silence.

"Halo." You took a step forward. Only their eyes moved as they tracked you; the villagers might as well have been made of stone. "Tolong batu kami…" *please help us,* "…kapal," *ship*—

As one, the children creaked their jaws open and a swift whirring issued from their mouths.

"Sial!" *Fuck!* Aayiz and the others stumbled backwards with cries of alarm: all of the children's tongues had been torn out.

The whirring changed in tone, becoming a rising chirr and the crew took another step backwards, clutching at each other. Small jewel-green heads, then thin, spiked legs and flexing, damp wings unfolded from deep within the children's throats, crawling over the mutilated remnants of their tongues. The grasshoppers spilled and flew from the children's mouths, swarming around you all. Needle-noses drilled into your cheeks, your arms, your hands, your chest.

You screamed and ducked, sweeping a thick branch from the ground and swung. The end struck a girl of about seven across the skull with a crack; her head snapped sideways and she tumbled, loose-limbed. The grasshoppers that teemed around her fell like stones, all of them twitching and dead. For a moment, the insects around you paused, trembling.

You stared at the villagers. They had not moved and their faces were blank.

Gently, almost reverently, the land took the child's small body into itself, folding over her lax and broken form like a mother's embrace. As soon as she was gone, the fierce green cloud again whipped into a frenzy, stabbing, scratching, buzzing.

The men seized branches, rocks, whatever they could find, and swept through the children, smashing, cracking, pulverizing. When all the young were gone, they turned on the men and women and elders, and still, the villagers made no move to stop them: they simply dropped, bloodied, one after the other.

Finally, you and your crew staggered to a standstill. Everywhere you looked was dressed in gore… the ground slick with blood but not a body to be seen. All the grasshoppers had vanished, leaving not even one jewel-green wing behind.

Why hadn't the villagers fought back? If only they had raised arms, that might have given you and your men pause enough to stop, to regain your civility. Perhaps their lives did not have value. Perhaps they were hantu, *spirits*, after all.

You waited.

The crew looked at each other in numb exhaustion. Kadek folded over and vomited. Aayiz absently wiped the tears streaming from his face, only smearing his cheeks with more red. Another man broke into giggles, the sound grating across your teeth.

You waited.

A furious rustling came from beneath your feet and the ground began to heave. Your men tottered away from the buck and churn, crying out weakly.

"Boss!" Aayiz shouted. "Let's go! Now, while we can!"

The men turned and ran, back in the direction of the *Fanrong*, back towards the beach.

Not yet.

You charged and swung, connecting with the back of Kadek's skull. He collapsed, cracking his cheek against a rock, never even putting his hands out to stop his fall. The ground shuddered, and you imagined it was with pleasure and vicious anticipation. Another crewman turned, confusion on his face when he saw Kadek's body. Without pause, you swung again, splitting the skin at his temple, hooking his eye free from its socket, and he tumbled to the forest floor with an ugly grunt. Again and again, you swung, until only Aayiz remained, weeping, hands held out in helpless pleading.

"Boss, tuan…please. What are you doing?" Snot and tears washed the blood from his face in lines. He looked every bit as young as Shi Lei had.

"I have to call her," you said, almost apologetically.

Then you swung a final time and all was quiet.

The *Fanrong* rode low in the water; her hold was full to the brim with sand and she chugged slowly. No matter. You were the only crew member left and there was more than enough supplies for your trip back to port.

Oh, Ngoi Goong. You're awake. Please don't look so upset. Here, let me plump your pillows, is your canula bothering you? Your mouth seems to be working at something; do you have something to say?

No? I see the effort it is taking you in the clamp of your lips, the tremble of your chin, in the tightness around your eyes. The doctors say it was a stroke that robbed you of your speech but I know it is the secret you swallowed so many years ago: what you consumed that became so much a part of you that you could not relinquish it.

Don't worry, you will be able to rest soon.

Your business boomed. The contract led to connections, guanxi, money. You supplied the government with all the building and land reclamation material it could require and you became one of the wealthiest, most influential men in Singapore—an island that increased its landmass by nearly twenty-five percent in two hundred short years. How many men could say they had a hand in creating *a quarter* of an entire country?

Our family grew. The child your wife had been pregnant with would eventually become my father, and was the first of eight sons and daughters. Those children married and blessed you with many grandchildren, and thanks to your wealth, they lived under one sprawling roof of your marbled manse on Nassim Road. Surely, it must seem to outsiders that the gods smile upon you.

Surrounded by so many filial children and grandchildren.

Yet none of them know you as I do.

CLANG.

Goodness. You startled me.

Here, let me pick up that bedpan. I suppose you hoped to rouse one of those many filial family members, hoped that they would come rushing to the rescue. I will go and check.

I pass from one room to the next—my mother and father's, my brothers', uncles', aunts', cousins', everyone down to Baby Caihong, the littlest one's, rooms—taking my time, knowing that the household will slumber on; they sleep untroubled, secure in the knowledge that I will always be there to care for you. The house remains still and quiet and dark.

"Just as I thought, everybody—" I stop.

Five-year-old Hao-yu, your favorite grandson, stands by your bedside, his head cocked to one side. "What is that noise, Ngoi Goong?" he asks in his little-boy voice, so sweet and curious. "Is it a lucky cricket?" He is transfixed, listening hard, and I am delighted.

He hears her too, now that I have spoken her story and drawn her to the surface and so close to freedom.

"Polong," I whisper.

You begin to shake and your eyes roll wildly, nostrils flaring.

"It didn't matter that thousands were displaced by your piracy, nor that villagers were slaughtered because they stood in the way, with no capacity to fight back." I lower myself to the chair I have spent so many hours sitting in, watching over you, listening. I am suddenly weary but I must continue. We are almost at the end.

"All that mattered was success. But they already knew they were dying, the people of the land. Perhaps they were already dead. There was nothing they could do to save themselves, but they could save the land, their mother. They created something, didn't they? That's what you encountered on the island. More than that, that's what you went *seeking*."

You groan.

"You went to the island, not by chance, but by design."

You strike out, almost falling from the bed. Hao-yu, good boy that he is, helps me to return you to your position.

"It must have seemed impossible when you set out from Jurong Port—how to convince your men to go beyond your usual mining grounds on Dibaham Island to the dark Riau Archipelago, where it was rumored the original crew was lost? It must have seemed like fate when the Malaysian Coast Guard almost intercepted you and you had no choice but to make for the unknown."

Hao-yu has grown drowsy and he climbs up beside you and lays his head on the pillow. His eyes drift.

"When Shi Lei was gone the next morning and the cloud of grasshoppers burst from the tent, you knew you were in the right place and your faith in destiny was strengthened. And when you came upon the blackened glass jars in the kampung, and the abandoned barge and the dead crew, it must have seemed like you couldn't lose. All you had to do was call to what you were seeking. You called with blood, slaughtering the villagers. But that wasn't enough. You had to call with the blood of those who were gouging the land, scarring its face, devouring it."

Hao-yu sighs in his sleep and tears trickle down the sides of your face. You flick your eyes towards your grandson, begging me to save him from this story. I get up and gently wipe your cheeks dry. "I'm sorry, Ngoi Goong, but it is good for him to hear. He needs to know who he is too."

I sit on the edge of the bed. I will need to be close for what comes next.

"The day after you were offered the contract, you came across the single surviving crewmember of the *Naga* and he told a very strange story. One about a tiny female spirit and her pet grasshopper. It reminded you of a tale your mother told when you were young.

"You plied the story from him with promises of money and freedom.

"A believer in many things, your mother whispered of a polong: a tiny female spirit created from the blood of a murder victim and kept within a glass bottle, which could be used to harm enemies and extract revenge. The polong had a pet, a pelesit, a sharp-nosed insect made from the tongue of a dead child under the light of the moon."

Your Adam's apple bobs in your throat. Something swells and rolls beneath the paper-thin skin like a baby eager to be born from a woman's womb. I lean in close to watch.

"The little grasshopper crawls backwards down an enemy's throat, then sings, calling to the polong so it can burrow into their bellies and drive them to insanity and death.

"There is only one way to exorcise such a terrible demoness. You must force it to name its creator.

"But Great-grandmother told you of a way to *gain* control of the polong. If *you* said its master's name, it would become your servant. Goodness. Just think what you could achieve with such a creature in your employ.

"You had the crewman killed, but not before he revealed a name."

Wild, you shake your head, turning thin strands of hair into a nest.

I clamp my hand over your nose.

"Orang yang hilang," I whisper.

The lost people.

"The people of the land created a polong from the blood of all those who had been murdered in the name of profit and progress. Then they created thousands of green, gossamer-winged creatures from the tongues of their dead children."

Your eyes bulge. You struggle, skin unpleasantly loose and tissue-thin beneath my palm, nasal cartilage flexed and compressed, the reek of stale breath and aged flesh thick in my face. Something roils again in your esophagus. The soft area at the bottom of your throat sucks in desperately as you fight to keep your jaw locked.

With a spasm, you gasp for air. And there, peering at me from inside your death-soured throat, is a tiny, black-eyed woman.

All those hours watching over you, Ngoi Goong. So many quiet hours tending, waiting, serving, that I began to hear the chirring coming from deep inside you; I began to hear her voice.

Withered and thin with straggling strands of long hair, a distended belly and sagging breasts, the polong pulls herself arm over arm from your gullet. You thrash. Hao-yu wakes with a cry and cowers.

I offer my palm and the polong grins a grey smile and climbs free with a sucking, shucking sound, releasing a roiling flood of pelesit, which fly out, filling the air with emerald buzzing. You buck against the bed, choking and gagging.

"She whispered from inside of you as you slept, and in these past few years, you have slept more than you have lived.

"This is how I finally know where I come from, where I belong. *Who I am.*"

Hao-yu echoes your throttled sounds. His mouth is as choked with grasshopper bodies as yours is empty of them. Instead of agony, his expression is one of calm: his brow is clear, his unblinking eyes seem full of knowing.

I know what I must do.

I leave you on your bed, soiled and gasping like a mudskipper flipped onto sand, and revisit each room in our grand household. Each and every person—elders, uncles, aunties, children—receives the communion of a pelesit as dawn arrives, with only the sounds of choking and my footsteps echoing in the halls.

The last is the baby, Caihong. She is a beautiful child, with smooth, round cheeks, inquisitive eyes and reaching, warm little fingers. She coos softly: as if not to wake the others, as if she has already learned to be considerate and dutiful. I hesitate, as perhaps you might have hesitated if the villagers had fought back. Do I spare her?

The polong shifts, warm and slimy in my hand, and I hold my resolve. The baby seems to gag at first, her tiny arms seizing and waving, her legs kicking in her romper, then when the pelesit has finally crawled down her throat, she stills and her eyes are dark with a new awareness.

Marina Bay Sands Resort glitters before me in the baking morning sun: three impossible towers on impossible grounds that shine as a symbol of Singapore's dominion over the natural world. I take a breath and step from the old island to the new.

A mighty hook drags at me. I double over as something squirms and chews at my gullet, slicing with spiked, bent-back legs and razored wings. I taste long hair at the back of my throat, and even as I choke, I smile.

At last, I have traced my line.

ESTUARY

THIS WAS NOT THEIR WAR

Angela Yuriko Smith

They came to the caves, but there was no room. Mother, babe and boy, the three begged shelter from the leaden rain, but begging doesn't make the ground open, doesn't expand rock and wall, doesn't make miracles. The men who turned them away felt their hearts shatter along with everything around them. It was a sad time when they didn't have even a patch of cold dirt in the dark to share. The boy cried and she tried to soothe him, tried to keep the terror from her voice but you can't fool children. Explosions and dirt rose up against them. Not only did it refuse to hide them, but it heaved violently to shake itself free of their touch. The boy pulled away and ran, the mother, bouncing babe nursing at her breast, tried to follow as another mortar impacted…

… things went quiet as she fell, still cradling her babe to breast, cushioning the blow, a flesh shield against the razor shards of steel that cut through trees, bit into the earth, bit into her life. The babe was saved, the boy returned and curled up against his mother. Ashamed he had run, he wrapped his arms around her bleeding neck and vowed to protect her. She gave no answer, no smile and if she saw his brave act it was from far away. The shrapnel had claimed one of the cave dwellers too, and the two corpses lay facing, sightless, eye to eye. When the breast went dry and the night and rain both fell, the baby wailed before falling into a last and final sleep. True to his promise, her brother never left.

The sun failed to rise
as did hundreds of thousands.
This was not their war.

JARS OF EELS

Kanishk Tantia

It started when Anwar replaced Mr. Booth. *Things were good before that, Amma swears it.* Flies hovered, eager to suck salted flesh and sweet blood from fish piled high on the wooden stall, but the fan kept them at bay. Hundreds of bulbous eyes looked up, unstaring, unseeing, shimmering in the golden sun. The whites were mottled gray, the dark black pupils turning blue and purple in the heat. But their scales, their scales were still lush, an iridescent pink-gray, the rainbow trapped within.

These fish were stragglers, the last few schools, the ones too weak to fulfill the primal call of their genes. The early schools passed without interference: the village fishermen would not touch them, for they would reseed the oceans, providing more bounty in the future. Not so for the ones piled on Amma's table: perhaps some of these had even tasted sea spray before being cruelly wrenched towards a heaven they neither yearned for nor belonged in.

"Amma. Good morning."

Mr. Booth had not learned Amma's real name, despite having known her for years. There were too many syllables, and they made him uncomfortable. He called her Amma as the other villagers did, a familiarity she had not granted him. But Amma forgave this transgression, and many others, for Mr. Booth brought other advantages.

"Mr. Booth! Good morning!" She planned on selling him fish, of course. But there was an implicit understanding between the coastal villages: Mr. Booth could pay more, therefore *should* pay more. They had not discussed it, simply mentally adjusted prices when he approached. "Mr. Booth, I have fish for you again sir. Fish and eels, local delicacy sir."

He would never buy eels. They sat in the back of the stall, the few not smart enough to slither out of the nets, the dregs of the ocean. Mr. Booth had no desire for them and averted his eyes when he saw them floating in glass jars of water. Amma enjoyed his discomfort and made sure to offer him some whenever he visited. The village enjoyed her retellings at night, exaggerating Mr. Booth's reactions, his gagging and retching and pretending not to see the eels.

Some of her other customers, the ones who had not been personally greeted, frowned. Most of the time, Amma sat on her stool, baking in the heat alongside her fish. She moved only when asked her the price of fish, but otherwise, she was a desiccated corpse, dry and leathery and barely awake. Except when Mr. Booth came by, for here was a customer to woo and coddle and mollify until he departed, pockets lighter and truck laden with fish.

"Mr. Booth, how much today?" Amma presented an ingratiating smile. When Mr. Booth arrived, she often found herself closing her store early. "For you, special rate."

"Amma, wait. Things are going to change."

He smiled at her and Amma found herself smiling back even though she felt not the slightest shred of happiness.

If Mr. Booth had just bought fish, things would be the same.

Instead, he gestured to the man next to him, a man Amma had ignored because he looked like her, and was therefore of no importance, like her.

"This is Anwar." Mr. Booth slapped Anwar on his back, pulled him forward. "I'm making the rounds, introducing him to everyone. He'll be here instead of me, new Requisitions Officer."

Amma took him in again, noticed the crisp white uniform he wore, the same kind sloppily stretched over Mr. Booth's more corpulent physique. His uniform was clean, starched, with none of the faded yellow mustard stains and green splotches she had grown used to seeing on Mr. Booth's clothing. He stepped forward, shook her hand, and Amma realized Mr. Booth had never, in two years of buying fish, done so.

"Anwar Singh. Pleasure to meet you."

Amma nodded at him, and for a moment was reminded of her own son, who loved the sea and the ships and wanted to be like Mr. Booth one day. She had always laughed, but today, she would not laugh. It was possible, after all. Anwar had done it.

"You'll see a lot more of me soon." Anwar smiled, teeth brighter than his uniform. "Dhyan rakhna."

He hadn't lied. Mr. Booth did not appear again after that day, but Anwar did. Every week, when the first boats came back early in the morning, when the first streaks of purple dawn still choked the skies, Anwar appeared on his little Honda motorbike. As if that would convince someone he wasn't Mr. Booth in disguise.

"How much?" Anwar pointed out the fish he wanted, waited politely for Amma to pack them up. He was always so polite.

"Thirty-five rupees per kilo."

Anwar did not argue. He simply bought the fish, directed his men to load them up, and walked away.

"How much?"

"Thirty-five rupees."

For a month, Anwar did not argue. Instead, he brought gifts. Trinkets and toys, little things the village could not easily make. Useless little things, but the children loved them, and nobody would head to the nearest city, a four-day journey by foot, to get spinners and playing cards and little balls with green fuzz and English words on them.

"How much?"

"Thirty-five rupees." Amma hesitated. Her son wanted a spinner, and the one Anwar carried was beautiful, all glass and marble, with streaks of glittering black. She could see him smiling now, showing his friends. "Thirty rupees and give me the spinner."

"Deal."

For a few more months, he did not argue. He kept buying fish, more each time, until the village sold almost every fish to Anwar. For a time, there were complaints. Favorite dishes were no longer made, fish curries and soups were taken off the menu entirely. Instead, the villagers ate eels. Amma made eel curry every night and eel kebabs every morning. Other customers were quickly turned away: They could not pay as much as Anwar did. The villagers complained, missing their fish, but the complaints were quiet, and easy to ignore.

Soon, Anwar brought other things. Portable music, the kind they only heard during Diwali and on the rare occasion there was a wedding where the groom wanted a band. Shoes, the kind Mr. Booth used to wear, though his were always streaked with dirt, whereas Anwar's shone in the sunlight.

"How much?"

"Thirty-five. But—" Amma peeked at the little bag of tricks the city-boy carried and chose from the treasures within. "Thirty if you give me a radio."

"It'll need batteries." Anwar handed over a radio and two shiny batteries, sun-warmed and smooth. "Here. Do you know how to use it?"

Amma's stall had music then. Those who had known her for a long time remarked on the change in her, in the way her hair was brighter, her eyes more alert, her skin slick and smooth. She played the radio and moved slowly, sinuously, still fixed to her stool. And behind her, the jars of eels continued to swim, but now they swam to the music.

On one memorable occasion, on Amma's birthday, Anwar brought her a *sari*, black and gold. He pressed the box into her hands with a smile.

Amma hadn't even known it was her birthday. The village kept no such records. But Anwar assured her it was, he had looked it up. He knew her name, with all its syllables, and there was a record in the city somewhere.

"How much for it?"

Anwar smiled, and it was a wide, beautiful smile, with little artifice and only honesty. And she looked at the sari and hoped it was the kind of gift her son would one day give her as well. Perhaps for her *next* birthday, whenever it was.

"You're like my mother. It's a gift for my family. Gifts don't cost anything."

She had accepted, hesitant to take the box, but more hesitant to give it up. And in all that time, Anwar never argued, never haggled, only paid the prices she set. He was truly so polite. Soon, the complaints died down, and it became the norm: the villagers ate eels and sold fish to the polite young man who never haggled.

Things were good. Things were very, very good.

"Thirty rupees, beta."

"It's too much, Amma." Anwar shook his head. "The other villages sell for twenty."

"I sell for thirty." Amma was not a young girl making her first sale. She would not be cowed by a little haggling, even if it came from one of her own. "Thirty rupees. You know the price."

She didn't know when Anwar started calling her Amma, or when she had started returning his familiarity. It was no transgression to be forgiven, not when Anwar did it.

"You've been fleecing Mr. Booth for a long time, Amma, and that's fine. You have to. Jugaad." He switched to their language, secret and shared and not for the Mr. Booths of the world. "But don't fleece me. I must make my boss happy."

"Twenty-five." She looked at him and saw her son laughing as a glass top spun, light reflected over their house. She heard music from the portable radios in every house. And she felt the sari, which she had never worn, but one day would. "Because you remind me of my son."

"Twenty-five this time." He smiled, gave her the money, and pressed a small sweet in her hand. "And this is for him."

If Amma had refused then, perhaps things would still have been different. But she took the money, and packed up the fish Anwar wanted, and gave her son the sweet and thought nothing more of it.

"Thirty rupees."

Anwar shook his head as Amma knew he would. He'd been back twice that week already, unhappy both times, shaking his head both times. But she tried again.

"Twenty-five, not one paisa less."

"Amma, no." Anwar shook his head again, and there was remorse on his face. "The price is fine. I just need more. There are too few fish, too little to take back. It's not worth it."

There were precious few flies, and precious few fish for them to suck on. The ocean did not often reach past the creek, towards the river, but there were seasons when its anger would not be contained. The men had tried, setting nets at the mouth of the estuary, but the ocean denied their efforts. Each morning the men pulled up the nets and Amma saw them bulging with eels so tangled and conjoined they may as well have been a single writhing mass, the beating and pulsing blackened heart of an ocean which refused to heed their prayers.

And now they sat, covering Amma's stall, twisting and untwisting within the glass walls of the jars they were trapped within. Music still played, and the eels swam, and wriggled, and watched, and waited.

"Buy the eels, Anwar. They're tasty. Nutritious." She coaxed him. Her own son loved eel curry, enjoyed the rich, flaky texture. She had not tasted fish in a long time but felt no need for such naïve prey. The eels gave her strength, and she was grateful for them, was sure Anwar would be too. "Tell Mr. Booth, I'll give him my eel curry recipe. It'll make him famous."

"Nobody wants eels. I can't bring that to him." Anwar had the same disgusted look for the swimming eels as Mr. Booth once had. "He can't load eels out to America, Amma."

"America?" Amma had only heard the word on the radio before and it pierced the veil of the saleswoman, startled her into a burst of pride. "My fish are going to America?"

Anwar, who, for a moment, looked worried, composed himself. A self-important air surrounded him, and Amma saw his back straighten, his chest extend as he spoke with carefully chosen words.

"Yes, Amma, America. We sell to American restaurants. Big restaurants." He smiled, held her hand, looked her in the eyes and pleaded. "They can't take eels, Amma. Only fish, good fish. And they'll pay a lot. Especially if there are no other villages selling fish, no other competitors. Hundreds of rupees, just for you."

"I can't do anything, Anwar."

"You have power here, Amma. Please. Help me." He held her hands then, and Amma was taken aback by how soft, how dry, how pale he looked. "Please. For me, Amma. For family."

He was just a child, helpless and naïve, begging Amma for aid. How could she not help him? He could have been her son, after all.

"We should start fishing the earlier schools, no?" It was a whisper at first, subtle words spoken to the right ears. The wind carried Amma's words until they rang in the ears of every villager. "They're there for the taking. Stronger fish. Better, tastier fish."

The villagers nodded. The fish were prey, the bounty of the ocean to be hunted and scavenged. The eels had done so for centuries. The villagers would do the same.

"Mr. Booth and Anwar will pay for the fish. So much money." And now a little nudge, stoking the embers of opportunity. A few well-chosen words to set the village ablaze with greed. "Will you let those rupees swim away?"

The villagers hissed, anguish and rage building within them at the mere thought of losing the money they were owed, the money they deserved, the money that, by all rights, was already theirs.

"There are other villages too. If we don't take the fish—" The last few words, left hanging in the air. A cold possibility that, overnight, became certainty. "They will. And then, where would we be?"

The villagers did not need more urging. Perhaps in days gone, they would have sent messengers, spoken to the other villages. But to do so now, when hundreds of rupees were at stake, was folly. To ask for opinion was to alert the other villages of intention. Instead, they sat, and planned, and decided in the confines of their village, surrounded by darkened rivers choked with eelspawn.

A few months later, when the first schools of fish, the strongest fish, came by, they found themselves hunted without reprieve. In years past, they would have found their path unhindered, would have swum through the river, felt the water turn from fresh, untainted blue to wild, salty green, and known they were past the estuary and in the ocean, about to fulfil their genetic promise. They would have multiplied, reseeding the waters with the bounty of the future.

This time, Amma watched the fishermen polish their boats. She watched as their skin shone in the sun, as they moved with the languid, fluid movements of the eels they ate, moved without mercy towards the ocean. She watched it all silently, for the music had long gone out, and without Anwar, there were no batteries, and no money to buy batteries anyway.

When the nets emerged from the water, Amma, for a moment, believed their problems were over. Barely a trace of inky black swirled amidst the silver fish, their scales luminescent, their death-thrashing strong. These were not the limp specimens Amma had grown used to selling. These were healthy, the best of their kind, the finest fish the estuary had to offer.

Anwar would be pleased.

"Forty-five rupees, Anwar." She had already packed the fish he would ask for, had already mentally spent the money on new clothes for her son, on maybe even going to the city for a weekend and tasting the fish she had been selling for years. "And don't argue with me this time, beta. These are worth it."

Anwar's uniform clung tighter on him, sweat seeping through the white and turning it gray. If he had been helpless last time, he showed no such signs of desperation, walking with the lazy, arrogant ease Mr. Booth once showed. His shoes had streaks of dirt and dust, and a new stain decorated his uniform.

No matter. He was still Anwar. She had called him beta, had labelled him family. That could not be taken back.

"And throw in some batteries." Amma missed the music, missed the way it thrummed within her soul. The eels behind her still swam within their jars, but their movements were chaotic, untimed, and Amma herself felt bound to her stool, felt unmoored. "Enough for two months, at least."

"Fifteen rupees, Amma."

"Fifteen? Anwar. Be serious." She smiled, a motherly smile, and reached for his hands only to find he had moved away and she could reach only empty air. "You promised us a lot more than that. Be reasonable."

"Fifteen, Amma. It's what the other villages are getting."

"You promised, Anwar. Hundreds of rupees." She spoke then in their shared language, hoping it was simply a matter of reminding him of the promises he had made. "We're not being greedy. We're being fair."

"Fifteen, Amma. We do *jugaad* too, and there's more fish than we need." He stared past her, past the fish, and Amma noticed how the whites of his eyes were gray and dull. "Every village got the same offer, Amma, and they've flooded the market."

For a moment, Amma believed he was joking. It was only when she saw how Anwar refused to meet her eyes, how he stared only at the fish, how he had already counted out the money just like she had already packaged the fish, that she realized there was no humor to be found here.

"Fifteen."

"No. Come back when you're thinking straight, Anwar." It wasn't the saleswoman speaking anymore. It was Amma, stinging and betrayed by someone she considered family. It was a scavenger, seeing her plans scattered and broken, feeling clutches of dark anger wash over her. "Or don't come back at all."

He didn't come back. Every night, Amma took home a jar of eels, and shared them with her son. Together, they slurped the eels, raw and hungry and vicious, felt them slide and thrash within their bellies, slick with the same dark anger Amma felt. Every morning she waited, and waited, for Anwar to come by. Every morning, the dark, instinctive anger roiled and grew within her.

For a week, he didn't come back, and by then the fish were rotting. Their once sleek, muscular flesh turning putrescent, the luster of their scales turning stale gray and necrotic black. The flies were back, belly sacks swollen with blood and liquid flesh, gorging themselves on the fish baking in unrelenting heat.

"Twelve rupees, Amma. It's more than I'm giving the others." He looked ashamed as he said it. Perhaps, deep down, he truly felt the shame. "Because you're like my mother. Like family. Take it, please."

What could she do?

She watched as he bought the fish. She watched as his men loaded the crates, taking them far away to someplace she would never go. She counted the meager notes he left behind, drenched in the slick moisture her skin secreted.

The notes, and a small sweet. For her son. But her needle-toothed son no longer craved sweets, would eat only the freshest eels from the jars Amma brought home every night.

She watched Anwar leave, bound to her stool, surrounded by jars of eels. And as she watched, so did the eels. They did not twist.

They did not writhe. They only floated, eels in the jars and eels in the village and eels within Amma's veins, all coated in the same dark anger.

As Anwar left, thousands of pairs of eyes watched him go, in complete silence.

"There's not enough fish, Amma."

In some ways, Anwar had changed. His uniform was more slovenly still, ill-fitting upon his body, a size too small for his now more corpulent physique. His shirt, once crisply starched, bore stains the same color as Mr. Booth's shirt once had, of not quite faded yellow mustard and bright green.

"I know." Amma did not care for Anwar's troubles anymore. She was surrounded only by jars of sleek, writhing eels. Hundreds of them, thousands, dredged from the estuary, caught in nets and on lines, and they swam now in jars, and they watched Anwar. They whispered hungering knowledge to Amma, expanding her world until Anwar no longer belonged. "There are no more fish."

"I can't go back to Mr. Booth empty-handed."

In other ways, Anwar had not changed at all. He wore the same expression, one of abject pity, boasting trust, offering promises he would not fulfill.

"So, you've said." In many ways, Amma remained the same. The same saleswoman, who manned the same stall from the same wooden stool. "So, you've said many, many times."

"Do something, Amma, please. We need fish." He paused, hesitated. For a moment, Anwar's eyes were drawn to the jars of eels, to the hundreds of eyes watching him. "We'll pay. It's been a bad season. We'll pay a lot."

In other ways, Amma had changed.

She saw more now. She saw with the eyes of the eels she had eaten every night, for there were no more fish in the waters, no gentle laggards or strong swimmers, no hatchlings or fish eggs. Her eels owned the estuary now, hungry and cunning, with eyes that watched every movement, with sinuous bodies that cut through the water and scavenged for scraps. Eels, who were lifted in nets by their brethren and bottled and jarred and swallowed so they could run through different waterways entirely, in the crimson rivers within a village of the wronged.

"Come back tomorrow, Anwar." Her voice dripped sweetness, needle teeth hidden carefully under her smooth, scaled lips. She watched him shift, watched the tension release from his shoulders, a pleasant smile plastered on his face, hope in his eyes. Once, she would have called him *beta*, would have taken him in. Now, she saw with the ever-watching eyes of an eel. "Come by early tomorrow, before the boats leave. We'll have something for you. I promise."

For a moment, Anwar took in Amma, whose voice sounded a little too silken, whose smile reached just a little too far back, whose skin and hair were slick with viscous secretions and gleamed in the harsh sun. He took in the eels, who had stopped moving even though the music still played, and instead watched him with unblinking eyes.

"I'll be here, first thing tomorrow."

He pressed another sweet in her palm, smiled, and wiped the slickness she left behind onto his rumpled uniform, adding to the plethora of stains.

"Amma. Amma, please."

She stroked his face under the net he was wrapped in,

and when her fingers left his pale skin, a thin, sticky trail followed, cool and moist in the warm summer heat.

"It's okay, beta." She whispered to him. "You're family, no?"

Amma sat next to him as the wooden hull of the boat cut through blackened waters, pushing eelspawn from its path. She hushed him as he begged and promised and pleaded, and then watched silently as he disappeared over the side of the boat, still wrapped in nets. She moved slowly, sinuously in time to the music of his crying, and then his screaming, and then his gurgling.

And when the net rose from the water, she welcomed the pulsating mass of eels, flesh-fattened and plump, the beating heart of the ocean that beat in time to her own. She welcomed the eels, for they gave strength and allayed hunger, and because her son loved slurping the eels down, raw and slick and vicious. She welcomed them, for they were family, both water and blood.

A few months later, when Mr. Booth returned, thousands of eels watched him behind glass jars, and one watched from the stool where she always sat.

"How much, Amma?"

"For you, Mr. Booth?" Amma whispered, and the jars of eels whispered with her. She could not hide her teeth any longer, but Mr. Booth never looked at eels anyway. "Special rate. But come tomorrow morning. Before the boats leave."

FED BY EARTH, SLAKED BY SALT

Jess Cho

T he house looks smaller and shabbier than I remember, bleached colorless by the sun and salt air. Built above where the river meets the sea, my parents saw it as the compromise between a man who pulled his living from the water and a woman who coaxed life from the earth. Together, half a world away from where they started, they built a home.

Home. The word tumbles in my head like a pebble turned over by the tides, invasive and unyielding and strange. I shift the package tucked beneath my arm as I regard the house—there's something almost accusatory in the way the empty windows stare down at me, a projection of the guilt I never let myself feel until now.

I can sense eyes on me as I stand in the sun, a rustling in the underbrush, almost drowned out by the distant roar of the surf. Motion flickers in the corner of my vision, too large to be a bird. I turn, but it's already disappeared into the scrub. Just one of the countless creatures who have more claim to this place than I do.

I grip the package tighter. I'm stalling.

Fishing the key out from under the planter is more muscle memory than conscious action, as if my body belongs to someone else. The rusted teeth stick in the lock and for a moment, I'm gripped by the dizzying certainty that this is all some kind of mistake, that this is the wrong house, the wrong door, the wrong life.

And then the tumblers click, the key turns and I'm inside.

In every compromise, there is a meeting place, a juncture where two things might stop being themselves and become something together, something different and new. Here, where the ocean opens its arms to the river, my father shows the child version of me the life that can be found in brackish water.

"Resilient," he says of the sleek shapes that glide beneath the surface. "Survivors. If you put an ocean fish in fresh water, or a lake fish in the sea, their bodies don't know what's happening and they'll go into shock and die. These ones…" His gaze drifts out over the endless blue-green of the ocean. "They've learned to adapt. They belong here now."

In the dirt of her garden, my mother teaches me the same. Crouched low, she cups her hands around a plant with yellowed leaves and gives a sharp tug, pulling up a pale, tangled knot of threads.

"Too much salt," she says. "It gets into the roots and makes them grow up twisted and sick, if they grow at all." She cradles the plant in one palm, while with the other she makes a note in the open book beside her.

"When I came here, I had to relearn everything I knew of growing things. The soil, the water—even the air was different. The ground spoke a foreign language; it took a long time and so many mistakes before we understood each other."

The trick, she tells me, is to find plants that can adapt to their environment, to nurture them until they figure out how to survive on their own.

To me, none of them seem adaptable at all. Just trapped.

In the quiet interior, I take my bags to my old bedroom from a lifetime ago, setting the package down on the bed before I examine the rest of the house. The living room and kitchen are both neater than I expected, though the latter has been stocked with staples, meat and vegetables by some enterprising nurse or neighbour. Ewan, perhaps. Whoever it was, I'm thankful for the foresight, even as the sight of food turns my stomach.

I leave the room that had been my parents' for last. Unlike the rest of them, this room at least feels lived in. Clothes in the closet, a few photos on the wall. My father's coat that my mother kept after he died. Her blanket chest, all warm wood and iron fittings.

Even here, though, the touches of home are sparse. Both my parents lived small lives, in the way that only those who understand the weight of uprooting know how. I look at the blank walls and feel a small flush of shame, though I don't quite know why.

There's an added feeling of sterility to this room, too, more than just recent disuse. The bed is made with clinical precision, not even a hint of a depression in the mattress when I run my hand over the coverlet. Someone had come through after my mother's passing and scoured the house clean of death, taking with it any signs of life.

She chose to return here at the end, once the doctors told her there was nothing left to do but wait.

"Tradition," one of the nurses told me after, as if that explained everything. I nodded, pretending I understood, that I hadn't been separated from both my parents by more than just the years and the miles.

Now, sitting here where my mother lived her final days and finding no trace of her, I feel a yawning emptiness rise inside my chest, waiting to devour me whole.

Leaving the bedroom behind me, I return to the kitchen, where I search the cabinets until I find what I'm looking for: stemmed plates of white porcelain, small, black lacquered bowls. Dishes we never used in our daily life, but I remember just the same. They sit heavy and strange in my hands, unused to their shape—it was always my parents who arranged them before. But though dimmed by time, the memory of their placement stands out in my mind, and one by one, I begin to lay them out.

At the funeral, an older white man introduces himself to me as Ewan, closest neighbour to the house. I recognise his voice from the phone, scratchy with static and poor connection. Did he tell me his name, then? He must have, but all I remember are the words that followed, that hooked into my skin, barbed and pulling.

...*sick*, he said. Sick in the way that didn't mean a cold or the flu. Not even in the way that sometimes means *old*, the body turning in on itself, bartering for just a few more years.

No, he said *sick* in the way that means *dying*. In the way that means—

—*your mother is dying.*

And buried beneath that meaning, another, one so quiet and foreign it took most of the conversation before I understood what was being said: *Come home.*

The ceremony itself feels surreal, unfolding in front of me like someone else's memory. When the pastor greets me with murmured condolences, I'm suddenly struck by the wrongness of it all— this should be my responsibility. I should be the one in his place, overseeing the arrangements and greeting the few scant guests. I should be mourning.

Instead, I move through the room like a stranger. I can feel eyes on me, the weight of their judgment as I lay flowers on top of the casket, but not tears. Throughout the eulogy, my own eyes remain as dry as they did when I hung up the phone, when I sat in my apartment feeling nothing, while the city moved on around me. No tears, no pain. Just an empty hollow, curled up behind my breastbone.

I blame it on the jet lag, the exhaustion, the shock. I blame it on everything but me.

As evening approaches, I leave my preparations behind and let my feet carry me down the mountainside, following the path that I've taken a thousand times before. I'm still wearing my funeral clothes, though I removed my shoes at the entryway of the house, the only habit I carried with me when I left.

Barefoot, I walk until the air thickens, turns heavy and moist with decay. The ground becomes spongy beneath me and when water begins to pool in my footprints, I know I've reached the marsh. The space I claimed as my own as a child—the ocean for my father, the mountain for my mother. And for me, the in-between, where life hatches from the mud and makes its home.

But that was before I began to hunger for something bigger, something more than just a small house in the marsh. Before I was ready to adapt to something new.

I step into one of the winding tributaries that branches off from the river, feeling the silky squish of the mud around my feet. I dip my hand into the slow moving current and touch my fingers to my tongue, the way I used to when I was young. The taste is almost metallic, rich with organic matter and threaded through with salt. It makes my mouth water.

It isn't until I'm in up to my calves that I feel the tension in my shoulders ease, that I realise how afraid I was. Afraid that this place had changed, or that I had changed, enough so that we wouldn't recognise each other. But more than the house, more than the mountain, stepping into the warm, rippling current feels like coming home.

Standing knee-deep in the brackish water, surrounded by the drone of insects, I let the dark and hollow thing inside me grow, let it balloon out and fill my chest, let it push away my lungs, my heart and reach up into my eyes and finally take over.

For the first time since I answered the phone—what seems like a lifetime ago—my vision blurs, turning the rippling grasses into a kaleidoscope of gold and green. I open myself up to my grief, letting the tears fall from my face into the river below, swirling into the current.

I let the water taste me. I let them know I'm here.

I have always been a creature of appetites. Of wants and desires. My father used to tell how I erupted into this world screeching and wide-mouthed, as demanding as a newly hatched chick who knows only hunger.

When I came of age, that hunger drove me eight states and two thousand miles away from home, ravenous for something I didn't recognise and couldn't name.

It's an easy thing to mistake for ambition, and so I hid behind that veil for a time, tearing through jobs, friends, lovers in equal measure. I went from city to city, in search of anything that would quench the desperate need in my core, even if only for a short time. And every time I moved, I left another piece of me behind—my parents, my language, eventually even my name. It just seemed easier that way. Fewer things to weigh me down and remind me of a life I didn't want.

I cut so many pieces out of myself, I feel like there's nothing real to me at all, leaving me nothing but a ghost.

It's nearly dark when my grief finally settles, leaving me wrung out and exhausted. My skin itches with salt—from tears, from sweat, from the brackish water, and the sound of the surf tempts me with its nearness. But more than anything, I'm starving. With the absence of grief, the hollow in my centre is replaced with a new emptiness, a deep, physical hunger that gnaws at my bones.

I feel a multitude of eyes on me as I climb back up to the house, watching from the scrub. I'm careful not to step on the small mounds that dot the edges of the path; they look like animal stashes, gathered fruit and fish and bits of seaweed, though I know of no wild animal that would leave food out in the open like this, piled almost like offerings. Which, in a way, I suppose they are, just not to me. Most of it's started to rot, and the sweet, cloying scent of decay follows me up the slope.

My insides twist with a feeling somewhere between nausea and need.

Around me, nightbirds call to each other, piercing the dark with their strange cries and from the shore, I hear a whistling sound, plaintive and low. In the softness of the dark, the sounds comfort me.

The day before Ewan's call, a package arrives, stuffed in my mailbox, the writing on the front of it crooked and smudged.

To Tae-young. For when you come home.

I must look crazy, standing in the lobby of my apartment building for long, uncounted minutes. The shock of seeing my name, the one my parents gave me, the one I thought I'd left behind years ago, roots me to the floor and all I can do is stare.

At first, I resent the presumption of the short message, and I leave the package unopened on the table. But the next morning, my phone rings and there's a man's voice on the other end telling me after twenty years, there's no time left, that I need to come home.

I'll never know how my mother found me, years after our last conversation, my last forwarding address. There are so many things I never understood about her, and now I never will.

Save for what I find wrapped in plain brown paper: a slender notebook, its cover scuffed and blank, pages filled with block after block of my mother's small, cramped hangeul. Her journal.

That night, I struggle through the twisting letters, each syllable coming slowly, through the mire of years. It becomes easier the more I read, each half-remembered sound and word paving the way for the next. Slowly, the details of my mother's life unfold with them, all the secrets she never shared.

Back at the house, I head immediately for the kitchen, rooting through the cabinets in search of something to appease my aching stomach. I leave behind me a trail of bags and boxes, their contents bland and flavourless, doing nothing to ease the cravings that hold me in their grip.

I open the ancient refrigerator. One whole shelf is filled with jars of bright red kimchi, and it's to these I gravitate, twisting one open to release the familiar, pungent scent. With my fingers, I scoop out chunks of fragrant cabbage, dripping with spicy brine. The bounty of my mother's garden. My stomach groans.

The thick leaves crunch between my teeth, flooding my mouth with a flavour somehow both sweet and salty, punctuated by the soft bite of ground red pepper. There's a brightness to it that sparks on my tongue, and I nearly weep as I eat.

And yet, even when I leave the jars empty on the counter, the hunger inside me continues to grow.

I learn that I'm not my parents' first child, though I'm the only one to survive beyond infancy.

She writes about it only briefly, but I can read the pain between her words. It's what drove my parents to leave Korea and emigrate to the States where my father held dual citizenship—a fresh start, away from the tragedy.

She writes of the mountain that was here to greet her, but instead of fir and hornbeam and branching snowbell, she arrived to find pitch pine and stunted oak, the rocky ground unwilling to receive her roots. Her family had been ginseng farmers back home, and it was from them that she learned her love of the earth. Here, the plant she cherished so much withered and died under her care.

It won't grow, she writes. *The mountain is too unfamiliar, the soil too strange, too full of salt. Everything I plant, the ground rejects and nothing I do will make them grow.*

And so, she adapted.

My arrival is met first with anxiety, then tentative excitement, and finally, once I reach my doljanchi, relief and unrestrained joy. I became her focus, her everything.

Tae-young, my miracle. My greatest success.

She never forgot about the ones who came before me. She carried them with her always, across the ocean and into her new life. It's only when I was born that she allowed herself to let them go, to focus her attention instead upon the living. But she always remembered.

And now, so do I.

The door to the cellar is warped with age and lack of use, but when I turn the knob, it opens without a sound. I make my way carefully down the steps, using the wall to guide me, until I feel the packed dirt floor beneath my feet, and grope for the light switch.

Even half-knowing what to expect, my heart leaps into my throat when I see them, stopping my breath. Pale, desiccated bodies press against the glass, some no larger than my palm, a few as long as my forearm. Infant bodies, too small to be fully formed, their limbs suspended in preserving fluid, broken and reaching like snarled roots seeking nourishment.

It's only when I somehow force my feet to bring me closer, one hand over my mouth to keep my horror from spilling out in a scream, that the image resolves. They *are* roots—gnarled and pale and shaped like broken children, but roots nonetheless.

Ginseng. The kind my mother grew before she came here, floating in thick, golden honey, jars sealed tight to survive the trip access the ocean.

Looking closer, I can see faint writing across the glass, letters swimming against the warm glow of light behind them. Most of it's too faded to make out, though some appear to be dates, others seasons. What might be names, words, small and broken up. Salang-i. Jip.

There are only a handful, no more than one young couple might easily carry with them. But it's enough. Enough to contain the memory of soil and water and the mountain that nurtured them. Enough to provide that slightest hint of home to something that might otherwise be unwilling to leave the place where its bones had already put down roots of their own.

Inside the glass, each root floats softly, nestled in a tangle of their own threads, as if holding themselves safe. Beside them lie others wrapped in burlap. Small, wizened things compared to their jarred siblings. I lift one up from the rough fabric, turn it over in my hands, breathe in the herbal smell of soil and root. I have to resist the urge to sink my teeth into the pale flesh, to devour it whole, dirt and skin and all.

Instead, I bundle them back up and carry them with me into the kitchen.

Is there any power on Earth like the desperation of a mother? Perhaps only the desire to be accepted, to carve out a place for yourself to belong. Combine them both, and they become a powerful force, with no end to what they might accomplish.

My mother learned more from her family than how to just care for plants. After all, nurture is nurture, and children grow just like any other thing.

The roots should be old, older than I am, but when I slice into them with the razor edge of my mother's kitchen knife, they're impossibly crisp, firm and juicy as if just pulled from the ground. Saliva pools in my mouth as the hunger from the marsh rises up in me again, practically a living thing; I slip one of the sliced roots into my mouth, the taste both bitter and alive.

I throw chunks of ginseng into a pot with a young chicken pulled from the fridge and stuffed with dried fruits and a handful of rice. Again, I whisper thanks to the neighbour Ewan. I wonder how much he knew.

It takes every ounce of patience to let it simmer, aromatic steam escaping through the cracked lid. The hunger in me is practically a living thing now, coiled and seething in my gut. To distract myself, I fetch the package I'd brought with me, wrapped back in the same brown paper it was when it arrived. With care, I set my mother's journal beside the stove.

The soup is still near to scalding when I take it off the burner, but I wait only long enough to ladle broth and meat and rice into two bowls, which I set carefully aside.

At the first taste, I'm lost.

The hunger that consumes me is unnatural, impossible in its intensity. I am ravenous, tearing the meat from the bones with my fingers, and when that is no longer enough, I crack the bones themselves between my teeth. I rip apart the carcass, swallowing flesh and gristle and skin until nothing is left but needle shards and a slick of fat at the bottom of the pot.

I lean over the stove to catch my breath, hands greasy and shaking, my stomach swollen.

It's still not enough. But it will do for now.

The items I prepared earlier are stacked in the corner, waiting. The lacquered surface of my family's jesasang groans beneath the weight of its contents, polished wood gleaming red in the light. Tiers of fruit lay stacked on white stemmed plates, while bowls of rice and fragrant soup line the forefront.

I've never set the memorial table before, and my hands are clumsy, untrained. Juice pools beneath split skins from where more than once I sent piles of fruit tumbling to the floor. I resist the urge to lick it from the plates.

I set a burning stick of incense in the center, watch as the smoke curls and mixes with the steam of my offerings.

It's the wrong time, that much I know. There's an order to things, one that I've fallen outside of, and there's no one left to teach me the right way. A pang strikes me, stronger than the hunger as I wish I had known to ask, back when there was someone to answer. Now, holding my mother's book in my hand all I can do is make my way through the prayers alone, and hope that it's enough.

Enough for my mother, for my father. For all the small lives whose names I never knew.

That night, I dream myself back to the marsh. Mud oozes up around my bare feet, heavy with organic decay and baked to ripeness in the sun. The smell of it is enough to make me salivate.

I drop to my knees, scooping up handfuls of the slimy muck, dripping with brackish water. I stuff my mouth full, gulping down the rich silt, grinding fish bones and cartilage to paste between my teeth. Larvae squirm against my tongue before they're swallowed, tiny insect eggs burst as I devour the life born in the in-between. I eat and eat until I'm bursting, until my stomach swells, and finally, I feel sated.

Even before I enter the room the next morning, I can smell it. The green, wet smell, somehow both earthy and cloying. The same one that rose from the path and followed me back from the marsh.

On the table, the offerings I arranged with such care are rotted and black. Mold covers the fruit in a sickening white and green layer, faster than it should possibly grow, even in the humidity already thickening the air. In the bowls, meat and broth have melted into a unified sludge. Flies dot every surface, small feet marching over the memorial to the dead. The only thing unchanged is the incense, the slender, uncorrupted stick incongruous amidst the spread of decay.

It feels somehow like both a failure and an acceptance.

I make my way down to the marsh.

The small piles are still there beside the path, mounds of decayed fruit and dead things, tiny mirrors of my own offerings back in the house. I gather them up as I pass, feeling them ooze between my fingers.

In the flooded space where the river cuts through into the sea, I see them fully for the first time. Furtive and shy, they cling to the muddy banks, hiding in the tall reeds. Their forms are small, stunted, and my mind flashes to the plant my mother pulled from the dirt to show me years ago, its roots tangled, salt-twisted and strange.

Sometimes things don't grow right, no matter how much care and attention they're given. Uprooted from their homeland, pulled up from the familiar earth and carried across an ocean to a place where the land won't receive them.

But they still grow. Ghosts and plants and children alike.

My mother brought them with her when she came, unwilling to give them up in her grief. She nurtured them as best she could. Then when I was born and her attentions were occupied, they adapted, cut free from her care and made their home in the marsh—an in-between, the only place that would have them. Survivors, my father would have called them.

I understand, now, why my parents never seemed to worry about me, alone so close to the water. Why out of all the things I felt growing up, trapped and irritable and small—loneliness was never one of them.

And when I left, they came back to her, stayed with her in her final days. To anyone else, the end of her journal seems to devolve into madness, the delusions of a mind pitted with age and loneliness. But she trusted I would understand.

Look after them, Tae-young. The last words my mother wrote and the only thing she ever asked of me.

They approach me, my strange siblings, limbs bent in impossible ways, their skin fish-belly pale. They're small, some of them no larger then the roots that lay in the cellar, and I can see slender, branching threads emerge from their fingers, seeking the soil and water of the marsh. They watch me with wary, curious eyes.

In their hands they hold familiar things, pieces of blackened fruit, seaweed baked ripe in the sun, the small bones of an animal, long dead. The rich smell of organic rot strikes me, sweet like incense. Offerings from the dead to the living.

The hollow emptiness in my stomach, finally, begins to ease.

Behind us, a compromise sits between river and ocean, mountain and sea. In a year's time, I'll lay the lacquered table again with fruit and rice, say prayers for the dead and watch it turn to rot beneath my hands. But from that rot, comes a place for life to grow. This is the gift I can give.

For now, surrounded by the ghosts that my mother raised, I take all their offerings of home and eat until I know fullness once more.

PIG FEET

Yi Izzy Yu

Have you ever played the game "My Other Arms," Ali? It goes like this:

You put your own arms down by your side or behind your back, and a friend slips behind you and pretends that their arms are yours.

This friend then peels an orange and nudges dripping slices between your lips or picks up knick-knacks and turns them this way and that—as if it were you examining them.

It's all very unsettling. You look down. "Your" arms, which are not your arms at all, emerge from beneath your armpits—much lower than you're used to. They seem stubby yet also long, like something distorted under water. Your mind tells you that these hands are not yours. Yet your body, a "knowing" inside your body, insists that they are.

My grandfather Yang Bolin, a street thug turned village shaman turned developer of hypnosis apps for SP3 Studios late in life, taught me this one afternoon when I was twelve. The rest of my relatives were napping after gobbling sea snails and long-life noodles to celebrate my grandmother's birthday. He provided the extra set of arms (hairy) and the orange (blood).

After he released me, I breathed hard and giggled at how strange his/my arms felt, splayed in front of my face, and ending in freckled, old man fingers that wriggled like sea anemones.

My grandfather laughed at my bewildered expression. "Unbelievable, isn't it? How quickly your body takes to another set of limbs?"

He explained that this trick was just the tip of the iceberg. Triggering words and rituals could dramatically strengthen the body's proclivity for accepting other meat as itself. In the old days, body hypnosis—"shenti cuimian"—was a high art and underlay everything from exotic tortures and theatrical performances to a special form of tantric yoga. More recently, it had been used—at least that portion recovered from Tang dynasty scrolls—to help amputees and cyborgs accept artificial body parts and gamers to disappear into virtual realities.

"How much does the triggering word part help?" I asked. I was fascinated by the power of language even then, by calligraphy and fu talismans, by sweet words and cursed.

"A great deal, Yaya," he said. "They're probably the most essential part. It's rare we see things instead of the words that color them. This is why you should never say or write words carelessly. Never say 'wolf' unless you want one to appear."

I took my grandfather's advice to heart for the rest of my life, Ali. Except not in the way he hoped. I in fact made lots of wolves appear. That's why you were drawn to me at my reading. This, although I was older and less attractive than your usual companions. A beginning webtoon writer, you wanted a bit of my magic to rub off. Nothing wrong with that. Except you didn't stay the course, did you?

A few weeks after my grandfather taught me the arm trick, on a fall day when vividly colored leaves lay everywhere like murder weapons, he tugged me to the side of a narrow country road during a morning walk.

"That's where he lived," he said, pointing.

The ruins of a dwelling place lay half in shadow, damp from the morning mist.

"Who lived?" I asked.

"Someone something terrible happened to, Yaya. Someone now not even bones. Not even a shadow. Listen close." He sat down in the dirt and motioned me to join him. "I'm going to tell a story. The type with many things to reflect upon.

"It begins when I was twenty-four and worked for the local gangs. I was not a nice person then. But Shan Bao? Although just sixteen, he was worse. You couldn't see this at first, mind you, because he was so pretty. Eel-black eyes, a tall nose. Add to this, plump lips that were red as if tinted—although boys didn't do such things in those days—and a wide smile. He looked like those K-Pop boys you sigh over. But once you got closer, you saw that his wide smile was sharky and perverse, and that perversity lay glistening like fish eggs in his eyes too. Of course, if you saw all this, it was too late. He was already hurting you.

"Shan Bao had quick hands that loved inflicting pain. That loved turning into fists and screwing into spines. That loved pulling out bloody hanks of hair. It was like he was panning for something shiny in his victims' pain that he'd lost. Maybe he would have lived his whole life like this. Just another miserable village bully. But one afternoon he went too far.

"Sanjo, the village doctor's songbird—a gorgeous creature with a crest like a chrysanthemum—escaped her cage. Shan Bao saw her in the morning market. A flash of red weaving between stalls and the smells of fried dough and skewered meat.

"Although his sweat stank like moonshine, he was still quick enough to catch her. After plucking her bald as a thumb, he ate her right there in the muddy street, slurring between grisly mouthfuls: 'Uncle! Auntie! Want some? A doctor's bird is good medicine.'

"Word reached the doctor within hours. Sanjo belonged to his wife who had died earlier that year. Enraged at what had happened to this precious remnant of the woman he loved, he wasted no time in contacting Butcher Peng, his frequent collaborator for cases difficult or dark. By that night, they devised a plan for retribution. It involved hiring two scary men. I was one.

"When we found Shan Bao, he thought we would be full of empty threats like most adults and hopped around, play-boxing. A slap stopped this quick enough, followed by a blow that broke his teeth and sent him sprawling in the dirt.

"'Don't let it go to your head,' Shan Bao said as we marched toward the abattoir section of Peng's butcher shop. 'Got lucky.'

"The phlegmy quiver in his voice undermined his boast though.

"I hesitated then, Yaya.

"Just seeing his flowerboy face made me flash back to him as a toddler at the night-market: gnawing on a roasted potato dipped in date sugar, while his waste of a father argued with debtors.

"But in the end, I shook the memory off. If we always remembered people as young children, how could we bring ourselves to punish them as they deserve?"

I've always remembered that line, Ali. Just like every detail about what happened next.

The heat hit him first in the dark room, my grandfather said.

Then a dead animal stink—full of decay, hair, and blood; of scraped entrails and buzzing shadows. The room was like the butthole of something recently dead ballooned into a living space.

Or, more accurately, a dying one.

The smells nauseated my grandfather. But confusingly, they made him hungry too. The odors of dead pig flesh and pig blood evoked memories of his nainai's sweltering kitchen, of a black pot of pig's feet, hooves fist-bumping in gelatinous boiling water.

I made my family's pig feet dish for you once, didn't I, Ali? You claimed to hate the cumin taste. But I knew it was the hooves that made your skin crawl—like a woman's feet bound in shoes too small so that they grow gnarled: pink toes crowded like teeth, distorted in size and sprouting at wrong angles. But maybe it was the smell too. That's the thing about meat, isn't it? At its bottom, no matter how good, you taste the rot. And rather than squashing your appetite, this makes you hungrier.

Lovers are a little like this too.

In the middle of all this reek, Butcher Peng loomed: thickly built, with a face as leathery as his apron, one dark mole in the middle of his forehead like a third eye. Perched on a stool beneath him, looking more capuchin than man, was the doctor.

Shan Bao froze sober when he saw them. Village gossips held Peng chose his current profession (after a youthful stint as a sailor) for two reasons.

One, the feeling of meat and bone in his broad hands—its honest stink and lusty give, its slick marbling and wet slap.

Two, the provision of raw materials for his occult pursuits.

The latter reason made Peng especially indispensable to the

doctor. Early in his career, the doctor recognized that combining magic and science was incredibly powerful and that it was in fact often difficult to distinguish the two. Was the placebo effect simply mind over matter? Was hypnotic trance spellcraft? Were dreams the creation of tulpa worlds? Peng's famous skill with ventriloquism also blurred the line.

"Put him there," Peng said and directed my grandfather and his accomplices to gag, strip, and rope-tie Shan Bao into a wriggling cocoon as he violently resisted. They then suspended him upside down, face-to-face with a disemboweled hog corpse whose drooping snout drizzled strings of black goo.

Despite the ball of dirty cloth plugged into his mouth, Shan Bao began to babble.

Or so it seemed at first.

"Look at you all here. Like a tribunal! Do you think this pretend game will scare me?"

My grandfather's guts lurched uncomfortably at Shan Bao's voice. How could he be speaking? He was gagged. More disturbingly, the voice wasn't coming from his body. But from the cutting table. There, heaped blue-veined pig organs lay, glistening like wet river stones in the room's dim lighting. Liver, heart, kidneys, stomach— all stickily piled together. It was they, my grandfather realized with shock, that were speaking with Shan Bao's voice.

"Are you crazy?" the organs shrieked, as the real Shan Bao thrashed, craning his upside-down head to find who had stolen his voice. "Do you think my father won't take revenge?"

Peng signaled everyone not to look at the original Shan Bao, so their bulging eyes followed him instead as he heaped the jabbering organs into his arms like a fisherman's catch and marched them to the hanging pig carcass where he shoved them inside.

"No, I don't think your father will," said Peng to the newly stuffed carcass. "He's been paid and likes money much better than you."

It was a horrible thing to hear, Ali. That one is not as loved as one thought. Such things should be kept secret out of simple human decency.

Now, Ali, to fully appreciate what happened next, it's helpful to know that there's a variation of the game "My Other Arms." It's called "The Rubber Hand Illusion."

The set-up is simple. A subject hides their real hand beneath a table. A helper then places a rubber hand in their line of vision on top of the table, tucked inside the subject's shirt sleeve—as if replacing their real hand. Next, the helper strokes the fake hand from behind while also covertly stroking the actual one beneath the table.

This confusion of tactile and visual data quickly convinces the subject that the rubber hand is not only their own but that they feel it being stroked. For a small group of people, this illusion works even when the rubber hand is replaced with something decidedly unhand-like, say an old cow bone. And for a yet smaller group of people, this illusion works even when something violent is done to the rubber hand.

While fascinating, this is all pure neuroscience so far. A kind of phantom limb syndrome trick. Mirror neurons, suggestion, visual resonance, the peculiar way the brain synthesizes and packages sensory data. Not a lick of magic. Yet. But the potential is obvious, isn't it? And that day in Peng's cutting room, my grandfather saw the full potential demonstrated in a ritual. It changed his life.

Peng's performance with the organs was part one. Part two required help—specialists from Xi'an who stepped out of the shadows like spiders when Peng said, "Now."

Identical twins, at one time cojoined like all those who practiced their art, they moved in eerie concert: gaits, facial twitches, hand movements. They even swallowed in sync. God knows how much practice it had taken them to manage such precise choreography.

As my horrified grandfather looked on—thinking of my infant mother gurgling and burping at home, needing him alive—and as the dead pig, sounding quite alarmed, cried in Shan Bao's voice, "What are you doing?!"—the specialists knelt, drew long acupuncture needles from leather side pouches, turned toward their respective patients, and——ffft! ffft!—simultaneously drove the quivering metal into the vertebrae of the pig and Shan Bao.

A humming noise began, one whose location my grandfather struggled to identify.

Was it coming from the pig?

Shan Bao?

The timbered ceiling?

He realized that the noise actually had several origin points. Two of them were the specialists. Two were Shan Bao's and the pig's needled bodies. And one more was Peng's slightly ajar mouth, pursed like the end of a woodwind instrument.

The five points of sound connected, drew a shape in the air, the hum throbbed louder, and the specialists—as if knitting at high speed—plunged more needles into cortical bone until the backs of their two patients bristled.

It was about this time, my grandfather said, that his hands began to tremble, and his mind was overtaken by an intense brain fog that made everything that followed seem strangely distant.

Peng kowtowed. Once. Twice. Thrice. To what my grandfather didn't know. Then he whispered words between the bodies as he slapped yellow fu talismans on them.

Shortly thereafter, the spasms began—initially out of step, Shan

Bao leading the pig, but then they moved in sync, faster, quicker, as if both were boiling from the inside until the pig made a wet, belching sound and abruptly Shan Bao's cocoon sunk inward. Empty.

The dead pig tried to speak then with its rubbery lips. "Plelemgwah. Wghah. Plelemgwah. Wghah." The words were mushy and misshapen, like a stroke victim's. Even so, my grandfather discerned that the pig was begging, "Please help," just like he discerned that its eyes were alive with a gleam that had once belonged to Shan Bao.

An hour? Two? How long did the pig keep up its screeching and babbling? How long before Peng finally cut its throat so deep that the head could no longer produce sound? My grandfather never could say other than it seemed like it went on forever.

Things didn't end there though. Even with the pig muted, everyone in the room could still feel Shan Bao's life energy inhabiting it, feel his consciousness diffused into its tissues—in that way you can feel someone watching you in the dark.

They felt his agony as he struggled to open his not-eyes, as he struggled to think through his crumbled dirt clod of a half-disintegrated mind, desperately wanting to scream with his not-voice—especially after Butcher Peng picked up his tools.

My grandfather was repulsed, but not once in his life had he been so fascinated either, not even when my mother was born.

"I decided right then and there, Yaya," he said, "that I would devote the rest of my life to mastering every technique I observed in that stinking, hell-hot room."

It was almost dawn when Peng finished butchering Shan Bao and wrapping him to sell that day in the front room as fresh and delicious pork. And here's the most beautiful thing of all, Ali, a true testament to the miracle of consciousness.

My grandfather felt, no *knew*, that even after what had once been

Shan Bao was cut into hocks and jowl and rib and chop and loin, after it was stripped of soon-to-be crispy skin and shorn of ears, that Shan Bao remained conscious, thanks to Peng's ritual. Conscious in each and every part. And he would remain so even as he was chewed, dissolved, and shit then eaten by something else and then chewed and dissolved and shit by something else still, for all eternity, flowing into one body and the next. How marvelous is that? Maybe in this way—and it's what I truly believe is the case—he found that thing that he spent the first part of his young life looking for so desperately in the pain of others. All along, it had been hidden like a jewel inside his own suffering.

So much time, Ali.

I've spent so much time thinking about that day in Butcher Peng's. I thought about it whenever someone bullied me in high school, thought about it as lovers left me one after the other, thought about it as well when I went to work for my grandfather's company. I was hired to edit AI story scripts for VR games but too I spent long hours in his science labs, watching monkeys wired with electrodes, convulsing in harmony with one another—playing out via the language of science a polished draft of what my grandfather had observed a rough draft of decades before.

Though Peng is now long dead, over time I've collected everything he knew and more—following in my grandfather's footsteps.

This is why I drugged your plum wine, Ali. It's why you're now bound on the table and the pig is in the refrigerated chamber next to you. A little something old. A little something new. Kind of like a wedding, I suppose.

NEITHER FEATHERS NOR FIN

Angela Yuriko Smith

Miya lay on her back, ears ringing with a high-pitched whine, gasping. Windless, she was like a koi out of water—eyes bulging, open mouthed. A weight pinned her to the floor, crushing the strength out of her. The buzzing that stopped up her ears morphed to screams. She stared up at a bird winging lazily across the sky where the roof of her house should be, too numb to wonder, too cold to feel, too weak to move.

When breath came back, it was like a typhoon, forcing her lungs to life with a fit of coughing. She choked on bitter, metallic air. Miya struggled to sit up, to push against whatever held her down.

It was her mother.

She was too still, not holding Miya down but not helping her either.

"Mother…" Miya pushed at her mother's shoulder. Mother gave no response, but from her new vantage point Miya got her first view of their home… what had been her home.

Only one wall remained, the rest lay as flat as she had been minutes before. They were exposed to the rest of the neighborhood, not than many remained there. Her small house had withstood countless storms in the past, but the wooden walls had been built to keep the storms from getting in. Her father had never imagined the threat that eventually tore their home apart would be from within… and from him.

Through the ringing in her ears, Miya heard the voices of men calling to each other in the strange language that identified them as the enemy. Panic brought her focus back. The foreigners were coming. Her father had meant to save his family from the horrors of capture, but somehow, she had survived. To be captured by the foreigners was a fate worse than death. Her father had only been gifted one grenade, no more. Miya was on her own.

With a strength born of desperation, she pulled herself free and tried to shake Mother awake. "Mother! Mother! We have to run!"

She rolled her mother partially over to see the mangled ruin that was her face and neck. Miya quickly closed her eyes and pulled her hands back. This could not be real. There had been promises, plans for the future, plans for grandchildren. "Wake up. Wake up… you promised…" The words shimmered out of Miya's throat, her world warping in their heat.

The sound of gunfire cut into her blossoming panic and brought her back to the moment, to the immediacy of survival. She slid halfway free, her left leg still pinned and pushed herself to her feet. It took her a few seconds to register what she was seeing, but once she understood she almost collapsed under the weight of it.

Her family lay scattered around her. Her father, who had been the one holding the grenade when it went off, took the brunt of the blast. Her sister must have survived as well, if only for a few minutes. She had been reduced to not much more than a torso, a trail of blood leading to where she had finally collapsed. Her sightless eyes stared at nothing; her face twisted in a frozen scream of agony.

The bleeding corpse in front of her was not her sister. The small girl that used to follow her everywhere was not this girl. A shout from behind the one standing wall that remained brought her back to herself, and the reason her family, and everything that mattered, was gone. Miya ran.

Like a frightened rabbit, she dodged between houses and out into the grassy wetland. Some of the houses were on fire, the sea bleached wood blazing. She raced, zigging back and forth as she imagined a swarm of bullets following her like lead hornets. She ran blindly, her vision turned inward to the carnage she had just witnessed. Her father had done this because the Emperor had commanded it. It had not been his choice. It was for honor. Miya knew this, but still, anger blossomed in her heart to become rage.

By the time she reached the brackish waters that bled into the sea, she could do nothing but collapse in exhaustion and grief. She had been abandoned by her family. Strangers overran her home. This island would be burnt to the ground until there was no place for her to hide. Once the foreigners caught her, she would be their toy, and when they were done playing, they would flay the skin from her flesh while she screamed. It would be slow, and they would keep the relief of death from her as long as they could. So said the Emperor, *tenno heika banzai.*

And yet, in spite of all this, she felt a bitter anger toward her father. He had always protected them, always loved them. She knew pulling the pin was the ultimate act of love and sacrifice for his family. She saw it in his face as they embraced, hoping to travel together into the next life. The tears that ran down his face to wet her hair had been real. This death was an act of love. But then, why was she still here? Was she unloved?

Gunfire erupted from the direction she had come. A cloud of

birds erupted into the sky, adding their cries to the cacophony. The shouts of men, again in that strange tongue, and screams spurred Miya to flee like the birds, with no direction but away. She wished she could fly, or swim. With neither feather nor fin, she was trapped. For the first time in her life, her island home felt claustrophobic. With no other direction open to her, Miya remembered her *babaan* who lived in the heart of Naha-shi. Miya still had family and somewhere to go. She wasn't entirely alone.

She started back, returning from a different direction, but as she came closer her hopes began to sink. So much of the city was already in ruins. The few buildings left standing were either completely destroyed or heavily damaged. The streets were filled with debris. An overturned cart spilled a small load of sweet potatoes into the road, abandoned. As she passed, Miya picked up a few, tying them into her loose top. She wouldn't come empty handed to her grandmother.

There were few people on the streets, and they moved quickly to vanish. Imperial soldiers, however, seemed to be everywhere, some setting up makeshift defenses, others tending to the freshly wounded. The smoky air choked her from all the smoldering buildings. Naha looked like a war camp. Miya moved cautiously, trying to avoid being noticed. She knew enough about the world to understand that attention from any soldiers, enemy or otherwise, was unlikely to end well for her.

It was late afternoon by the time Miya made her way to Shuri gusuku. The last time she had been here, the red lacquered walls made her think of a dragon ornamented with intricate carvings and bright colors. Thousands of red clay tiles had lined the roof like scales. Now, the palatial building was covered in grime. The once-brilliant walls blackened from explosions and flames, the lacquer showing through in patches like wounds. Missing red tiles from the roof left large empty holes letting the elements ravage the interior. Outside, the grounds were pockmarked with craters from artillery shells. Once a place she dreamed of, now the gusuku was an extension of the nightmare Miya found herself in. She looked away. Like her mother, she wanted to keep her vision of Shuri intact, as she'd last seen it.

"You. Girl! Stop."

Miya looked up. A soldier pointed his gun in her direction, motioning to stop. In her shock at the state of things she had failed to remain unnoticed. She'd never seen a gun so close. She stopped, trembling, her mouth going dry, and put her hands up. The two sweet potatoes she had in her shirt slipped out.

The soldier examined her with a look of hunger and motioned for her to turn completely around. He slid the tip of his rifle under the hem of her baggy tunic and started lifting it. Miya pulled it back down without thinking. Angry, he smacked one of her hands with the metal. It hit her wrist bone and she fought tears. He studied her without expression for a long minute before he spoke.

"How old?"

"Thir-thirteen."

"Where is your family?"

Miya couldn't answer at first. She mouthed the word *dead* three times before it came out as a whisper.

Again, he just stared at her, blank, before he spoke.

"You are very pretty," he said. "Do yourself a favor and throw yourself off the cliffs before the Foreigners catch you. Unless you want to be raped to death."

Miya shook her head, gasping for air. She trembled violently.

Again, the soldier used the tip of his rifle to lift up the front of her shirt, exposing her small breasts. Miya closed her eyes, praying, trying not to move. Finally, he let her shirt drop back down.

"Yea," he said. "They will have a lot of fun with you. Listen to what I say."

Miya just nodded without opening her eyes. Everything was sliding off-kilter and she felt like she might collapse. She had to hang on.

Finally, he spoke again.

"Go. Turn around. Get out of here. You might not like what would happen to you if you stay here... but I bet you would like it compared to what those foreigners will do."

Miya didn't move at first.

He jabbed her in the stomach with his rifle. "I said, go! Go away."

She staggered back, momentarily winded and then took several steps back. Once she was out of his reach, she turned and ran as fast as she could. She expected him to shoot her, but she left him behind soon enough. Miya didn't stop until she was completely out of the town.

The rural landscape fared no better but maybe she could find somewhere to hide within the abandoned fields and destroyed homes. The roads littered with the remnants of battle, of the dead, but Miya also passed a few of the living; groups of people, mostly women, children, and the elderly, all trying to flee. They all seemed as lost as she was, carrying what little they could, their faces etched with exhaustion. Night was coming.

Miya got off the road as the dark settled in and made herself a shallow nest in a patch of long grass. She had never felt so small, so alone. The universe seemed too vast. It was no longer filled with the friendly stars she was familiar with. Overhead wheeled a black void, threatening to swallow her and everything she knew. All her life she had felt lucky to live on an island, safe from the rest of the world behind their ocean moat. Now, it was a trap.

She had no wings to fly. She had no fins to swim. She wished the earth would swallow her. Maybe she could bury herself, and only come out at night like the tanuki. Then it hit her. She couldn't go away, but she *could* go down.

Miya wasn't sure she knew the way to Gyokusendo Cave, but she thought it wasn't too far from where she was. She had only been with her family a few times. It wasn't much, but it was something. She would go to the caves at first light. She could stay there until all the soldiers were gone, whatever side they were on. With that thought, miraculously, she slept.

She opened her eyes with the rising sun, the sky a clear blue blushed with pink and gold and the birds chittering. Other than waking up in a bunch of long grass, this morning could have been like any other. Miya had a plan. She was going to find that cave and wait out this war safe underground. After, she could find her *babaan* and her aunt. She prayed they were safe in town.

She remembered the soldier last night, his gun under her shirt and shook it away. She sealed away all the events from the day before as another life, one she couldn't think about at the moment. Now everything depended on getting underground, getting a little food and staying away from the foreigners. The sound of water led her to one of the many estuaries that fed into the ocean. Parched, she drank before she sat up and breathed in the morning, inhaling the moment of peace. She needed this. And then it was over.

A plane, two planes, a handful of planes broke the peace with their droning roar, smoke trails smudging away the sunrise. Miya hurried back to the road. She would not be safe until she was underground. She needed to reach the cave.

Apparently, the planes sent the same message to everyone. People popped up from the grassy land, some in pairs or small groups, but most alone like she was. They all moved with a sense of urgency, gathering their few possessions in bundles and heading back to the road. A few people had a little something to eat. Miya's stomach rumbled and she thought wistfully of the two sweet potatoes she'd dropped at Shuri. Most people, like Miya, seemed to have nothing. They were all going in the same direction, and it occurred to her then that other people must have thought the same thing and were also headed to the caves. She was relieved to think she wouldn't be alone. Encouraged, Miya began to trot in the same direction.

Her boost of energy faded fast, and before long she ran slower, winded and listening. The cry of morning birds was drowned out by distant gunfire and the frequent roar of aircraft overhead. After the noise of the planes passed over, everything became too silent, the stillness electric with tension. When Miya felt like she could no longer run, she would try to rest but it never for longer than a minute.

She had to navigate through the chaos carefully. The landscape was hilly and rugged, providing some cover but not enough. She saw soldiers from both sides, some hunkered down in foxholes, others moving in groups. Like an infestation, strange men were all over the island. She was beginning to think of them all as foreigners, all of them as invaders.

The final stretch to reach Gyokusendo Cave was the worst. The forested area helped to shelter her from the open fighting, but the Imperial Army also used the natural terrain for guerilla tactics. Miya moved cautiously, painfully aware of the dangers and praying she wouldn't get caught in an ambush. The dense vegetation acted as both a refuge and a trap.

When she did finally reach Gyokusendo Cave, it became apparent that too many people had had the same desperate plan. Imperial soldiers scattered throughout, taking advantage of the hills and dips to use as convenient bunkers and hiding places. The cave entrance was already surrounded by other refugees setting up a temporary camp. Miya still tried to slip inside but an old woman stopped her.

"Don't bother. The cave is full."

Miya shook her head. This was not possible. The cave was large. Surely there was room for everyone on the island. "How?"

"Lots of people. Lots of war. Everyone wants a hiding spot. Did you think you and I were the only ones to think of this place?" Her tone came out bitter.

Miya felt stupid. Of course everyone would have the same thoughts. They were all wingless, finless and trapped. It seemed obvious now. She wasted time and energy getting here, and now where? She slumped to the ground, defeated. She had no other ideas.

The old woman studied her.

"Don't feel bad. It seemed like a good idea to me as well." Her expression softened. "My family is gone, and I suspect yours is too. We can be family for each other, maybe."

This woman was not her *babaan*. She could never replace the mother she just lost, but what choice did any of them have now? She hadn't had a say in who her family had been the first time. Maybe that was just how families worked. She noticed a small pot of water ready.

"Are you trying to build a fire to cook something?" Her stomach audibly growled, emphasizing her words.

The old woman laughed. "Yes, it isn't much. A few potatoes and a handful of dried pork. I would be happy to share with an adopted granddaughter. Especially if she could help me start a proper fire. I really need to find some large stones but I don't want to leave my few things unattended and I'm too tired to carry it all much further. I was also disappointed to see I was too late, but perhaps we can bring each other hope."

And as simple as that, Miya was no longer alone. Because things were so busy outside the cave, they wound up relocating to a sheltered bluff that overlooked the sea. There was a freshwater stream nearby that flowed past them and into the sea. With the old woman settled in, Miya went down to the beach to dig up clams. As tenuous as it was, having a connection to someone made all the difference. It wasn't a home but having a place at that small fire and a cooking pot mattered.

As dusk fell, Miya and the old woman fell into a sort of peace. There were plenty of people camping around them now. Small groups lit by tiny fires, each light represented someone displaced like herself. Darkness set in, the horizon turning pink, then purple and then darkening to black. As the stars began to show, she thought of how much they mirrored what was going on below. A thousand lonely fires all over her island, a thousand lonely stars in the sky. Her little island, her world, was so tiny compared. How could it survive this war? Two giants had chosen to fight in a house that wasn't theirs. It didn't matter to them if they flattened it.

The moon rose then, shining silver on the waterway as it flowed past them, a ribbon of light going into the sea where it shone bright, lighting up the vast expanse. "Perhaps that will be us," she thought. Her belly full, warm beside the fire, she was no longer alone. "We are not this place. We are a people, a *monchu*. As long as we find each other, we will survive. We don't have feathers or fin, but we have spirit. On that, we can travel."

BEDROCK

HOW WE SURVIVE

Christina Sng

The roses whisper my name

When I feed them his skin.
I carved it from him while he slept.
I do not think he is waking.

These monsters—
They crawl inside from the bedrock
Into your bones, into your mind.

They cast fog inside
And make it impossible
For you to think.

They convince you
To believe
You cannot do anything.

Until the day you snap

And give him a proper send off,
A lighter one without his skin.

In the end, when your brain
Has nothing but cotton and poison,
You can only act.

GUILT IS A LITTLE HOUSE

J.A.W. McCarthy

Candace, the landlord's housekeeper, brings us dinner at seven-thirty. Tonight, it's tamarind chicken, green beans, and sticky rice, all arranged in precise scoops on a platter edged with silver vines. On another plate, there are six small almond cookies ringing a tomato cut into the shape of a flower. The tomato seems out of place considering Candace isn't much for garnishes, but there always has to be something red at every meal.

I watch from the window as Candace lays the plates on our porch then hurries back to the big house, glancing over her shoulder several times along the way. I wave, but she stopped returning my greetings a long time ago.

As she does every night, my mother tosses the plates out the window right after I bring them in. She doesn't even look at me as she crawls back into bed. My mother is never hungry. She never eats.

Once she drifts back to sleep, I go outside. Sitting cross-legged on the ground, I pick chunks of chicken and green beans out of the grass before the ants can get to them. My hands are slick and smeared orange as I push this meal meant for two into my mouth faster than I can chew.

It's always the same: later, after I'm done, I slip back into the house, curl up on my bed, and scrape my tongue against the backs of my teeth. No matter what we've been served—garlic bread or habanero salsa or blue cheese with grapes—all I taste is a thin mustiness, like the way mothballs smell. All I feel is smooth, wet enamel. I remember sitting in the grass, the way the meat threaded between my teeth, the way the cookies ground into the craggy surfaces of my molars, but I don't remember what any of the food tasted like. Unlike my mother, I am always hungry. I always feel hollow.

Though it's only one room and its upper levels are ornamental, the little house my mother and I live in is a replica of the landlord's big house up the hill. Three stories of bright white with dark red trim and a red roof. We have a terrace like the big house, except ours can hold no more than two people; it isn't grand enough for dinner parties and dancing to a live band like I've seen them do at the big house.

Where the landlord's house is surrounded by three acres of land, our little house is close to the street, next to the gate. It sits several feet up from the ground atop a concrete platform, as if under all the soil and pebbles this support tethers us to the earth's core. The columns in front are chipped from where neighborhood kids have poked them with long sticks over the years. We're an oddity, my mom and me, as if we're on display in a rich kid's dollhouse. I know it's strange to see a mini replica house like ours here in the US, but Joy says houses like this are common in Thailand.

Joy is the landlord's daughter. Like me, she is the first in her family born outside of Thailand. She doesn't visit me in the little house anymore because my mother says we aren't the same. When Joy and I want to see each other, I walk up to the big house.

"Val! Guess what?" Joy chirps, leaning out her bedroom window at my approach. Though her parents aren't home, I stiffen on the back patio. The one time Joy's mother caught me in the house, she chased me out with a shriek and a broom. Through the glass, I can see Candace in the kitchen mopping the floor. She sets the mop aside and lets me in without a word.

Upstairs, Joy's standing in her doorway with a mouthful of glossy white teeth and a big cream-colored envelope in her hand. "I got in!" she squeals, waving the envelope over her head.

Stanford. In the fall she will head to California to attend the university she's been talking about for the last two years, and I will be left with only my mother. I will never set foot in the big house again.

"Congratulations. I knew you would," I say, stepping into her embrace. As she squeezes me, I catch the scent of fennel seeds in her hair.

Joy ushers me into her room and shuts the door. "I wasn't so sure," she says as we flop down on the loveseat by the window. "I mean, my grades are good, but there's a million other people with the same grades, and they probably did more charity work than me, and they're better at piano and…" She laughs, giddiness thinning her voice. "I just can't believe it, you know? Like, how the hell did I get in?"

Your family's money. All your father's promises.

She reaches across the loveseat and pulls my hand into hers. Her dark eyes are big and glassy because she cries easily, because she knows what I'm thinking. Though she doesn't sense the resentment—or she doesn't let on, anyway—she knows her every achievement leaves me further and further behind. I will never go to college in California, or even here in town. There will be no empty spaces to carve into my own. Without Joy, I won't have this room anymore, where I spend most of my days while my mother sleeps. I won't have the unlocked patio doors after Candace leaves for the night. I won't have the back stairs, Joy with her finger pressed to her lips, the *c'mere* pull of her hand as she waves me into her room while her father drinks in his study and her mother nods off in her bed after a handful of pills. Even though I'm a year older than Joy, I'm bound by rules. As an only child, I have a filial duty to my housebound mother.

"I really am happy for you," I assure her.

She nods, but any excitement has been eclipsed by the things I can't hide: the corners of my mouth straining, the wobble of my chin, the dry air making my eyes tight in my head. She's both a chimera and a mirror, a thousand *me*s reflected in the droop of her mouth, the tightening of her brow. So, we do what we always do when we're sad: we get in her big bed and pull the covers over our heads.

Here, we're warm and safe and the same. There's nothing on the other side of the pale blue sheets and fluffy white comforter. With our arms straight at our sides, our shoulders are level and our fingers end on the same invisible line. I can imagine going to sleep like this and waking up with my arms and legs spread in this big fancy bed, not curled and alone on the front porch of my own little house.

Joy turns to me, propping herself up on one elbow. "I'm serious, you know, about my dad. He'll give me money, and I can fly you out to California. Whenever you want. He doesn't have to know."

"My—"

"Your mother can do without you for a few days. You can help me settle in. Please? It's a new place, and I don't want to be there without you."

I want to remind her of all the times she tried to sneak me out for shopping trips and double dates, the time she came to the little house and tugged on my arm until my heels caught on the wooden porch planks and it felt like she was going to tear off my forearm. The times she stood outside my window crying that if I really was her friend, if I really loved her as she loved me, I would leave my sleeping mother and go with her to this concert or that party. Even with her car waiting and promises of experiences no girl my age should miss, I never made it past the gate.

Every time, as Joy pleaded and yelled my name, no matter how hard I tried to stay calm, something deep in my gut would take over and I would start screaming—that hollowness, that emptiness I always feel would fill itself with its own screams—until everything went black and I was back home in my bed again.

Remember that, Joy?

"Please," she tries again when I don't respond. "I haven't told anyone this, but I'm scared. I really need you, Val. We'll have fun. I promise."

"You'll make friends right away. You'll be fine."

"I can't be myself with new people. I need *you*." Her eyes latch onto mine. "Listen, before you say anything, this isn't charity and it's not just for me, it's for both of us. You deserve a break from your mom, from all this. We'll go to San Francisco and we'll go dancing and meet guys and—"

As she prattles on about all the things we'll do in the city, I can see the mounting desperation behind the bright animation of her hands and face. Though I've never seen pity in Joy's eyes, it's clear she aches for me, for my situation. She describes the museums, how we can sketch in Pioneer Park and eat dim sum at Hang Ah Tea Room, all the things she reminds me I love to do. Do I, though? I've lived inside her every discovery and adventure as if they were my own, but my enjoyment has always been secondary, the diary waiting for her at home. I've never had a chance to grow and discover what I'm good at, what I want.

"Val, please. At least consider it, okay? Candace will take care of your mother. You're almost nineteen—you can do what you want. Your mom can't stay mad at you forever."

All the times I said yes. All the times I thought it would be different because I wanted it as badly as she did. Her wounded eyes when she believed I simply changed my mind and went home. How easily Joy forgets.

I roll over on my side, away from Joy, because there's nothing I can say to make her stop. She's got her chin on my shoulder, telling me all about City Lights Bookstore, when I feel that build-up in my gut, a hollowness filling with the sounds I can't control, sweat seeping from my hairline and down my temples as my lips go white trying to keep that scream behind my teeth. I can never hold it in for long.

When I wake on the front porch of our little house, it's already dusk. There's a small dish with two bright red apples by my head. A large platter of lasagna and blue cheese-dressed iceberg wedges rests by my feet. This time, I eat everything with my hands before bringing what little is left to my mother.

She doesn't rise from her bed when I enter. Her eclipse-dark eyes dart from me to the dishes in my hands. Without breaking eye contact, I take a big juicy bite out of the apple I saved for her, then turn and toss the dishes out the open window.

My mother wasn't always like this. She used to be in love with my father. She used to sing to me in her belly, read to me before

I could even comprehend language, take long walks on the beach with her head on my father's shoulder as they talked about all the places they would go when I was old enough to travel. I remember her laughter. I remember how she used to love to eat, garlic sauce glossing her lips and chicken grease snaking down her wrist.

My father died before I was born. He was killed serving in some faraway war, though which war changed often, back when my mother still talked about him. My mother gave birth to me alone in their first house on this very patch of land. She named me Valley because my father thought the word was beautiful, a joyous exclamation of awe. Right after my birth, our house burned down, and the man who owns the land—Joy's father—built his big house in the back and a little house for us in the front.

It was not only pity, my mother says, but guilt and fear masquerading as generosity. Our house burned down on his land, but the landlord acted as if he was appeasing a pair of unreasonable women for the displacement he caused.

This is what my mother tells me, but I know not all of it is true. How can my father have died before I was born if I have memories of him? Time has faded most of the images from those first few years of my life, but the screaming rings diamond-cut in my head. His screaming. Her screaming. Crying, then silence trailed by the scents of fennel seeds and lime.

Sometimes I stand over my mother's bed and watch her sleep. If she knows I'm there, she's never let on. There were times I took the pillow from my bed and held it over her face, waiting—hoping—for her to struggle as I pressed down, even though I knew it was futile. What kind of life is this, only waking to throw dishes and stare at me with spite burning her eyes to soot? Why would she want me to live like this?

The big house unfolds endlessly as Joy leads me through all these rarified spaces. We staunch our giggles every time we hear Candace working down the hall. Joy's father is out of town on business again, and her mother is at a bottomless chardonnay lunch with her friends. I know this place with its heavy draperies and ornate woodwork is meant to be impressive, an illustration of her family's wealth, but it's strangely sterile to me, like a museum. Only Joy's room smells like someone lives there, smells familiar, like her.

Her father's study is sweet lignin, as I imagined, but there's nothing human—alive—behind those heavy double doors. We trace the nooks and crannies of built-in bookshelves and hulking furniture until we find the bourbon.

"When you visit me in California, we'll have a bottle of this," Joy says, raising a cut-crystal rocks glass. A wave of amber liquid licks the glass's rim but doesn't escape. Her pours are generous this afternoon, and I imagine all the parties she'll throw in her new apartment, all the men she'll seduce for liquor runs and validation.

"Maybe you'll visit *me* if I take all the bottles," I say, grabbing at the thick glass rectangle cradled in her lap. We're sitting in a book-lined alcove, in matching leather armchairs facing each other, our toes tapping together on the ottoman between us. The stretch feels good, reminding me that I can still feel my muscles, that my body doesn't have to be a phantom. "I'll keep them under my mattress so my mother doesn't throw them out the window."

Joy laughs. She doesn't let my bitter note spoil her fun. "This isn't even the good stuff, you know. My father hides the really expensive shit."

She tips her head towards the imposing mahogany desk in the center of the room. Its gilded drawers and cabinets coddle secrets that form a fortress of protection and power. I imagine her father behind it, sipping the good stuff while he congratulates himself for the charity of allowing my mother and me to live on his land.

"I think we deserve the expensive shit," I say.

Not that she was waiting for my approval, but Joy downs the last of her bourbon and races to the desk. Together, we crouch behind it, pulling open drawers and cabinets. We find half a bottle of Pappy Van Winkle Reserve in one cabinet, Nolet's Reserve in another. Kneeling on the floor, we pass the bottles back and forth, sipping directly from them as if that's the greater rebellion. Warm spices and bright botanicals light a soft flame across my chest, but it doesn't last, any lightheaded sway evaporating before my vision can go with it. Joy burps, looks embarrassed, so I burp too, then we're both laughing. I'm emboldened to touch everything in this room, and she joins me in rifling through fancy stamps and golden coins. When I find a small, locked drawer hidden in the base of a cabinet, she points me to the key taped under the desk.

"What does he keep in here?" I ask.

She shrugs.

I unlock the drawer and pull it open. A puff of dust and scent escapes, fennel seeds and lime tickling my nose. The only thing inside is a photograph.

Joy rests her chin on my shoulder as we both study it. A young woman stares back at us from the glossy print. Big brown eyes, golden brown skin, puffy lips shaped into a confident smile. Her short black hair frames her face in a wispy haze. I can see myself in her face, ten years from now. I can see my mother as she might've looked twenty years ago, if I could remember her smile.

"Who is this?"

Joy takes the photo from me and turns it over. No name or place or date is written on the back.

"I don't know," she says, flipping it to face her again. "She's pretty."

I lean forward so that my face is level with the photo. The movement makes everything in my vision swirl, all the polished browns and glistening crystal smearing into Joy's dark hair, but it passes quickly, same as all the other times I drank to little effect while Joy giggled and marveled at how she saw two of me. Can she see straight enough now to notice how this woman's lips and nose and eyes are so much like my own?

"Huh?" I nudge, raising my eyebrows up and down. I'm silly, playing drunk so she doesn't feel alone.

She takes a swig from the Pappy Van Winkle and presses it roughly to my chest. "He has this hidden in his desk. Like, in a secret drawer with a key and everything. What if…" She whips her gaze to me, pupils swallowing her irises. "Val, what if my dad's cheating with this woman? What if she's his secret lover?"

"This picture's old. No one wears their hair like that anymore."

"If she's just some old girlfriend, then why is he hiding this?"

I lean back against the desk and take a couple sips of bourbon. With all these bottles going back and forth between us, with the influence of how loose and sloppy Joy's gotten, we've been loud, careless. Maybe I want Joy's mother to come home early and find us. Maybe I want her landlord father to throw open these doors and banish me back to the little house with my mother. What can they really do to me? The worst has already happened.

"She looks like my mother," I say.

Joy grabs the bottle from me and takes a long drink, grimacing as she studies the photo again. "It's so weird, right? I know our parents had lives before us, but God, I can't imagine my dad, like, flirting and asking out some random girl."

Some random girl who looks like my mother.

162

"Oh my god!" She holds the photo up to my face. "She kinda looks like you. What if—There's a reason we click right? I always wanted you to be—"

At that, the study's double doors swing open. I grab the photo from Joy and slide it under my butt as Candace steps into the room.

"What are you doing in here? You know your father—"

"Sorry," Joy says, though her giggling betrays any remorse. She's still got the bourbon bottle in her lap. "Just one last hurrah with my very best friend. You won't tell, will you?"

Candace looks from Joy to me, her gaze catching on the shiny corner of the photo peeking out from under my thigh. Her eyes soften but her mouth twists in stifled glumness. "Watch over this one," she tells me after an uncomfortable moment. It's the first time she's ever spoken directly to me.

Joy falls backwards, laughing.

After Candace leaves, Joy sits up and lets out an exaggerated breath. I think about all the times I watched from the little house as she snuck down the driveway, winking at me, as she slipped out to meet some boy waiting for her on the street. I find it hard to believe she's ever experienced such thrill when there seem to be no consequences.

"Watch over this one," she mimics Candace, her words as crowded and heavy-bottomed. "See, even Candace thinks you should go to California with me." I open my mouth, but she cuts me off. "Seriously. Your mother won't even know. She'll sleep right through it."

This again. As if I'm the one being stubborn. "Okay," I relent, even though I know she won't remember any of this when the booze wears off. She presses the gin bottle into my hand then clinks it with her bourbon bottle. I take the obligatory swig with her. There's no point in arguing, not when the scream is building in my gut, crawling up my chest, pounding against the back of my tongue.

I've tried to tell her so many times: being a ghost doesn't mean I can go anywhere I want.

It makes sense, really, and I think in a way I've always known: Joy is my sister. The landlord is my father.

Though time and grief have weathered my mother's smooth skin and gentle features, it's obvious now. Many years ago, she loved the man who became our landlord, and they made a family. Then, the screaming started, so he left her and made a new family. His guilt built us this house, where she's trapped with me, a constant reminder of the screaming, and Joy and her mother in the big house up the hill, a constant reminder of what she should've had. We're the ghosts of his past, sealed in the amber of his guilt. Appeasement takes centuries, and they're safe and dumb and happy as long as my mother and I remain in this little house.

I grasp my mother's shoulder and shake hard, wanting her to acknowledge this, but she rolls away from me, pulling the covers over her head. Every time I marveled at how much Joy and I look alike with our gummy mouths and red-black hair, my mother would get angry. Now I know how much that hurt her, to see her daughter love her own replacement.

I get in my own bed and imagine Joy on the bathroom floor, puking up bourbon and gin while Candace rubs her back. I've never tasted vomit, only imagined its foulness from the pinched face Joy made as she described the hitch in her stomach and the acid rushing over her tongue. When I run my tongue along the backs of my teeth, I don't taste warm spice and mineral burn; it's the same thin mustiness, the usual nothing. My fingers don't smell like rare books or antique coins. My hair is the nothingness of ozone, not fennel seeds and lime. Not like Joy. Not like our father.

I've always known I'm dead—my mother never kept that from me. It's the how, the what happened, that she would never answer, even when she still spoke. I remember screaming because it's in my DNA. I'm a ghost made of my mother's anguish.

When Candace comes with dinner tonight, I'll make her stay. I'll make her tell me everything.

"Your mother died in childbirth," Candace says, staring up the hill at the big house where Joy and her mother are both sleeping off their hangovers. Her hair has come loose from the slick ponytail she always keeps it in, a thin fringe of grey frizz framing the harsh lines of her face. "The baby—you—you were early. Your father was away on business. He didn't know."

"When did I die?"

"You were stillborn."

We're sitting on the edge of the porch—not too close; Candace never likes to be less than ten feet from me—each of us absently nibbling on our slices of red velvet cake. Tonight's beef pot pies lay broken with the plates in the grass.

"Is that what he told you?" I ask.

Candace still won't look at me. "I was there."

"Then why didn't you help my mother? Why didn't you take her to the hospital?"

"I lived up the road at the time. I didn't know she'd gone into labor. When I found you both, it was too late."

"So, his whole family died and he—my father—went and got a

new family, just like that." I toss my fork down into the grass below. I think about breaking my plate, then Candace's, then the serving platters, creating a cacophony that will not only wake my mother but pound in Joy's and her mother's heads all the way up the hill. I want them to start screaming so I'm not the only one. "He built a big fancy house for his new family, and put me and my mom in this little house where he doesn't have to look at us, never has to think about us again."

Candace looks down at her cake, all the swirls of white buttercream in perfect division from the red cake below. "The big house was meant for you and your mother. You lived there for a time, all three of you. Your father, he didn't believe me when I told him you were dead, that he was living with ghosts. Then one day he met a woman and she told him, and he finally understood. He built this little house for you and your mother so your displaced spirits would have a home."

"He trapped us. He moved on, and now Joy is moving on and my mother and I, we'll never leave this place. We're trapped here forever."

"No, Valley, he didn't move on." She turns and looks right at me, same as this afternoon when she caught Joy and me in the landlord's— my father's—study. This time her jaw softens with her gaze, her eyes a wet reflection like Joy's. "Why do you think he works so much? Why do you think he gives Joy whatever she wants, except his time? He looks at her and he sees you."

Candace scoots towards me, placing a tentative hand on my knee. She looks surprised—by her own action, or by the fact that her palm lands on fabric and flesh instead of slicing through thin air. I feel the scream building again, branching out from the center of my chest, over my shoulders, up my throat, forcing itself against the back of my tongue. My mother screaming in pain, me screaming in the womb, Candace screaming as she stood in a puddle of my mother's blood, my father screaming as his new love held him. It takes everything I have to force it all back down, to pull away from Candace's touch.

"I wasn't sure how much you knew," she says. "Joy can't know any of this. Promise me you won't tell her."

"You asked me to watch over Joy," I remind her. "She goes to California soon, but I can't follow—not when I'm trapped like this." Up the hill, dots of light prick the darkness, every window bright and bold and unashamed. Knowing that I was meant to eat and sleep and dream and succeed behind those brocade curtains doesn't mean as much as I thought it would. My mother sleeps and glares and hates me because she knows, but that is still not the eternity I want for her.

I turn back to Candace. "If you want me to watch over her, I need you to do something for me."

On the morning before Joy leaves for California, we get in her bed and pull the covers over our heads one last time.

"Don't be mad at me, but I did something," she says, her breath making the blue satin billow out. As always, we are in perfect symmetry, beginning and ending in all the same places. "I told Candace you're coming with me. She's going to help. She'll do whatever we need so your mother can't stop you."

When I don't respond, she rolls over to face me, lips pursed in a held breath. She wants my gratitude, my surrender. I concentrate on the blue sky of the sheets, the fluffy white cloud of the comforter above that, the sunlight pouring in from her many windows making our little bubble glow. Why protest? Joy hears what she wants, talks and cries until she's drowned out any objection. All the times I tried to make her understand that I'm not alive like she is, that I'm anchored to the bedrock of this land. If she actually listened right now, would she even believe me? For eighteen years we've hugged and held hands and pulled fistfuls of each other's hair in backyard scuffles. She's never said a word about how cold my skin is, how I have no scent, how when we get in her bed the sheets lay flat against my face, no breath to ripple the fabric. All this time she's never acknowledged my limitations, of how my mother and I cease to exist beyond the gates of her home. She's been in denial just like our father was.

"You're mad, aren't you? Well, if you weren't so stubborn, I wouldn't have to do this. You can't hide from the world forever, Val."

"I'm not mad," I tell her. "What will I do while you're in class?"

She brightens. "Well, first, the campus is huge. There's an arts center, and galleries, and a sculpture garden…"

This is what makes Joy happy, describing all the things she loves. The more she talks, the more I realize that none of this was meant for me. She'll plunge her hands into clay or warm skin, but those same actions will be no more than an echo for me. My hands will never retain the shape of what I touched. My tongue will never relive the phantoms of flavors I enjoyed. I will always be hungry and hollow.

"So, what do you think?" she asks, squeezing my arm with a fingernail prick of expectation. "I mean, there's so much to do there, you'll never be bored. And then we'll have all night to see the city."

I pull her hand into my mine and squeeze as hard as I can. It helps to tamp down the scream building in my chest. "I'll start packing."

After dark, Candace brings me the things I requested: five bottles of gin, oily rags from the garage, and a box of fireplace matches.

"Are you sure?" she asks, watching me bunch the rags beneath the door and window frames.

Inside, my mother is in her bed. I wonder if she knows what I'm doing, if she can smell the gin as I empty the bottles all over the white wood front of our little house. Will she wake, or will she remain in some lovely dream of my father before the big house, before me?

When I strike the first match, Candace flinches and starts up the driveway. I touch the flame to each rag, the odors of sulfur and benzene slick on my tongue. I light more matches, tossing them haphazardly towards the structure, every individual flame linking limbs to outline the door and windows, long orange fingers smudging the crisp edges, climbing, multiplying, licking the roof, devouring the little house's screaming face all at once. White and red give way to the black of destruction quicker than Candace can make it up the hill. I don't need to stand back.

I'm sure.

I brace myself for my mother's screams, but they don't come. There is no echo in my head, no memory—false or not—of my father screaming in another woman's arms. There is no scream building in my own chest, forcing itself against my tongue. Instead, as the little house becomes nothing more than a rough-hewn block of solid fire, a stream of white smoke rises from the roof, cleaving the black smoke with such force that it makes an audible crack against the dark sky. The white smoke swirls upward in a graceful column, a ribbon twirling into the night. The acrid sting of burning fades in my nostrils, replaced by the scents of fennel seeds and lime.

Up the hill, windows light up across the big house. Candace is no longer visible, perhaps already inside rousing the landlord. Soon, there will be sirens and firemen and neighbors gathered on the other side of the gate. Tomorrow, the neighborhood kids will take their long sticks to the remains of my little house. They'll take turns scaring each other with ghoulish new tales about my mother and me and what they think we were.

When I turn back to the little house, the white smoke of my mother is gone, but the scents of fennel and lime remain, a hand beckoning me upwards. I may have been tethered to this land, but I was not born here; this world was never meant for me. The little house reaches its long, burning arms out, out, out and I don't resist. I walk into its warm embrace.

THINGS TO KNOW BEFORE YOU GO

Nadia Bulkin

Della had just closed her eyes when she heard a shriek from the direction of the pool. A small child splashed frantically, having apparently slipped off the edge(?), and her towel-draped relatives—as well as a hotel lifeguard—were trying to help her back out with great fanfare. Della's Indonesian was rusty, but she understood enough: *she can't swim,* and *she just jumped.*

The thought exploded in her mind, unbidden, coarse: she could just jump. Into the pool, with her sarong and sunhat on. Or from their hotel room balcony on the third floor. Or off the curb. It wouldn't have to be a jump, even, just a step. That was important, actually, a critical aspect of the whole thing—it had to be *easy*. Really, stupid easy, or she'd never do it. It had to be just a flick of a wrist, a simple lift of a foot. Something easy and then everything would all *go away*.

She heard a plastic squeak and a sharp clearing-of-a-throat from the adjacent chaise lounge. Mary was preparing to read aloud a page from *Things to Know Before You Go: Indonesia.*

"This jungle hike sounds cool." Mary sounded out the name of what was apparently a jungle, over and over until she felt that she got it right. "It says it's considered sacred. There's even a special waterfall that's off-limits to everyone except members of the spirit world."

And then she laughed uproariously, and Della glanced around to see if anyone was giving them dirty looks. It felt like she had spent the whole trip embarrassed. Embarrassed when the waitress at the restaurant slowly repeated her order back to her, eyes searching her face for some mental defect that would explain her awkwardness. Embarrassed with how badly her comfort with Indonesian had dissipated over the years, because she had no friends to speak it with and her parents now only spoke it when they got emotional, which these days happened very rarely.

Embarrassed, too, as Mary then took it upon herself to order in bungled Indonesian as well, with the same try-hard shamelessness she'd shown in Comparative Religions. Her pronunciation was worse, but she'd gotten a smile from the waitress. "A" for effort considering her straw blonde hair, Della guessed, but that was a lie. Mary had always been the smarter of the two of them. That was true in the front row of Comparative Religions. It was true when they were freshman roommates, trying to push their way into the company of their cooler, surer betters.

No. That sear in her nerves when Mary *pushed* wasn't embarrassment. That was something else.

"Where is it?" She typed the name of the jungle into her phone, and upon zooming in and out, felt the clench in her stomach. (The clench sat in that sacred space in her soul where Mary had the push. She didn't know what the push felt like, but it had to be better than the clench.) "I don't know. I have no idea where this is."

Mary cocked her brow in impatience. She was tired of being held back by Della's misgivings; Della understood that. But for all of Mary's whip-smart wit, there were things that Mary didn't understand about this country, about misery and malice and lack. And there were also things about this country that even Della didn't understand, except as half-remembered stories passed down by the teenaged girl who used to be her babysitter, back before the family moved to the States. "So we can only go to the places you personally know? Kind of limits us, huh?"

All their years in college, Della had used her heritage as a party trick, an icebreaker, a small means of distinction from the sea of neurotic middle-class youth. Like Ravenna's chronic Lyme disease, and Krissy's affair with an ethics professor. At Mary's house for Thanksgiving, she'd regaled the Crowders with every story she could remember about her exotic homeland—*the traffic!*—because it was quite simply the most interesting thing about her.

But now that they were here, the truth was spilling forth like bottled water into the hotel sink, like piss into a squat toilet; she was not a *real* Indonesian.

She willed herself to move past the note of disappointment in Mary's voice by responding urgently. "I'm serious. Look how remote this place is. It would take us half-a-day to get there."

Mary laughed. "I don't even know how anything could be remote in this country. This island is literally sinking from being jammed with so many people." It was a joke, but it wasn't funny. "Come *on*, Dell. We didn't come all this way just to hang out at the bougie hotel pool, did we?"

Della's cheeks burned, because she really had tried to pick a hotel that Mary would like. She imagined the spreading pink to be the same color of the skin slowly searing on the upper center of Mary's back—the fiery spot Mary couldn't reach, the spot Della promised she'd covered on her behalf. It was just a very little lie.

Their destination was a six-hour journey by bus into what passed in Java for mountains. The hotel concierge looked confused when Della asked him to confirm the route they would need to take – evidently it was not a hike that tourists embarked upon often. "We like to go off the beaten track," Mary declared, but even the power of her inner push wasn't enough to settle her stomach as the rickety bus heaved its way uphill, like an old water buffalo trying to get out of the mud.

They switched seats so Mary could suck sweeter air through the semi-open window. Della imagined herself stoic like the other Indonesians, rocking to and fro like she was made of water instead of rocks, like she was one with the road and the bus and the hillside. By the time they reached the trailhead she was so nauseous that she couldn't think—it was Mary who figured out where they were and commanded the bus driver to stop.

An old woman sitting behind the driver with a bundle of plastic bags grabbed Della's arm as she descended the steps—long fingers, a deeper brown than Della's own but with a similar root-like boniness. She spoke fast, using more Javanese than Indonesian, and although Della's ears were catching the syllables the old woman was throwing down, her brain couldn't string them into any particular meaning.

"Dell, come on!" Mary was calling from off the bus, loud and stabbing enough to quicken Della's pulse – people like Mary didn't need gimmicks to make their mark, they simply *made it*, boldly, carving their way into fresh earth without losing a single precious moment to self-doubt—but the old woman's focus didn't veer. She didn't seem to notice Mary at all.

Tuk, that was one of the syllables the old woman kept repeating. *Ku-tuk*. She didn't know how to translate the way that word made her nausea swell anew.

Ultimately, she couldn't disguise her ignorance. Stupid Della. Della the ill-prepared. She shook her head, apologized, pulled her arm free as politely as possible. The old woman pulled back, and her grim expression curled into greater frustration. Repulsion?

Mary had done well, as usual. After the bus rattled away, they could see that they were only about fifty feet from the trailhead. Reinvigorated by the glory of her navigational victory, and the relief offered by the window seat, Mary was jovial—even bouncy—as they deposited the requisite access fee into a little wooden box posted by the trailhead, secured only by a rusty padlock—ten thousand rupiah for Indonesians, fifty thousand for foreigners.

Della felt Mary's eyes rummaging in her wallet along with her own fingers. She waffled, but eventually pulled out a bright blue fifty-thousand-rupiah bill. "Really?" Mary asked. Della tried to explain that she really wasn't a local, despite her passport, but Mary urged her to put in a magenta ten instead. She said the fifty could come in handy if they needed to bum a ride off someone – a thought that nearly sent Della into a panoply of hives.

She wondered why there was no one manning the wooden box, official or otherwise. Normally at least a few enterprising locals would be hanging around selling snacks or tour guide services, but this stretch of the road was disconcertingly quiet. Not even a stray goat. The word *remote* popped back into Della's head, as did *kutukan*. Amid all this vacancy the mouth of the trail had been allowed to clog with web of waxy leaves and prickly vines, and for a moment Mary frowned and Della was sure she was going to let them go home—but then Mary simply pried apart the vines and stepped into what looked like darkness. Della followed, reminding Mary that they had to be out before four p.m. to catch the bus back down the mountain.

"Christ, would you relax? Act like you want to be here?"

But she didn't want to be here. She wanted to go home. She did not like the way the unkempt thicket had suddenly given way to a trail so well-maintained it looked plucked from a storybook. Gentle ferns lined the trail with such precision they could have been planted; the winding path ahead basked in a sunlight uncomplicated by either heat or shadow, despite the weight of the canopy like a green cathedral hanging overhead.

"What exactly are you so scared of? This place is beautiful!"

"Snakes." There was something else, too, some itch where her heart should be. Rationally she knew that warnings to keep out of sacred spaces were just part of a larger pattern of social programming through storytelling. She'd written an essay on it in Comparative Religions. She'd cited her own childhood babysitter, warning her not to go near wild bamboo because it was home to ghosts, when really it was just home to thorns. "Crazy people."

"Is that it?" Mary asked. "Oh no. Don't tell me. You think we're crossing into the *spirit world*."

She said it in such a wretched, crooked voice that Della instantly wished, in a flash of heat, that she hadn't agreed to come on this trip at all. She forced her tongue against her teeth, a method of peacekeeping that she'd taken up in college to protect her limited social capital. But several years had passed since then. They lived much further apart, now, than a grimy linoleum hallway, and through her rustiness a bite of honesty slipped out—"you wouldn't get it."

Mary's eyes narrowed. She wasn't accustomed to being excluded. Disappointment was catching up to the dream, but Mary knew how to turn frustration into a push. "Okay. So, tell me. How do we protect ourselves? Are there any prayers? Code words? Since you're the expert."

But she didn't know. She had no goddamn idea. The warnings

were about staying out of forbidden spaces, not staying safe within them. The only thing she remembered Mbak Susi saying was to not eat any food the spirits offered, or she'd never get back home—a thought that had seriously concerned her considering how loose and permeable the barriers between the two dimensions seemed to be. "But how will I know if I'm in the spirit world?" she'd asked, and Mbak Susi said, "You'll know."

Except what if she didn't?

Mary started up the path and Della reluctantly followed, surprised to find her ankles straining under the force of its slope. From a distance, the path had looked effortlessly flat, but now that they were on it pebbles were flying out from beneath Mary's sneakers and Della's eyes were level not with Mary's head, but with that sunburned patch on Mary's back. She could even hear it in Mary's voice, gone thin and hurried in the rush for breath.

"You don't want to go to bars. You don't want to go clubbing. Now you don't even want to do this. Go on this quietest little nature walk. Just the two of us. Anytime I make a suggestion, it's *no, no, no*. I don't think I'm asking for a lot here. Just wish you'd… you know, chip in."

"I wish we'd gone to Thailand," Della replied, and with a sudden burst of energy, squeezed the straps of her little backpack and pushed past Mary.

She was expecting a snide remark to follow as she strode ahead—a valid if cutting observation, maybe, that Della never spoke up for any of her preferences so how could anyone be expected to know what she wanted? But what she heard instead was, "what is that?"

She turned and saw the path behind her empty. Nothing else had changed; it was as though some divine photographer had simply double-clicked on Mary and edited her out from between the trees. A cold coil wrapped around Della's guts and jerked. "Mary?"

And then all at once it came to her. "Curse," it meant. *Kutukan* meant "curse."

Della's parents had not been happy about her returning to Indonesia. Or at least her mother hadn't been. The two of them decided not to tell her father, for fear of worsening his blood pressure. He was the one that hadn't wanted to give up on the country, but the results of the last "free and fair" election were his last straw. "I don't know why you want to go back there," her mother said, and stopped replying to any messages Della sent about the trip.

So maybe, Della was thinking, her parents wouldn't even know when or where to start looking for her if she never got out of this forest.

Of course, that was an insane thought. Neither she, nor Mary, could be far from the path. How long had they been walking when she vanished, five minutes? Fifteen? Surely Mary, in her bright yellow shirt, was lying in a crumpled heap just under these here bushes, her ankle probably broken and her voice shocked into silence after having slipped—so quickly, so quietly!—off the path and down a heretofore invisible hill. Now all Della had to do was find her, so they could get back to the main road and back to America and…

Never come back again.

Where had that thought come from? Had an agent of the spirit world put it there? Some long-haired jinn slunk down from the trees, boneless and whispering and full of teeth?

A perverse, nervous giggle burst out of Della, because she had pulled back the bushes that she was sure were hiding Mary and once again seen… nothing. The flash of yellow that she thought had to be Mary's shirt had turned out to be nothing. Nothing except a little swarm of ants that had found something to take back to their queen.

She was losing it, she thought—she had to be. Thinking about ghosts and goblins when really she was just dehydrated and scared, and regressing—understandably—into Mbak Susi's horror stories. Those stories were only ever meant to help keep her alive—away from strangers, out of the night—so of course they were going into overdrive now.

What had happened to Mbak Susi, anyway? The last time Della saw her was through the rearview mirror of their car as they drove to the airport. She'd been standing in front of their house in flip-flops, arms crossed, brow furrowed. All this time Della had imagined her frozen in time in that old south Jakarta neighborhood with the sea of turquoise roof tiles and tiny broken streets, but of course that wasn't how time worked. That wasn't how life worked.

And unless Mbak Susi had been replaced by a plastic mannequin, of course she would have moved on. Taken another job, gone back to her village, found other children to frighten. Of course, this volcanic land had not stopped churning, shifting, grinding in the years that she'd been gone. She was a fool to imagine otherwise.

She was a fool to leave the main trail to look for Mary, too. She should have just turned around and used that fifty-thousand-rupiah bill in her wallet to hail anyone who passed by for help. Because now she couldn't even find the hill that Mary had presumably slipped from, the hill that she could have sworn she'd stumbled down—the elevation had changed while she was busy looking under bushes and now, she was somehow up *high* again. But now the light was muted.

After she stepped into a loose hole in the earth and nearly twisted her ankle, she decided she needed to stop for the night and hope for better luck in the morning. With her stomach in a rage, she tore open her backpack, hoping against hope that she hadn't eaten all the airline cookies—but praise God, she'd somehow remembered to pack granola bars. She mashed them between her teeth, chewing as fast as possible without regard for the dirt and sweat on her fingers to distract herself from the visions of fanged ghouls trying to pry into her head.

It was just a trick. Just her mind thrashing against superstition like a fever, like an infection. She could fight it off like a fever too, she realized, and now the rest of Mbak Susi's advice came flooding back to her in a softly reassuring wave: *There's no reason to be afraid.* The words were so clear, so precise, that she could almost feel the woman's cool skin against her arm. She had always smelled so charmingly of frangipani. *The spirit world isn't evil. It just knows how to bring out the wickedness in you.*

The further she walked, the harder it became to go backwards. She would turn around to test herself and immediately lose track of the direction from which she'd come. She lost track of other things too; sometimes she tried to conjure up Mary's face, to prove that the Mary-figure she saw floating between the trees wasn't *really* Mary, but found to her dismay that she could never get the details right. Eyes never in the right place. Mouth too big, no matter how much she'd try to shrink it in her mind's eye.

But she didn't need to make sense of all that to keep walking. Walking was easy. She wasn't even hungry anymore. Maybe it would be fine, she thought, to walk forever.

Until, finally, she saw light, and every buried wish came back. Not the light of the sun catching on leaves but white light in the dark, artificial light. She had to be near a road, she thought, except had she seen any street lamps near the trailhead? Yes, there had to be. This wasn't the 1950s, there was a bus route, this trail was listed in

180

Things to Know Before You Go, for heaven's sake. But *look how remote this place is.* Of all the voices that were buzzing in her ear she trusted that one the most, because that voice was her own.

She kept charging forward, stepping back, until finally she remembered that even if there were no street lamps, there would be roadside stalls, single-bench trap-draped huts serving black coffee and instant noodles under a cloud of cloves and citronella. They would make light.

It was a police station. A small white outpost under a simple gable roof, only large enough to house a few rooms but maybe that was all they needed, up here in the would-be mountains where no one seemed to live. Once inside, she saw that it was even smaller than she'd thought. A single police officer sat at a wooden desk, patiently polishing a small rock collection.

"Please help, sir," she said, "My friend is missing."

The police officer put down his rock. "Missing? You mean you lost her?"

"Yes. I mean... we were walking on the path, right at the start, and I passed her and then I looked back, and she was gone. I've looked everywhere, but..."

"Surely, not everywhere. Surely, she must be somewhere."

She took a deep, hard breath. "Okay. Yes. I think she maybe tripped or slipped and fell down the hill back there..." an attempt to imagine the hill in relation to a blinking "you-are-here" X for her current location resulted only in a sea of mental static. "I don't know where. But I think she might have gotten hurt."

"Wasn't that what you wanted to happen? When you pushed her?"

The static cleared out. "What?"

"Are you sure you didn't see her walking in front of you..."—because Mary always walked in front, from the cafeteria to the library, and Della the Dutiful always followed—"… and think to yourself, I could just give her a push. She wouldn't see it coming. All you'd need to do is reach out your hand and let yourself…"

It would be so easy.

"No!" Della squeezed her fingers into her ears. "She saw something! After I passed her, she said, 'what is that?' That's when she disappeared!"

"You resented her, didn't you? You were jealous of her. I have this right here from Mbak Susi." From the filing cabinet under his desk, he pulled out a folder and opened it to a page she couldn't see. *"Della is always jealous of her friends.* That's sad, no? Aren't you proud of who you are?"

She shook her head so vigorously she imagined her brain leaking out. "Mbak Susi didn't say that. Mbak Susi—Mbak Susi couldn't. She hasn't seen me in years. And it doesn't matter if I was jealous of her, what matters is that she's gone!"

"She's not gone," the police officer said with a gentle laugh. "She's here with us."

A cold mist drenched her body as he indicated the forest that surrounded them with a flick and sweep of the wrist. "I think if you looked under the bushes, you'd find her. Waiting for you." For a moment, the walls dissolved, and the police station became a police pavilion, open to the elements. She averted her eyes, not liking the feeling of all those yellow eyes staring back at her from the dark.

"I swear," she begged, chin tucked in supplication, "I can't find her."

The police officer sighed. "Okay, okay. Then just sign this missing-persons report and we'll start looking." He slid over a piece of paper heavy with ink that didn't look at all like a missing person's report, but the words squirmed when she tried to read them. It was curious, she now realized, how well she'd understood him. How smoothly her own language had flowed. She hadn't even felt the stress of her brain trying to reconfigure English thoughts into Indonesian words, and now she was afraid that if she tried to speak again, it would stop. And even more afraid of what it meant if it didn't.

"Is this a dream?" she asked.

"No," he said with a smile that looked sympathetic if not apologetic and offered her a pen. She clicked it open, and it hissed.

M ary would be found first. She was not far from the trailhead, at least in Cartesian terms—topographically speaking, she was several hundred meters below the main path, having apparently fallen down the hill. The locals who found her—so alone, so pretty, so *white*—were worried, because they could see the story of her death rapidly spiraling into ugly themes of madness and darkness and evil.

Della would be found later, much deeper in the jungle. The locals would conclude, based on the nature of her necrosis, that she had been bitten by a pit viper. Her discovery would greatly calm the locals' nerves, because they were allowed, now, to tell a story free from murder.

It would be a familiar story, a story that would surprise no one, about two young American women who had gone to a remote forest without a guide and fallen prey not to predators but to their own inexperience, their naivete, their loud and unrelenting ignorance. Their profound unbelonging in a land that did not spend its fleeting energy trying to forgive.

NEW ANCESTORS

Robert Nazar Arjoyan

*T*hey are mirror images of one another, their twinned faces at rest in identical attitudes upon either window of the backseat. One left, one right, the tattered leather armrest this tableau's folding crease. *Armenia's green countryside flies past these reflective brothers, meridians there and gone, there and gone. Blonde plumy hair, lips pursing and relaxing, long legs bent at acute angles so near their strapping chests. The single distinguishing deviation which spoils the otherwise perfect illusion is a broken nose, Liam's. Where Logan boasts the subtle bump of their father's Irish line, Liam's nose more resembles their mother's kin, a burst mess of bone and flesh, one smashed pomegranate fallen from the highest branch of the tallest tree. A spill of mauve stains Liam's proud cheeks, his upper lip, his forehead.*

The siblings blinked in sync when a halting baritone broke the silence.

"This you are did was your premiere fighting?"

Liam and Logan looked up in stringed unison, as if one's movements determined the other's. The man in the passenger seat of the Mercedes V-Class watched them through the rearview mirror, waiting with his bushy monobrow raised for some sort of a reply. An evil eye dangled on a chain of suncatcher jewels from its perch.

"He asks if this was your first fight," said the driver, a woman of fine feature steering the luxury van along the meandering two lane blacktop. Her English sounded English.

"Yeah," said Liam, unproud. "First fight."

"Good!" said the stout man and clapped. "You are did a very good!"

He reached between and below his legs to rummage and produce a mason jar of clear liquid, its idle sloshing an invitation.

Liam and Logan spoke wordlessly in their womb-written language.

"Mulberry vodka," the woman clarified. "Homemade."

"You are will to drink this, eh? Strong for strong!"

"OK," they both answered, stereophonic instinct, and drank.

Sips interspersed with coughs, their neophyte throats at once living kilns and tear ducts corroded pipes.

"First time for that too I would wager," said the woman, amusement assuaging her sentence. The palm of her hand smoothed the knitted rim of the steering wheel, that soft caressing sound, and the boys nodded, their tongues too slick with fire for speech.

"Also, your first visit to the homeland from what I understand."

"That's true, ma'am," replied Logan, and cleared his larynx growling.

"Yes, Armenia is a place of many firsts," said the woman. She honked at a roadside fruit vendor and twiddled her manicured fingers. "Well, many forgotten firsts, let me say. We founded the first winery and laced the first pair of shoes. We were the first country to ever officially accept Christianity, this was in the 4th century, and the first genocide of the 20th century, as you two doubtless are aware. We turned folks on with the first color TV then saved their souls with the first MRI. When you need cash and stop at an ATM, kiss the mouth of the first Armenian you can find. Yes, we even mapped the heavens with the planet's very first observatory, a site you will soon behold."

"We're excited to behold it," said Logan, adulthood and youth still wrestling for supremacy in his vocal cords. "Aren't we, Liam?"

"Oh, sure, nice consolation prize, a four-hour drive to Core-a-hunch," Liam replied through the wreck of his nose while staring at an arterial clot of sheep, jumbled wool as far as he could see. The Mercedes slowed to accommodate this passing flock.

"Karahoonj, not Core-a-hunch," replied the woman, the gentlest of corrections. "Predates Stonehenge by a whopping 4,500 years, but..." Her eyes smiled all-seeing as they sized up the twins and crow's feet danced there on her olive skin. "Your Armenian is not very good, is it?" she asked, finally at full stop. The cross-eyed sheep bleated as they trod the pavement, a further cacophony of hooves and bells.

"Between us combined," said Logan, "there's maybe one decent talker." The words stumbled out from behind the fuzzy line of his teeth. Logan licked his gums and tried to taste.

"A repulsive crime that will be remedied," she said. The paunchy passenger hissed under his breath and that blast of spit fluttered his unkempt whiskers. Liam and Logan looked at each other and saw twins of their own twin.

"What... what did you say that drink was again?" inquired Logan as best he could.

"And we at Dear Diaspora are only too happy to provide such a service for you, this little daytrip, in return for your commendable courage and valor."

Sheep billowed now on both sides of the car and pinioned it. The jostle of their progress stirred the boys' whisking stomachs.

"Hey, my brother ast you a queshin," slurred Liam. "He ast whawas in the jink-"

"That poor girl! And at the hands of her very countrymen, no less. If we do this to ourselves, I ask you, why shouldn't our enemies be so inclined to follow suit?"

"Logah," spluttered Liam, "Logah, cuh."

"Thank goodness for you brothers saving that young woman."

Liam pawed at his door handle like a lame cat and finally found purchase.

"It's just a shame, really," bemoaned the driver. "Your corrupted blood."

Liam nudged the way open but an instant aroma of animal clawed its way through the ruined tunnels of his nose and ramped his spinning head into a cyclone.

"Intermarriage perpetuates genocide, you know," offered she, as if sharing her favorite thoughts on how best to wrap dolma or book thrifty travel.

Logan crawled across the back to join his brother in escape but those two feet of distance seemed a chasm stretching far beyond his capability. At home in LA, he captained the water polo team of St. Francis High to victory and gold. But just then in the unknown town of Sarnakunk, stuck amongst tidal livestock, Logan felt weak and powerless.

"What good is half an Armenian?" she asked no one in particular as anonymous sheep slammed shut the backseat getaway, all trace of her joviality eradicated alongside all hope of their freedom.

Liam and Logan trapped in a tunneling world.

"God has poisoned this country, boys, has spread her festering legs open for rape and pillage and death. Well, Armenia is a land of firsts and today will be the first day of the rest of her life."

Logan took hold of his brother's limp hand as night somehow came at noon.

"What... whajya say at jink was–"

"—**A**gain? It just tastes like gas, bro, Jesus."

"Bartender said it was gin but it probably is just gas."

"Or lighter fluid."

"Fucking Armos."

Liam and Logan intoned this condemnation together, the umpteenth time after their arrival. Mom had never been back since immigrating to the States as a preteen and Dad had come to test the reputation of Armenia's brandy straight from the cask, liquor said to be loved above all others by Winston Churchill.

The boys didn't have a choice.

Summer before college, Cancun might have been their ideal destination.

"Cheers." Logan raised his glass and Liam clinked it.

"Cheers." They drank the foul concoction and grimaced.

Mom and Dad were enjoying an evening at the opera while their sons savored the pub scene of Yerevan. The twins walked the capital city streets, a head and half taller than most of the locals, broad shouldered and fair. By the time they set out from the Marriot and ambled past the fountains in Republic Square, Liam and Logan had drawn stares at every turn, leers which harbored little love. One dude even tossed a crumpled pack of smokes at their feet. Liam stopped, the scuff of his Allbirds audible over a busker's accordion.

"Forget it, Li, let's m–"

"Do I look like a trashcan to you?"

The hunched man also stopped.

"Vat you says?"

"Put your trash in the trash, asshole. It's not rocket science."

"Liam, fuck it, dude, th-"

"No, Lo, Mom and Dad and fuckin everybody sends money to these people all the time, oh, we're poor, we're starving, the Turks and the Azeris are taking everything from us, please help us, but this cocksucker throws his cigarettes at me?"

While Logan led the water polo team, Liam was the Friday night star of St. Francis, the football team's major deity. He hinted at that with his bold bearing.

"Way to make us feel welcome, dipshit."

On they went, sussing bad from worse and letting Liam simmer while the sultry evening enveloped them close as might some sweaty uncle. In the open air between beat up brutalist apartments, they could see the penumbra of Mount Ararat haunting its former home, a hungry ghost waiting for a dying friend.

"Do you think Noah really landed up there with the ark and the animals and shit?"

"It's in the Bible, bud, so it must be true."

"Liam, for real, man, like, don't you feel… I don't know, different here? Of all the spots on Earth, why choose Ararat for Noah's Ark to park, huh? I even read-"

"You? Read?"

"-about these ancient cartographers mapping Armenia as the Garden of Eden. Again, why, why here? It's like we're walking through a myth or a fairy tale."

Liam was quiet as they skirted a park.

"Remember in history class, the Silk Road stuff? Armenia was like the revolving door, they said."

"This is an old place."

On Pushkin Street, a group of similarly aged kids were entering a bar, maybe seven of them, and the twins heard with relief the unmistakable patois of Glendale, California.

"Down?" they asked each other as one.

"Down," they answered in the same fashion.

Now wiping his mouth clean of gin dribble, Logan looked about the place and saw one of the girls from the group, one that had shone under the pub's neon sign.

She was tall for an Armenian, tall like him, with long hair which might in private tickle her waist.

"Li, see her?"

"Who, Lo?"

"That girl by the painting."

"The blonde?"

"No, man, the-"

"The tall one?"

"Yeah."

"She's pretty."

Logan squinted.

"I think I know her, bro."

Liam clicked his tongue and flicked his finger, evidence of ancestry.

"Those are Armenian school kids, dude, probably on a senior trip, we don't-"

"Kindergarten."

And as if that answer was *the* answer, the tall girl cut her big eyes across the crowded tavern right at Logan. They then widened like an aperture primed for illumination at the sight of two such lifeforms. Mom had a favorite song, a ballad titled "Hayi Acher" sung by a bearded badass named Harout. From what Logan could glean, the lyrics expounded upon the depth and breadth of Armenian eyes, how they cry but laugh, how black clouds always smother them but somehow still strive as ponds of light.

Feeling those Armenian eyes on him, Logan picked up what Harout was putting down.

"Kindergarten," he repeated and set off for a hello when three men encircled her as if they were vultures and she carrion. If not for their drunken swaying—or their grabby hands—it might have been a funny moment, a trio of sleepy tots looking up at their tired mommy. But when the center guy dropped his hairy paw from her shoulder to her breast, Logan moved on the son of a bitch in a second, closing the space between them in four practiced bounds.

Liam watched as his brother yanked the offender's Caesar bangs and loomed over him, daring him to do something. Even from Liam's distance, the flush of furious embarrassment burned the older man's face as his outnumbered cronies dragged him off. Liam snickered at the trio's hasty retreat, his twin backed up by the tall girl's schoolmates and towering like the mast of a ship. It hit Liam then how they really did stick out in this place where they were meant to fit in.

"Nothing we can do about that."

It also hit Liam then that he needed to find a restroom.

Three tries it took, Liam searching for the *zukaran*, when at last a merciful barkeep pointed out the path. Liam shuffled past Logan and the tall girl and ducked into an ill lit corridor.

"Umm?"

There was a turnstile at the bathroom's entrance and Liam's buzzing brain didn't compute its presence. He tried to shove through but the thing had no give, so he simply hopped it. After a long pee and an internal discussion with his gut about throwing up, Liam washed his hands.

When Liam stepped back into the toilet's fenced anteroom, he found Logan's three rivals, chests out and scowling. Caesar snarled at Liam in Armenian, racist garbage about his whored-up heritage.

"Fuck off with that shit man and anyway you got it all wrong that was my brother bro that wasn't me even though you had it coming aren't you guys married or some shit you're like forty and molesting a teena—"

The punch came from the left and it came low. It bent Liam at the waist and stole his oxygen. His gut reprised those vomit conversations and let loose a bilious flow on the attackers' Gucci loafers. So stained, a foot found Liam's face and thus he heard the foremost crunch.

After that, it was just a volley of dizzy pain.

Liam sank into a well of his making, deep and dark, each percussion of agony an added weight pushing him fathoms further. It was quiet there in his shaft and he rolled in its cold waters until–

—Something nuzzled his ear, an incendiary huffing so opposite the mute chill from which he was now disturbed.

A pleasant wind laced through the skein of his hair, and he felt it twice, the same sensation looped double.

Oh, fuck.

The van!

The drink!

They must have drugged him, drugged—

He shot up and a wave of misery slapped him down.

From the crown of his skull to the tip of his penis, heat paralyzed him, sharp and insistent, nearly alive. It radiated outwards in a terrible stria within and without, the throbbing nexus of his heart pumping deaf to any rhythm he might recognize.

He realized a horse had awakened him and already it stamped some fifty feet away, cropping the grass of its wild abode. Flies harassed the horse, and its flank rippled. He alike detected such spasms electrocuting his body.

Some unsupported voice slithered out from nowhere. "How do you find Karahoonj, young man?"

He attempted to sit up once again, and while the torment was immutable, it was no longer novel. He found himself in the middle of a field ensconced in a circle of squat stones, themselves surrounded by a gallery of hard-edged rock jutting out of the soil like a chthonic monster's dentition. Beyond these megaliths, plain and pasture spread beneath a sparkling star-blown firmament such as he'd never imagined. The primeval boulders leaned at odd gradients, their strange slant made weirder by a pattern of perfect wounds, circles bored with purpose into their granite integument. And through these numerous spirals he saw curious eyeballs glinting and groping.

From behind the nearest monument emerged the driver, the kind tour guide.

"Predates Stonehenge by 4,500 years but do people know that?"

A chorus of VOCH rang through the meadow, a unanimous NO.

"Peering through these proto telescopes, our forebears hailed the heavens and charted celestial migration while Europeans were still negotiating their way down from trees. Legend even says we held court with intelligentsia from space as depicted in the petroglyphs before you."

He looked about as prompted but only saw more people emerge from the prehistoric pillars.

"Where's my brother, ma'am?" he asked and wondered to whom he referred, Liam or Logan. His head hurt, as if holding on by a thread.

"God saw fit to plant His Garden here, here!" she declaimed with a downward finger, ignoring his question. "Adam and Eve were meant to kickstart life along these hills! This was the very center of the world!"

Another chorus boomed, "AYO," a redoubtable "YES."

He began to stand and at last took note of his nudity. A lurid red suture crawled its way up the length of his torso starting from his groin. That gristle looked to him like a marching army of fire ants. His hands traced this surgical seam up, up, up, and it never stopped.

The boys often woke in the middle of most nights to trade dreams, see if they shared similar reveries. But there in that place where time and sanity were diaphanous, where God had apparently cursed, razed, and salted the earth, he discerned a single nightmare, a horrible truth made visible by the sick lamp of moonlight.

A corpse sliced vertically in half lay face down on the dirt, two pieces of geometric meat. He heard the woman, but her proclamations were dim, dim.

"People have forgotten all the things we've given to them and all the things that have been taken from us, don't even know about it in most cases, don't even care. Just as the old maps have wiped Eden from Armenia, so too does our atlas neglect its modern erasure."

He inched toward the victim and was anew unsure if he'd meet Liam or Logan.

"We have yet been trained by our rapists to bend over at will, to freely give what belongs to us!"

Closer now but more afraid than ever. The cut was so precise, so clean, as if this thing was made of clay and not skin or skeleton. Even the organs were chopped with museum perfection. Cross section of intestine, lung, spine, heart, tissue, colon, rib, and brain. Fresher than fear, an opaque sadness slouched upon him.

"Armenia is a losing place, a place that is being lost every day, a rotting cadaver still being cannibalized, picked apart until not a bone will be left, where no patch of grass can ever again be called Armenia."

He could feel the baking fever of his audience and it transported him back once more to Los Angeles when he and his twin starred in the school play, a production of *The Comedy of Errors*. He reached down to flip over the carcass because he had to tell Mom, right?

"But you boys are winners."

That plural paralyzed his progress. Boys?

"A new Armenian to make a new Armenia!"

The "AYO" which erupted at this jingoism came from the ground itself and toppled him amidst the bisected remains.

"But what good is half an Armenian?" she asked, and pleasure perfumed her revelation.

He lay in the middle of butchery, him the disgusting result, an enantiomorph made manifest—by what magical means or medical he could not say. He scrambled away, pushing himself gone with heel and wrist, wishing to die. His braided back struck stone and he spun round and screamed.

A band had begun to perform and the reedy insouciance of a zurna matched his shattering volume as if it were his cloven mouth emitting the squeal of celebration while a deep throated drum hammered shut any semblance of his original being.

Reflecting rock showed him to him, twins halved and stitched as one. The right side of his face was Logan, handsome and unmarred, with Liam the left, nose broken and hideous.

"It's a little bit a lot, I am sure, but now that you are whole, you shall make us whole."

The witnesses cried out like champions, coming conquerors.

"Ashot!" she hollered. "Bring her out!"

He, for he no longer knew a name, craned his neck to discover the chubby passenger from eons ago, the man who had offered the jarred narcotic. At the escorting elbow of this Ashot, the tall girl let herself be led.

"Rise!" yelled the tour guide.

And he did.

Ashot released the tall girl, and she kept gliding closer to him as might a swan propelled by the calmest breeze.

"Barev," she said to him, hello.

"Barev," he replied, his accent immaculate.

Music swelled like orgasm in concert with the cult's exultations as these new ancestors linked arms. He felt a twoness then at the naked touch but those conflicting inputs soon fused into a singularity.

The land of many firsts plays host to their first kiss.

He tumbles into her gaze, round ponds of light smothered by black clouds.

They are Armenian eyes, he thinks. Hayi acher.

And so are mine.

IN TWAIN

Rowan Cardosa

"You know we don't have insurance," my mother told me that December. "What if it turns out to be nothing? Then you're on the hook for four hundred dollars just because you decided to be dramatic."

"It *hurts*—"

I turned, perhaps a little too sharply, as I worked, and felt a fountain of tingling and pain spray forth from my hips. Everything felt disjointed, like someone had taken off my torso like the lid of a box and put it back on wrong. My mother rolled her eyes, her gaze searing hot as I tried to set myself right again.

"You just have to live with the pain. I'm almost sixty years old, do you think I have the time to sit around like you do?"

There was never a point in responding to any of her questions. Ever since I'd arrived home for holiday break, she'd never missed a day telling me how I had been doing nothing. There were other issues at hand. Soy sauce, milk, vegetables, some bread from the discount section of the bakery aisle. I'd wanted to pick up some shrimp paste later from the Asian grocery, but Mom reminded me how my father, a pink-hued man from West Virginia, would be put off by the smell. I said nothing, letting my vexation bubble below my skin, and turned my attention back to putting away the rest of the groceries.

I needed to talk to someone about my condition. Just Googling my symptoms gave me nothing but more anxiety that it might be something fatal, but I wasn't dying. I was shifting, *becoming*. I lay in bed for ages until my body sunk into the mattress, pondering my options until I remembered *her*.

My mother had buried most of herself long ago when she married my dad; twenty-five years of culture and memory, now smothered like grass under pure white snow. But she couldn't keep everything contained. The number of times I'd seen my Lola in person could be counted on one hand, but our meetings never failed to make an impression. I was whole back then, my tiny child body as solid as those of my parents and brother. I played idly among Lola's prized orchids before she called me in only to be scolded for tracking sand and seashell bits into the house. Sliced-up mangoes awaited me on the kitchen table and Lola fed me one with rice that was just a bit stickier than my grubby juvenile hands. She often fussed over my hair: dark with a blood-crimson shine when the light hit it just right.

"It's just like your mother when she was your age," she'd say, her voice full of nostalgia and just a hint of regret.

Lola knew many secrets, and revealed what crumbs she could whenever we met in person. The one time she was able to scrape up enough funds to visit us in America, I was sixteen, heating up soup on the stove before a cacophony of reedy whispers called for me from out the window.

"Probably a bird or something," my dad had said then. Lola knew better.

"Close the window and don't say anything," she had advised me.

It was the middle of summer then, and there was nothing else to be heard outside. No birds, no traffic, not even the rhythmic shrieking of the cicadas.

I knew which one of the adults in my life had the better instincts, then.

If there was anyone on earth who could tell me what was going on, it was her. For the first time in months, I logged into Facebook.

The first post that graced my feed was a distant cousin posing with an oddly familiar Coach bag my mother had sent her in a grand show of generosity. So *that's* where it went. A real shame; I had saved up for weeks to seize it for myself. But I couldn't let my indignation fester. Not now, when there were bigger issues at hand.

It felt like days, scrolling through a timeline that had been neglected for years. Lola's most recent post was a simple one, with her enjoying a cup of coffee in the company of her orchids. I began typing my message to her.

Lola, it's Madison. I need to talk, it's kind of an emergency.

I was about to put my phone down until I saw that Lola was typing. Even with a dozen time zones between us, I could smell her panic.

Her answer was brief: *What is it?*

I decided to tell her as much as I could.

Something feels different, I typed. *I feel like putty. Almost like I'm going to split in half.*

A pregnant pause followed my reply, and I knew the child that would soon be born from that silence would be a crying, screaming mess.

How long has this been going on? Her inquiry on my condition continued.

I struggled to imagine a time when things weren't this way, even though I knew I had memories of a world without the pain. A time where I wasn't falling apart.

The last time we had this in the family, Lola continued, *was about 80 years ago. Do you have garlic?*

Just the minced stuff in the jars, and there's only a little left. You know how my dad is.

Damn. Grappling with this revelation was bad enough, but I cursed myself for forgetting some of the items on the grocery list.

Try not to eat any meat for the time being. Her response was brief but worrying.

Why?

I'm not sure what else I can do, she typed. *I will need to talk to someone in town tomorrow about your condition. There is a lot going on.*

How long is that going to take? I asked her.

I will let you know, she replied. *There may be things I will need your parents to do too, can you get your mother to call?*

I don't know if she has the time for this.

Lola's response came quickly: *I'll talk to her asap. If she cares, she will listen to me.*

She won't, I typed, but my protests went unanswered.

Mom talked on the phone for hours later that night. She always found someplace away from the rest of the family whenever homesickness overtook her, as if hearing the words that escaped her lips was something to be embarrassed about. I tried to eavesdrop once, to trace every syllable with my lips as if I understood anything at all. I was eight years old. Mom just saw me hanging around the corridor and whispered for me to scurry off somewhere else.

So I never learned the language my Lolo and Lola spoke. I didn't even know which of the myriad dialects graced their tongues, because my mother deemed this forbidden knowledge from the day she married my father. Centuries of her people living under the heels of another land's boot had taught her to savor the taste of leather. I could only imagine how many times Lola must have held her tongue in shame.

This time, she holed herself up in her own bedroom. As I pretended to use the bathroom in the hallway, I found myself struggling to make out her muffled words until the conversation grew more heated. Even if I didn't understand the particulars, it wasn't difficult to imagine English words in their place.

I can't believe you're enabling her, Mom probably said at some point. *She really has you wrapped around her finger, doesn't she?*

Her tone grew more blistering by the second until I could hear Lola sobbing. Just when I thought I would need to play guessing games for the rest of the call, Lola delivered a plea in English:

"I need to talk to her, Isabela. For the love of God—"

But I didn't get to hear what she said next, nor would I ever. Mom hung up the phone and walked right past me into the kitchen, with neither of us saying a word. I stayed up later than usual to make sure she was gone when I headed over to the fridge.

I was hungry.

The next day, my parents screamed for my brother Arthur first. I followed soon after, figuring that Dad's demands that we head to the living room *now* couldn't go unmet for a second longer.

That was when we saw *her.* A woman in her twenties or thirties, dressed in baggy clothes and lying limp and cold on the floor.

Anxiety bubbled in my blood as I smelled the gin on Dad's breath and realized just what he'd done.

Mom and Arthur had a million questions. So did I, and the three of us were met with Dad's fountain of excuses, all perfumed with more gin.

"Nothing but pitch black out there. How the hell was I supposed to even know she was crossing the road?" My father gestured to the woman's wrinkled black shirt that draped over her, reaching almost to her knees.

"So, what, y'all just fucking brought her home?" Arthur's voice rang through the hallway. "What are we gonna do when the police find her here?"

My mother shot back in a sliver of a second: "Don't you *dare* talk to me that way."

"He has a point. We were probably better off if you had just left her there," I said.

"Who's going to support us if your father ends up in jail?" my mother asked, her voice beginning to show its cracks. "Do you know what they might do to him in prison? Do you have *any* idea? What if he never gets out? I just don't think he deserves all of that because of one little mistake."

"Do you really think the police won't find the body?" I replied.

"They won't, sweetie. Trust me. They won't."

No one said anything as my father wiped the blood and sweat from his brow with the sleeve of his shirt. I couldn't even look at his face. So gracious of him to give his family even more evidence to dispose of. My mind raced with exit strategies. If I could survive this pisspot until I'd graduated from college and found a better job for myself, I'd never have to think about any of this again.

But my plotting was interrupted by my mother inhaling all the tension in the air before spitting it out again. I saw Arthur's stance grow more rigid.

"We were doing *so well,*" Arthur grumbled, his gaze fixed on Dad's face. Mom wasted no time with her reply.

"I've known ever since I married your father that love requires sacrifice. We need to clean up this mess."

Mom's words were clear: I should be the one to do most of the heavy lifting. Arthur had spent all of twenty minutes beforehand washing away the excess blood and burning her clothes. Part of me wondered if this was some sort of punishment for daring to dream a little bigger, but I would have the last laugh. I reached into her skull, and as I pulled out my bloody hand, I resolved to make sure my parents would be the ones that would have to dispose of her teeth.

Mom had plans for the rest of the cadaver, though, and the fact that I hadn't brought home any meat earlier in the week had not gone unnoticed by her.

My life had hit a new low. I deftly removed her heart, kidneys, and other giblets before tossing them into a metal bowl. Mom scolded me for splattering blood on the cabinets and the tile floor, as if mops had never been invented. My mind inexplicably drifted to what I could do with all this meat. I had seen a blood soup, rich with vinegar and spices, on a cousin's Instagram months ago. Dad had mentioned how grateful he was that Mom never cooked up such "strange" and "honestly kind of disgusting" cuisine in his own home, and I never brought up the subject again.

As I pulled another lung out, another thought manifested: *Fuck it.* I brought my bloodied arm to my lips and ran a togue all the way to the tips of my fingers, in a show of flexibility I never knew I had. Perhaps I never had it until now.

I'm not sure what the new me was shaping up to be, but she certainly was a good kisser.

Gutting the poor woman my father had so generously murdered took far less time than I thought it would. I had just finished removing her intestines when I found— my prize: a pink, swollen prison of water and flesh. A freshly ripe uterus with a fun little surprise inside.

I reached for a smaller, more precise knife and plopped the freshly extracted womb into the sink. It was somewhere in between lancing a giant boil and popping a water balloon, with blood and amniotic fluid spraying all over the bottom of the sink. But I was able to peel back the tissue and grasp the delectable filling inside.

Here's the thing about fetuses: it takes a long time before they begin to look like a little person. What I saw lying limp in the sink was an apple-sized blob of viscera and veins, indistinguishable from any other organ save for the tiny umbilical cord that had begun to form on one side. Little bumps and ridges could be observed from the rest of the flesh, the beginnings of limbs that would never grow fingers nor toes. I unwrapped the embryo and held it in my hands for just a moment, pondering what needed to be done.

I found myself reaching for the blender.

The fresh meat and coconut water was harder to clean out of the blender than I thought it might be, but getting the kitchen spotless was easy. The product, sadly, of too much practice after no one else in this family wanted to do the damn dishes. My little pre-dinner smoothie had been the emperor of all guilty pleasures. A private spiral into depravity, all just for me, and the only evidence it ever happened was a blood-spattered plastic straw in the trash.

The rest of Dad's roadkill was now roasted, unseasoned, and festively placed in the center of the table alongside undercooked carrots and discounted rolls made of moldy bread. It was Christmas Eve, and I'm pretty sure we were the only the only family on the block who had a roast like the one he had managed to bring home.

His hands clasped together in a desperate attempt to pretend he was the good Christian man... someone he probably never wanted to be.

"Our Father, who art in heaven, hallowed be thy name..."

I fidgeted in my seat and hoped no one else would notice. Dad never said grace before meals save for holidays and special occasions. I guess it was to make him feel better.

"She's way too tough," my father said, chewing on a mouthful of the overcooked flesh with his mouth open.

I took a bite of the roast. It was far tougher and more flavorless than I'd have preferred it, just as Dad said. But I thought for a moment how much sweeter her flesh would have been if she had been medium rare. Or perhaps even blue, the muscle charred at the surface to seal the succulent flavors within.

"That's because she didn't have much fat on her," replied Mom. She played around with the food on her plate, hoping no one would notice. But I noticed. "You don't exactly get to pick who you accidentally run over unless you make a habit of it, Carl."

Arthur didn't eat a single bite of the roast, simply picking at the vegetables before prematurely moving on to slicing the store-bought pecan pie I'd bought earlier. He shot me a judgmental glare and I averted my gaze. Still, I could feel my father smirking at me. *Not so high and mighty now,* I assumed he thought.

There was nothing but skin, bones, and void inside my core now. My skin softened like dough that could be pulled apart and shaped into distinct loaves. If I just had enough strength, then maybe I could force those loaves together again. And if I proved too weak, I would have to make do with pretending. I swayed and wobbled in my chair, hoping the rest of the family didn't notice.

My plate now empty, I silently tried to hold back tears and grab myself some pie.

I don't know how long I cried. It must have been more than an hour wrapped tightly in a quilt, soaking its fabric with my agony. My face grew heavy with the tears building up underneath my skin. There was nothing I wanted more than to make myself lighter, to become small as a songbird and fly far away from humanity.

Her supple flesh is one of the finest delicacies we've ever sampled, said a terrible yearning whisper in the back of my skull, like a fucked-up Jiminy Cricket. *But the youngling? So tender, such a mild little creature. A most refreshing beverage, all wrapped up and delivered right to us.*

"No…"

Madison, no, I tried to tell myself, still wanting to believe that there was even the tiniest scrap of hope that I could turn back the clock. But as the night's chill wrapped itself around more of my bisected torso, another sentiment sprung forth, bigger and bolder. *Madison, yes. Madison, absolutely yes.*

There were three knocks on the door of my bedroom. Then four, five, six.

"Madison?" I heard Arthur's muffled voice on the other side of the door.

I didn't move, and nothing else disturbed me as I sat in stillness and silence.

As the sun burrowed its way far below the horizon, my knees

buckled, leaving me shuddering against the chill of the laminate floor. It was more than emptiness now. Behind my navel, my innards caved in, sucking in what paltry flesh remained until my waist was cinched into a messy knot. Before I could try to get up and move towards my bed, my torso popped clean off.

There was no pain, just the shock of watching my legs and pelvis slumped over the floorboards, oozing far less blood than I thought it should. Reverberating in the halls were the muffled sounds of the TV in the living room. Mom yapped on the phone, oblivious. Pulling myself up from the floor was impossible and all I could do was try to drag myself away as my screams crumbled and died inside a parched throat.

"Help me," I wanted to shout, but the words stuck in my throat like rust in an old drainpipe. "HELP ME!"

As my mouth opened, my tongue, now hollow and serpentine, fell out onto the cold floor. Sinew and bone cracked and twisted my shoulders. Whatever this was, it wasn't finished with me. My ruined lower half looked as if it had almost sunken into the floor now, like the stump of a gnarled and rotting tree. The scent of copper and cold sweat filled my nostrils, and as I closed my eyes, I could feel myself floating.

Inside the cavity of my ribcage I felt not apathy, but hunger.

ROOTS

AGROUND

Rena Mason

Up he goes, the eagle ascends,
His eager flapping sure to please.
Below, her feet on firm ground,
He makes no effort at amends.

Fly away, she waves at air,
She wants him gone, you see.
His beak and talons pointed, sharp.
Pain she can no longer bear.

Again he stays away, she yearns,
Disappears, and melts into her land.
She waits still for his return,
Contemplates whether to outstretch her hand.

THE FOX DAUGHTER COMES TO GLENVIEW

Seoung Kim

1

"*They say he had another family in Korea…*"
"*…I heard no one wanted the girl…*"
"*…if I was his wife, I would be humiliated.*"

The girl arrives at the airport in the middle of the night after thirteen hours on a flight from Incheon International: rigid-backed and four feet tall and clutching the handle of a purple plastic suitcase.

She does not look like Jiyeon's husband whatsoever, who is currently at a work conference in Texas. Unlike her own sun-browned American child, the girl is pale and bloodless. Her eyes are not brown or black but a dark honey color. Her legs look too long for her body. The choking Midwestern humidity makes her crooked bangs stick to her forehead.

"You can call me Imo," says Jiyeon. She thinks for a moment, then repeats herself in Korean.

"Umma." Her son tugs at her hand. "She doesn't speak English? Like Halmoni?"

"Halmoni speaks English," says Jiyeon.

The girl remains silent during this exchange; in fact, she remains silent for the first two weeks she spends at their house.

2

In July, her son goes away to camp, one that she and her husband had to pay a lot of money for. Jiyeon called the camp director and begged her to accept the girl as well, but she wouldn't relent, talking about the long waitlist and how they had to be fair to everyone.

With her husband still on his business trip, Jiyeon is left alone in the house with the girl.

The house: 5 bedrooms, 3.5 bathrooms, 3,128 square feet. She and her husband decided on it together after months of searching for something close to his job and large enough to host her family. It is built on a filled-in swamp, and clouds of insects fill the air after it rains. Jiyeon keeps the doors and windows closed in the summer and turns the central air down to 60 degrees.

The girl: when Jiyeon was little, around the girl's age, one of her brothers took in a stray dog without their parents knowing. Her parents were generally opposed to pets, who needed to be fed in addition to their children. The dog was a rangy, fawn-colored thing. It did not have an easy life, and when her brother let it loose, it slunk around in the shadows, watching them and avoiding contact.

She doesn't remember what happened to it in the end – probably ran away. She thinks of the dog each time the girl appears in a doorway to stare at her.

For the most part, the girl stays in her room all day, and only comes out at night to eat. Jiyeon tries to help her adjust to the time zone changes, serving her warm milk or slipping her crushed sleeping pills with dinner, but she seems determined to become a nocturnal creature.

After Jiyeon is already in bed, she hears the girl's bare feet on the hardwood floor, the doors creaking as she wanders through the house.

And sometimes, from her room, a dragging, scraping noise that goes on for hours. Whenever Jiyeon goes to check on her, the girl is just sitting on her bed, like she's been waiting for her.

3

The girl speaks her first words to them after Jiyeon's husband returns.

He has just taken his shoes off. They are standing in the entryway of the house.

"Go back," she says in Korean, and then she repeats herself in broken English. It is unclear to Jiyeon whether she is requesting to return herself or making a demand of her husband.

If her husband is unsettled by the child, he does not show it. Perhaps he is already used to her staring from the time he spent with her in Korea. It is difficult to imagine him cradling her as a newborn, as he did with their son.

"That's right," he says, patting her head. "You'll go back soon."

"Should we hire an English tutor?" she asks her husband that night.

He scoffs. "What for? She'll learn at school. Besides, we never had English tutors growing up."

As a child, Jiyeon was the English tutor for her younger siblings, and the translator for her parents. Her parents scraped and saved when they first came to the US from West Germany, where a lot of Koreans went to find work after the war. Eventually, her aunts and uncles followed from Korea along with their children.

She hasn't been back to Korea in decades. She can't picture what the girl's life was like with a single mother – what meals she ate, what stores they shopped at – so she transposes her own childhood on top of it: the seaside village, the nearby G.I. base, the little market.

They probably lived with her grandparents, like Jiyeon's family did back in Korea.

How does this big house feel so small to her now? Didn't they sleep 10 people to a room growing up, cousins, nieces, and nephews? Didn't they grow soybean sprouts in the bedroom from the heat of their bodies?

4

Jiyeon was making lunch when the woman called on the phone and told her she was his wife. Bokkeumbap, her husband's favorite.

She looked blankly at the phone in her hand, thinking, *this is something that happens in dramas, not real life.*

"You're probably wondering why I'm calling," said the woman. Her Korean was unlike her own family's, with their humble accents and old-fashioned speech. Seoul maybe? Her husband is from Ulsan.

"Do you want money?" Jiyeon asked.

There was a child. Jiyeon wasn't so naive as to think a man as handsome as him had never been with a woman before, but they'd been together for years now, and he never said anything about a marriage.

She thought back to the wedding, tried to think of some sign, his family shaking their heads or laughing behind their hands. The memory of her happiness eclipsed everything else.

The problem, Jiyeon learned, standing dumbly in the kitchen as the woman went on talking, was that nobody wanted the girl. The woman he had left behind in Korea decided she wanted to remarry, to have a fresh start, and she no longer wanted this girl, this reminder of her past life.

As the woman spoke, Jiyeon thought to herself: who the fuck

is this woman? What kind of mother sends her daughter away to another country?

The woman interrupted her thoughts. "Can I speak to my husband?"

The rest of the week dissolves in her memory. There were a lot of tears and screaming. She fled to one of her sisters' house for a few days. Her sisters were outraged on her behalf after they found out about what happened. But they all told her she couldn't leave him, not while she had a young child to take care of. They prayed over her for hours.

She found out later that, at first, her husband tried to refuse to take the girl. The matter was decided when his mother called from Ulsan and threatened to kill herself if he didn't take her in, effectively ending the conversation.

It was the right thing to do, of course. Unbearable all the same.

5

Across the dining table, Jiyeon watches the girl methodically peeling her chicken nuggets, trying to construct the other woman from her features: long legs and a thin frame, where Jiyeon is short and round. A pronounced nose bridge and wide, golden eyes, unlike Jiyeon's flat nose and monolids. Silky black hair that shimmers red in the right light.

The girl eats everything in the house. Jiyeon finds granola wrappers stuffed in odd places, empty bread bags on the counter, plastic berry cartons placed back in the fridge with nothing in them. Jiyeon's son complains to her about the snacks disappearing overnight, although Jiyeon never catches her at it.

She hoped the girl could be something of a playmate for her son, or at least a babysitter, but her son seems terrified of her, won't go near her room. He's more prone to tears now, throwing tantrums, picky eating. Jealous of sharing his parents. She can hardly blame him.

There's a kind of bird she remembers hearing about – it pushes an egg out of a nest to lay her own, leaving the nest-builder to raise her young. The imposter baby grows bigger and bigger until the good mother bird's chicks starve.

She slaps the girl's hand.

"Stop that," she says. "Don't play with your food."

After dinner, while doing the dishes, she hears her husband speaking to the girl in the living room. His voice is uncharacteristically soft.

"...your mother. That doesn't mean..."

She switches off the water and stands still at the sink, listening.

"Try to remember that, ok?" says her husband.

If the girl replies, Jiyeon doesn't hear it.

"What were you talking about?" she asks when her husband comes back into the kitchen.

He goes to the refrigerator and pours himself a glass of water from the filter. He takes a long drink while Jiyeon waits.

"You need to be kinder to her," he says, wiping his mouth with the back of his hand. "She is still my blood."

"If I wasn't kind, I'd let her act however she wants." Jiyeon switches the faucet back on, hot enough to steam up in the sink. "I'd let her turn into an animal."

6

For as long as Jiyeon has been alive, she has been going to church: from the village chapel, to the dirty brick Presbyterian church when they first moved to America, and now their spiritual home in the suburbs, a modern concrete-and-glass marvel with bright, wide-open rooms.

That Sunday, the pastor preaches about Daniel in the lions' den. Although he gives sermons in English, he is Korean, and many other Korean families attend the church.

Jiyeon takes short notes, balancing her notebook and her Bible on her knee: My prayers are heard, through Him all is possible, God won't give me more than I can handle.

She underlines the last one.

He said, now is the needed time

Now is the needed time

He cried, now, Lord, is the needed time

Jiyeon sways to the music and puts out her hands.

The service ends, and the children return from Sunday school. Everyone files into the atrium for the church luncheon and piles plates full of jeon, kimchi, and rice.

The children go to run around at the other end of the room, and she sits down with her Bible study friends, a group of middle-aged Korean women, most with families of their own.

The first thing they ask about is, of course, the girl, in whose provenance they seem already well-versed.

"She's staying with us for a little while," says Jiyeon. "We're not sure how long yet."

The pity on their faces makes her stomach churn, seeing those hidden feelings reflected back to her.

"She speaks English?" one of them asks.

"All of the kids in Korea learn English nowadays," another woman assures her.

"We missed you at small group," says another.

Jiyeon smiles apologetically, folding her jeon in half with her chopsticks and putting it in her mouth rather than responding.

"We've been praying for you and your husband," a woman pipes up.

My husband? she thinks. Why are you praying for him?

Her husband, at the other end of the table with his golf buddies, laughs loudly at a joke. She glances at him in profile: his heavy brow, strong jaw, the gray at his temple, and for a moment has the odd sense of not recognizing him at all. He looks like a complete stranger.

On their wedding night, their parents rented them a room in a bed and breakfast not far from the venue. The two of them had been too exhausted to do much of anything.

Her husband propped himself up in the bed and watched her undress. "What?" she asked.

"Just thinking about how you are the most beautiful creature I've ever seen."

She didn't think it was strange, at the time, but in recent weeks and months she's taken to playing all of his words back to herself, holding them up to the light and examining them like film negatives.

"Thank you," she tells the woman from Bible study, "for thinking of us."

She has to peel the girl off the food table on the way out. As they pass another family, Jiyeon overhears a whisper: "They say her real mom sent her away…"

7

Jiyeon is upstairs folding laundry when the screaming starts and abruptly stops. She throws the clothes down and takes the stairs two at a time.

Her son stands in the middle of the playroom, his crying muffled by the girl, who has a hand covering his mouth. His arm is covered in blood up to the elbow.

Jiyeon grabs the girl by both shoulders and pulls her away.

"She bit me!" he screams. "She bit me!"

The girl is standing a few feet away, expressionless. There is a smear of red on her chin.

"Go to your room," she tells the girl. "Right now."

She hushes her son, helps him to the bathroom, and lifts him up to the sink. His skin is cold and damp to the touch. Her own pulse pounds in her ears. She holds his arm under the running water. The blood, when washed away, reveals a set of four neat round punctures. They are not human teeth.

She puts her son in his room and goes across the hall, to where the girl is sitting on her bed.

Before the girl came, Jiyeon used the bedroom as a guest room for visiting family. It hasn't changed much since then. The girl's suitcase stands by the door, as though she is ready to leave at any time. Some of her clothes are lying on the floor.

When she first arrived, many of her clothes were too small or had holes in them. Conscious of how it would reflect on them, Jiyeon bought her a whole new wardrobe. She had thought it might be a little bit fun, one of the pleasures of having a daughter she missed out on, but the girl was totally uninterested and had to be hauled from store to store in the mall.

"Why?" Jiyeon asks. She kneels down in front of her.

The girl looks back at her calmly. Her hands are relaxed at her sides. The blood on her chin drying and turning brown.

Jiyeon's voice grows sharper. "How did you do this? What did you use?"

The girl lifts her head and smiles, showing white teeth.

When her husband gets home, their arguing goes on late into the night.

"What do you want me to do? Call the police on a little girl? It's just a few pokes."

"Doesn't her mother have any family who can take her?"

"We can't send her back to Korea. No."

"What about your mother?"

"She's 84."

"I can't do this."

"I'll call my sister tomorrow. See if she can watch her for a few days while you calm down. I'll call tomorrow."

8

Long ago, there lived a poor salt seller - or perhaps he was a farmer. He had three sons, but wished for a daughter.

One night, as he prayed for a daughter on the mountainside, he caught sight of a fox on top of a boulder, holding something between her paws, grinding it against the rock.

"Go home," said the fox, and the man saw the object was a human skull. She slid the skull onto her head, then shook it off and continued grinding it against the rock.

The man fled, terrified, and never told his family about the encounter.

Sometime later, a daughter was born, healthy and beautiful. But every night, one of the farmer's cows disappeared.

Or maybe the salt seller didn't run away. Maybe he followed the fox into the valley, where it went in the form of an old woman to the house of the richest man in town.

When he asked the three sons to watch the daughter, one by one, they reported the daughter was stealing the livers of the cows to devour.

He went to confront her—

"You should know better," she said, opening her jaws, "than to wish for a daughter."

9

The weather report that night calls for a severe storm, with the potential for flash flooding. The clouds open up and shake the windows with torrential rain. Thunder crackles continuously and lightning arcs sideways across the sky.

Jiyeon is still awake when she hears a voice.

"아버님." *Father.*

The girl stands in the doorway of their room.

"What do you want?" her husband asks sleepily.

She hooks a thumb under her jawbone and lifts the skull off of her body. It comes away cleanly, and the girl's body twists and elongates until a fox, eyes glowing, is left in her place.

The fox makes a graceful arc as it leaps onto her husband and tears out his throat. Its head dips down beneath his ribcage and comes up, muzzle covered in blood, with a dark shape clutched between its jaws.

The fox turns to look at her with its luminous eyes. Blood drips steadily onto the pillowcase.

Somehow, Jiyeon understands what is being asked of her. She staggers to the window and unlocks it. The latch and the window itself are rusted and jammed from years of disuse, but she manages to wrench it open.

The fox leaps past her and lands on the wet grass. It crosses the lawn and disappears into the swamp.

Jiyeon breathes in, clutching at the sill. The night air is thick and warm on her skin. Frogs call into the night like a distant chorus of bells.

She leaves the window open, then goes to put the blood-stained sheets in the laundry.

HAIR

Saheli Khastagir

My mother was 33 when she began pulling her hair. It was summer, she said, one of those 100% humidity days, when her blouse clung to her back with her sweat, angry red rashes formed everywhere her skin folded, and her scalp itched and itched. It wasn't the first time her head itched so much that she wanted to yank it all out. But she had never considered pulling it before.

Why not? I asked her.

I didn't think it was mine to pull, she said to me. But that day, with her three-month-old son wailing in the heat, and her eldest son throwing a tantrum, and the house echoing all their sounds back at them, she stood in front of that long mirror her father had given them as part of her dowry, and she pulled. She didn't yank it out in bunches. Instead, she held a single strand between her thumb and her index finger, and she plucked in a quick swift motion…like she plucked the red hibiscus every morning for our gods.

What did it feel like? I asked her.

Imagine you are constipated for a week, and you drink some of that disgusting isabgol your father takes, and finally…after a lot of huffing and heaving…you let out a big satisfying dump, she said, tickling my stomach.

Ewwww, I giggled.

By the time I arrived, she became meticulous in her pulling. She waited for the boys to leave for the day and then she would lightly close her bedroom door and begin. What started as an occasional pleasure, became more and more frequent; once a week, once a day, twice a day, three, four, five times a day. When there were guests at home, I saw her getting restless, her feet would start tapping, she would snap at us for something small, but I knew what it was. She couldn't wait to go into that room and start plucking. She was addicted to it, like a hair-junkie except that she wasn't consuming anything, only pulling and pulling.

After I turned five or six and she began to confide in me, she would let me watch, as long as I didn't interrupt her. I felt special, I was an accomplice, it was our secret. I was mesmerized by the cold precision of her fingers, how deftly she found a single strand every time and without flinching, without a second thought, she tugged, and out it came. She never had to pull twice. She would then take that strand and stroke her lips with the root end of it, and smile at her reflection. By then she knew what the pulling was doing to the people around her, and with every pull she seemed to be willing it… willing the thing to happen.

I wonder now why nothing happened to me. Amidst all the illness, deaths, unemployment and insanity that her pulling brought on everyone, why was I left unblemished. Was it because I knew?

As her hair began to fall, she started having a spring in her steps. She could move her head and body like she had never done before. The aches did not go away, but she no longer felt so hot all the time, she could feel the cool monsoon air on her neck and back, she could match her pace to the pace of those around her. When I came along, her body had started to relax and she had begun to laugh often. She made us laugh too.

I never saw her cowering the way my brothers had. In my mind, she was always strong, lithe, and often terrifying. She would not let me grow my hair. There was to be no argument about it. Every month, she cut my hair herself, and no tears or begging could keep those shears from nipping away at my strands.

You will not let me be beautiful! I screamed at her one day. She slapped me across the face. *You are more than your hair. Your beauty is more than your hair* she hissed at me.

I heard the tales about her hair. The longest it was measured at was 60 feet. That was before her grandmother died.

60 feet. How to fathom a force that big? I imagine it filling their house—the one she grew up in. The hair would have thumped down on the floor, *thud*, pulling her scalp with its weight, and then it would have spread through that room she shared with her sister and grandmother, pushing through the doorway, running across the long corridor, some strands might have entered the kitchen and the living room, jostling with the chairs, the divans and the tables.

How did you wash it? How did you comb it? I asked her one day. *I didn't*, she said.

Every two weeks, her grandmother spent a whole day patiently lifting up one foot of her thick dark mane at a time, to oil and braid them. After braiding it, her grandmother coiled it to her small back and then tied it with a belt to her body so it would not break her neck with its weight. Every year, right before the Bengali new year in April, her mother performed the annual cleaning of the hair. *She hated it,* she said about her mother. It took three bottles of shampoo and hours of back breaking labor to clean it. I imagine my mother kneeling in the back yard by the tube well with a saree wrapped around her body like a towel, and her mother cursing in frustration as she tries to untangle the hair, lather it, and wring out the mud-colored water. Her mother used a big wooden brush, a steel bucket and a mug, she used them all to beat her daughter as her own frustration grew. Sometimes, her grandmother tried to intervene. *Let me do it,* she would say, but it was her mother's job, and everyone held their breath the whole day and once it was done, they could all relax for another year.

She never relaxed though. Every day, her neck and back throbbed with a dull pain. *It felt like the earth was pulling my bones, and my bones were tearing my skin to join it,* she said of the aches.

It was not just the pain, but also the heat and the rage. There was no air-conditioner in their house and summer temperatures hovered close to 97. Her hair was like a thick down blanket that she could never take off…her braids alone covered her entire small back. Her head and her back were always wet and itchy with the sweat. Her grandmother wrapped a wet cloth around her neck and waved a hand pankha when she did her homework. The heat turned to rage and migraine. Her book of sums would be splashed in red, streaks of light flashing through the pages of her poetry book, black and red spots filled her vision every day.

The doctor warned them that she wouldn't make it past her 20th birthday with hair that long, and she never did grow taller than 4 feet 10 inches, weighed down by the weight of her head. But the family astrologer said cutting her hair would mean cutting their fortune. *Your family's fortune is coiled in that girl's hair,* he told her father, *keep it safe and the fortune will also be protected.*

What were they to do? She was just one of five children. Should they relieve the pain of one—a daughter at that— and bring misfortune on the other four?

My mother was her parents' second child and their eldest daughter. Her three brothers shared a room between them, and she shared one with her younger sister and her grandmother. The brothers never much cared for her, she was sullen, silent and slow. Her hair made her move laboriously. She slowed down their games, and didn't seem much of a help around the house either. Her little sister envied the attention she seemed to get for her hair, the more time to rest and nap that it afforded her, and how her days appeared to be filled with leisure while the sister's was filled with labor. On monsoon days, when my mother's bones screamed with pain, she spent whole days in bed. Her parents did not let her stand for too long or carry heavy loads. Instead, she was given work that she could do sitting down like shelling peas, rolling rutis, pulling the leaves from the coriander stems, sewing buttons, cleaning the gods, feeding the youngest son. While the younger sister carried big loads of laundry, swept the floor, dusted the ceiling fans. *You've always had it so easy, you never had to work for it*, her sister would complain.

The sister also envied her bond with her grandmother, and the silence that seemed to engulf them both. How they sat together for hours, each engrossed in a book, a sewing pattern, or just watching the street from their window. Her sister would insist on sleeping between them, to force them apart…and to force them to contend with her.

The dispute between the two simmered and grew when my mother started taking music lessons, another privilege that her younger sister was deprived of, and then again when the unsuccessful attempts to find her a groom, delayed the little sister's ability to marry and leave their dreary home behind.

In anger, her sister pulled her hair, kicked her in her sleep, dunked her music sheets in water, and hurled hurtful things at her. Sometimes, after one of these outbursts, her sister would embrace her in remorse and demand her forgiveness. But my mother neither fought, nor forgave. Not her sister nor her brothers or her parents.

She locked her rage in her throat. She had to stop talking, and smile with her mouth closed, to not let it escape her throat. When the anger grew in size and hardened, she had to stop eating and could only sip the starch water that was drained from cooked rice, the cloudy soup floating above the dal, and the thin broth of the mutton curry that her grandmother stealthily scooped out for her. She was hungry often, but she could not swallow any solid food. It wasn't until she began to sing that she could safely release some of that anger bit by bit into the air, without wounding anyone.

I don't remember hearing her sing. She stopped singing when I was still very young. Music was forbidden in our home. We were not forbidden to listen to it, we could listen on our headphones or outside the home. But no music was allowed to enter her ears. I did not dare hum a song, or switch on the radio in the car. There was no question of music lessons, how can there be when we couldn't practice at home?

Growing up, she was also forbidden music. Her mother found out music made her hair grow, so she did not let a single note enter their home. Her hair had become life threatening. She had shooting pain across her neck and back. But they didn't dare cut it, fearing the repercussions the astrologer warned them about. The sheer weight and size of it seemed to be a testament of its power. If that was how God made her, who were they to intervene, after all? Unable to relieve her daughter's pain, her mother did the only thing she could do—kept it from getting worse, and banished music from the house.

But her hair yearned for music the way skin yearns for sunlight on a winter afternoon. It was pulled towards it and pulled her with it. Which was why, even though she never dared disobey her mother, every afternoon when her mother took her nap, she ran to the balcony and strained her ears to listen to the tunes wafting from their landlord's radio upstairs. *That's how I learnt my first songs*, she told me.

When my mother was 17, her grandmother left her body. In grief, my mother's hair started leaving her scalp. This was different from the pulling she did later on. This was unbidden… it was a shedding, and she was a helpless spectator of it, and what followed because of it. Balls of black hair filled their house, woolly, dense and knotted. They started clogging the drains, until one day the bathroom flooded to the ankles and the kitchen sink pooled with water mixed with gravy and brown-yellow clots of food debris. Her father slipped and hurt his back. He couldn't go to work for a month. The younger kids got typhoid. Her mother looked around at the deluge, in a house that was still in mourning, her sick children and an injured husband, and she knew that her eldest daughter's hair must grow. And she knew exactly how to do it.

They found a classical Hindustani vocalist to give her weekly lessons, and they bought her a harmonium and a tanpura. As music entered their home, her hair stopped shedding and started growing again. The music not only made her hair grow, it also muted her aches. Every time she sang, her hair became light as feather, her bones reclaimed the skin of her body, she felt the air fill her lungs and her body became, briefly, pain free.

Why did you stop then? I asked her.

Because of the echoes, she told me.

I never heard her sing. There were no lullabies for me, but I have heard the stories. How the crowd gathered around our house every morning she sat down to sing, and then how it all changed when Daddy remodeled the house.

She met him when she was 27. Her parents had been searching for a groom for many years, unsuccessfully. Her hair and her music did not help. Her hair never grew to its earlier length, but it was still an expense that no future husband wanted to take on. Especially since it came with the caveat from her father that she be allowed to sing after marriage

When Daddy first met her, he fell in love with the way her shoulders bent like a bow under the weight of her hair and with the soft curl of her lips that so diligently stayed shut. *She was not a talker, your mother…unlike the other girls…she knew how to listen,* he said. He also liked that she was so short, and how, unable to move her head from side to side, when she looked at you, she *really* looked at you. *She was like a secret waiting to be cracked open,* he told me many years ago, *and I thought, I will be the one to do it.*

In Daddy, she saw an escape.

He was tall, broad and handsome. In every room he walked in, he commanded space and attention. He also never stopped talking, not ever, and he was never far from ears hungry for his words. She thought that her silence would fill the space around his words. Rumor

234

has it, and I can verify that it's truer than most rumors, that he used to speak even in his sleep, that even in slumber he was not silent. His way of listening was also to speak, to say constantly, *yes, I know I also had something similar. You are right you are wrong and hearing you say that makes me think that...*

When they married, she was 27, and he was 39. The perfect age gap, the elders said. Her father had elicited his promise for her music to continue. Every morning after he left, and she had cooked and cleaned for the day, she sat with her tanpura and sang. Her hair back then was only about 15 feet long, and she could clean and tie it herself. But her neck and back still ached as before, and singing still made the weight, temporarily, lighter to carry. Home alone, she could give free reign to her voice, it echoed through the neighborhood and brought curious ears of the street dogs, the snakes, and the neighbors. Soon the news spread, and every day by 11 in the morning, a crowd gathered around their house, some brought dhurries to sit on, a few started carrying hand-held recorders to record her, and many brought and shared snacks and cha during these gatherings. Oblivious to the crowd, she sang and sang.

When Daddy found out about it, he was livid. He didn't know he was sharing her gift with the entire neighborhood. He felt betrayed, his pride hurt. His incessant voice became louder, faster, and took on sharp teeth., the words hurt her and made her sick and she started vomiting from their assault. She told him she would stop singing, but her hair still recovering from her grandmother's passing, started falling as soon as she stopped.

Her father came in to intervene. *This can't go on, you promised,* he told Daddy. *Your house will flood due to clogged drains and it will bring misfortune to your family and my family.* Then he told him how intimately the fortunes of their families were linked to her hair.

That's when Daddy remodeled the house and turned it into an echo chamber. The windows caught every sound inside the house and threw it back into it. No sound could leave the house. So, when she sang *Sa Ni Dha Pa*, she heard an echo of *Sa Ni Dha Pa* two seconds later, and the echo created another echo, so that she became immersed in *Sa Ni Dha Pa* repeatedly hitting the walls. *It took away the joy out of my singing,* she told me bitterly. Of everything that Daddy had done, this slow poisoning of her music was the thing she hated him for most. The day she began pulling her hair, that hot day at the age of 33, was also the day she stopped singing. This time, no intervention could make her start again.

The windows in our remodeled home were nonpartisan—it wasn't just her singing they echoed back, but also Daddy's voice. Whenever he was home, the house rang with his voice, overlapping each word with the ones he said before. Like when he says, *I think some people haven't evolved beyond the sheep, so they want to vote for a shepherd to guide them.* The sentence came to her like this: *I I think Ithink some thisome peothinkple somepeopl havensome evolpeople havebeyon Ithinkpeoplesheep-somepeoplesheepvotevoteevolveforvoteforshepwanttoshephardwantbeyon-peoplguidtheseforthemvotevolvethinkthem...*and so on.

The weekends were the most challenging, he was home the entire day and she felt like she was drowning in words, gasping for breath. She sometimes ran up to the terrace and looking up at the sky prayed that the Gods would take away her hearing.

When the house filled with her children, there was no longer any silence, not even when Daddy went to work. Though we tried. We tried so hard, to be quiet, to speak in whispers, to walk softly, to not run or bump into things. But we failed repeatedly. One of us might exclaim in delight at something, or cry or fight, and the sounds would echo back and forth for hours and hours.

Her rage was silent though. She never yelled or screamed. You might hear a loud *smack* of a slap ring through the house, but we knew to take it quietly to not infuriate her more. But mostly, she expressed anger noiselessly—by a sharp turn of her back, a souring of her face, a refusal to feed or bathe us. She refused us her presence, her love, until we proved we deserved it again.

When she began pulling her hair, she also stopped tending to it in any form— whether through oils or through songs. This time, it was more controlled, and there was no clogging of drains or flooding of rooms...or if there were, then she took care of them before anyone found out. But the misfortune that astrologer had promised arrived, one after another.

When did you know, for sure? I asked her.

It was when Daddy started having those stomach aches, she said. It was the first time since he began talking at the age of three, that Daddy became quiet. He was in so much pain, he just lay there perfectly still, scared to move or utter a sound, to even moan in pain, worried that it would only make the pain worse. The doctors couldn't figure out what was going on. They prescribed medicines for a stomach infection, scanned him for appendicitis, checked his stool for worms. They could neither explain nor relieve his pain.

I must have had a smile on my face, my mother said. *I was sitting in the bedroom, looking out the window, and I must have had a smile on my face It was just so peaceful. Finally some quiet in the house. He must have seen my smile, because he whispered to me. The first thing he had said in days, "are you poisoning me?" It came out of nowhere, that accusation. As soon as he asked that, I knew...I knew that I was. And his pain went away soon after.*

Did you ever feel guilty? I asked her.

I felt...powerful.

And soon she started observing the effects of her pulling on other people. You can map my mother's anger by mapping the misfortune that each person received. I was the only one left untouched.

Her elder brother lost his job, her father's pension barely enough to sustain his son's family. One of her younger brother's son was diagnosed with a heart condition that required regular blood transfusions. One of the sisters-in-law went mad and ran out of the house. Her mother broke her hip and the doctor who was operating on her collapsed on the day of the operation. Her sister had rashes all over her body that made her itch and scale. The sister also had three miscarriages and the sister's husband beat her in disgust and frustration.

Daddy began to stutter. It made him flounder and get frustrated every time he spoke, and people no longer flocked to him like they used to. And he often... had that inexplicable ache in his stomach that made him go quiet for days. Even though he never knew for sure, I think he suspected that she was behind it all, and I would sometimes catch him looking at her with a strange expression on his face...something close to terror.

My brothers were not spared either, but they had it light—a scrape here, an ache there, illnesses and fractures, those were the only times that she seemed to have any remorse about it. I would see the dark gloom on her face when one of them fell ill, and how she would offer them extra love and leniency as penance.

People offered unsolicited advice to manage the hair fall. They gave her hair masks, oils and pills, and recommendations of doctors to visit. Her parents urged her to start singing again. Whenever someone slipped an ointment or a medicine into her palm, she would sometimes wink at me when no one was looking.

I never saw my mother be sullen or slow. She tickled and chased us, and played hide and seek with us, and lifted me into the air. She also punished and hit us. Her anger was sharp and biting, unlike Daddy's which was dark and brooding. Even though she was so much smaller than Daddy, she seemed the more powerful of the two, and she would sometimes have fits of quiet rage when we would all hide from her because everything we did just made her angrier. But she could also be playful and energetic, and funny and charming. Daddy just seemed old and tired.

I was seven when she began to lose her hearing. When she began to hear less, she also began to be angry less. It relieved her from the echoes. She could just take out the hearing aid whenever it became unbearable. That was also when she began to talk more and she started telling me about her childhood. My brothers were teenagers and more interested in their friends than the old stories of their mother. But I listened, and even when she stopped talking, the house continued to echo her voice, so that I could not help but absorb and remember.

When I was 21, she had only a handful of strands left on her hair. By then, her scalp no longer sprouted new hair. People told her to wear a wig, but I know that she liked to flaunt the emptiness of her scalp, like a blank piece of paper. She carried it tantalizingly, as if threatening the world of its possibilities—*imagine what I might write on them,* she seemed to say.

A few weeks before I left for college, she plucked out the few remaining strands. I stood by her when she did it. This time, instead of smiling at her reflection...as she pulled out that last hair, her chest heaved and she crumpled up in sobs. I held her and rocked her till she quieted down.

It's like mourning the loss of an abusive parent, she later explained it. *Who am I without my hair?*

Whoever you want to be Ma, I told her.

Soon after, Daddy lost his voice. That was the last blow she brought on anyone. Daddy never again had those stomach pains, and the house never again echoed his voice. With the last of her hair gone, she also began to forgive everyone, or maybe she just began to forget what she had been so angry about.

Her memory loss progressed rapidly. It allowed for a rekindling of her relationship with Daddy and her siblings. She would forget who they were, so when they visited her at the Care Home, she could open her fists, relax her shoulders and approach them like strangers. Some days, she would have flashes of recognition that would make her frown at them, but most weeks, she rediscovered them like new. She would smile and press their hands warmly.

Maybe Ma's idea of the person she wanted to be was a person without history, without the baggage of memory and past associations. Maybe her memory loss was a blessing that she willed on herself. Every time I visit her now, she seems younger than before, livelier...lighter. She is a model resident in the Home. Always ready with a laugh. She doesn't always recognize me either, but she always seems pleased to see me. And every time she sees me, she runs her hand through my hair, which now touches my shoulders, and then she touches her own bald head. And this act of touching my head and then hers seems to please her, she giggles and squeezes my hand conspiratorially. If she ever has an errant hair that tries to come out of her scalp, I shave it for her. She never protests.

Last Tuesday, she turned 70. We were all there. Daddy, her sister with her family, my brothers and their families, my ex-husband and both my kids.

We were sitting around her room eating ice cream cake, when I asked her if she wanted something for her birthday. I leaned close to her and spoke loudly and slowly, so she would understand what I was saying.

"It's your day Ma. Your birthday. Is there anything you want for your birthday?"

It took me a few tries to make her understand. And when she did, she had a new light on her face.

"*Anything* I want?" she asked, her face opening like a child's with the possibility of that statement.

"Anything at all." I repeated.

She nodded, there was something after all. But she couldn't remember the word. "I want...I want...," her face scrunched up in concentration trying to clutch at the world. The room went quiet. "I want...I want!" she emphasized.

"Take your time, there is no hurry...it will come to you." I encouraged her.

"I want...a...a...a *song*" she looked triumphant at finally finding the word. "A song." She repeated and then looked around the room at us. "Do any of you know one...a *song*?" She said the word like it was something foreign, something hard, tangible and...foreign.

Her sister sucked in a sob. I saw Daddy's hands start to shake, and I felt something clutch at my throat. And then we all started singing. We sang her the birthday song, we sang her Rabindra Sangeet and Nazrul Geet—music from her past. Daddy mouthed the words soundlessly, but the rest of our voices got louder and louder, making sure she would hear us. One of my daughters played her a Taylor Swift song, her sister played her some A.R. Rahman tunes. My ex got a guitar from the Home's recreation room and started strumming a blues tune. And as we filled her room with songs, my mother, small, hairless and past-less, began to slowly rise up into the air.

My youngest daughter pulled at my sleeves, "Look Mamma, Dida is flying!"

IN THE HEART OF THE FOREST, A TREE

Gabriela Lee

the present

The bougainvilleas were in full bloom that summer. This was perhaps the first thing that surprised Triss when she came home. It was only two years since she left the Lagrosa household in Quezon City, but it seemed like everything had changed. The garden was now a riot of color; the bright magenta leaves of the bougainvillea vines hanging heavy over the clusters of arrowhead bushes that lined the perimeter of the property, hiding the pockmarked gray cement walls that separated their home from the neighbors. Gumamela flowers winked and nodded in the afternoon breeze. Ferns, spider plants, and monstera grew in abundance, framing the neat stone paths that now crisscrossed across the front yard. Grass flourished in the cracks between the stones, leading towards a shaded area at the back of the house separated the outdoor kitchen from the rest of the living space.

Triss had already seen the family car parked outside the gate but wasn't sure who owned the other vehicles that lined their side of the road. She was slightly upset that nobody offered to pick her up from the airport and she had to pay the GrabCar driver an exorbitant amount for the ride. What she imagined would be a couple of hours turned out to be at least a four-hour ride, the traffic moving sluggishly across EDSA. In contrast, Singapore traffic was quick and efficient; qualities Triss immediately missed.

She trundled up the stone path, dragging her small carry-on luggage behind her. Triss traveled light, unlike most of the other Filipinos she encountered at the airport with their large suitcases that seemed bigger on the inside and their cardboard boxes held together by tape and rope and a prayer. Nobody asked her to bring pasalubong, and she never offered to buy anyone anything from her travels. Any souvenirs she purchased were for herself, and if she didn't like it, then she would give it away. She constantly disappointed her mother and her older sister, Ate Hattie, whenever she came back without anything except maybe some duty-free chocolates (and only if she remembered).

But today, Triss didn't think they'd mind that she was coming home empty-handed.

The entry room was dark and cool, a contrast to the afternoon sun beating down on her head. Triss slipped off her shoes and kicked them towards the pile of discarded footwear by the door, and maneuvered her roller bag beside the wall, away from any foot traffic. Shucking off her jacket and backpack and dropping them beside her luggage, she made her way through the formal living room (dark wood, old furniture, giant Virgin Mary statues), the dining room (dark wood, old furniture, wedding china displayed in glass cases), and finally up the smooth wooden stairs to the second floor of her childhood home, her hand tracing the slope of the carved railing of the stairs.

When Triss was younger, before Ate Hattie's accident, they would slide down the wide banister and race to breakfast, with Ate Hattie making it to the dining table seconds before Triss stumbled in, sweaty and laughing, her school uniform already askew. Their household helper, Manang Rose, would scold them for behaving in an unladylike manner and try to straighten Triss's clothes before the school van would arrive. Triss remembered Ate Hattie in her neat blue-and-white checkered blouse and dark blue skirt, her straight dark hair pinned neatly away from her face, her eyes sparkling with mischief as she calmly ate her breakfast while Manang Rose struggled to make Triss presentable for school. Ate Hattie would grin widely at Triss as she took dainty bites of her pan de sal and Lady's Choice sandwich spread, never rushing even as the clock ticked to 6:30 a.m. and the school van would arrive outside their gate, honk-honk-honking to let the two girls know that the driver was there.

Triss remembered the dusty, barren garden of her childhood with the spindly trees and tired bushes, the bougainvilleas hanging limp and exhausted over the walls, drooping down almost to the ground. The soil was dry and cracked, and there was barely any grass growing on the ground. Sometimes, when Ate Hattie could still move her legs, they would play outside until the sun had set and Manang Rose called them in to take a shower and eat their dinner. Triss wondered where her parents were, but Manang Rose always said that they were busy and working late and needed to make sure that there was food on the table. Ate Hattie always looked sad whenever Manang Rose said this, but Triss was always happy when it was just the two of them at the dinner table. They could watch TV while eating. There were no sad sounds coming from her mother, or uncomfortable tsk-tsk-tsking from her father. Triss could put her elbows on the table, and eat with her hands, and swing her legs so hard that sometimes her toes would touch Ate Hattie's toes underneath the table.

Triss couldn't remember the last time she had even *seen* her older sister's feet.

Triss finally reached the top step and wandered slowly, almost reluctantly, down the second-floor corridor. Ate Hattie's open-platform elevator was tucked to the side of the stairs. From the master bedroom voices rose and fell like waves rolling across the ocean. She passed the bedrooms before arriving at the end of the hallway. The doors were shut; the dark wood still shiny from years of polishing, the knob turned easily. Triss took a deep breath and stepped inside.

A hospital bed dominated the entire space. The old bed had been pushed to one side and piled high with unnecessary pillows and blankets. The new one stood out in a room filled with dark wood and rattan furnishings. Wires and tubes snaked around the bed connected to IV lines and beeping machines. In the corner, like a sentinel stood a dark green tank of oxygen, guarding over the entire scene.

Two doctors fussed around the bed, tweaking tubes and tightening wires. Triss wondered if they were in the same class as Ate Hattie, or if they knew her as a patient. Triss's older sister wanted to be a doctor, wanted to go to medical school, wanted to follow in the footsteps of their father. Triss wondered if her sister resented her for leaving, for not wanting to stay, for escaping the dark confines of the house.

Ate Hattie was ensconced in her wheelchair beside the hospital bed, dark hair neat and pinned away from her face. She looked regal, a queen comfortable on her throne. Triss reached up to pat down her own hair, which was starting to frizz in the humidity. Nobody noticed her. Ate Hattie conferred with the doctors, her voice low and soft. Her hands crossed daintily over her blanket covered lap. She appeared competent and sure. Triss turned away, not wanting to eavesdrop. Instead, her eyes swung to the small, tired figure in the hospital bed, swallowed by softness.

Her mother was never a formidable woman. In her youth, Katrina Lagrosa was small and bird-like, her features almost elfin in appearance. She wore large spectacles that amplified her eyes to an almost comical point, and her wardrobe consisted of hand-me-downs from her two older sisters. Unlike the rest of her family, who migrated to the United States as soon as they were able, Katrina had decided to stay in their ancestral home, marry young, and have two daughters while working a government job, which she stuck with until she retired. Even before she left, Triss was painfully aware of how much taller she was compared to her mother, of how frail her mother was, how delicate her bones.

Now she seemed even more delicate, with wires and tubes coming out of her arms and from her throat and mouth. They had rotated the hospital bed and raised the head so that she could see outside the large windows, where the bougainvilleas helpfully lifted their leaves so that they could be seen. From above, the garden looked almost riotous, wild. Triss wondered who tended to the greenery, especially now.

Ate Hattie looked up as the door closed behind Triss. "Oh good, you're home," she said, her tone flat. "As always, just in time to do nothing." The doctors ignored the conversation between the sisters, averting their eyes.

"I came as soon as I could file my leave." Triss came out small and submissive.

"It's fine." Her older sister's voice was cold. "You did your best, I'm sure."

Triss stepped closer to the bed. Up close, she could see her eyes were closed, the pale skin stretched taut over her mother's cheekbones, across her mouth. Her hair, thin and scraggly, was mostly gone. Her chest barely rose and fell, her breathing burbling as she struggled to take in air. Beneath her loose nightgown, Triss could see the wires sticking to her mother's chest and leading to portable monitors mounted at the head of the bed, the squiggly digital lines unreadable to her. She barely heard her sister introduce the two doctors to her.

"...even after the last round of chemotherapy, the prognosis remains the same. While the spread of cancer seemed to be controlled by the latest round of treatment, she is still too weak to withstand another surgery to remove the growths in her stomach," one of the doctors was saying, turning to Triss.

"How long does she have?" Triss wanted to hold her mother's hand but couldn't make her body move.

"One, maybe two months? We are strongly suggesting shifting to palliative care."

"Can we bring her to the hospital?"

Ate Hattie wheeled towards Triss, her eyes dark and filled with frustration. "She didn't want to die in the hospital. You should know this. You also signed off on the papers."

Triss felt her thoughts scrambling in different directions. Where was the anger coming from? She knew that her sister probably didn't like she was left behind to take care of their mother in such a state, but she didn't think it was reason enough for this vitriol.

"I didn't think—"

"That's right, you didn't think." Ate Hattie's voice was venomous. "You never do. You just go in and out of this house, in and out of this family, like it's a volunteer position you can drop in and out of whenever it's inconvenient. Well, guess what, Maria Cristina, it doesn't work like that at all." Out of the corner of her eye, Triss saw the doctors step aside, shifting away from the bed and the window and the wheelchair. "Mama is dying and you did nothing."

"I can't do anything against stomach cancer! I'm not a doctor!"

"Neither am I, and yet…" Ate Hattie took a deep breath. "I want you to leave."

"No," Triss felt bile rise up in her throat. Exhaustion threatened to slam against her with the force of a typhoon. "This is my home as well as yours, and she is my mother as well as yours, and I have every right to be here."

"Get out." Ate Hattie turned her wheelchair towards Triss, rolling so close that their knees touched, nudging Triss's legs backwards. "Get out."

Tears blurring her vision, Triss turned and walked out of the room, closing the door behind her.

the past, some time ago

The house could hear everything. For its entire existence, it had kept everything in secret: the words whispered in the dead of the night, the dance of betrayal and heartbreak, the tears shed for names and faces that passed through the house. The house remembered the world outside, and the ways in which the fireflies floated briefly into existence, before disappearing into the void. Its family was like that; people who burned bright for a moment, lighting up the world, before sinking back into darkness. It loved to watch the young ones brought in after a day or night of disappearance, of the young ones becoming old ones, and the old ones closing their eyes in forever sleep. The house never learned the shape of their names, but it knew whose child was whose, and how the branches of the family connected to one another, and how all the branches were still connected to the house.

The house cared for the family that lived in it as though it was its own roots, its own trunk, its own leaves. It protected the family that lived inside with every desire in its wooden being.

The creature in the heart of the house did not care about any of these things. The creature only listened for what the house desired and enacted the house's vengeance.

The first time it slithered out of its hole, there was only the sleeping man on the floor. The creature writhed and shifted. This was no mere bird or rat or snake that the creature could easily smother with its dark, elastic body. It stretched and elongated, fueled by nothing more than hunger, until it resembled a pleasing shape for the man.

Patricio Lagrosa was not supposed to be in this bedroom. In fact, he was not supposed to be in the house. But his brother and sister-in-law were not yet home, and here in the sweet darkness, he could wait for them for as long as he needed.

Fuck Tomas and the laws of inheritance! He was supposed to own this property, not his younger brother. He was supposed to have the money and the property and the wife. And now here he was, breaking into the family house, where he was no longer welcome, and hiding beneath the bed that his brother and sister-in-law slept.

He didn't mean to cause trouble. He didn't mean to tarnish the family's reputation. But clearly, his apologies fell on deaf ears. So, he decided to take matters into his own hands: a small gun, easily concealed, and six rounds. Now all he needed was for the couple to arrive.

As he lay on the cool hardwood floor, Patricio closed his eyes and allowed his mind drift towards the future. The woman in his imagination looked exactly like his sister-in-law. She crawled over to him to lay beside him, her head a comforting weight on his shoulder. Her cool, nimble fingers skipped across his chest as she tilted her head towards him for a kiss. She tasted of midnight and rain. There was weight and heft to her body as she pressed against him. He allowed it—this fantasy spinning in his mind, in which he was given access to the most intimate parts of a woman who was inaccessible to him. He allowed her to straddle him, her legs parting, soft and inviting. She made no sound as he shifted to touch her in ways that only his imagination permitted, and he found himself moving faster and faster, his heart racing in his chest as he dismissed reason and fell into the pure, instinctive bliss of lovemaking.

He opened his eyes to blackness. The woman-weight on his groin became heavier and heavier, legs wrapping around his until he felt his limbs become numb. His pleasure-addled brain did not realize that with each thrust the creature's body became larger and larger, pinning him down. Flesh met flesh as the creature sank against Patricio's body, consuming him beneath its weight. Patricio sighed once in relief as the creature's flesh covered his mouth, his nose, his unseeing eyes. He no longer needed to breathe.

the present, again

Triss stepped outside and breathed in the humid evening air. Light pollution from the city obscured most of the stars, but she could still see the faint light coming from Venus. She wanted to step outside the gate, but she didn't have the keys and anyway, given the sudden temper tantrum, she was sure that Ate Hattie would lock her out. She pulled out her phone from her jeans pocket and tried to snap a picture of the garden, but the battery bar was at 5%.

She wished, for a brief moment, that her mother would wake up. A miracle! But Triss was never a big believer in miracles. Otherwise, her sister would have been saved from the accident, and she wouldn't be in a wheelchair, and they would never have had a fight like this right now.

Triss knew she should talk to Ate Hattie, that she should figure out a way to walk back the mistake she made.

There was something about the way in which Ate Hattie spoke to her that made Triss feel numb. There was something about her tone that felt dangerous, almost feral. Perhaps it was also her fault. Triss never denied she dropped the ball, all those years ago: she felt set aside, ignored, invisible while her sister was treated like a princess after the accident. Not that she wanted to lose her legs—Triss flexed her sandal-wrapped toes and watched them move in the light of the garden lamps. The guilt weighed her down. The guilt of being the able-bodied sibling. The guilt of not wanting to deal with Ate Hattie's loss. The guilt of blaming herself (for what? She wasn't there during the accident. She was in school.) and never really receiving absolution for that guilt. But Triss had never been religious and wasn't about to randomly attend some kind of church confession just to feel better.

Maybe she should go inside and apologize, start over. Maybe there was still a chance for them to patch things up. Isn't that what happens in the movies? Doesn't everyone get a happy ending?

the past, recent

The first month after the final operation, when they told her that she could no longer walk, Lualhati Lagrosa did not weep. She held her mother's hand as they both sat in the doctor's office and listened to the prognosis. She did not want her mother to see her cry; her mother had already been crying all this time. Lualhati had to be the strong one. She had to be the perfect daughter.

But she was now *imperfect*. Her legs were useless. The doctors suggested amputation, but she refused. Lualhati promised them that she *would* walk again.

She was unable to keep that promise.

Weeks turned into months, and Hattie stayed in her wheelchair, in the house that she was supposed to inherit from her mother. They built a small elevator for her, an open-air platform that went up and down, giving Hattie access to the ground floor of the house. They installed ramps where there were steps, allowing her a modicum of movement. Her mother poured a portion of her inheritance into outfitting the house into a home that could accommodate Hattie and her chair. While grateful, Hattie could not stand to see her mother slowly crack under the pressure of realizing that she would be taking care of Hattie for the rest of her life, not the other way around.

And Triss! Triss avoided Hattie as though she carried some kind of deadly disease, as though she was a rabid dog that would bite. Triss never met her eyes across the dining room table anymore; Triss disappeared after meals, until she was no longer taking her meals at home. She would be gone at odd hours, and come home at the crack of dawn, her bedroom door always locking behind her. Hattie wondered why her sister never spoke to her after the accident and the operations. Had she become invisible?

She was becoming an expert in one-sided conversations. She spoke to the walls, the plants, the garden outside her bedroom window. Whenever her mother checked in on her, she was either at her computer or on her phone. Her mother tried to encourage her to attend community sessions with other quadriplegics, join Facebook groups with other people who had been in car accidents, talk to other people with nerve damage. Hattie was uninterested. As far as she was concerned, she could still use her legs if she tried hard enough.

It was only at night, lying in bed in the deep, heavy darkness that seemed to seethe with a life of its own, that Hattie could freely admit to herself that she wanted to die. That she wanted to end this farce of a life, where each day simply tumbled into the next without any kind of change or improvement. She whispered to the wooden wall beside her bed, telling herself how she dreamed of disappearing, of never existing, of how her mother and sister would be better off if she died in her sleep like her father, or her grand-uncle Patricio, whose body was found underneath her grandparents' bed with a crooked smile on his face.

Bangungot, her mother called it. Suffocation brought on by a creature that weighed hundreds and hundreds of pounds, sitting on someone's chest until they choked. The victim usually died with a smile on their faces, as though they simply had a pleasant dream before they ran out of air. Hattie tried doing that once, pressing a pillow against her face to cut off her airflow, but her arms tired out easily and she threw the pillow across the room in silent rage.

How does one court a bangungot anyway? Was there a call, a ritual, a way to summon it? Hattie found herself diving into the weird corners of the internet, chasing down links from sketchy websites that hadn't been updated in decades. The bangungot lived in a hole in a house post, likely from the tree where it was chopped down from. Sometimes the creature was a tiny, wriggly, slimy creature. Other times it took the form of a beautiful man or woman and seduced the person while they slept before smothering them with their weight. Hattie liked that option; if you were going to die, you might as well die in pleasure.

When Triss announced that she was pursuing a job opportunity overseas (her eyes firmly on her mother's face and never once glancing at Hattie), whatever fragile thread binding Hattie's fraying thoughts together slowly unraveled. She congratulated her sister, and wheeled out of the living room, towards her little platform elevator, and moved to her room. She was careful to lock the door behind her. She didn't intend to be disturbed.

Using her hands, Hattie shifted her entire body from the wheelchair to her bed. She didn't care about her clothes, but she did care about her appearance. She laid in her bed, turning her body so that it faced the wall, and pressed her palm against the wood.

She wondered if the house was listening.

She wondered if anyone was listening.

(If anyone ever listened.)

But she heard it first: the soft slithering sound, the wet *plop* of a creature shifting itself from a small, tight opening and dropping on the floor.

She kept her eyes closed even as she felt the first tentative otherworldly touch. Her mind's eye conjured a boy of her desires: a shy smile, a soft touch. It was easy enough to allow the heft and weight of the boy/creature to encompass her body, to be taken into the arms of a dream and be loved. Hattie gave in to the heaviness of the moment, anchored to a fantasy that was sure to be the death of her at any moment.

A small flicker of logic told her that this was *not possible* that it was *not happening* but Hattie immediately dismissed it, lost in a flurry of open-mouthed kisses that drew down, down, down to the core of her being. Doctors said that she would never feel sensation here, that her reproductive parts were no longer capable of feeling, of creating and carrying a child.

And yet here she was.

Here she was. She waited for the weight of the creature to crush her chest. She waited for the moment when pleasure would transform into pain, the helplessness that she knew was coming. She was familiar with those feelings, knew them like the back of her hand. She wanted all of it to end.

But there was no ending. She felt the creature enter her, its large swollen body insisting that it belonged inside her; slithering and sliding inside her until she felt it burrow into her abdomen and settle there, wrapping itself into itself. When she finally opened her eyes, Hattie realized that she was all alone, that there was nobody else in the room but herself. She reached between her thighs and found nothing else but her own flesh. Sitting up, she swung her legs over the bed and walked over to the dresser to find something to wipe herself with.

It was only when she was halfway across the room that Hattie realized that her feet were touching the floor, unassisted. She looked down. Her legs were dark and mottled, pulsing softly as though there was something breathing just beneath the skin. She reached down to run her palms up and down her limbs, feeling her skin ripple beneath her fingers as though she was touching the dark surface of water, knowing that there was something deadly just out of reach. Unbidden, a though surfaced in her mind: *hunger*. Her palms skimmed her belly, surprised at its sudden fullness. Was the creature inside her?

Hunger.

Hattie stared at her reflection in the mirror. She still looked the same: thin, wan, her complexion lacking the sunlight. And yet there was something else there.

Hunger.

That was a good word. She ran her the tip of her tongue across her teeth. Hunger was a good word. Hunger was better than sadness, or pain, or loneliness. Hunger could do so many things. Hunger could be satiated over and over again.

From behind the door, Hattie could hear her mother calling her.

"Coming," she said, walking back to her wheelchair and covering her legs with a blanket from her bed. No need for her prey to see her in her newfound glory. She needed to feast.

the future

This is what will happen when the sisters meet again: the house will be set on fire.

Or perhaps we can also say, the house will catch fire.

Perhaps there is a chance that the sisters will reconcile. Triss will apologize for all the small, innumerable faults that she accumulated over the years, like sand in an hourglass. Hattie will let go of the resentments that tethered her down. They will hug in front of their mother's hospital bed as the sun rises over the horizon. The sisters will forget that, over the course of their long, long conversation that someone had left an open flame. Perhaps a candle left flickering in front of the altar of the Virgin Mary, or a kitchen flame untended? (There are so many ways that wooden houses catch on fire in the Philippines.)

The sisters will try to save their mother, but they will be unable to. Triss will barely be able to save Hattie. They will emerge from the smoke and the flames in each other's arms, crying as they try to explain to the firefighters what happened. Thankfully, there will be nothing more serious than dehydration and smoke inhalation. The house is insured. The sisters will be able to rebuild.

There will be a happy ending.

But perhaps in another ending, the sisters will not reconcile.

Instead, Triss will find her older sister standing in front of their mother's hospital bed, her mouth over their mother's. Triss will see the seething mass of blackness on her sister's bare legs, like a tangle of snakes writing in the grass. Triss will see how Hattie's mouth is painted black, as though she had swallowed shadows, and will be revulsed by the sight. She will run away, down the long hallway, down the stairs, and she will find something flammable (a canister of gasoline? A box of matches? There are so many flammable things in a wooden house).

The fire will spread across the house. Triss will run outside with her small roller bag and watch as her older sister scream and rage against the fire. Old wood catches the flames easily. She will call for firefighters, an ambulance. She will hear their sirens echo in the night. She will watch the house of her childhood, of her mother's childhood, of her grandfather's childhood, burn down, taking her entire family away from her. She will not cry, not in front of strangers. Instead, she will hold the hollow, burnt-out shell of her heart and mourn quietly.

She will not hear the death-cry of the wooden house that used to be a tree in the heart of a forest. She will not hear the angry hiss of a hungry shadow creature burn away like dark smoke. Thankfully, there will be nothing more serious than dehydration and smoke inhalation. The house is insured. She will be able to rebuild.

the past, long ago

The house remembers being grown from a seed. The house remembers the sunlight and the water and the long dark slumber beneath the earth, where its roots burrowed deep into the shadow, seeking answers to questions that were not yet asked. The house remembers the lash of rain and wind, the fierce bend of its body as it resisted the storm. The house remembers branches reaching the sky, leaves silver beneath an ancient moon. The house remembers.

Even before it was a house, the tree that was the house remembers the creatures taking shelter within it; the vermin scurrying across its trunk, the birds entangled within its branches, the myriad insects taking leaf and bark and sap and, occasionally, other insects. The tree remembers. The tree remembers when the creature first took up shelter in its trunk, slithering its way into a hole in the middle of the tree and curling up inside to escape the rain. The creature was heavy like a stone, settling into the stomach of the tree. Unlike the others, who left the tree as soon as the rain stopped, setting out to hunt or forage or be hunted, this creature stayed. It burrowed deeper into the heart of the wood, until the shadows could no longer tell the difference between the creature and the tree.

At first, the tree did not concern itself with the debris of the dead. It understood that when a life was extinguished, another life emerged. The tree considers the fireflies that surrounded it at night. They dashed and flashed and flew like reflections of light on the water, disappearing and reappearing in the dark corners of the forest. The tree knew that no two fireflies would visit its patch of land for more than a moment, that the creatures would live for no more than a breath.

And yet, there were always new fireflies.

But the dead seemed to grow more and more around the tree, while the creature living at the center of the tree seemed to grow heavier and heavier. It stretched and shaped the hole it lived in, forcing the trunk to bulge and swell. The smell of decomposition overshadowed the smell of mulch, the slow digestion of flesh and bone and carapace into new soil. Bacteria ate at the tree, from the inside out, and the outside in. The tree remembers its roots struggling to draw food from the soil to feed the creature, to feed itself; its leaves turning yellow and then brown and then falling to the ground to cover the bodies of the creatures' many victims. Living things began to avoid the tree. The tree remembers those days, when neither sunlight nor rain nor soil could satisfy the dark creature that seemed to grow fatter and fatter inside it.

The tree, which is now the house, remembers the bite of the blade that eventually took it down. In the morass of its trunk, the creature shuddered and shrank as the roots and the wood were separated from each other. It remembers the relief as it crashed down on the ground, the freedom of finally becoming a firefly, of flickering and then disappearing forever. There will be no more remembering.

But I remember —

The house, which is no longer the tree, awakens without roots, without branches. One end is buried in the ground, but nothing grows. The other end reaches up to the sky, but there are no longer any branches or leaves to soak up the sunlight, the rainwater. The house, which is no longer the tree, wonders what will happen to it. The house now realizes that it has been planted somewhere else, that it has been given new roots and new branches and a new lease on life.

The house remembers the fireflies, and the sunlight, and the rain, and sighs in contentment.

The house, which is no longer the tree, but used to be the tree, did not notice the tiny hole in the middle of its new body. The small, insignificant hole, where a child's finger could barely push through. Maybe it was a quirk of construction. Maybe it was a carpenter's accident. Maybe it was nothing more than a surface embellishment, nothing to be concerned with. Maybe, maybe, maybe.

Inside the hole, a shadow stirred.

It was hungry. It had been hungry for so long. It did not remember the tree, nor the forest, nor the light of the moon. It did not remember anything except for the comfort of the darkness around it, and the gnawing, tearing hunger that consumed it. It was ready for a meal.

MINDFULNESS

Rena Mason

"The clearest way into the universe is through a forest wilderness."
—John Muir

Flung from slashing machete blades, warm droplets pelted Kessa's face. The Thai guides up front, head-to-toe in camo, strobed between umbrage and polka dotted sunlight, their movements disjointed and jarring. The men shapeshifted, became rainforest and then human again in a hypnotic dance. Sluggish and a tad nauseated, they reminded Kessa she nursed a hangover and of the night club the guys had dragged her to the night before. *"Let's toast to an award-winning episode of GHOSTS ABROAD!"* Walt had said.

Tinny 80s glam rock blared from cheap speakers in small tent bars lining both sides of just one aisle in the night market. Every opening no more than ten to fifteen feet wide, a different song played from each one. Discordant music blasted into throngs of tourists looking for all the things they'd heard about Thailand and the locals ready to make good on it.

Dirty plastic chairs and sticky folding tables lined the fronts along with women and men in various stages of dressed to sell. The guys finally settled on a place called the Monkey Bar. Aptly named for the small Jar gibbon that sat atop a wooden post with a rope tied around its neck.

"Well, would you look at that." Walt nudged Kessa as if she'd never seen a monkey before. Well, maybe not in a bar, she thought, but still.

"They've got a macaque for a mascot," Don said.

Fabrizio laughed and then went up for drinks.

"In addition to being inhumane," Kessa said. "I doubt that's sanitary."

Don shouted after Fabrizio, "Bottle for me, Fab."

Fabrizio, ahead of the game, headed back carrying four bottles of Singha.

Many beers later, the tent was standing-room-only packed. The guys shuffle-danced under a dizzying glitter ball with local women circling them as Kessa sat at the only table the annoyed proprietor hadn't broken down to make way for more patrons.

Walt shouted and waved her over. Ready to go ten minutes after they'd arrived, Kessa left the last sip of warm beer and stood.

"Come here and meet these lovelies," Walt said.

As she headed their way, Kessa casually tugged at the moist, moisture-wicking trek pants stuck to her rear and thighs.

"Ladies, this is one of my film crew, Kessarin," he shouted over the bar din. "I'm her big boss."

The ladies offered a quick fake laugh and then glared at Kessa up and down.

"She one of you," Walt said. "She Thai too."

That incited immediate death stares. One woman said, "No. She *farang*." The woman turned away in disgust.

Walt laughed and then said to the women, "She no *soy* like you though."

They all giggled and cackled once more but meant it that time. When Walt had asked, Kessa never should've told him that *soy* was Thai for pretty. And why the hell had he spoken in broken English just now? These women probably understood several languages better than he knew the one.

Kessa was born in Thailand, but her parents had moved to Homestead, Florida when she was three. She remembered only a few Thai words because her father had forbidden a single word spoken in his presence. "Speak English or don't speak at all," he'd said.

A part of her understood why the women called her a *farang*, a foreigner, in her birth country. People treated her as a foreigner in the states, too, even though she was born an American citizen abroad because her dad was in the U.S. Army. Being in Thailand reminded her of an identity she'd lost in relocation, and probably why she always preferred haunted places and to be among ghosts. They existed somewhere in between, like her.

"Gee. Thanks, Walt," Kessa said. She wondered what these women really had against her. Kessa hoped they didn't think of her as competition.

Deep down though, Kessa knew. Somewhere in her subconscious, she turned her nose up at them the same way they looked offended by her presence. Kessa disliked their career choice most, but she also hated that the people of her birthplace knew with a mere glance she was a *farang*. She couldn't blend in anywhere. But truly, who was she to judge them? Kessa had used all her wit and charm and threw herself at the guys to be a part of their viral paranormal series.

Maybe the women disliked her because she worked for these men, these white men, these outsiders, looking to exploit them and their country, when they worked only for themselves.

Walt yanked Kessa against him and yelled into her ear. "Bet I could get 'em all to come back with me tonight," he said.

Pressed into his damp clothes, rife with body odor, and forced to inhale his beer breath made the room spin.

"Back?" Kessa said. The thought of Walt making sex sounds and more giggling keeping her up all night through the rice paper walls of their cheap hotel, wasn't the least bit enticing. "No way," she said. "Have some respect. These are still my people."

Walt laughed again. "No, they aren't. That gal just said so to your face. You're one of us. A *farang*."

Kessa rolled her eyes. "I'm heading back. Remember, we have to get up early tomorrow."

Walt grumbled and freed her wrist. "Yeah, yeah. You're no fun, Kessarin!" he shouted into her hair as she walked away from more laughter.

They'd hiked for six hours, harnessed into mountaineer-sized packs, through rainforest, in temps soaring over a hundred degrees, during an unseasonably wet monsoon downpour. Kessa had given up swiping moisture away after the first twenty minutes. She'd never been outdoorsy. If she didn't drown walking upright, perhaps bug swarms, or maybe even a Burmese python, would swallow her whole. More than two days of this hellish footslog, and she'd beg for a quick end.

The weather explained how Walt found such a great flight deal. Despite him being the oldest and something of an uncle figure to them, they clearly needed to start fact-checking the travel details themselves.

At least she'd gotten some solid rest. The guys, much more

hungover than her, with a lot less sleep, trailed behind. They'd groaned and complained behind her all morning.

"Is it much farther?" Don yelled. "Kessa, ask them."

The guides hacked away and ignored him if they'd heard him. No way would she approach the two men from behind while they wielded machetes. And just because she looked Thai didn't mean she spoke it well enough to make a coherent sentence. The guys probably assumed she could translate. Their mistake. Don of all people should have known. She went to high school with him in Homestead. *Go Broncos!* He wasn't too sharp back then either, and they'd graduated seven years ago.

Kessa came because she wanted in on the episode highlighting her birthplace—lend it some authenticity and prove to the guys she belonged in the crew. She hadn't known much about Thailand before reading up on it ahead of the trip, and she regretted that the more she learned.

Everything came together during a poker game in Walt's mother's basement.

"What do you all think about doing an episode in Thailand?" Walt said.

"Oh shit," Don said. "That would be epic."

"Mix a little business with pleasure while we're there too," Walt said. "We'll promo the crap out of it beforehand. This one might even get us to a million subscribers and over that five hundred thousand views mark, fellas. Oh, and you too, Kessa."

"Thailand," Fabrizio said. "My cousin's been there. He told me anything goes."

"You have a cousin that's been everywhere, Fab," Don said.

"What can I say? I'm Italian," Fabrizio said. "And Walter is my—"

"Yeah, yeah, we know," Don said. "He's one of your American cousins."

"I'm Thai," Kessa said.

"What?" Don said. "I thought you were Chinese."

"You don't look Thai," Fabrizio said.

"Oh, cause you go there a lot, huh?" Kessa said.

"You don't though," Fabrizio said. "From what I've seen."

Kessa knew better than to ask after that last remark.

"Eli Roth wrote *Hostel* because he'd heard you could pay to kill a man in Thailand," Walt said.

"No way," Don said. "That true?"

"I'd heard that too," Fabrizio said. "And anything goes for sex there."

"Gross," Kessa said. "Wait, this is a *Ghosts Abroad* episode, right? You're not going there to make an illegal movie, are you?"

"Don't be ridiculous," Walt said. "We're PIs for chrissakes."

"I'm being ridiculous?" Kessa said. "Fabrizio's the one who keeps saying anything goes. What does that even me—"

"Just stop," Walt said. "I got a tip from a guy there's an 'off the beaten track' tour of a government off-limits temple that's supposed to be haunted as fuck."

"It's never good when it starts with *I heard from a guy*," Kessa said. They all stared her down.

"What? You know I'm right," she said.

"What's the story behind it?" Fabrizio said.

"You won't believe me," Walt said.

"Try us," Don said. "Fab just told us anything goes, so it's bound to be off the rails."

Walt looked side-to-side and lowered his voice. "Old Army

buddy of mine told me that years ago, a group of monks went rogue mafioso and cultivated poppies for opium to export. Stuff would blow your mind," Walt said. "I mean top notch, grade triple A."

They all leaned in closer to hear him.

Kessa crossed her arms and shook her head. She doubted any of them had ever even seen an opium poppy. She hadn't.

"Well, the government found out about it. And rather than get into trouble with the public who revered these monks, they went in armed with automatics and gunned them all down right there in their temple."

"Oh shit," Don said.

"And get this," Walt said. "To avoid attention of what they'd done by burning it down, which is probably bad luck too, I guess, they left everything as is and just took off. Bodies strewn about and all."

"No way," Fabrizio said. "That's…that's…what's the word… san…sancti—"

"Sacrilegious," Kessa said.

"Yeah, that's it." Fabrizio nodded.

"Anyhow, I've been looking into it," Walt said. "No solid info online, but I found two sketchy tourist clips. One's a fake filmed in Mexico. The other might be legit. My buddy says the few folks he's recommended the place to, he never hears from again, and I have no idea if that means they went or didn't. He's always looking to be mysterious and talk shit up."

A giant leaf smacked Kessa in the face. She shoved it aside and started at the guide holding the bulky stem. He shook it at her to take it and then pointed up.

"*Fone,*" he said, although it sounded a little bit like 'fun' too.

The canopy roared above. "Ah, rain," she said. "*Fone.*"

The guide nodded and smiled. He moved the leaf over her head. It was the biggest one she'd ever seen. "What kind of plant is this?" she said.

"It's called an elephant ear," he said.

Kessa laughed. "That makes perfect sense," she said. "Nature's umbrella!"

The guide nodded once more and then went back up front. It took the rain several minutes to actually fall, but when it did, it hit her like the ocean was the sky and someone sliced open the bottom.

White milk sap ran down her wrist and dripped off her elbow onto the ground where rainwater washed it away. Kessa rubbed some of it between her fingers and brought it up to her nose. Her fingertips stuck together and smelled the same way they did after pulling weeds.

Drenched, she turned back to complain, but the guys had lagged farther behind. Kessa couldn't even hear them anymore, so she slosh-jogged over slick leaves and mud to the guides. When she got their attention, they stopped.

"The uh, American guys," she said. "They might be lost. We should stop and wait for them to catch up."

The men nodded and cleared an area under a massive tree. Its trunk was as big around as a zoo's carousel, and it ruffled around the bottom like a long skirt. The roots bore into the rich soil as if someone had dug their toes in and planted themselves there.

"What kind of tree is this?" she said.

"Takhian," the other guide said.

"Takhian," Kessa said. "It's beautiful."

Both men smiled.

"I'm Kessa by the way."

"Your name's not Kessa. It's Kessarin," the elephant ear guide said. "But all Thais have a nickname. You should, too."

"I'd love a nickname," she said. "What would you choose?"

"How about Mai," he said. "It means *new*."

"Oh, I love that. Yes, please. Call me Mai from now on. What's yours?

"I'm Moo."

"Your name is pig?" she said.

He laughed. The other guide shoved him and laughed too.

"And what's your name?" Kessa said to him.

"Mee," he said.

"Bear," she said. Kessa smiled. "So a pig and a bear walk into a bar—"

"Hey!" Don said. He stumbled and slid over to where they sat under the Takhian and then leaned against it, hunched over, and panted. "You guys are way too fast."

"Where's Walt and Fabrizio?" Kessa said.

"They're way behind me. Walt made me run ahead to find you and ask for a rest."

"That's what we're doing," she said. "You guys get lost?"

"No. It's easy to follow the path they made. You'd never get through without it. We just kept a slower pace than you. Then the rain from hell started, and we gave up."

"I was just following the guides," she said. "I never felt like I was chasing after them or like they were getting too far ahead of me though."

"Yeah, whatever," Don said. "Just let me catch my breath. You know I've got all my sound equipment, plus some of Fab's heavy ass lenses in my pack."

"I'm carrying stuff too," she said.

Don waved her off.

An hour later, Walt and Fabrizio step through foliage and warm mist rising off the forest floor.

"Jeezus, this is one helluva hike. Are we getting close, I hope?" Walt said.

Kessa turned to Moo and Mee. "How much farther?" she asked.

"I thought you said you couldn't speak Thai," Fabrizio said.

"I can't," Kessa said.

"Then what did you just say to them?" Walt said.

"I asked them how much farther?"

"Ask 'em again," Don said.

Kessa turned to the guides and asked again.

"About six more hours," Moo said. Mee nodded.

"Well, what did they say?" Fabrizio said.

"They said about six more hours. How are you guys not understanding them? Their English is pretty good," Kessa said.

"What the hell are you talking about?" Walt said. "They answered you in Thai. You asked them in Thai. How else would they understand you?" Walt shook his head.

"Hadn't you talked to them about where we're going?" Kessa said. "How'd they understand you then?" Kessa said.

"I didn't," Walt said. "My buddy set this all up. Told me to meet them in front of the hotel in the morning and then they'd guide us to the haunted temple. He gave them explicit instructions so we wouldn't have to communicate that much knowing the language barrier and all. I figured they'd be able to understand some basic English, and that you said you remembered a few words, but I had no idea you knew more than that. You even have an accent like them."

"Stop messing with me," Kessa said. "I didn't drink nearly as much you guys did last night, and I'm not still drunk. I sweated out any alcohol that may have been in my system ten minutes into this damn hike."

"Whatever," Don said. "The important thing is that they said six more hours. You guys want to continue or set up camp here for the night?"

"Let's start out early tomorrow," Fabrizio said. "Tell them, Kessa."

"You tell them," she said. "That's Moo on the left and Mee on the right."

"You even know their names," Walt said.

"Well, that's just a common courtesy when they're guiding us through their land. And if you haven't noticed, they also have big ass machetes, so I thought being friendly and exchanging names might be wise."

"Guess you're right about that." Don eyeballed the long wide blade protruding from Mee's palm.

"These American guys want to rest here for the night and then get to the temple tomorrow, if that's okay with you?" Kessa said to Moo and Mee.

"No problem." Moo nudged Mee with his elbow. "Let's set the tents."

Mee got up and went to their packs, unzipped them, and pulled stuff out.

"What did you tell them?" Walt said.

"How did you not hear me, Walt? You're right there. Oh, never mind." Kessa stood up, unbuckled, and then let her pack slide down her shoulders. "We're staying here for the night."

She dragged her stuff away from the guys, and nearer to the guides, but not too close.

Once she got the EMF meter and ghost box out, she could get to her things. She wanted badly to get out of her wet clothes but changed her mind when she realized she'd be soaked again as soon as she dressed.

Kessa had her tent set up in no time. Mee even came over to make sure it was tight.

"You hungry?" he said.

"I am," she said. "Is there a restaurant nearby?" She laughed. "I only brought protein bars with me." Kessa took two out and handed them to Mee. "Give one to Moo to try too."

"Thank you." He put his hands together and bowed a little bit.

"Welcome," she said. Kessa bowed her head, the response immediate and instinctive.

Later, Walt barged into her tent while she tossed and turned, unable to sleep. "You got any more of those protein bars? I ran out of room and hadn't really thought about bringing food."

"I do." She pulled two out of her backpack and gave him both.

"Thanks," he said. "You uh, got maybe one more?"

"So, none of you brought anything to eat?" she said as she handed him another.

"No. But that's why we let you tag along. You think of all these things, Kessa." Walt held up the bars.

"Yeah, because food isn't really so important." She zipped up her pack.

"We've got plenty of water at least."

"Well, that's good. Hey, I hope you weren't planning on filming for too long tomorrow. I didn't bring enough to last us two more days."

"We'll just need a few hours," he said. "We'll edit, and eat, when we get back."

"Sounds good." Kessa followed Walt out of her tent and went over to the guides to ask about where she could go to the bathroom with a little privacy.

Moo nodded, jumped up, and grabbed his machete.

"Stay close behind me," he said.

"Absolutely." Kessa followed him through the forest.

Finished, she walked to where she last saw Moo. He stood waiting with his arms crossed and his back to her.

"Thank you so much," she said. "And I'm grateful I didn't see a python."

"Harmless," he said. "They're more afraid of us. People hunt them for their skin now."

"Better than them swallowing me whole."

"They don't eat people," he said.

"What about pigs?" she said and then laughed.

"We're smart enough to know not to bother them," he said and then smiled.

The two headed back to camp. Kessa pulled her tent flap open. A bunch of miniature bananas sat on her sleeping bag. She glanced up. Mee waved and gave her a nod.

"*Kha*," she said, and then went inside.

Everyone woke before her the next morning. By the time she dressed, the others had already packed up. The guides broke down her tent while she ate a few more bananas.

"It's about time," Walt said.

"Sorry," Kessa said. "I was dead tired."

"So were we, but all the animal and tree noises kept us on guard."

"Tree noises?"

"You know, the short squeaks and long creaking sounds when the tops sway, only there was no breeze or any wind. It's creepy."

Kessa laughed. "You're a paranormal investigator, Walt. Creepy is your thing."

"Not *Blair Witch* creepy. Anyway, Don and Fab just want to get to the temple and knock out the recording."

"Sounds like a plan." Kessa went to get her pack from Moo and Mee.

"How'd you sleep?" Moo said. He helped her get the pack on and buckle it.

"Wonderful," she said. "You?"

"Very good," Moo said. "Your friends didn't though it seems."

"Don't worry about them," she said. "They don't really do nature."

As soon as she had her pack squared away, Moo and Mee started out, slashing and hacking a path. Kessa observed them more closely and noticed they moved in a precise rhythm, their motions mesmerizing. Before she knew it, the American guys had trailed way behind again.

Don was right yesterday, and it comforted her to know that the only path in or out was theirs, so Kessa walked back to find them. The further she went, the more foliage she came across. Huge Jurassic ferns and vines, the kind she visualized when dinosaurs roamed the earth. It couldn't have been thirty minutes since the guides cleared this, and she would've noticed stepping over and going around them. Kessa stopped and scanned the area, wondering if she had in fact gone off the path. The ground, soft from the rain, made her shoe prints clearly visible, except where the vegetation seemed to pop up through her tracks. No other footprints marked the trail.

The landscape changed between jungle and rainforest and all of it indistinguishable. The topography bled through from one to the other with no precise delineation or significant landmarks. A bush under a tall tree to her right shook. Something snorted behind it. Fast and small, an animal darted from undergrowth across the path. Wiry hair sideswiped her pant leg. Fangs protruded near its snout. Kessa let out a short scream and then laughed while patting her chest, thankful for a small boar and not a bigger one.

"Kessa, that you?" Fabrizio called out.

"Yeah, I'm on the path," she said. "Follow my voice."

"Okay."

"Are the guys with you?" she said.

"The guides aren't with you?" Don said.

"No, not the guides, the guys." Then she saw them. All three headed her way.

"How did you get so far behind again?" she said.

"It's like you and those guides just disappear," Walt said.

"And we were staying up this time," Don said.

"But then as soon as something caught our attention for just a second, you'd all be gone. Then we'd chase after you, even run, and we still couldn't catch up. We'd yell and shout ahead, but you seemed so far off, we figured you couldn't hear us anymore." Walt wiped the sweat dripping from his forehead.

"I'll stay with you this time," Kessa said. "Come on. They're only about thirty minutes ahead."

"Okay, good," Don said.

About twenty minutes into hiking back toward the haunted temple, Kessa noticed more growth than she had previously.

"I know Moo and Mee cleared these earlier," Kessa said. "Doesn't it seem weird they've grown back so fast?"

"What are you talking about?" Fabrizio said. "The path has always looked like this. They don't chop everything away."

"Yeah they do," she said.

"Come on. Two men? They're not superhuman, Kessa." Fabrizio shook his head.

The path wound on for three more hours, and they still hadn't caught up to the guides. Dense growth crowded them closer together, their packs bumping into one another. The path narrowed. Even the trees seemed conjoined. They weaved around and ducked under long vines; some touched their heads. Kessa kept her eyes on the dangling creepers. She didn't want to bump into a python.

"There's a big hole ahead," Kessa said. They came to an opening cut through dense shrubs. A tunnel lined with every shade of green imaginable. They crouched low and took small steps to get their packs through and stay balanced. Kessa marveled at all the work Moo and Mee had done. They'd be exhausted and resting outside, near the exit.

Kessa stepped through to the other side first. Into a clearing free from soaring trees. Not ten yards ahead, carved green stone steps led up to a temple with tiered golden roofs that pointed to the sky. Four massive columns, a natural shade of Phthalo green, held up the main roof at the entrance.

"Holy shit, is it carved out of jade?" Don said.

"No way," Walt said. "My buddy would've said something. The amateur-hour tourist video on YouTube didn't mention it being jade either, or all green like this. But it was filmed at night of course. Now, I doubt it was even legit."

To the left of the temple, one tree remained. Kessa assumed it meant something, had to be sacred. A Takhian tree, not as tall as some of the others, but its crown was full of thick branches packed with lush leaves.

"Let's gear up and test everything *before* we set out this time," Walt said. "Fab, go ahead and roll. Our viewers love the outtakes."

Kessa knew Walt meant what he'd said for Don. When they'd

recorded in Vancouver, B.C. last month, Don hadn't tested the mikes, and the sound quality was shit. Walt had to buy some expensive editing program to fix it.

They took their packs off and slid them down. Green leaves, half a foot deep, covered the entire ground. As they moved around, twigs and branches snapped underfoot.

"Exactly what are we stepping on?" she said.

Don kicked his leg side to side. Walt kneeled and brushed leaves away with his hands. "They look like bones," Walt said.

"Animal bones?" Fabrizio said.

"Not quite," Don said.

Kessa reached through the greenery, slid out what she'd stepped on, and brought it up to her eyes. Pinched between her fingers, a pristine piece of white skeletal finger. She dropped it, stood still, and whimpered. All around, the more she scrutinized the leaves, the more human bones revealed themselves.

"Geez, my buddy wasn't kidding about this place," Walt said. "Look at all the skeletons."

Vines wove in and out of skulls, from eye sockets, bullet holes, and through separated jaws. One to her right appeared frozen in a scream.

"I hope you're getting this," Walt said.

Fab gave Walt a thumb's up. Lifting the camera, he panned the clearing slow and steady.

"This doesn't feel right," Kessa said.

"Wait, Kessa. That's good. Say it again." Don held the mike toward her.

"Forget the sound," Walt said. "We'll clean it up later. Don, get your camera out and film, too. We need shots from every angle."

"On it."

"Get the reader and box out, Kessa."

Kessa trembled and shook her head. No equipment necessary. Violence happened here. The air came down thick and heavy. Damp woody smells and ozone filled her nostrils.

"Unbelievable." Walt waved her off and rolled his eyes. "I'll do it then." He took two steps and fell forward. "Ow! What the hell!"

"The vines." Kessa's voice squeaked out. She pointed, her finger shaking. "They're around your legs."

Walt kicked and struggled then screamed.

Beneath the squiggly shoots, blood blossomed across his khaki pant legs.

"They've got thorns," he yelled. "They're squeezing! Cutting in!"

"Stop moving!" Fabrizio said. He took one step before his legs got yanked out from under him. The camera flew from his hands. Leafy ropes pounced and wound around his body, immobilizing it, as if it cocooned prey.

"Dammit, get the camera," Walt shouted. "Don't stop filming. I'll get free."

"Fab's down, and you're bleeding for chrissakes!" Don said. "What the hell is happening?" Don tossed his camera and held still. Vines rose through the leaf layer and encircled his legs up to his thighs. "No!" Don screamed.

They crept from her ankles toward her neck, winding around and around. Kessa tilted her head back and looked up at the patch of clear blue sky. She waited for pain from the thorns, but none came. Kessa mentally blocked out the crew's screams and focused on her own. Her feet left the ground. The vines carried her across the courtyard to the tree. They placed her against its trunk and bound her to it.

"Get them off!" Fabrizio raised a bloodied hand toward Don.

Don reached for him, but vines pulled him down.

One darted through Fabrizio's palm. He shrieked as it snaked up his arm under his skin and burst from his shoulder in a spray of blood. Stringy gore hung from its leaves and thorns. Then it plunged into him again and back out, separating dermis from muscle. Again and again, exposing a bright red underside. Kessa gagged. White stars swirled in her eyes. She turned to Walt. Fabrizio's scream became a gurgle.

A vine entered Walt's ear. His eyes went wide, and he frantically shook his head side to side. Then it came out the other ear, and Walt screamed again. His body bucked and convulsed under the mass of ropey plants pinning him down. Kessa looked away, closing her eyes.

"Kessa!" Don screamed. "He—" It went quiet.

Tied to the tree, she spun with the stars until everything went white.

When Kessa woke, she lay at the tree's base, alone. All corpses, equipment, and packs had disappeared under new layers of thicker and lusher vegetation. The temple appeared to fade into the woods, there but not. She placed a jittering hand on a large leaf and pushed herself up. The ground dropped beneath her palm. Kessa closed her eyes and shook off the lingering vertigo.

Her clothes had changed. She wore a red and brown silk skirt and matching wrap-around blouse. She'd seen similar outfits at the night market—sold as "traditional Thai costume." Kessa stood, leaning against the tree for balance. Then she pushed off and headed back through the tunnel into the forest.

She heard voices ahead and called out. "Guys? Moo! Mee! Are you there?"

At the edge of the jungle, a dirt road. A man with a hardhat and orange vest stood on the flatbed of a truck, trimming trees on the opposite side.

"Help!" she said.

He turned. His eyes went wide. "Nang Mai! Nang Mai!" His pole saw hit the tail gate with a clang. He hopped to the ground, scrambled around, got in, and then sped off.

Kessa stepped onto the road and fell down, down, down until she once more stood at the base of the tree.

It won't let me leave.

Determined to get her bearings, she tucked the skirt between her legs and then climbed the Takhian's trunk. Too many taller trees obscured her view. Not far away, a bear climbed one of the high ones carrying a bundle of small bananas.

Near the top of Kessa's tree, out on a thick branch, sat a little house. An acute familiarity came over her, and she recognized it.

"Hello," she said, half in question and half in answer.

Kessa opened the door. A large bowl of fruit, plated foods, and glasses full of drinks in vibrant colors sat on a table next to a pitcher of water—offerings. Kessa drank and ate and cried. In the back of the house, a sleeping mat and long triangular pillows waited for her. As she lay down, she remembered a line from Cynthia Kadobata's *A Million Shades of Gray*, "The jungle changes a man."

For me though, she thought, sometimes it changes us back.

AIR

CHARCOAL SKIES

Lee Murray

we descended from celestial clouds
sons and daughters of the crane, we hungered
after life, a new world to rest our bones
the bitter Tang of sulphur in our throats

sons and daughters of the crane, we hungered
taxed in holds, the powder at our back
the bitter Tang of sulphur in our throats
we were damned and blasted to Kingdom come

taxed in holds, the powder at our back
our voices stolen; our lungs scorched to dust
we were damned and blasted to Kingdom come
breath after breath after breath after breath

our voices stolen; our lungs scorched to dust
foul corpses laid in monuments of blood
breath after breath after breath after breath
building iron roads across hostile lands

foul corpses laid in monuments of blood
we spanned oceans, we bridged generations
building iron roads across hostile lands
it was all they were after, all they asked

we spanned oceans, we bridged generations
they suckled the life from our blackened lungs
it was all they were after, all they asked
we gave it, and our sons and daughters, too

eternal travellers, alchemists of hope
we descended from celestial clouds
to explode, saltpetre on charcoal skies
afterlife, a new world to rest our bones

THE HEAVEN THAT TASTES LIKE HELL

Ai Jiang

Y ou were only twelve the first time you heard about the deity, but you were already helping your sister carry wooden buckets filled with bricks to the home of the village builder—always only after school, always only after she had already made several trips to and back before she arrived at the school entrance to wait for your afternoon dismissal.

She stands at the same spot each day, under the shade of a balding tree, buckets by her feet, the rust-coloured bricks piled well above the buckets' rims, threatening to topple over, yet somehow always remaining balanced—not dissimilar to herself, to mother, to your family.

You shove the remainder of the bun you stole from a monk on your way out of classroom, a makeshift space of desks and chairs that get cleared away from the main temple space when all the students leave. Sometimes you lounge on the cushions they lay back out for those who visit to pray to the Buddha, until they kick you out for the lacking respect.

Lao Da chastises you when you come bounding towards her with squirrelled cheeks, picking up one of her buckets with both your hands. Your arms strain from the effort, practiced not in manual labour but in mental ones instead—mathematics, science, literacy and language; both the tongue of your village, the same one your family speaks as well as another language, one not your own.

"If callouses appear on your fingers and palms..." your sister grumbles, casting her eyes downwards at you, expression thoughtful yet conflicted, her teeth worrying at her upper lip. Even though she's sixteen, sometimes she seems much older, stress already lining her forehead like mountain skylines during sunsets. The expression reminds you of the boy who sits next to you in school, the one who always received the top grade in class, the one always with sweat pouring from his temples. Those glistening droplets rest at the bottom of his chin from concentration as if each word and number he scribbled down could change his entire life—and perhaps, it really could. At least, everyone seems to believe so.

Would it be so bad? To have callouses on your hands? To be as strong as your sister? As your mother, the iron widow of the village?

Just before the two of you reach home, your sister does what she always does—sometimes successfully, sometimes unsuccessfully— and urges the bucket of bricks from your hands, the clamminess of her palm and fingers giving away her nervousness. Her eyes dart about, no doubt seeking out Mother, even though you and her both know she is likely still in the fields and will continue to be until well after the sun sets.

"Let me help—"

She shakes her head, lips pressing into a slender downwards curve. "I heard you have a test tomorrow," her tone almost accusing, unamused at your failure to offer the information voluntarily.

You pull your chin low, look at the worn edges of your straw shoes, and wait as your sister's shadow lingers. She releases a tired and exasperated sigh, the sound trailing her as she steps away from you. She says over her shoulder when you finally look back up:

"Lao Er must be still at the market. Finish your homework before she returns."

"Okay."

You don't.

You are up the mountain, searching for your friend Hongxi when Lao Er finds you and drags you home by the ear the same way she hunts and snatches rabbits to bring home from the stretches of tall, wild grass left unruly and untended near the rice patties. At least it is her and not Mother, who in comparison is quick and merciless and free when littering welts from her hand across your body. You wonder if she is trying to make up for the discipline you do not receive from your late father.

The village cat strolls in after you and Lao Er, silently snaking through the sliver of the wooden sliding door left open. Sweat pours from Lao Er's temples whether from exhaustion or anger, maybe both. Dinner sits steaming on the dining table chipped in more places than where it remains unmarred, and the laundry is left abandoned, half done, near the well behind your home.

Lao Da and Mother sits in front of untouched rice with chopsticks neatly placed on the side of the blue and white ceramic.

No one seems to mind that the way the worms hang from the village cat's belly too closely resembles the pale, fleshy fingers of pork mixed with the mossy green choi sitting at the centre of the table.

Lao Er, after setting you down, returns to her chair, *accidentally* dropping a piece of pork onto the table, then pushing it off onto the floor with the flick of her elbow. The village cat nicks the meat and darts away. You wonder about how it feels to be hungry—food is always tight, the tickets your family receives monthly sparse, and yet, your stomach is always full. Your sisters however…

Instead of eating, your eyes fixate on the cat and her worms. There's no doctor in the village for the people, much less for beasts—only someone who had studied, somewhat, herbal medicine and remedies, a friend of someone whose cousin is an apprentice of a zhongyi. You are reminded of the time you caught a high fever; you were offered a bitter brew of medicine that seemed too expensive for your family to afford. And you are reminded of the time your sister had fallen ill, her cough persisting, and yet all she received was a cold towel, and yet she was still expected to deliver her usual quota of bricks the next day.

"Your test is tomorrow," a statement from Mother, not a question. That is all anyone ever speaks about here. At least when you're present. And it is hard for you to imagine your mother and sisters speaking about anything else that does not concern you and your past or your present or your future.

Mother has high hopes you can become a doctor—a proper one, with a degree, a license, from a prestigious city university—so you may be able to help others like your late father.

You wonder what the zhongyi might look like—perhaps an old man with a long, wispy beard and matching eyebrows trailing like blanched horsetails, and you wonder if city doctors look similar, and you wonder why you would ever aspire to become such a thing, even if they save lives, even if they appear immortal, if you can't even save yourself from the drowning weight and pressure of being in this family, of your mother's expectations, solely because you are her one and only son. You wonder if it would have been better if your father was still alive—or perhaps it would have been worse.

Y ou had failed the test. More accurately, you had barely passed, but anything below the class average is unacceptable, anything below top three, really. This is not the first time, far from it, but it is the last time that Mother seems to have the patience for. And after Mother's harsh whispers last night and your sisters' pitying expressions when their eyes quickly flick to the bruised edge of your lips the next day, your failure was forgotten. Or so you thought. You should have known that something as everlasting as failure would never be forgotten. Not by Mother. No, never.

I t is at night, when the candle in your room has become more wax than flame, that you hear the murmur from the wall connected to your mother's room.

"The deity…" your mother whispers, then follows a long, long sigh like a gust of wind tumbling through fields of wild grass. "He will have to go to the deity."

You scramble from your cross-legged position, push your ear right up against the wall, squeeze your eyes shut in hopes it might somehow help you trespass the limitations of your hearing.

"But Mother, he may never return," whispers Lao Er.

"So many have left without returning," mutters Lao Da.

"Then so be it," Mother says, resolute, tired almost in her response. "If he cannot find success here, there is no reason for him to remain." Silence, then, "And if he is able to offer us passage, one day, like the way Yaoyao has for his family when he went to the deity, then we may consider ourselves lucky, fortunate, blessed."

You could hold your curiosity back no longer, and so you scramble upwards, knocking your shoulder into the wall in your haste, no doubt alerting your mother and sisters to your eavesdropping, and rush next door to Mother's room.

"The deity?" You ask, breathless at the entrance. Your sisters scowl at your disruption of their private discussion. Mother's gaze remains fixed on her weathered hands clasped in her lap. All three kneel on a bamboo mat as if praying.

"I do not wish to leave," you whisper, voice a thin rasp.

Then, reanimated by fury, Mother tosses her head up, whips her chin in your direction, and stares you down, and even though you are the one standing, it feels as though you're bowing beneath her. "Do you want to become like your father? Like me? Stuck here in this village forever? Do you?"

Your sisters' fervent stares urge you to stay silent—Lao Er picking at her nails, on the verge of tearing the white crescents from her fleshy fingertips. Lao Da's lips are pressed so tight together they have become white, the skin around them spotted and speckled from the pressure.

You know you shouldn't speak back, go against Mother, and yet—

"...Would that be so bad?" you whisper.

They all look at you, the three women, as if your tongue had detached, crawled out of your mouth, and slapped each of their faces.

That night, you curl around the village cat for the first time regardless of her worms, the back of your legs aching, your forearms too. Your spine stiffened and stooped from listening to the whispers of sisters and mother continuing to speak about you. They no longer try to hide their discussions, as if you will soon be gone to a place they cannot follow. You wonder why such a place exists, and why they describe it as a heaven, yet their tone suggests that it is instead a hell?

Yes, that was the first time when you had heard about the deity, and that was the last time you saw the village cat. When you woke in the morning, she was gone, and even though you waited for her by the entrance of your home after dinner each evening, she never returned.

The next time you hear about the deity, you're about to turn eighteen.

"Uncle Liwen left last night. No, no... not through the air, through the soil... He... didn't wake..." It is Mother, and that is the first time you have ever heard a hint of fluster in her voice, the subtlest urgency in the way she dragged out each word.

"I... see." It is an auntie who often visits Mother on her day off. Another widow. But her husband had not passed in the confines of the village—her husband had gone to the deity and has yet to return. It's been ten years. Lao Da says the auntie still holds hope. It takes a certain courage to cling onto hope, and for so long.

Uncle Liwen's son Hongxi had left the village, not by air, but by foot. You know not where he has gone, though he is almost always gone more than present, like a living ghost of the village, and you know for certain that you will not be able to follow.

You remember Uncle Liwen asking you to make sure Hongxi goes to school each morning. Instead, Hongxi always leaves you halfway there, darting up the mountains, shouting behind him, "Keep it a secret, will ya?"

And you wonder if Hongxi ever regretted not listening to his father when he was still alive, or if he does now, if he even knows his father is gone. You surely did—do. Maybe you should have tried harder to convince Hongxi to go to school with you. But would that have made a difference?

Can you convince him? You are his closest friend.

You know in the end you cannot convince Hongxi of anything he does not want to do—friend or not. He has never been known to listen to anyone but himself. Sometimes you envy him for the way he blocks out the rest of the world, the way even though his family attempts to place him on a pedestal, he hops right off and kicks it down, tramples on it even. Though you wonder if that might be seen as the strength of his individuality or a sign of deep disrespect.

For a moment, you consider also running away into the mountains and looking for Hongxi. Or perhaps head in the opposite direction to where they say the deity will appear in three moons' time. And return when the deity is gone. Except, if you do, will Mother allow you to re-enter her home?

Will the deity look like the statue of the Buddha at the temple? Will the deity look like the monks who chastise you for falling asleep in class? Will they resemble the immortal zhongyi who is the master of a friend's cousin? Or—

"There is nothing for us here, but you, for *you*… the deity will take *you*," is what Mother says in an even tone as she steps out of your home first.

You imagine yourself running, right at this moment, past her, up the mountains, away, away, away—until you miss Mother and remember your father again. You imagine returning home from the mountains when the night has already fallen, your sisters and Mother already asleep. Mother's breath comes deep and even. Her back is turned away from the entrance as though she already knew you would return, and for that, for some reason, you loathe her. No, you loathe yourself for always bending at the will of others.

And still, you follow her out—

By the entrance, straw shoes sit all neat in a row, uniform except for size, except in the level of wear given weight, stature, division of labour: Lao Da's has a hole, two, the second slightly hidden. Once you tried to switch your shoes with hers, being similar in size, only to be reprimanded by Mother who said you needed to be presentable in class. But Lao Da walks for hours each day, where you only sit, unmoving except for your hand holding a pencil pressed against paper. Lao Er had ended up mending Lao Da's shoes to maintain the dwindling peace, the tension already boiling from the time you mentioned you wanted to become a police officer, an athlete, a chef, instead of a doctor.

This is the last time you will see those shoes, and the last time you will wear them.

You are told to tread to the deity barefooted. You won't need shoes in the air, just as you won't need shoes when you're buried in the soil.

Mother does not look at you as the two of you walk past the long narrow alleys and wide winding main roads filled with neighbours peeking out from their wood and brick homes, past the rice patties, past the temple that used to be your school, and out the village where the grass is almost taller than the people.

Your mother said your father died, like Uncle Liwen, like her own family, because they stayed, because they did not go to the deity.

Your lips feel as though it has been running parallel to a river and never meeting its waters.

Sweat clings to the loose fabrics of your cotton shirt, plastering against your spine. In front, there is a tell-tale ring around the curve of your neckline, perspiration drenching the row of slightly uneven stitches from Lao Da and the neat, hidden mending from Lao Er who desired nothing more than to be a fashion designer in the city.

When Mother leaves you alone, in the dark, in the middle of the field where Lao Er usually hunts the rabbits, you feel a warm body caress your ankles. The village cat. And you think of the worms in its belly, the decay. Then, the sensation is gone, and you are left with the single thought of sacrifice. The one Mother has prepared you for just as she has done herself all her life. What the deity seeks—an offering of skin, bone, blood, and marrow.

How can those who seek out the deity toss everything away for the unknown?

You wonder if you had worked harder, maybe Mother would not be sending you away. You wonder if you had worked harder, would it mean your sister would not have to carry bricks? Would it mean your mother would not have to labour in the fields, if your sisters would be able to go to school?

If you go to the deity, could the deity grant you these desires?

The grass around you flattens in a circle, pressing down into the soil, then you are uprooted and whisked into the air. An invisible torrent slices and caresses your body at the same time. Blood runs down every cut, each wound like a hungry mouth, crimson saliva dripping down into the upturned soil.

The deity—

—is here.

I do not want to leave.

You don't realize you'd even voiced the thought aloud until a ghastly image of Mother floats in front of your eyes. She glares, the age lines in her face deepening like the shadowy crevices of hidden mountain caves at night.

Your skin begins to peel, flake, mixing with the tornado of grass around you like flesh-coloured ashes. Your muscles tear, the sinews snap and dislodge. Each of your bones detach, collapse, swirl around what remains of you—if there is anything that remains.

Why do you want to stay?

Is it because you think it would be easier to live with comfort in the village for the rest of your life? To be like your friend who escapes up the mountains when he should have been in school instead; the same one who leaves you staring at his empty seat with a weary envy? Or because you have been pampered by your mother and sisters and know nothing of what it is to live outside of such a life, outside of the village, where perhaps your worth will be reduced to nothing. Is that how your mother and sisters have always felt?

The crickets collect around your body not body, scream into the night their farewells as every piece of you is whisked upwards into the clouds, over the sea, where humidity dampens you, chokes you with its warmth rather than calming you.

They say water is rebirth.

Yet here, in this village, it is air. Because everyone wants you to rise, and you have no choice but to, and everyone is below you, hands reaching towards the sun, towards you, palms up, and you cannot tell whether it is because they worship you like a deity or because they are waiting to catch you if you fall, if they already expect you to.

Do not look down. Do not look back. Not until you have arrived at your destination, only then.

Mother's voice: *I will be waiting.*

I will come back for you, but you do not know if it is a lie. You do not know if these thoughts are what you truly believe or what you have been raised to believe, a duty you are bound to.

You feel like a god controlled by the people who made you, the mother who birthed you, the sisters who enjoyed no rest. You feel as though you owe them, you feel as though you have almost become entitled. Yet there is that nagging, lingering, guilt that because they have raised you upwards, you should not—cannot, must not, even fall below the clouds, become mortal, become any less than the deity they made you believe you are.

You land in a place you never knew existed, to a place where you will have to piece yourself together again and hope that becoming whole might be possible. Even though you know that it is not. But you think of the auntie and her hope, and perhaps you might be able to gather the same courage to hold on to it, to yourself, for a decade, a lifetime, in death.

You think about the smooth stretch of muscle resting bloodless on your body now put back together. Your veins and the pulses they hold echoing to the rhythm of a metronome—almost too steady to be human. You think about all the men who have collapsed into heaps of bones and sinew and skin and—

—in front of the deity, leaving all the women behind, because they have to, because they were told to, because they have no choice but to, not knowing when they will be able to return for them, months, years, if ever.

Mother's last words: *Carry our family name and make sure it survives, even if we do not.*

On the ground there is a thin thread of golden silk, so faint it seems as if a mirage, and yet with your new feet, you follow it as if walking on air, hoping it might take you to the place your mother had spoken about—the heaven that tastes like hell.

UNDER BLADES WE LIE STILL

Christopher Hann

It should have been strange, how the hands of the wall clock glowed in the pitch-black darkness of the summer's night. Dongwoo noted it was eleven past one when he heard the bleeping of the electronic door lock.

Then the rummaging of luggage. A familiar chatter. His parents must have returned from the airport. They came up the stairs towards Dongwoo's bedroom and gently knocked on his door.

"Son? Son? Jah-ni (asleep)?"

"Yes?"

They entered, still carrying their luggage.

Huh.

"Son? Jah-ni (asleep)?"

"Well, not anymore," replied Dongwoo, sitting up on his bed. "What's up? What's going on?"

"Ah. The airplane crashed during takeoff, so we had to come back."

"Oh," said Dongwoo. "That's not good."

Mother. Father. They stood there in the shadow, silent.

"That's not good," repeated Dongwoo. "How are you going to make it to Dongha's graduation?"

The hands of the wall clock were so clearly visible, as was his desk, his chair, the closet, the posters on the wall. But by the life of him, Dongwoo could not make out the expression on his parents' faces.

"Wait, *what*," said Dongwoo. "What do you mean the airplane cra—"

Father placed his hands over Dongwoo's mouth and began to press. Father smothered him, whilst Mother piled the luggage on top of his torso. Then they climbed into bed with him—Father to the left, Mother to the right—and cast their arms around Dongwoo's neck and *pressed* him tightly into the mattress.

"Jah-ni (asleep?)"

They strangled him for six hours. And in the morning he woke up, and saw it on the news.

C ritical engine failure. Or so said the alleged report. Only twelve hours had passed since the incident and nothing was clear yet— nothing at all—except that there were no survivors. The bodies lay in remnants, so the authorities were sensible enough to conduct identification by items only.

Father's watch. Mother's rosary wristband.

"So, so, sorry for your loss," said an officer, or something along those lines. It was all a bit of a blur because Dongwoo had to make plans now.

Is the funeral going to be here? In New Zealand? Or Korea?

Surely it must be in Korea. Most of the family is there. Funeral parlors? Who to contact? But wait, how to *bring* them? What was the word... *Jar*. No, not jar, you fucking idiot, what was the word. *Urn*. That's right, urn. He needs to cremate them here first, then bring them over on the airplane. But **(don't go there)**.

Do they do it in a church? Both parents were Catholic. But Father's side is all Buddhist. So church or temple? But **(Jesus, don't fucking go there).**

What goes in the urn, Dongwoo? Bits and pieces, fished out from the fiery rubble –

Dongwoo paused the thought. He had plans to make now, so he had to remain calm.

See, he was an adult. He had just graduated from college, had a weekend job, and paid taxes. He planned to move out too, right before his twenty-fourth birthday, and by Korean standards that was pretty quick. He was head of the family now. An old-fashioned sentiment, yes, but it rang truer than ever. First born son, pillar of the household, guardian and breadwinner for his little sister Dongha, who was about to graduate from a university in Baltimore –

Yeah, Dongha. She doesn't know yet.

Dongwoo began to shake. It dawned on him; not so much the knowledge, but the sensation itself. His parents died screaming as they fell through the midnight air, crashing into flames, extinguished abruptly in a whirlwind of dust. Mangled. Scorched. The sensation of having to convey that knowledge to his sister.

He called her, hoping she would not pick up.

"Hey! Hello?"

Dongwoo could not speak. He wept like a child.

"Umma, you really ought to think this stuff through," Dongwoo had told his mother, slouched before his laptop.

His parents' flight plan to Baltimore. As itineraries go, it was *terrible*.

"Seriously, six hours layover in Sydney?" he asked. "You've been to Sydney a dozen times. What were you going to do there for six hours?"

"(Hmm. Haven't thought about that)," she replied.

"Plus another four-hour transit at Hong Kong… You're doing yourself a disservice trying to save pennies, you know that? Look," said Dongwoo, flicking through the web. "Go through Honolulu. Stay the night there. Go see the beach with Dad or something."

"(Well, that'd be nice but)," she protested. "So expensive!"

Dongwoo grinned. "What day is it, next Sunday?"

Mother thought. Then she grinned back. "(Hmm. *My* day.)"

"I'll take care of the hotel. Five stars and all. Not bad for a Mother's Day gift, right?"

"(Lucky for your Dad, he gets to freeload!)," she said, then held up her thumb and announced proudly, "Very helpful son! I raised a good one!"

Dongwoo chuckled. She had never been a tiger-mom per se, but that didn't exclude her from the familiar stereotypes. Homework this. Extra curriculars that. "A" grade stands for "Average." All that fun stuff.

Teenaged Dongwoo had perceived her as such: both kindhearted matriarch and relentless nag-master; the gift that kept on giving with the occasional bamboo smack if you talked back too hard. Sitting here now, himself on the cusp of adult independence, Dongwoo could see her a little differently. A person of her own. A human as herself. Who could say, perhaps even a friend to her son.

"Alrighty," he said. "Let's make those bookings. See here? Click. Click. All done, as easy as that."

Yes, it was easy indeed. *Click. Click.* Just like that, Dongwoo had booked the flight that killed both his parents.

✦

It should have been strange, how the nightmare of his parents' visit coincided so precisely with the crash. Dongwoo paid it no mind. Pure chance. Or maybe they did come back for a final farewell. Whilst their presence was up for debate, the phenomena itself was in no way supernatural. The body switches off out of sync with the brain—a glitch in the sleep cycle, as common as lucid dreams.

"Sleep paralysis (gawi-nulim)." Roughly translated to "pressed by evil spirits"." In twenty-four years he had never researched the term, and had always assumed that "gawi" stood for "scissors." Pressed down by scissors. Pinned in place under the edge of a blade. That's what it felt like, when his parents came back to strangle him.

Summer was coming to an end, and Dongwoo was feeling the pressure.

Shit, I don't have a stable career yet.

Shit, our house is on lease and I can't pay the rent.

Shit, Dongha and I have to relocate to Korea, where we have some family at least.

And *shit,* I don't know a single thing about this place.

As soon as the funeral swept past him in a blur, the subsequent *shits* bludgeoned him like a hammer—a harsh brick wall of reality that stood so monstrously high and dark. Before he knew it, he was back in his homeland; a "black-haired foreigner" as the locals called him.

"*Tsk, tsk,*" they said. "*That's why you should never forget your mother tongue. Tsk, Tsk.*"

Never in his face, of course, but he felt the condescension which at times weren't so subtle. The siblings stayed with their aunty until autumn. They both got jobs as English tutors and found themselves a two-room flat in Incheon city—a few miles west of the ossuary where the ashes lay in rest.

Dongwoo settled in for the first night in his new home.

It was eleven past one, when he heard a knock on his door.

"(Asleep?)"

He didn't answer. He twitched his fingers. He twitched his toes. He could not move. He was pinned to his mattress.

"(Asleep?)"

The door creaked open, and something approached his bed.

Just another one, he thought. Just another paralysis, onset by stress. It should have been strange, how Dongwoo had his eyes closed but could still see the wall clock. Through the pitch-black darkness he could see his room: the desk, the luggage, the messy pile of clothing strewn about in the corner. Only this time he could see his parents, carnal and vivid, staring down at him without an ounce of emotion.

Mother didn't have her jaw. Her tongue drooped down to her bosom, scorched in black. On her forehead there were eyes – one blue, one brown, bloody and lidless. Her ribcage pierced from her torso in a twisted knot, jumbled out of place.

Father was crawling as he didn't have legs. Fingers and toes sprouted from where they shouldn't. Neither of them were clothed. Scabs and blisters covered their flesh.

"(Asleep?)," they asked, climbing on the bed.

They hugged him, crushing his windpipe.

"(Bits and pieces from the other passengers. The blue eye is from an attendant. The brown one from a baby.)"

They hugged him.

"(Bits and pieces got left behind. And bits and pieces got mixed in here with us. As ashes. Cremated. In the jar. Asleep?)"

Dongwoo screamed. In silence he screamed, for hours.

IMF means "International Monetary Fund," but for those who lived in Korea in the late 1990s, the acronym really stood for "Incredible Motherfucking Financial-disaster." To put simply, the country went bankrupt – or at least came close to it. Companies went under. Veteran employees were laid off without a hitch. Dongwoo's family was no exception; bludgeoned by the gale of economic crisis, his father's business scattered to thin air.

Father had always planned for Dongwoo to study abroad. See the world. Learn some English. Then return to the homeland as an "international elite." Never could he fathom uprooting his own foundations: to leave behind the familiar in embrace of the unknown.

"(I see clouds. Beautiful, long white clouds, under which your clan shall prosper.)"

Said a shaman, apparently. Father was no superstitious man, but when the going gets tough, one seeks guidance in whichever ways possible.

"(Screw it)," he had said to Mother. "(We go where the winds take us. We go, and we make do. We do our best.)"

And so it was chosen: New Zealand, Aotearoa, the Land of the Long White Clouds. And prosper they did—but not without a price, paid in full by the struggling patriarch. The former CEO worked at patrol stations, cleaned schools and cut grass. Mr. Boss Man was now a simpleton, rapid-fire words and phrases flying over his head in every direction. But he persevered. For the coveted Citizenship he persevered—always stoic (he cried in secret), always proud (he felt like a failure) and always with strict discipline towards his son and daughter (he adored them to death).

Yes, he adored them to death, and perhaps there beyond. Dongwoo wished he wouldn't. Because even now – on this winter night, many months after the tragic fall that took him – he crawled toward the bed, limbs missing, skin oozing with scabs and pus.

"(No room in here)," he said, arm clutched around Dongwoo's throat. "(No room in here at all. So stuffy. So very stuffy.)"

Why, thought Dongwoo. Why this torment, why this torture towards your own flesh and blood? Like his Father, Dongwoo was no superstitious man. For the first few weeks he attributed the nightmares to his mental state; mere hallucinations generated by stress. But not anymore. Every night they came to press him, their apparition more hideous than the last. Tonight, Father seemed especially talkative.

"(No room in here. Can't breathe in here. So stuffy. So, so stuffy.)"

Could it be? That Father was not fond of being stuck inside an urn – and the scattering of his ashes will free him of this curse?

Fine, thought Dongwoo. *Fine. Very good, actually. I'll do it tomorrow. If that's what you wish, I'll do it. So long as you both (leave), (me), (alo-)*

Father removed his eyeball and shoved it down Dongwoo's throat. Dongwoo **choked** – and for the first time there was a fear: not of any ghosts or apparitions or nightmare induced paralysis – he was well over that stage. There was a fear; a tangible and visceral concern that Dongwoo could actually die from this.

He writhed under the sheets. He glanced at his parents through the corner of his eyes, begging them to stop. He looked at Father. He looked at Mother—who was caressing his cheeks.

She tore off the skin on Dongwoo's face and wore it atop her own like a mask. There was a voice in the air. It whispered, softly, even tenderly. It was a voice so bizarre, yet eerily familiar.

"But you *are* alone."

He woke up. A blockage in his sinuses. He blew his nose, and felt fine. But he did not go back to bed.

It amplifies, thought Dongwoo. *Gawi-nulim* does that; it amplifies trivial discomforts into life-threatening woes. He peered out the window and saw so many crosses. Neon crosses on the horizon; peppering the labyrinth of a never sleeping cityscape. They glared back in apathy—in mockery, even. Dongwoo was no superstitious man, but when the going gets tough, one seeks guidance in whichever ways possible.

But he had already tried church. And prayers did nothing against the terror that pressed him.

The blooming of spring may be the coldest time of the year. The sun shines bright yet the gust blows frigid, and just as the seedlings sprout through the icy soil, the ocean birds return home to roost. Over half die during their flight across the Pacific – or so Dongwoo had heard.

He watched them flock around the cliffside of the shore; birds of all kinds, swallows, gulls and herons and all. They congregated in a cyclone of synchronized chaos, quacking, chirping and hovering about—as if in rackety celebration of their migratory exodus. They would settle, so long as the ground yields food and the air offers warmth. For now they would settle—and in summer they would fly to wherever the winds might take them.

"(Young man!)," yelled a gentlemen in uniform, scurrying towards Dongwoo. ("Young man! Hold up!)"

"(Yes?)," answered Dongwoo. He waited for the man to catch his breath.

"(Hey, uh –),", said the man. ("Are you alright?")

Was he alright? Not exactly, thought Dongwoo, but gave the perfunctory answer.

"(Yeah, sure. Can I help you?)"

"(What are you doing here?)"

What was he doing here? "(Bird watching,)" he replied.

"(Oh. Good)," answered the man, looking a little embarrassed. "(Uh, well. I'll leave you to it then. But take this. Hope you're not offended.)"

A suicide prevention pamphlet. *Ah,* he thought. *Makes sense.* He would learn later that the cliff was a so-called "hotspot." He didn't blame the man. Dongwoo hadn't a good night's sleep in months, so surely he must have looked like a wreck.

"Thank you," he said to himself, long after the gentleman had disappeared.

The ocean breeze sliced through his jacket, but there was an inkling of warmth – a candle that thawed the corner of his heart. The man was just doing his job, and was completely wrong about Dongwoo's intentions—but he had looked out for a stranger. A black-haired foreigner, no less. *Yeah,* he thought. *People still give a shit. People care.*

He felt better.

He might have felt good, in fact, if it wasn't for **them.** The monsters. The nightly tormentors that denied him any peace. He feared to go to sleep. He feared to close his eyes. For tonight, as with every other night, they would return. They would return to press him, with all their agony, suffering and grief. They would return to pin him with the blades of their anguish, ever dull, yet unbearably heavy.

When the going gets tough, one seeks guidance in whichever ways possible. And thus Dongwoo found himself in a shaman's house.

"What the *hell* is that?" asked Dongha.
          "Just a painting."
"It's fucking creepy."

"Ignore it. It won't be there for long."

The painting cost eighty-thousand Won, which was about the price of a bottle of whiskey. Was Dongwoo scammed? Sure, perhaps. But he didn't care. *Anything* to rid himself of the nightly terrors, he would try. Anything to rid himself of the ghosts of his parents.

"Uduk-shini," the shaman had said. "(Dark sprites. They come to press you at night, I see.)"

Not bad, thought Dongwoo. He knew most of it was "cold reading"—intuitive observance of the client in question, as opposed to some divine jibber jabber. But still, people buy the lottery, don't they? They carry clovers for luck, right? Was this so different?

"(The best way to battle it is to challenge it head-on. To face it with courage)," said the shaman. "(But you're afraid to do so. Why?)"

Because they're my goddamn parents, he thought, but said nothing out loud. In the end the shaman gave her prescription:

"(Hang this)," she said. "(Hang this portrait of the Dharma in your house. He will capture the dark sprites when they come to visit. Once they are captured, burn the painting.)"

Dongwoo laughed to himself as he followed the instructions. His sister was right, it was indeed fucking creepy. The Dharma was apparently a revered monk and shaman. His likeness kept in households as a protection against demons. He certainly looked the part: brows furrowed and expression grim, ready to go to war.

What's there to lose, thought Dongwoo. *What's there to lose, other than the price of a bottle of booze?* He turned off the lights and went to bed.

It was no longer strange, how the hands of the wall clock were so clearly visible through the pitch-black darkness of the night. *Here we go again,* thought Dongwoo, mocking himself for being so gullible. *Dark sprites. Dharma. Yeah right.*

"(Asleep?)"

He did not answer. Minutes passed. But there was no press.

"(Asleep?)"

The voice came from the living room. Dongwoo got up. And went outside.

There they were. Lumbering, crawling, as grotesque as ever. But something was looming behind them. A man, a giant – holding them by their scruffs.

"(Asleep?)"

"Yes," Dongwoo answered, and was surprised he could speak. Come to think of it, it was his first time to do so. To actually speak to the apparition of his parents—out loud and clear, free from paralysis.

"Yes," he said again. "Or at least I'm trying to."

Mother and Father nodded.

Then, ever so gently, the giant withdrew from his pocket two sets of clothing, woven in silk. Its glow was that of ivory and starlight, luminating the dark in a tranquil shimmer. He wrapped both parents in the garments and lifted them softly into his arms.

Dongwoo saw it. It was a fraction of a moment, but he saw it. As they entered the painting—to return to the world of the nether, to rest in serenity in a place there beyond—they looked back on their son and smiled. As if the months of torture they inflicted was no torture at all.

"Jal-ja (Goodnight)."

Dongwoo woke up at noon. He felt refreshed. He felt strange.

He burned the painting that same evening. The ashes vanished without a trace upon the snow.

"Promise me you won't call me crazy," said Dongha.
"Sure," replied Dongwoo. "I promise?"

"I'm being serious."

Indeed, Dongwoo could tell. Ever since the funeral, the two never had a heart-to-heart. No "deep conversations," so to speak. If his sister wanted a sit-down, the topic had to be serious.

"What was the deal with the painting?"

A pause.

Dongwoo offered a lame excuse. A good luck charm. He said he got rid of it because—she was right—it looked too creepy. "No big deal," he said. No big deal at all.

"It was a Dharma portrait, right?" asked Dongha. "The scary looking monk. Used to ward off evil spirits."

"Yeah, something like that."

"Don't call me crazy, okay? Here's the thing."

And what a thing it was.

Mother and Father had been visiting her also. Ever since their passing. Every night, without fail.

But they had hugged her gently. They had held her hands as she shivered in the dark—trembling at the thought of being left alone, trembling in fear of the tides of the future. And when she told them *I miss you* they said:

(Our girl, our lovely girl)

(So sorry we're not here)

(So sorry you have to live here like this)

(In a house cramped like this, no room, so stuffy)

(No room here to breathe)

(We'd give anything to be with you right now)

(We'd give anything, we'd give an eye)

(Look at your pretty face: takes after your father, takes after your mother)

(We miss you too, but we're always here, do not forget)

(Asleep? Goodnight now. Go to sleep now).

They had visited, without fail. But not after the arrival of the Dharma.

"Did they, by any chance," said Dongha, then paused. She cleared her throat. She knew it was ridiculous, but had to ask. "Did they visit you as well?"

Silence.

A thousand emotions raced through Dongwoo's head, and a thousand more churned his stomach.

"No," he lied.

Why, he pondered. Why the difference? Why the hellish visage when they visited their son? Why not the hug, why not the lullaby, why not the gentle comfort he yearned for so much—why, why—but he knew why, didn't he?

He had killed them.

"Dongwoo?" asked Dongha.

Her brother was crying. Tears streamed down his cheeks as he recognized the truth of his ailment; the core of the curse that defiled his dreams. It amplifies. *Gawi-nulim* amplifies—moments of regret into crippling self-hatred, a passing imagination into terrifying nightmares. All he could think about in relation to his parents was the crash. How they died. How they burned. And how he had a part in it.

So he had refused to remember them at all. He avoided cherishing their memories in life, and all the while it grew—the darkness, the sorrow, the ever-irrational blade of guilt that pressed him this very moment.

The dark sprite was within him all along.

"I have to tell you something," muttered Dongwoo. "It was me. I booked their flights. I *changed* their flights. I should have just left it. It was me. It was my fault they died. I'm sorry."

Silence. The evening traffic droned outside as the sun glided gently into the west. A family of magpies cawed in the distance.

"Dude," said Dongha. "How on earth is that *your* fault?"

"I'm sorry. I'm so–"

"Fucking hell, Dongwoo. That is **not** your fault."

Yes, he knew. But it hit different, hearing it from another voice. Dongwoo bawled his eyes out as Dongha hugged him. It was embarrassing, to be consoled like a baby in the arms of a little sibling. But it made him feel better. Much, much better.

He went to bed early that night, tired from all the weeping. He waited till his eyes adjusted to the dark.

The wall clock was there. But he couldn't tell the time.

Was it insane, he thought, to wish that his parents would visit one last time? They could look as hideous as they liked, Dongwoo didn't care. He hoped to converse with them. He wouldn't know what to say, but that didn't matter either. Just to talk. Just to chat. Just to recognize their grasp as the embrace that it was.

Dongwoo wished they would visit, because he was no longer afraid.

The hands of the wall clock hit eleven past one. Then twelve. Then thirteen. Dongwoo fell asleep.

His parents never returned.

It was a bright summer day, exactly a year since the incident. The sea stretched before the siblings into the azure horizon; the ocean birds chirping from the cliffside to the right.

Dongwoo looked at them. The hatchlings had grown feathers now, awkward and clumsy, gawking at the air to learn the ropes of the wind. For what it's worth, they seemed to be doing fine.

They opened the urns to cast the ash. Dongha agreed with the idea. After all, their parents used to talk about a trip to Barcelona, or to Jakarta, or wherever – once their kids had settled in their careers. Mom and Dad, just the two, for a trip around the world.

Dongwoo still felt the pain. The dull ache of grief and the occasional sting of passing anxieties remained within his heart—but that was okay. Under blades he lay still, so all he could do was grow a thicker skin.

They cast the ash towards the western sea. It drifted – first low, then high – then dispersed under the mist of sunlight, to travel to wherever the winds might take them.

MOHINI'S WRATH

Priya Sridhar

Kriti's lungs shrunk from the pressure as she tried to sleep; she couldn't breathe. Heat, humidity, sweat; it all weighed on her chest. And the dust. Good God, all the rolling dirt from the roads and construction. It smelled burnt and clogged, trampled by cars and rickshaws.

The green-flecked idol of Vishnu stared at her from its nook in the living room wall, frozen mid-dance. Her grandmother had draped him with a fresh jasmine garland. The sweet scent gilded the heavy air.

She wiped her brow with the cotton bed sheet and flipped the pillow on the couch. Just another day in Chennai before the monsoon season. But she had another reason to sweat.

Peony had insisted on coming along on this trip to see her grandparents. She had obliterated all of Kriti's objections: that no Indian believed in being gay, bi, or pan, that it would be a long and excessive trip, the costs would make it a once-in-a-lifetime experience, and if they got kicked out then they would have nowhere to stay. Kriti was the last unmarried girl in her family, and she had just wanted to visit before her grandparents got too ill. She didn't want to add more drama to the dressing up in pavadas that covered her legs and seeing relatives that asked about her career prospects as well as her love life. The kids hid their faces and refused to talk only made her feel worse, though she understood them out of all the family members. Kriti had done the same when she was their age, hiding from the large grown-up strangers that wanted to hug her.

Peony had been too jet lagged and dehydrated to hear her explain to her grandparents that Peony was with her and let them draw the conclusions. She had said "Namaste" to them and folded her hands. Nana had raised an eyebrow at her that was more white fuzz than hair.

"Is she a yoga instructor?" he asked Kriti when Peony had gone to shower.

"A pastry chef actually," Kriti replied. "She works at a three-star restaurant in the Wynwood area."

While the flat had air conditioning, the humidity weighed around them. They slept on couches in the living room, while Nana and Nani slept in the only bedroom. Kriti was not going to displace her elderly grandparents, especially after Nani had recovered from a broken hip.

Peony kept insisting she could rough it out. She wanted to explore the city, try new foods, and walk by the seaside. There was so much that they could both do and explore as a couple. And surely Kriti had earned this time alone.

Kriti ran her hands through her sweaty hair. Sure they could do all that, but Nana and Nani would want to spend time with her. They wanted to show her off to relatives, and potentially Indian men seeking young wives with Green Cards. She couldn't just be a tourist.

"Don't you care about seizing the day?" Peony would ask. "You've been here so many times, and it's my first trip. I think seeing the beach would be great, especially since you rarely go."

Kriti had to admit, poking at a hole in the cotton bed sheet, that Peony wasn't wrong. She had visited this city so many times, but it felt too unfamiliar. Always bordered in by expectation and social visits. She would bury herself in Indian mythology comics called *Amar Chitra Katha* and American television to cope. They helped her abide by Nana and Nani's rules. And that meant definitely not snuggling together on the couch.

Her lungs protested about the heat, but she fell asleep. Eventually.

The curtains fluttered. Kriti peered with trepidation while wiping her furrowed, sweaty brow. A silhouette draped herself around the white linen. Dark in the shadows but gaining color with each step.

She blinked and rubbed her eyes, more sweat dripping down her back. The figure stayed there. Probably another sleep paralysis demon; maybe she had fallen asleep and was dreaming that she was awake. Normally, Kriti told them to go away, and they would. But this one came into focus. Long hair that coiled like ink spirals, kohl outlining large shining eyes, navy-blue silk that gleamed with gold thread. It looked like a familiar figure from her Indian mythology comics. She could hear her grandfather reading them aloud. His voice carried with the humid night breeze, though he was in the next room sleeping.

Kriti did not say bug off. And opening her mouth, she knew she was screwed.

"You are beautiful."

Footsteps. The figure turned. It melted into the curtains, and vanished.

"Kriti-rani," Nani said, stumbling down. "Are you asleep?"

If Kriti weren't scared, she'd find that a stupid question. Nani used to roam the house more often before breaking her hip, and would wake the grandkids up to check on them. But looking into her grandmother's eyes, Kriti realized that's not what Nani was asking.

"I…" Kriti tried to explain. "I saw something…"

Nani patted her hand, nodding.

"You've seen her too?" she whispered.

Kriti nodded, not understanding.

Nani disappeared and returned before Kriti could fully process her words and found her grandmother shoving a book into her hands. It was old and smelled like incense and long-ago knowledge.

"This will explain," she whispered. "I'm going to add more garlands to Vishnu."

She shuffled away. Kriti opened the book. She flipped to a page:

Mohini is an avatar of Vishnu, created when the gods (devas) allied with their worst enemies (asuras—called demons, but probably powerful humans because many Indians are colorist) to churn immortality out of the ocean. A jar of amrit emerged, along with other precious objects and the goddess Lakshmi in her form as Shree. This amrit nectar flowed out in golden streams and tasted like a cloud. Those that drank it would become immortal.

The asuras, according to the devas, charged forward and wrestled over who would take the first sip. They had forgotten the alliance in their quest for immortality. When the devas prayed for help, Vishnu the protector god took the form of a beautiful woman. His blue skin softened into a creamy beige, and his curls straightened into long locks. Even his signature peacock feathers became golden bangles.

Mohini was so beautiful that the asuras stopped fighting and asked her to distribute the nectar fairly. She pretended to hesitate, but agreed on the condition they would not question her decisions.

Rahu, one asura, noted that only the devas received the nectar as the alleged demons waited their turn. He disguised himself as a god and tried taking some amrit for himself. Before he could swallow it, the Sun and the Moon exposed him. They pointed and shouted he was not a deva.

Mohini beheaded him with Vishnu's discus, and his conscious head flew into the sky. He chases the sun and the moon to swallow them in vengeance, hence how we get eclipses. Yet no one can hear him scream when the darkness gathers.

The ocean attracted crowds. Kids ran by the beach while vendors offered popsicles from ice bins with wheels. Locals could appreciate the beauty of the masses. Tourists would note how the grains of sand were stickier here compared to the Western beaches, with the humidity and the churning water.

Kriti packed her inhaler in case she has another asthma attack. Back in the States, she would not have to worry about breathing, but every time in Chennai, the air would attack her lungs. It meant she couldn't do long social outings unless she wanted to choke. Nana and Nani thought she was being shy, even when she was prone to coughing fits.

Peony didn't notice. She had consented to wearing a dress that covered her legs, but the short sleeves showed the burns from splattered oil. Years of working the fryer at her family's restaurant manifested in angry red marks. She took pride in announcing to Nana and Nani how clumsy she was, and how often she would grab a hot tray without realizing.

Kriti tried not to look at the scars as they strolled. Other people did.

She didn't want to judge Peony for natural burns — several occupied her knuckles from accidentally touching the oven once or twice when upset—but it did concern her that Peony missed the judgmental looks, the quiet whispering. You had to know how to navigate the alleys of gossip in this neighborhood, to avoid the heavy judgment that would settle in her lungs. Nani asked with her eyes why not wear protective equipment when handling hot ovens, while Nana turned away and muttered in Tamil about reckless Americans. He had spoken more opinions since retiring from the government.

Maybe she was being too judgmental. At home, she admired Peony for not hiding her body and talking openly about the dangers of grocery store bakeries before she had gotten her Wynwood position. When Kriti was here, though, in a familiar place that trapped her? It all weighed on her, the expectations with the heat.

"It's such a beautiful day!" Peony said. "Do you think you want to go to the aquarium?"

"I've never been," Kriti responded. "But I do agree, it is a nice day for Chennai."

"First time for everything!" Peony pointed. "It's just a short walk."

"I need to see how many rupees I have, and what time we have to be back," Kriti said. "It's on me."

"Oh, come on, let me pay for it." Peony swiveled. "I made sure to exchange enough. And you've covered a lot already."

Clouds passed over the dripping sun. Kriti wiped her face. When she removed her hand from her forehead, a familiar figure in blue stared at her from a distant dune.

"Whoa," she said.

"What?" Peony asked.

"Nothing," Kriti said. "You just don't see many people wearing silk on the beach."

318

Peony followed her gaze. The woman stared, her long hair curling around her. A breeze made the sari flutter and sand grains spin around her.

"It's just a woman by herself," Peony said. "Not many of them are out here alone. That's why she's standing out, though that outfit is definitely helping. I wish I could rock something like that."

"You could," Kriti reassured her, fighting the unpleasant feeling in her stomach.

So Peony could see her too. Her grandmother was one thing, since Kriti was sure she inherited the insomnia and sleep demons from Nani, but her girlfriend?

Kriti felt her lungs gather grit. The figure watched as they navigated down to the aquarium and the dunes. And more of the book came back to Kriti, that she had flipped through after a breakfast of idlis and coffee:

When the ocean was churned, a blue poison emanated from the waves. It suffocated gods, demons, and the humans in-between. Beautiful as a sapphire, but slippery as oil sliding through your lungs and twisting around the heart. *Halahala*, the victims called it when they could still speak.

The gods were not yet immortal. They fell to the ground, choking and spluttering. Some shuddered before laying still.

Those that could still pray asked for Brahma and Shiva to help them, choking out their pleas. Brahma was a creator, so he could do nothing. He watched from his abode, brow furrowing with worry.

The god Shiva controlled death. It also meant that he could control life. So, he came from his mountain home, gathered the poison in his hands, and swallowed it. The blue gathered at his throat and concentrated there. As a result, Shiva's other name is Neelakanth, named for the shimmering blue throat. He had to breathe around that poison, so that the world would not suffocate in blue fog.

So, the churning of the ocean continued, and Vishnu waited to introduce the asuras to Mohini.

Kriti mentioned nothing to Peony; how would she even explain it? That she had dreamed of a gorgeous Indian woman, with bangles that gleamed even in rooms with the lights turned off and a slender figure draped in the finest of saris? Neither she nor Peony had slender bodies, and she wasn't going to be wearing gold bangles anytime soon. They interfered with her typing at her day job.

Peony would just assume that it was adjusting to the different time zones and that Kriti's nightmares were trolling her. And her grandparents? Forget it. They'd just say it was a woman with no values who didn't fear for her safety. Nothing to fear, just judge and gossip about with friends at the Madras Club.

Still, Kriti kept looking over her shoulder. Any sign of blue made her cough. She had to rely on her inhaler when either the anxiety, hot wind, or air pollution would get to her. The little puffs barely kept her going through the aquarium despite the relaxing fish. Blue followed her, from the water in the tanks to the painted walls. She clenched her inhaler.

Peony didn't notice. She ran ahead to admire all the fish and the mermaid show. Kriti didn't bother calling for her. Admitting that she needed help in a foreign country would possibly provoke an argument about fighting for your independence.

Back at her grandparents' flat, she ate a few vegetables and rice. Peony complimented the meal, telling her grandparents about how beautiful the city is. She even tried a few phrases from Tamil and wore a long-sleeved shirt. Nani offered her memories of Chennai after the war of independence, and when India and Pakistan sent bombs after each other. Nana stared, still raising those white fuzz eyebrows.

Kriti tried to relax, seeing that Peony was getting it. The coconut chutney went well with the green bean curry, and she tried her best to keep it down.

Her lungs kept closing.

At night, the heat lay over them like a sweaty fog. Even with a shower, Kriti felt sweaty, and she struggled to breathe. Peony offered to cuddle with her and whack her back if needed, but Kriti refused. She didn't want her grandparents to wake up randomly and get the wrong idea. They still didn't know about them, but even if Kriti told them she was bi and in a relationship with a woman, they would forget a few days later. She had seen it happen with her older sister.

If Kriti were religious, she'd pray to the Vishnu idol, wash its feet and offer flowers. Instead, she turned away from it, feeling that a false prayer to save herself would be worse than being honest. Plus, her Tamil was nowhere near fluent to come up with a mantra.

Peony put on her sleeping mask and curled up on the couch. She was getting used to this distance. Kriti wasn't, in all honesty, remembering how Peony had run ahead of her while she choked, surrounded by glass tanks.

Kriti stayed up, reading with a cup of tea. Her cell phone provided the right amount of light for the book she had packed, a treatise on the science of honeybees. The *Amar Chitra Katha* comics were too old and weathered to travel. The book Nani gave her lay by her bedside.

This time, the figure didn't bother appearing in the shadows. Light emanated from the folds of her sari. And it was obvious that she was no monster.

"You are the slayer of demons," she said, "the most beautiful avatar of the protector and the most beautiful woman in the world. Mohini, the third avatar of Vishnu. Why are you here?"

The figure brushed a clump of hair over her shoulder. When she smiled, her lips grew even redder. And she stroked Kriti's lungs. They filled with ash immediately, and the smell of jasmine.

That scent drowned her in sweetness. It had a promise of joy and destruction. This avatar would come and take Kriti away from the world with heavy materials of love that threatened to weigh her down. She would float like the demon's head in the sun, her body filled with a holy blue poison that could kill gods. All she had to do was agree to leave behind the world's problems.

Kriti coughed. It came out in hacks and blue smoke. The figure clapped her on the back, icy chills running up and down. Kriti struggled for air, grabbing her inhaler. It fell to the ground. The carpet muffled the clatter.

"Yeah, I have a girlfriend," Kriti said, surprised that the words came out while she was struggling to breathe. "Sorry."

The figure did not move. It stroked her again. The poison built up again. So did the jasmine scent.

"Please," Kriti choked. "I can't go with you."

She slipped to the ground. The figure hovered over her. Kriti fumbled, grabbing the inhaler. She used the glow to force the plastic into her mouth and puff.

Breathe. Breathe.

She had to close her eyes, to concentrate on the regular air coming into her lungs and not that jasmine scent. The figure was not grabbing her at least, with those long fingers around her throat. Not that it would need to, with that blue scent.

"I don't love you," she said. "I don't need you or your beauty."

When she opened her eyes, the figure was gone. Just the dim

light from her cellphone and an askew book. Her throat was still throbbing.

A nightmare. Perhaps the choking from the humidity and air pollution had woken her up, the body warning her that she had to breathe. But then how had she dreamed of the woman before seeing her on the beach? And if it was just a nightmare, why was Peony able to see her?

She couldn't think. This meant going to the bathroom to splash some water on her face. Kriti turned on the light. Then she gasped.

Blue ran from her chin to her neck, in the shape of droplets. It was a navy color and twinkled under the light.

Kriti rubbed the spots. Then she went back to the bed and dug for the book. A page nearly tore out. She took a deep breath, and turned to another page:

Vishnu did not limit his Mohini avatar to helping the gods achieve immortality. He also used this form to slay other demons, or those that crossed his path.

One time, the god Shiva granted a demon named Bhasmasura the power to kill anyone by touching the top of their head. Bhamasura tried it on the god of death, who vanished into the sacrificial fire. That did not deter the demon, who persisted in finding Shiva in any form, to test out the power.

Shiva called in Vishnu for a favor. So, Vishnu returned in the form of either Mohini or an ascetic, coming to ask the demon why he sought death. Bhasmasura, charmed, explained that he wanted to test his new powers. Mohini invited him to a dance, while the ascetic suggested Bhasmasura test it on himself. Either way, the demon ended up dead, causing his own destruction when seeking another's.

Such deceptions are not nice. Shiva himself expressed sadness that the demon had to pass in such a way, despite being the god of death.

Vishnu explained it was a test; if the demon had truly sought no harm, he wouldn't have made such a request in the first place. You could resist a god's requests if you truly wished to hurt no one. But otherwise? You would end up dead, the air stolen from your corpse.

Kriti stopped reading. She touched her throat. A god had tried killing her, just because. And made sure that she would never forget.

She would get some flowers for the Vishnu idol. This time her prayer would be real, and angry.

THE POPPY CLOUD

Lee Murray

Beneath your feet, the deck heaves. Already unsteady, you grip the wooden rail, your knuckles white with worry and your face scoured by wind and wishes. Nevertheless, you revel in the cold-keen gusts that slough off the sea. It is a new day and you have arrived. At long last, currents of wind and water have brought you to the land of the long white cloud. Aotearoa. Your hair whips in frenzied excitement and you shiver with possibility. Brace for the possibilities…

winter pond / the reeds tremble / concerto

Revelling in the rich fragrance of the breeze, you almost giggle. The air had been anything but fragrant when you stepped onto this steamship in the harbour of Hong Kong on the cusp of the century, leaving behind your village in the Pearl River Delta, leaving behind all you have ever known. Instead, everything in the old country had reeked of rotting vegetables and unwashed clothes and weary hopes, but now in this brave new land, each intake of breath is redolent with salt and sanctuary and second chances.

The ship takes forever to berth, so you watch the gulls vying and crying and the people bustling and hustling on the docks of

Wellington. A beautiful, brown-skinned Māori woman carries her catch of shellfish across the sand; she catches your eye, her own brown eyes as warm as the blanket she wears over her shoulders. *Welcome*, she seems to say, in that instant. *Welcome.* Your own shoulders soften, and you return her smile, then you step down the rocking ramp, teetering on your lotus feet, ignoring the slice at your instep, at your every step to begin your new life.

There! Your clever enterprising husband is waiting for you. You stifle a gasp. You barely recognise him. In the twelve years since you last saw him—since his last visit home to see his sharp-tongued mother, his sharper-tongued First Wife, and his children— he has changed. Always older than you, he is much older than you remember. His face is meaner and harder, and his once-glossy hair is flecked with coarse white threads, like the frayed hem of a tunic or the left-over grains of rice at the bottom of your bowl—the sort that bring bad luck. Yet he is your husband, so you smile and bow respectfully, hiding your teeth politely behind your hand, hiding the ache in your step, putting your ungrateful thoughts behind you on such an auspicious day.

bowing / a wooden pontoon

An almost-stranger, he greets you, his Second Wife, and leads you to the wooden customs office to complete the paperwork that will allow you to persist on this golden mountain land. Your husband does the talking since you do not know the language. A good wife, you stand several steps behind him and grip your bag, your head lowered and your shoulders lank with hair and hope. In that instant, you are grateful for this clever man who stands between you and the world, who speaks the white-flour sounds and understands the whale-bone ways of these strange white-cloud people.

*the husband sings / the wife follows**

On the other side of the desk, the custom official smells of wilted flowers and old sweat despite his crisp white shirt and shiny shoes. He looks you up and down, shuffling the yellow papers in his ink-stained hands, and before your eyes, he becomes an angry bear, bellowing in loud brutish sounds. He fills the wooden building, thundering with noise and nuisance and dragging the air out of the room. You clasp your bag to your chest and shrink back against the wall, teetering on your twisted toes.

What have you done? But when you glance at your husband you see that he has shrunk too, cowering like a stray dog who has taken too many beatings.

You dare not raise your eyes. You dare not look, and yet you see the bear-man thrust the papers at your husband. Your husband has stepped out of line. You follow him as the bear ceases its braying. The other passengers swirl forward then, segueing seamlessly to fill the space where you once stood. In an instant, it as if you were never there.

a leaf in an eddy / the river rushes by

Your husband leads you to the edge of the customhouse. Your ribs tighten with worry. What is wrong?

Chinese people must pay the new poll tax before they enter, your husband says.

You listen while he tells you the sum. It is a fortune. A life's toil. More than you are worth. More than your husband can pay. You listen, your head bowed as he tells you that he must leave you here in this no-place. There will be no second-chance second life in this new land for you. Since he does not have the fare to send you back, he has decided he would fare better without you.

327

It would be better for everyone if you were to die here on the wharf, he says. Better if you were no longer a burden to him. Better if you did not breathe at all.

You tremble with fear, and your cheeks burn with shame. You know you cannot go forward and, even if your husband had the fare, even if he could spare it, it would not spare you because you certainly cannot go back to the village in the Pearl River Delta. A broken egg-wife cannot be returned to the shell. Already, you are a waste of rice.

But wait! The bear-man is looking up. He holds up a hand and, like ants who have hit a crack in the pavement, the line of passengers halts. Now he gestures to your husband, who hurries over. Across the rickety desk, they put their heads together, two ants with their antennae touching, and they talk in hush-hush tones. You do not know what they say. They are too far away, and anyway, you do not know any ant words.

Still, your chest bubbles with hope.

When your husband returns, he is triumphant. It is an auspicious day, he says. Your clever husband has found a way for you to pass into this land of golden dreams. There is still a toll to be paid, of course, but you may enter today for a small fee. A downpayment on a lifetime of toil. So lucky. It is almost inconsequential.

You can hardly believe it. You hold your breath in hope.

You listen while he tells you the price: you must give up your lungs.

low tide / exposing the crabs

You have no say in the matter. You will have nothing to say ever again, as minutes later, they are carving your lungs out with a fishing knife, swish-swish, left and right, slicing out your wife-lungs right there on the floor of the customhouse. While the butchers do their work, the line snakes by, white women with their bonnets and their bags, who flick their eyes at you as they pass. They need not pay a toll. No price, no poll for them. Instead, they pass by the desk, laughing and chatting with their lungs still intact.

When you have been fully flensed and flayed of your lungs, and the frothing pink air sacs have been carried away in a fish bucket by a small boy, your husband stands alongside the custom men as they consider the ruin of your body. Wide-eyed you watch them, while fluttering on the floor like a gutted fish, and you realise that they need you alive. There is a toll to pay, after all.

within the four seas / all men are brothers*

At last, they elect to simply sew the segments of your severed windpipe together, tying off the ragged vessels with a piece of baling wire. That done, they carry you out of the customhouse and into the street, where they leave you on the concrete.

Hours later, when you sink to the mattress in the tiny cupboard-room of the shared wooden house on the Chinese People Street, you are weak from lack of breath. Nor is there any food to eat. One look at the thin mattress and the grubby linen tells you your husband is not the worldly man he once claimed. In fact, as of very recently, there is nothing left of his gold mine, the once-lucrative claim lost in a game of chance. But no matter: your husband is a clever man. He will make his fortune yet, just as soon as he has a stake. Didn't he get you past the custom men without opening his purse? Such a clever fellow; he does not expect to be feeding on the northwest wind for much longer. He already told you as much as you followed him here earlier through the city streets from the customhouse to the celestial quarter, while you tip-toed and teetered behind him, rasping and rattling and sucking in your desperate half-breaths. Everything will be just fine. He knows of a game, he tells you, and he wagers he'll have his own business soon. Possibly today. After all, it is an auspicious day. Haven't you arrived to soften his stay? Putting on his hat, he throws a handful of coins at you, telling you to go out and buy some rice for his supper. Maybe some nice wife-lung tripe to go with it. He chuckles at his joke. The door opens and a rush of air enters, then he is gone.

A good wife, you collect up the coins and shuffle to your feet. A good wife, you do not complain, and in any case, you have no breath to spare. You pass through the open door, stepping painfully into the darkened hall, past the slow-moving sloe-eyed Chinese men who share the shabby house with your husband, and step into the street.

even a good wife / cannot cook without rice*

Without lungs, even that short distance has left you shaking with effort. You stagger sideways and steady yourself against a wall while you consider your surroundings. One thing is certain, the celestial quarter is no heaven. The narrow lane is tired and mean, and the people are bent and bitter. The air is steeped with the stench of offal. A dog barks in a nearby yard.

You clutch the coins and hurry on when a wagon barrels around the corner from a side street. A cart full of white-cloud people charges down the lane, pulled by two frothing horses. You want to shout a warning, but you have no voice and even less breath. Someone else shouts though, and in Chinese, a dialect not so different from yours, because you recognise the word police.

Police. No, no, no. A good wife doesn't put herself in the way of trouble. You can't afford any trouble. Terrified, you stumble away from the thundering hooves, hurry, hurry away, but your treacherous bound feet betray you. You trip. Sprawl in the dust. The coins spill from your hand and tumble away. You do not see who scoops them up. They are gone before you can look, and the wagon is still coming with its screaming white-cloud men and screeching horses. No trouble, no trouble.

You do not bother to get up, crawling on your hands and knees into an alley, into the narrow gap between a house and a fence, where you squeeze your body against the wooden foundations and lie heaving for breath, gasp-grasping for the smallest gulp.

On the street, horses stamp and snort. The wagon has stopped, the policemen jumping down in thuds. Clouds of dust billow into the alley. You wish you could cough.

A door slams open and the planks of the house tremble, or perhaps it is you? Inside the building, someone shrieks. Then all at once a board on the side of the house swings out and someone tosses an opium pipe into the alley, and it dawns on you that it is a raid and that opium is not allowed here.

You stare at the pipe. It doesn't appear to be damaged. The stem is bruised, scarred by multiple scratches, but the instrument looks sturdy. The poppy scent wafts your way and an idea trembles in your ribcage. A tiny pipe dream. You roll sideways and reach out, snatching up the pipe and slipping it under your tunic.

a spinifex seed / drifts in the dunes

With the coins gone you have no way to buy rice, so when the police wagon has gone too, you retrace your painful steps to the shabby shared house and the rented cupboard room, and while your husband is still out trying to make his fortune, you slip the opium pipe from under your tunic. Pushing the mattress to one side, you take the bowl your husband uses to shave, and clean the dust off the pipe's horn stem. You wash the opium residue from the clay bowl, wishing all the while that the pot was not so small.

slowly fuming / geyser

Everything is ready. Taking care not to spray the mattress, you slice your chest open with your husband's razor. Still fresh, the scars offer no resistance. You work quickly. With your lungless chest exposed, you pick at the baling wire to release your windpipe, and a wail of air escapes the severed ends. Those ends are a problem. You solve the issue by opening your mouth and shoving the apparatus down your throat, the pipe passing through your connective tissue like a needle through cotton. You do your best not to gag as you thread the clay pot to your diaphragm. This is the hardest part. The muscle is taut and hard to pierce, but you push the torn point of the wire through the fibres and grit your teeth through the pain. When the flaps of your chest refuse to close, you heat the razor's blade and cauterise the flesh; the smell of roasted skin momentarily reminding you that there is nothing for supper.

When it is done, you are shaking with shock and panic. You put away the bowl and the razor and push the mattress back to its place on the floor, and when you have done that, only then do you test your new pipes. You shiver with possibility. Brace for the possibilities…

Your chest heaving, you haul in a breath… The passing breeze burns inside you. Brutal. Bruising. Each inhalation is an agony, wire points at your nerve endings. You realise that the clay pot is too small and rigid, and the horned pipe is too thin, yet your heart lifts with hope. You can breathe! Not the way you breathed before you came through customs, not in the customary way, instead your breaths are shallow sallow things, and pierced with pain, but it is enough. You can live with this. You are so relieved that you almost giggle.

a life sentence: I choose life

Your clever enterprising husband, when he learns of it, has another idea. Because there is the still the terrible toll to pay, the lack of coin and no rice for his supper, and the unfortunate outcome of his game.

A cloud hangs over you. A poppy-scented cloud.

What choice have you given him? He marches you out of the shabby shared house, down the street, past the place where the police wagon stopped, to another shabby run-down house of planks and paint. Inside, behind shredded cotton curtains, behind a curtain of opium smoke, the run-down house is full of run-down Chinese men, who lie reclined and recumbent behind their pipes. Young or old, their eyes are dull. They are soporific, come to escape their sojourn on this white-cloud land, come to escape into poppy cloud dreams, into their wheezy-breezy dreams.

smoke curls / calming / ancestral spirits

Your husband's idea is pure inspiration. He tells you so himself. You are to become a pipe for hire, he explains. Providing pay-per-puff pain relief, you will become a decorative piece, a conduit to pleasure, a service to whisk away your countrymen's worry-weary care-worn woes. Your husband can barely contain his glee at his clever enterprise. At this rate, he will have his stake in no time. Even faster if he is lucky tonight. He leaves you there in that squalid opium cloud, while he rushes off to chance his luck.

OPIUM PROHIBITION ACT, 1901:

7. IT IS UNLAWFUL FOR ANY PERSON TO SMOKE OPIUM.

Unfortunately, it seems your husband is not a fortunate man. Clever and enterprising but not so fortunate. You realise that you will have to do your part to pay off that prohibitive poll. It is the custom. So while he toils at the mah-jong table, you spend your time in the crowded, clouded opium den. There is no call for you to return to your husband's rented room. No need, no need. Your husband is happy to come to the den to collect your earnings. He comes every evening on his way to make his fortune at mah-jong.

Other men come to the den, too, although officially, it is not a den but another shared house for retired Chinese miners. Night-after-night, day-after-day, a ghostly train of lonely disenfranchised Chinese men come to the share house, hungry to mine the sweet taste of your poppy cloud lungs. They come in a slow-moving fog, craving opium as you crave the air. Ghosts desperate to feed, they suckle at your throat, stealing your breath even as they suck at their poppy-poison pleasure.

Sometimes, they steal other pleasures, too.

What can you do? You are a woman with no voice.

*within the four seas / all men are brothers**

Months go by. You cannot speak, you have no words, yet it seems word has gotten out because now you are in high demand, offered as a conduit to another realm. These days you never leave the cloudy couped-up den. You are so weak you can barely walk. The edges of the pipe poke through your ribs. It can't be helped. It's all that puffing by the Chinese punters, the lingering opium residue that resides in your windpipe, and the poisoned second-hand air hanging in cumulus cotton clouds between the curtains. But despite your wretchedness, the poppy cloud has become the silver lining of your existence, sweeping you off to the solace of your dreams…

featherstitched / flesh and air / flying

You have made a friend in the dreamscape. Her name is Kuiarau, and she is a creature of this cloudland: a woman of no substance, a child of the mist, who hovers in the blurry billow of space above the living.

She is as lonely as you are.

Let us share our breath in a hongi, she says, as she swirls around you, pressing her body close to yours, and in the whirling, twirling spiral of her embrace, your heads touch and you catch her breath. It is heavenly. You hold the precious lifeforce in your mouth and savour its scent of bracken and earth and birds' eggs.

Just as quickly it is spent, overpowered by the poppy.

Kuiarau can't be tethered. There's no catching the Māori maiden. You know that now, although she visits you often. She is a spirit, a haunting of the air and the sky.

You marvel at her freedom.

But I wasn't always this way, she tells you. I was a woman like you.

The dreamscape softens and she appears in a forest glade that is deep green and dense with mist. She is bathing in the thermal waters of Taokahu, clouds of drifting mist spooling off the surface of the pool. You tingle with embarrassment. You should hide your eyes. There are men here—

Wait, the clouds are parting...

A serpent-monster with hungry eyes!

Surging upwards from beneath the water.

The taniwha drags her down bodily.

She is gone in a breath.

Smothered.

Submerged.

No!

All at once, the pool boils with churning mud. It spits and hisses with anger. The serpent is scalded to death. You see its carcass bob to the surface, belly up, the flesh boiled away. Nothing left of him but bones and broth.

Kuiarau!

You blink, searching for her in the clouds. There! She drifts off the surface, her head thrown back and her mouth open in a gasp. Your only friend in this desolate luckless place; you cannot let her die. You open your mouth and knead the clay pot with your hands, desperate to share what little breath you have with her…

Her laughter carries through the cloud.

Don't worry, I am saved, she says. I still live.

But how? What magic is this? It is too late. She is going, until the next time.

In the moment before she fades out, you imagine she calls you by your name, the real one, the one that isn't Second Wife. The name she mustn't use, for fear of attracting attention from the gods.

You wake on your mat, the Chinese punter snoring beside you.

It seems you have spent too long in your dreams. While you have been incapacitated, intoxicated in your dreamworld distraction, word has gotten out about another opium den in the Chinese quarter, and a crowd has gathered outside to protest. You catch a glimpse of them when the door opens, through the threadbare gaps in the shredded curtains.

It's a crowd of white-cloud women. Thickset, thin-lipped women, made of cotton and cruelty, they have come to rid the country of the sin of smoke. They wear white ribbons, mostly white, that flutter on their righteous breasts, and in their hands, they flutter white broadsheets.

Fearsome warriors, these women wage war with petticoat pledges and pious petitions. They are trouble, looking for trouble.

Half-aslumber, the men scatter.

Opium Prohibition Act, 1901:

8. A SEARCH WARRANT SHALL NOT BE REQUIRED IN THE CASE OF ANY ENTRY ON PREMISES OCCUPIED BY CHINESE.

As for you, when the police arrive in their horse-drawn wagon, thundering down the lane and making noise enough to wake the half-dead, the man who lets the rooms, needs only to lift a plank in the floor and roll you in. He takes care to ensure you are tucked away in plenty of time, the mat pulled snugly over the spot. You are so wasted; you barely touch the sides. And he can hardly let you be seized by the authorities, can he? Not now he has made a deal with your enterprising husband. Besides, you're the best pipe in the establishment, as the French would say.

You wouldn't know because you can't speak French, nor English, nor even Chinese. Nor can you walk on your rotting lotus feet, but you can sleep beneath the planks as well anywhere. If only the ladies outside would allow you to slip sideways into your dreams. The raid has yielded just two sleepy Chinamen, too intoxicated to roll away in time, and it seems the ladies are not happy at all. They grumble and gripe even as the police haul the men away in their wagon.

Temperence is hard work, and it has made them ill-tempered.

Their voices carry on the wind:

—Nothing against the poor dears, of course.

—No, of course not. It's for their own good.

—Not their fault that they're descended from weaker stock.

—If only they were the decent sort of Chinamen, the ones who clean and repair clothes and supply us with vegetables.

—We must deliver the nation from this peril, ladies.

You have no idea what they are saying, but one of them sounds just like First Wife.

You drift off.

dark clouds cluster / around a crescent moon

The house is dark. Since the raid earlier in the day, the Chinese men have stayed away, as is their usual custom, in case the police pull a swift one and come back. The proprietor, who scuttled out the back door when the police came through the front, is no fool and he has stayed away, too. Only you remain in the painted opium house, quiet beneath the planks, sleeping quietly when a noise nudges you awake.

Voices. Quiet white-cloud voices, so quiet they barely carry in the still night air.

Whoosh.

All at once the smell of earth and poppy flowers is replaced with something sharper. The building is burning. Wide awake now, you tremble in terror.

Someone has set the place alight. In the aftermath, it will be passed off as an accident, of course. These run-down old homes. And there was a police raid earlier. Illegal opium. Lots of paraphernalia in those places. Tins and pipes and seconds. Perhaps the Chinamen left a lamp burning. You know what they're like.

rimu trees / old bark peeling in the sun

It doesn't matter! It doesn't matter who it was or what they say. Nothing matters anymore because the house is ablaze, and you are stuck face up beneath the floorboards with no way to get out. You would crawl, if you could, if you weren't so weak, if there were space to turn down here. With no way out, you clench your clay pot lung, desperate to squeeze every bit of air from the rigid container, and you scream and scream and scream.

No one hears you because you are voiceless. Soundless. For the life of you, you cannot conjure the smallest breath. Even the floorboards manage to creak as they warp and twist under the fire's flaming fingers. The fire is alive. It has turned into a voracious dragon, the serpent-monster cackling as it chases along the planks, curling the paint and devouring the wood. Not just the wood, he is gobbling up the air. Swallowing it down in greedy gulps.

The monster consumes everything. He has reached the bottom of the plate and is licking the last planks.

His fiery drool drips through the gaps.

Smoky breath burns your face.

He smothers you.

You are submerged!

Your flesh bubbles and blisters.

Breathless, you scream.

You will die soon. Consumed by fire, your body shrivels and curls, turning to ash and smoke and sparks like joss paper offerings lit to appease ancient ancestor spirits. Your husband will not be appeased. No, unfortunately he will not be appeased. There is nothing you can do. Delirious with pain, your mind drifts, retreating from the agony.

Wait! Your scorched heart leaps. Kuiarau is here! Your friend is here. The mist-woman swirls around you, her body blurred and blended with the blanket of smoke, and in the whirling, twirling spiral of her soft embrace, your heads touch.

She shares her precious lifeforce with you in a hongi.

You smile.

She tastes of bracken and earth and birds' eggs.

"Come now." She calls you by your true name and pulls you from the serpent's grasp, dragging you up through the burning building. The gods chuckle as you are carried away together, lifted on flakes of burning ash, eddying upwards, upwards into the cool sanctuary of the long white clouds.

under moody skies / two willows / touching

Days later, the building's scarred skeleton collapses, although you are long gone. Your bones are still there, crushed to dust, along with some scraps of horn and clay, which the authorities say may or may not have once been part of an opium pipe.

---

*Chinese proverb

Aotearoa	Māori name for New Zealand; land of the long white cloud
hongi	Māori word for a traditional gesture of greeting, literally sharing breath
taniwha	Māori mythological serpent monster

GLIMPSES INTO THE HISTORICAL CONTEXT

COLONIALISM IN TAIWAN

(informing Shawna Yang Ryan's story "The Squatters")

The story of colonization and displacement in Taiwan is a complex one. No one can say definitively what would or would not have occurred without the disruption of the West throughout Asia. Western imperialism exposed and aggravated preexisting fissures and weaknesses in Asian governments and societies. Simultaneously, we cannot excuse, forgive, or forget acts of Asian imperial violence including the massacres of native Taiwanese at the hands of the Kuomintang (KMT) government. The road to these atrocities includes the history of Western imperialism, Cold War powers, economic and political instability, and civil war. But the acts of violence were directly committed by those who came to power in Taiwan—those who were ethnically Chinese and affiliated with the KMT. The victims were Austronesians, the indigenous peoples of Taiwan

History tends to work in a domino effect. Overwhelmingly, the narrative is familiar where Western imperial powers colonized peoples and lands to serve its interests and enrichment. To muddy the waters further, competition and conflict between groups have in various instances even welcomed Western hegemony.

The road starts with six centuries of Western economic manipulation, imperialistic infiltration, and abuses that did much to further weaken the Qing Dynasty's rule in China[1]. The result would be the ultimate overthrow of the Qing by the KMT establishing the Republic of China (ROC) in 1912. (The imperial ambitions of Japan made upheaval worse with the 1931 invasion of Manchuria.) Later, with the rise of Mao Zedong's Red Army, a Communist-terrified West threw support behind the KMT. In the subsequent Chinese Civil War, the KMT would lose to Mao's Chinese Communist Party (CCP) leading to the creation the People's Republic of China (PRC) as we know it today.

Taiwan's native peoples have been colonized and/or brutalized by multiple powers including the Dutch, Spanish as well as Asian powers including Imperial Japan and most recently the KMT. Fleeing its loss in the Chinese Civil War to Mao Zedong's forces, the KMT arrived in 1945 and took control of the island, establishing the ROC government there. Anxieties of control and beliefs in racial superiority, the Chinese KMT displaced indigenous Taiwanese from their homes and lands. Schools forbade the use of the many Austronesian languages of indigenous children. Often dissidents disappeared and were never heard from again. In addition, ROC forces committed multiple massacres of native Taiwanese, including the one featured in Ryan's story, the 228 Massacre (1947), and others such as the 1987 Lieyu Massacre.

The nation of Taiwan continues to struggle with this legacy and the government (as also depicted in the story) has made efforts to recognize and honor the memory of the violence. As with any colonial

1   Please note this is an exceedingly shortened version of a complex history. There are many history books on Chinese history that can discuss this in greater depth. Here's one: Ranbir Vohra, *China's Path To Modernization: A Historical Review from 1800 to the Present*, Third edition (Upper Saddle River, New Jersey: Prentice Hall, 2000).

power, "sorry" is *never* enough. Greater discussion of the massacre has been used as a political example of the dangers of authoritarian rule encouraging and emphasizing an identity of Taiwan as a nation of true democracy. The 2000 election which ousted KMT control is considered an example of Taiwanese anti-authoritarianism in action. Indeed, Taiwan is considered a vibrant democracy today.

Nonetheless, this idea simplifies and excuses the ongoing societal problems that persist against native Taiwanese peoples, who continue to experience systematic racism and prejudiced treatment from many ethnically Chinese Taiwanese. Much of this violent history has only just begun to receive greater attention. The indigenous people of Taiwan have not only been disenfranchised of ancestral lands, but all too many have stories of loved ones who never came home. It is likely that many of the vanished were victims of racialized massacres and other instances of violence.

Enriching Far Away Worlds

(informing Kanishk Tantia's story "Jars of Eels" and Ayida Shonibar's "An Unholy Terroir")

The British Empire as well as the West at large grew enormously wealthy from the plunder of raw materials from colonial holdings, such those produced in India. As the direct result of colonial practices, the West was able to industrialize, spurring the growth of economic and military power into the modern age. Simultaneously, those plundered found their own economies broken, native goods difficult to obtain, and policies forcing the purchase of products in further support of the colonizer economy.

The impact continues to echo in India as well as other formerly colonized regions. In India, British colonial policies are credited with over 100 million deaths from famine, disease, and other tragedies linked to this history (a number that does not even include those who died in the Partition of 1947, an event stemming from British rule and arbitrary, uninformed, and uninterested-in-being-informed drawing of political lines[2]). Even during periods of historic famine, food goods from India were still exported to the rest of the British Empire, resulting in even more human loss.

These policies left many civilizations utterly robbed of generations of advancement and wealth. This is by design. Imperial powers purposefully created systems in which goods and wealth benefit them while making the colonized dependent on the colonizer.

An Ancient Land

(informing Robert Nazar Arjoyan's "New Ancestors")

A rmenia has been continuously inhabited since prehistory and is the home of many ancient palaces, religious sites and other ruins. Through the ages, it has found itself part of many empires and civilizations, including the Hittites, Mitanni, Hayasa-Azzi, and the Kingdom of Urartu[3]. All of these civilizations have left their mark on the land and people of Armenia.

Yet the Armenian people have maintained a distinct culture with their own vibrant traditions, inventions, and architecture. Among these are the great standing stones, *Zorats Karer*. Estimated

---

2   Dylan Sullivan and Jason Hickel, "How British colonialism killed 100 million Indians in 40 years," Aljazeera, 02 Dec 2022, https://www.aljazeera.com/opinions/2022/12/2/how-british-colonial-policy-killed-100-million-indians.

3   S. Payaslian, *The History of Armenia: From the Origins to the Present*, (Palgrave Macmillan, 2007).

dates on their construction include 5500 BCE, but this is contested. More broadly, other estimates believe it was built anywhere from the Middle Bronze to the Iron Age[4]. Its original purpose is also contested. Soviet archaeologists suggested the site had been used as an observatory to chart the movement of the stars and the equinoxes. Most recent studies hotly disagree with these claims (2000), hypothesizing instead that the site had multiple purposes throughout its history with the most significant as a necropolis.[5] Today, Armenian scholars use historical documents and folk tradition[6] to provide greater context in understanding how ancient Armenians saw the stones. Based on these studies, Armenian archaeologists theorize they were likely linked to ancient cult activity.

Western scholars have often called Zorats Karer the "Stonehenge of Armenia." Statements like this can be especially problematic as they center Stonehenge, a European monument, as a standard against which other stone monuments are defined. Certainly, as Arjoyan's story suggests, terms like this feed further into forgetting the sovereign identity of the Armenian people.

---

4   Karine Vann, "Unraveling the Mystery of the 'Armenian Stonehenge,'" *Smithsonian Magazine*, 27 Jul 2017, https://www.smithsonianmag.com/travel/unraveling-mystery-armenian-stonehenge-180964207/.

5   Ibid.

6   Some of the legends include the belief the stones were once giants who had been petrified. See: Hayk Avetisyan, Artak Gnuni, Levon Mkrtchyan and Arsen Bobokhyan. "Armenian Standing Stones as an Object of Archaeological Study," in *Systemizing the Past: Papers in Near Eastern and Caucasian Archaeology Dedicated to Pavel S. Avetisyan on the Occasion of His 65th Birthday*, ed. Yervand H. Grekyan and Arsen A. Bobokhyan (Oxford: Archaeopress Publishing Ltd, 2023) 6-21.

AFTERWORD

An antique upholstered chair, over 200 years old has been spliced open in the video, its insides on display. According to the restoration craftsman's account the chair had been passed down through the generations of a wealthy family in the American South.[7] It's an image that remains seared into my mind because of the horror of what they find stuffed inside. Evidence of the inescapable darkness of American history, the sins of the past that will always catch up with us—it is filled with the hair of countless enslaved people.

And I can't think of a better metaphor for the United States.

Imagine how generations of this family have sat upon this chair, buffeted by its cushion yet completely unaware—or perhaps in denial of—the fact they sat upon a comfort fashioned from the suffering of enslaved people. For generations, this truth had been buried, going unnoticed yet existing just under their derrieres. For any American family, this chair holds a lot of symbolism. But that symbolism and meaning may vary based on the identity of *who* sits in it.

Now, I want you to imagine someone sitting in that chair, someone who is—*Asian American*. How does the story you've been telling yourself change?

---

7   Rebecca Flood, "Furniture Restorer Finds 200-Year-Old Chair Filled With 'Human Hair,'" Newsweek, 24 Aug 2021, https://www.newsweek.com/furniture-restorer-finds-200-year-old-chair-filled-human-hair-slave-1622452.

Made you stumble a little, didn't I?

Folk horror, like any other genre or subgenre is a way of categorizing. It is a lens through which to view a story. Howard David Ingham articulates the statement, "we don't go back," as the central conflict of folk horror.[8] For the white family who has derived years of comfort from the chair, this conflict may ring true. For Black Americans, there may be no "back," as racial horror isn't relegated only to the past. (The irony of the term, "we don't go back" and the frequent racialized statement many in the Asian diaspora hear, "*go back* to where you came from," does not escape me.)

American folk horror often digs into the soil to force a reckoning with bloody colonial history. The misleading trope of the "Indian burial ground" reveals more about the anxieties of the descendants of European settlers than it does about any historical truth. It is a subconscious understanding that they stand on blood-soaked soil and that history can come back to haunt. It is also a specter that raises questions about ownership and their relationship with the land. Jesse Wente's powerful quote in Shudder's documentary on folk horror, *Woodlands Dark and Days Bewitched* drives this idea home, "If non-indigenous people are going to be afraid of the Indian burial ground, then I've got some news for you. It's *all* an Indian burial ground."[9]

Matthew Cheney aptly states in his blog:

> As the United States continues to fight over the American past, few modes feel as contemporary and meaningful as folk horror. Partly, this is because so much of the U.S. self-conception is a folktale, a tale

---

8   Howard David Ingham, *We Don't Go Back: A Watcher's Guide to Folk Horror* (Room 207 Press, 2018).

9   Quoted in *Woodland Dark and Days Bewitched*, directed by Kier-La Janisse (Severin Films), 2021.

of benevolent Founding Fathers who created a sacred Constitution and set forth a great Experiment in Freedom that continues to this day in the land of the free and the home of the brave. The soil of that folktale sits wet with blood. It's all Indian burial ground — and it's all slave plantation, too. It's all exclusion acts and espionage acts, demonic anti-communism mixing with the dark arts of imperialism, with the grand duke of individualistic capitalism as Lord High Executioner. In America, we make human sacrifices every day.[10]

Dr. Chesya Burke starkly articulates the Black experience in America saying, "Black people do not need you (white people) to justify our experience. We don't need you to justify our horror. You are our horror. We exist within your terrorism."[11]

Asian Americans understand these sentiments well. We often share them.

The question of an Asian American sitting in the chair perplexes because no one seems to know our diasporic history—including us. Despite the "perpetual foreigner" stereotype, Asians have been in North America for a long time. From mutinying sailors, abducted and forced laborers, living curiosities on display for the public. Immigrants, refugees, and citizens—our history in the Western world is tinged with violence, sorrow, otherness... and hope. To answer these questions, we need to understand Asian-American history, as well as Asian history, a history that includes the meddling of Cold War powers, crises of war and poverty, atrocities of ethnic cleansing

---

10   Matthew Cheney, "The Folk Horror Moment," The Mumpsimus Blog, 05 Mar 2022, https://mumpsimus.blogspot.com/2022/03/the-folk-horror-moment.html.

11   Chesya Burke, "Horror Niore," panel presented at StokerCon, Denver, CO, 2022.

and political repression, and being both victims and perpetrators of imperialism. These histories have frequently been erased so skillfully by the dominate culture that many of us don't even know our own family stories, which makes creating a cohesive personal history a challenge. In an effort to become Western "enough," we've been forced to forget much.

We aren't supposed to have any claim. We aren't supposed to have a place. But throughout the diaspora we have found homes and forged lives even in the face of dehumanization and racial violence. We have been part of the building of nations and all the complexity that comes with such an endeavor. The truth is that we often have identities that span multiple cultures and nations. Whether in the U.S. or elsewhere in the diaspora, many of us have had to forage for knowledge of our family histories in Asia, only gleaning bits and pieces, sewn together from the shine of tears. Yet somehow, we carry it all. We taste the bitterness, feel the ghosts. Too often, we cannot name them, but they torture us just the same.

When I attended a folk horror panel in Denver, back in 2022, one element of the discussion really stood out to me: how often in folk horror, a dark ritualistic past resurfaces from the soil. I found myself struggling over this definition because I understood it was not meant to include me, a child of the Asian diaspora in America. It certainly did not include someone like my Korean immigrant mother and her presence in the United States. I chewed on a single question, "if folk horror is derived from what is dug up from the soil, what does it mean for the experiences of the Asian diaspora—those whose relationship to the soil is complicated and varied?"

I thought about the hardships and trauma my family endured from Japan's occupation of Korea, the Korean War, and the subsequent years of turmoil that followed. I sat with the stories I'll never know but have glimpsed, such as how my mother spent the young years of her childhood surviving war and grew up without electricity in the rural mountains of Korea. How she endured domestic violence throughout most of her too short life. She carried all these things with her, all the trauma housed in her body, living within her as she immigrated and became a citizen of the United States only to be subjected to more violence.

It was then I realized the very bodies and psyches of the people of the Asian diaspora are the "soil" of folk horror. The more I turned this over in my mind, the more I understood and even further the more I understood myself. I also recognized how we of the Asian diaspora have been conditioned to make ourselves small, even convinced to see ourselves as the perpetual foreigners we are so often labeled as. Not only is this inaccurate historically, but especially in places like the United States—a nation of immigrants (as well as a nation of murdering colonizers and land thieves)—it's a ridiculous idea.

For many Asian Americans living with the resurgence of white nationalism and anti-Asian sentiment, daily life has become a tangle of fear and fury. We worry for our loved ones, especially our elders, our children, and ourselves. More of us have grown *unquiet*[12] and many of the younger generation have just begun the work to challenge the "perpetual foreigner" idea head on. Many also carry a growing fury over the lack of conversation and reporting as we have watched elder after elder, woman after woman, subjected to racial violence. But we also know, racism is nothing new. Anti-Asian sentiment is nothing new. It's rooted in why some immigrant parents like my mother want their second-generation children to appear as Western as possible. If we can't access our Asian heritage, if we erase that part

---

12   A reference to the title of the breathtaking essay collection: Lee Murray and Angela Yuriko Smith, *Unquiet Spirits* (Black Spot Books Nonfiction, 2023).

of ourselves, we might find greater safety and success.

But then one day, we might reflect and wonder, "is this truly good? Is this *really* better?" Why do we feel like we are missing something vital within us?

Are we waking up and realizing, that perhaps… we needed the ancestors, after all?

That Asian American sitting in the chair—and there's a chair like it for all the diaspora, whether that be Canada, the U.K., New Zealand, Australia, etc.—the meaning is complex with many tendrils into many histories. I don't have an answer, but I do know pondering the question is important for us to understand ourselves and for non-Asian people in the places we call home to see us. We are here, but so too are the ghosts of the past, that we are never fully parted from them even when we cannot remember.

But that's the whole point of digging up the soil. Just don't be surprised when we turn the earth over and discover our own bones.

Kristy Park Kulski

BETWEEN THE WORLD'S ENDLESS SHADOWS I KNEW

Bryan Thao Worra

Confucius opined wisdom begins
When you call things by their "proper" names.
In India they warn you, without doubt,
All kings must once behold Hell.
Along the Mekong, if not every shore, beware,
When the water is high fish eat the ants.
When the water is low, ants eat the fish.

To meet true monsters is to discover almost
Infinite endings of what could have been,
And the beginnings of everything you wish would end:
Some mysterious, others obvious as a fear-laced breath.

At the present rate we'll all return enough times
To learn every countless unspoken rule
Of our shadowy worlds of flame and blood,
Fluid and edge, curving teeth and jade labyrinths,
This half-baked phoenix beneath a full moon.

Remember them by ten thousand terms.
Perhaps phi or yokai, rakshasas or asuras,
tatsu, bhut, or aswang, naga, oni, weretiger,
or something we dare not write down even here

Only to find, it does so little good
To know so many true names
At our true ends by true evils.

You recognize this, but cannot resist,
Seeking last words if not wise or caring,
At least as fine a sound to scream as any...

ACKNOWLEDGEMENTS

Thank you, my dear friend Effie Rose, for saying the fateful words, "you should do an anthology about that." Thank you, Lee Murray, for throwing your support and enthusiasm behind this project (and me), for making sure I had everything I needed… for reminding me often that I am enough.

Thank you to those I call the Founders: Lee Murray (our spiritual guide and force of nature), Rena Mason (our weapon wielding, trailblazing foundation builder), Geneve Flynn (our kind, compassionate believer in the human spirit), and Angela Yuriko Smith (our curious and adventurous spirit) for throwing your mighty support behind me and this project. Thank you for your wisdom, advice, and the immense work you've done to ensure Asian horror writers have a voice. (It is also no serendipitous mistake to find Lee Murray, Rena Mason, Geneve Flynn, Christina Sng, and Angela Yuriko Smith opening each segment of this book with a poem. This book stands on the foundations they built with their own work to bring Asian storytelling to the forefront of the horror genre.)

Thank you to each and every creator who contributed to this book with your words and art. You gave me your absolute best and with such vulnerability to make this book something more special than I could have ever dreamed. You own every part of this book as much as I. It has been an absolute joy to work with and get to know each of you.

Thank you to my husband, Mike, for your support and many pep talks. For listening with joy as I rambled with excitement over each story, poem, and art. Letting me talk out ideas and offering perspectives. For the hugs and comfort. For offering solace from painful memories. Even more, thank you for sharing my excitement and encouraging me. (Also, thank you for copyediting because you know commas will always be my bane.)

Thank you, Doug, for believing in the project enough to put your press and livelihood behind it.

Thank you, Maeve, for your part in this journey. For your hand in pushing this book when it was still a baby.

And as always, *Omma*. Thank you for not only your genes, but for your sacrifices that put me in a place where I can write words like this and say all the things that you should have been able to say in life. My voice will be loud and American while my spirit will always be fiercely Korean.

CONTENT & TRIGGER WARNINGS

SOIL

MOTHER'S MOTHER'S DAUGHTER
child abuse, violence

THE SQUATTERS
descriptions of corpses, political violence, Taiwan's 228 Massacre, domestic/child abuse

AN UNHOLY TERROIR
racism, colonialism, violence, illness, body horror, sexism

IF I AM TO EARN MY TETHER
violence, child death, entomophobia, racism

ESTUARY

JARS OF EELS
food insecurity, racism, colonialism

FED BY EARTH, SLAKED BY SALT
pregnancy loss, child loss, parental loss

Pig Feet

alcoholism, animal cruelty/meat eating, bullying, corpses, body parts, drugging, infidelity, mutilation, occult rituals, paralysis, teen violence, torture

Neither Feathers or Fin

suggested rape attempt, war related violence, mutilation, racism

---

BEDROCK

Guilt is a Little House

gorging on food, alcohol consumption, child death (mentioned not shown), death from childbirth (mentioned not shown), fire

Things To Know Before You Go

death, corpses (referred to)

New Ancestors

body mutilation/ body horror, sexual harassment, anti-miscegenation sentiment

In Twain

(extra caution advised) fetal remains with fetal body horror and cannibalism, general cannibalism, mutilation and gore, racism, corpses, pregnancy loss

---

ROOTS

The Fox Daughter Comes to Glenview

child abuse, violence

Hair

coercive control in relationships

IN THE HEART OF THE FOREST, A TREE
terminal illness, sleep paralysis

MINDFULNESS
misogyny, violence, blood, gore, mild racism, mild gaslighting

---

AIR

THE HEAVEN THAT TASTES LIKE HELL
violence, abuse, body horror

UNDER BLADES WE LIE STILL
parental loss/death, airplane crash, body horror, infant death (referred to), sleep paralysis, notions of self-harm

MOHINI'S WRATH
choking, claustrophobia

THE POPPY CLOUD
implied body harm, implied rape, abuse

ABOUT THE AUTHORS

Rena Mason is an American horror and dark speculative fiction author of Thai-Chinese descent and a three-time winner of the Bram Stoker Award as well as a Shirley Jackson and World Fantasy Awards Finalist for co-editing *Other Terrors: An Inclusive Anthology*. Her co-written screenplay RIPPERS was a 2014 Stage 32 /The Blood List Presents®: The Search for New Blood Screenwriting Contest Quarter-Finalist. She is a retired operating room RN and currently resides in the Pacific Northwest. For more information visit: www.RenaMason.Ink

Lee Murray ONZM is a writer, editor, poet, essayist, and screenwriter from Aotearoa. A five-time Bram Stoker Award-winner, Shirley Jackson Award-winner, and recipient of New Zealand's Prime Minister's Award for Literary Achievement in Fiction, her latest work is prose-poetry collection *Fox Spirit on a Distant Cloud*. Read more at https://www.leemurray.info/

J.A.W. McCarthy is a two-time Bram Stoker Award and two-time Shirley Jackson Award finalist and author of *Sometimes We're Cruel and Other Stories* (Cemetery Gates Media, 2021) and *Sleep Alone* (Off Limits Press, 2023). Her short fiction has appeared in numerous publications, including *Vastarien, PseudoPod, Split Scream*

Vol. 3, Apparition Lit, Tales to Terrify, and *The Best Horror of the Year Vol 13* (ed. Ellen Datlow). She is a second generation immigrant of Thai and Slovak descent and lives with her spouse and assistant cats in the Pacific Northwest. You can call her Jen on most platforms @ JAWMcCarthy, and find out more at www.jawmccarthy.com.

GENEVE FLYNN is a multi-award-winning editor, author, and poet. Co-editor of *Black Cranes: Tales of Unquiet Women* and collaborator for *Tortured Willows: Bent, Bowed, Unbroken*; winner of two Bram Stoker Awards, a Shirley Jackson Award, an Aurealis Award, and a 2022 Queensland Writers Fellowship.

AI JIANG is a Chinese-Canadian writer, Ignyte Award winner, Hugo, Astounding, Nebula, Locus, Bram Stoker, Aurora, and BFSA Award finalist, and an immigrant from Fujian currently residing in Ontario, Canada.

BRYAN THAO WORRA is one of the most widely-published, award-winning Lao American writers. He previously served as the first Asian American president of the international Science Fiction and Fantasy Poetry Association.

AYIDA SHONIBAR (she/they) writes dark and wistful speculative fiction about misfits, monsters, mischief-makers. You can find more information about their short works at ayidashonibar.com.

YI IZZY YU works, writes, and cavorts in the weird wilds of Pennsylvania. She is the co-translator of *The Shadow Book of Ji Yun;*

and her fiction, nonfiction, and literary translations have appeared in magazines and anthologies ranging from *New England Review, Strange Horizons,* and *Copper Nickel* to *Unquiet Spirits.*

ANGELA YURIKO SMITH is a third-generation Ryukyuan-American poet, authortunist, and publisher of *Space and Time* magazine. A two-time Bram Stoker Awards® Winner and HWA Mentor of the Year, she serves as the HWA President, coaches authors and shares the Authortunities Hub, an algorithm-free community for aspiring authors at authortunitieshub.com.

CHRISTINA SNG is a three-time Bram Stoker Award-winning poet. Her work appears in numerous venues worldwide, including *Interstellar Flight Magazine, New Myths, Penumbric, Southwest Review,* and *The Washington Post.*

KANISHK TANTIA (He/Him) is a BIPOC immigrant from India. A south asian author, his work has been published in *Apex Magazine, Dark Matter Ink, Planet Scumm,* and others. Find him on his website, kanishkt.com, on Twitter @t_kanishk, or by scattering eels into the wind.

ROBERT NAZAR ARJOYAN (he/him) was born into the Armenian diaspora of Los Angeles. Aside from an arguably ill-advised foray into rock n roll bandery during his late teens, literature and movies were the vying forces of his life. Naz graduated from USC's School of Cinematic Arts and now works as an author and filmmaker. Find him at www.arjoyan.com or on socials @RobertArjoyan

CHRISTOPHER HANN (he/him) hails from New Zealand – a distant yet charming pair of islands on the far side of the globe. He is of Korean descent (a 'Kiwi-Korean', so to speak) and hasn't thought twice about his love for horror since reading 'The Black Cat' by Poe. His shorty story, 'A Dampened Embrace' is due to appear in the *Beyond the Bounds of Infinity* cosmic horror anthology in 2024, published by Raw Dog Screaming Press.

AUDREY ZHOU is a Chinese American writer from North Carolina. Her fiction can be found in *Strange Horizons*.

SEOUNG KIM is a Korean librarian who lives on the lands of the Council of the Three Fires near Chicago. He has published work with *Strange Horizons, Cast of Wonders,* and more. Find him at seoungkim.com or haunting the aisles of his local craft stores.

ROWAN CARDOSA is a Filipino-American writer who lives in Texas. They specialize in speculative fiction and TTRPG content, and have a particular love for body horror.

NADIA BULKIN is the author of the short story collection *She Said Destroy* (Word Horde, 2017) and novella *Red Skies in the Morning* (Dim Shores, 2024). She grew up in Jakarta, Indonesia with her Javanese father and American mother, and currently lives in Washington, D.C.

GABRIELA LEE is the author of the short story collections *A Playlist for the End of the World* (University of the Philippines Press 2022) and

Instructions on How to Disappear (Visprint 2016). She teaches creative writing and children's literature at the University of the Philippines.

Shawna Yang Ryan is a Taiwanese American author and formerly a creative writing professor. Her works include the novels *Water Ghosts* and *Green Island*, which won an American Book Award.

Priya Sridhar has been writing fantasy and science fiction for fifteen years. She lives in Miami, Florida with her family.

Jess Cho is an award winning writer of short fiction and poetry. Born in South Korea, they now live in New England, within close reach of both the ocean and the trees.

Saheli Khastagir is a writer, painter and international development professional from India, based in Washington DC.

ABOUT THE EDITOR

KRISTY PARK KULSKI is a Hawaii-born Korean-American author, historian, and career vampire of patriarchal tears. Channeling a lifelong obsession with history and the morose she's managed to birth the gothic horror novel, *Fairest Flesh*, and novella, *House of Pungsu*. She bartered nine years of her life to the U.S. Navy and Air Force for food and later taught college history for a captive audience. Trapped by a force field, she currently resides in the woods of Northeast Ohio where she (probably) brews potions and talks to ghosts.

ABOUT THE ARTIST

Eileen Kai Hing Kwan is a Freelance Illustrator based in London. She primarily illustrates in publishing and games, and loves to illustrate haunting and beautiful dream-like moments and particularly enjoys exploring horror, gothic romance & fantasy in her work. Find her at eileenkaihingkwan.co.uk and on Instagram @whereiseileen.